TI

THE GATES
OF HELL

Stuart Seaton

FONTANA/Collins

First published by William Collins Sons & Co. Ltd 1988
First published by Fontana Paperbacks 1989

Copyright © Stuart Seaton 1988

Printed and bound in Great Britain by

For Val, John and Richard

PART ONE

THE
EXECUTIONERS

1944

They shot her on the 19th of July, just as the sun was rising beyond the hazy hills which climbed from the mirror-calm of the sea.

No one could be found who knew exactly what happened, for the only witnesses were the surviving soldiers, and soon their identities were lost in the confusion of war. But it would all have been different in the end if on that same morning two pilots had not flown their Corsairs off the deck of a United States Navy carrier and turned in low towards the Mediterranean coast of France, looking for trouble; because what they saw and what they did gave me a remarkable chance, much later, to recapture a ghost from my own past and, in so doing, to soothe the spirits of guilt which had haunted others.

A little earlier she had been taken from her cell in the German security headquarters at the Hotel Montfleury in the centre of Cannes and pushed with a dozen others into the enclosed back of a lorry. Two more lorries were alongside, one containing prisoners from the German hospital in the Hotel Grand-Bretagne. Altogether forty-three people were taken out of the town in the dawn light and up the steep, winding road to the trees and the hills above the heat-soaked sea. And as they went, beyond the horizon the big carrier steamed briefly at full speed so that she could launch two of her aircraft into the windless air.

When they reached their chosen place the drivers of the lorries turned off the road into a grassy arena surrounded by dark pines. There she and the others were ordered out and herded into a group by the rifle barrels of the soldiers; and watched in dumb, dawning despair as a machine gun was dragged into view. Then as the first rays of the dawn sun slanted through the silent trees around them, the man behind the gun pulled the trigger and held it hard against its guard.

The soldiers probably had orders to bury the bodies straight away, at the edge of the ring of trees. But as the machine gun's death rattle echoed across the hillside, the two American pilots lifted their heavy gull-winged aircraft away from the deserted beaches of the Cote d'Azur, up the terraced mountain face, across the trees which encircled the arena, and saw the soldiers and the doll-like bodies of their victims. They rolled into vertical banks, turning fast and hard, strafing the grey-clad figures and the lorries in a thunder of 2000 horsepower engines and gunfire. Most of the soldiers died in the confusion and terror as the lorries erupted in flame and smoke. Hours passed before a fatigue party was sent out from the near-by German army headquarters to bury the evidence of the slaughter.

But before then the Resistance had come, shadows moving through the morning pines . . .

LE PAGE

—◆◆—

1947

1

Charles Le Page was well over six feet tall and weighed around 18 stone. He sat hugely behind a wide oak-topped desk which supported nothing except a telephone and a note pad; and he beamed. The fat around his neck rolled over the collar of his spotless white shirt.

'I have a proposition for you, m'boy,' he said. 'But first tell me how you are, how you've settled down to the peaceful life.' His voice evidenced his public school education and his recent years at senior army rank.

I said: 'As well as most of us. I'm glad to stand still for a time.'

'Don't know how you did it.' Le Page was condescending. 'Charging all over the world with a microphone instead of a gun. Couldn't have stuck it myself, I can tell you. You chaps did a tremendous job. Though how you coped with the damn' censors I can't imagine.'

I shrugged. Censors had been a fact of life, and not only for war correspondents. Le Page was making small talk, but that was his privilege. He was my publisher – still is, come to that; and to a writer a publisher is a Very Important Person Indeed who can make small talk any time he likes. So I took my cue and said: 'Censors were necessary. We couldn't have had every war correspondent under the sun reporting everything he saw. German Intelligence would have had a field day.'

A broad pink hand waved dismissively.

'Know it full well, m'boy. Spent three years attached to a certain Defence Ministry department myself. But never mind that. The world's full of old soldiers reminiscing. Let's talk about the present. How do you like the book now it's in the shops?'

'Fine,' I said. Le Page's company had just published my first biography, a study of the Britain-hating Joseph Kennedy, American Ambassador in London at the outbreak of war and head of one of the most influential families in the United States. It had taken a year to research and write, and I was pleased with the way Le Page had presented it.

'Fine?' He lifted his bushy eyebrows in mock surprise. 'You should be delighted. It's going to make us both a packet of money. People are going to sit up and say "Who is this Neil Cameron who writes so brilliantly?" It's outstanding. You have a talent for biography, for making it live, for making it an entertainment. We must exploit it.' He stretched an arm and pressed a button on his desk. 'We and you have a long way to go together. Publishers are looking for new writers now we can start printing quality work again, and we're particularly happy to have found you – as I'm about to demonstrate. I want you to do another book. And this time with an advance before you write a word. How's that sound?'

His door opened without a preliminary knock. A woman came into the room, quietly. 'Neil and I would love some tea, m'dear. I don't think you've met. Neil wrote the exquisite Kennedy book, y'know. Anne Henshaw-Reid has just become my personal assistant. Straight out of the Wrens, and fearfully well connected. Way above my station, of course.' His laughter boomed.

I stood up and extended a hand. Her fingers were cool and firm. Her hair was dark and shorter than the current fashion, and by any standards she was attractive: late twenties, good features, tall and slender, and clearly an expert manager of her clothes ration coupons. I murmured courtesies and she responded distantly. Then she left.

Le Page said: 'We chose her carefully. One day she may sit in my chair.' Then he grinned and his chins creased. 'But not

16

before I'm ready to leave it. How do you fancy a commission, then?'

I dragged my mind back to business. 'Very much. Money out in front is music to an impecunious writer.'

'Impecunious? Like hell. You have articles in half the magazines I open, you've a column in The Times once a fortnight, I hear you on the radio, you write pulp fiction under another name, and any day now you'll be hailed across the nation for the Kennedy book. And I'm delighted, m'boy. A writer worried about money isn't relaxed. And you'll need to be relaxed to do what I want you to do now. A lot of research; and a delicate – nay, sensitive – hand at the end of it.' He snatched a fountain pen from his pocket and clutched it in his thick fingers by way of illustration.

I said: 'Who?' Monosyllabic interrogation is a habit I have long struggled to eradicate, without success.

'For one who writes with such humanity and awareness, you can be remarkably abrupt in conversation,' he said amicably. He put the fountain pen away. 'It's a biography, as you assume. The public will expect it from you, after Kennedy. Do you want to write anything else?'

'Not particularly. Who is it?'

He wagged his head, and his fat neck rolled over his collar.

'Let me tell it my own way. It's different. This time you won't be interpreting a famous personality; you'll be making an unknown famous. Absolutely unknown, m'boy. But you and we will change that. You'll give the public a new idol. Maybe a film will come out of it. You'll need to do a lot of research to unearth all the facts, and some may be very difficult to come by; but the little I know tells me that it will be a beautiful story, a remarkable story. Especially when you've given it the Cameron treatment. The whole world will lap it up.'

'Humour me, Charles,' I said. 'Just tell me who it is.' I was not impatient; just slightly irritated that he should be mysterious about it. He did not need to give it this build-up to excite the interest of a professional.

He grinned and his cheeks dimpled. I wondered if he cared that his weight made him repulsive.

'I'll tell you in my own good time,' he said. 'But I'll whet your appetite by confessing that I chose Neil Cameron for this special commission not only because he's among our most promising young authors – and you are still young, you know, m'boy, in spite of the odd grey hair I see distinguishing your temples – but because he will have a personal interest in the subject. There: does that intrigue you?'

It did. But before I could explore it Anne Henshaw-Reid brought in the tea on a silver tray and set it on the desk as if it were only a little less valuable than the Crown Jewels. I looked up at her and said, 'Thank you, I shall enjoy that,' and she inclined her head. 'My pleasure, Mr Cameron.'

She turned and walked out; but as she closed the door I glanced across for a final glimpse of her and caught her looking back. She did not blush, which improved my humour: I cannot abide women who colour when they are detected in assessment of a man.

I said: 'She's an interesting lady. Tell me about her.'

His eyebrow shifted.

'You surprise me. I had the impression that after your – ah – unfortunate experiences, you regard women as only a little less unattractive than the plague itself.'

'Perhaps. I'm not lusting after her. What's her story?'

He leaned forward and began to pour the tea. The cups and saucers were of fine bone china, delicately patterned. I wondered how he had come by such a set only two years after the war, when most people could still find only heavy utilitarian crockery.

'Odd that you should ask,' he said. He offered sugar and I shook my head. 'Because she's the source of the story I'm about to tell you. Don't flatter yourself, m'boy. If she's slightly curious about Neil Cameron, I'll give you a straight fiver to

18

nothing that it's only because she's wondering how you'll react to our proposition.' His fingers wrapped around his cup – the handle was lost inside them – and he gulped tea. 'I met her back in '43. She'd been seconded from some Navy department to the War Office. Then she was posted away, and I never knew where until last winter when I ran across an old War Office friend and he told me about a highly intelligent girl who was about to resign her commission in the Wrens and was looking for a career. The girl was Anne. And you know what? After I'd lost touch with her in '43 she'd gone to the SOE. You know what that was, m'boy?' I nodded, but he still went on: 'Special Operations Executive. The department run by the SIS for liaison with the Resistance on the Continent. No wonder people were a bit vague when she left the War Office.'

'Did they turn her into a field agent?' I was more than interested now. SOE people had been a rare breed.

'No. She was one of the assistants in the department dealing with sabotage – organising, arranging supply drops, training field agents. You had to be special to have anything to do with that lot. So I wanted to meet her again, because we were looking for potential editor material – the next executive generation, if you like.'

I was beginning to get the picture. I said: 'And she told you a story from her experiences about someone you now think is worth a book.'

'Absolutely right.'

'Then what's she doing out there making tea while you and I are deciding the fate of the world in here? If she has the story why don't you let her tell it?'

He raised both his hands, palms outward, in admonishment.

'My dear Neil, you don't understand these things. One can't let the children run amok. She has to understand that I make the decisions. I negotiate with authors, discuss their plans, describe ours, and set the whole show on the road. Then she comes into the picture. She's an excellent reader; considerable powers of analysis, a highly developed sense of drama and character. Of course you may talk to her later about this thing if you wish. But for the moment it's just between you and me.'

I had reservations. But I said: 'All right. Tell me the story. Get back to the point where I'm supposed to have a personal interest in it.'

Again the hands came up between us, as if to push me back into my chair.

'Don't be hasty. We have a long way to go. So think back a few years. To '42 and '43. What were you doing then?'

'I spent most of '42 in North Africa, telling the world the dismal story of the British army being driven back from the gates of Tripoli to within sixty miles of Cairo. Then they brought me home – just before Alamein – with a spell in Malta on the way. Which was no fun.'

'And?' Le Page's eyes were heavy-lidded and half-closed when he was concentrating.

'Three or four months covering the Home Front. Boring after the desert – though a lot less frightening – until they attached me to the RAF.'

'Precisely. And you did a spectacular job. Graphic stuff.'

'How the hell do you know about that?' I stared at him. 'I've never told you.'

Le Page smiled widely, the flesh creasing under his eyes.

'We only met for the first time a year ago, and you're a reticent man. But I know exactly what you did in August 1943.'

'How?' I was not expecting this; and I resented the implication that someone had been checking on my life.

'Because I have retained some of my friends in the War Office,' he said. He was clearly pleased with himself. 'It's a long tale and I won't bore you with it. But by a happy coincidence, when I was fishing around with Anne's story, trying to get some background to help me decide if it was worth following up, I ran across your name. And it was there because you once flew with Alan Tamworth.'

He looked at me expectantly, waiting for reaction. And I looked back, determined not to satisfy him. But somewhere inside, my nerves had tightened, and my memory raced back through the pigeon holes which housed the countless episodes from which thirty-five years of life had been fashioned, and instantly found the one labelled Alan Tamworth, Flight Lieutenant, Distinguished Flying Cross, who up to a certain night in August 1943 had flown fifty-six operations over Germany in night bombers. Then he flew the fifty-seventh and I went with him in the great four-engined Lancaster so that I could tell the people at home what it was like to ride the flak and dodge the night fighters in a major raid on a vital German target. It had been done before by more distinguished broadcasters than I; now it had become my turn because there was a new story to tell.

But before then I had spent weeks getting to know the men with whom I was to risk my life. I had spent time with them on and off duty. And I had met Alan's wife. That was why my nerves tightened; and I took care that my face was expressionless as I digested the shock which Le Page's memory-jolt had administered.

'I remember him – and the flight. Why should the War Office still have a record of it?'

'Because of what happened to him later,' Le Page said. 'Did you know he was killed?'

That was the second shock. I had lost touch with the aggressive, polished Lancaster pilot soon after the raid, when I had been sent back to North Africa ultimately to cover the invasion of Italy; and it had been deliberate, for while I would dearly have liked to retain his friendship, it was necessary for everyone concerned that I should keep away from his wife. Yet somehow, and illogically in the circumstances, I had always imagined he had survived the war, for he had seemed indestructible. Now, suddenly, I was saddened.

'I didn't know. And I'm sorry to hear it. Tell me.'

Le Page poured more tea and pushed my cup back towards

me. He said: 'Some time after you knew him he was asked to undertake SOE work, flying those extraordinary Lysanders which could land and take off in small fields, picking up agents and Resistance workers. One night the Germans got him while he was on the ground. But before he was chosen for jobs like that the authorities checked on his background. Your name was an incidental one in his file. As soon as I saw it I knew I had to offer this book to you.'

So that was it. Such a simple thing. Yet something which had dragged the deliberately-forgotten past back into memory's daylight. But that part of it was my own secret.

'All right,' I said. 'Now I'm hooked. Tell me the rest.'

His cheeks creased. He was satisfied. He wrapped a hand around his cup and drank until it was empty, dabbing his mouth with a spotless handkerchief, and settled back in his chair.

'You had better understand that we have an Official Secrets Act problem. A lot of SOE work remains highly classified. Methods, names, places. Anne told me her story only because she knows I'm covered by the same blanket after the work I did at the War Office. There are things I can't tell you because if I did I'd end up in the Tower, or wherever they put people like me who open their mouths too widely.'

'I understand,' I said tactfully. 'But so far you haven't told me whom I'm supposed to be writing about. Is it Alan Tamworth?'

He shook his head, and a lock of hair flopped across his wide forehead.

'No. Not Alan Tamworth. His wife.'

This time I could not conceal it. What had he said? That I would have a personal interest in the subject? There was surely no way he could know how personal it would be; how often, as I had sweated with the assault troops on the shores of Italy, I had thought about her, and had sworn that I would never try to find her when it was all over. I had kept the promise to myself and time had clouded the memory until it had been safely tucked away in its pigeon hole and the little door firmly closed.

Now Charles Le Page had opened it and the images took colour and form and I heard a voice and sensed a perfume and felt the torture of a strange chemistry I could explain no more in retrospect than I could at the time.

I knew my face had betrayed something, for he was watching me closely from beneath the heavy lids which half covered his eyes. But even though he had released the memory, the secret was mine.

And hers.

I said: 'His wife? You'll have to explain.'

'I knew you would be interested,' he said. He locked the fingers of his hands together, bent them backwards until they cracked, and inspected them closely. Then he looked up again. 'Of course, you'll have to do the story without giving a clue how you obtained some of the information. Certain people may guess; but as long as we don't tell the world anything which officialdom decrees should not be told, it won't matter.'

Suddenly my exasperation got the better of me. I snapped: 'Charles – will you kindly stop playing games? You're still talking in riddles and it's beginning to irritate.'

He raised his eyebrows and tried to look hurt, but it was transparent.

'My word, I didn't know you had a temper. Never mind. I suppose I have been difficult. Call me a frustrated dramatist. Did you ever meet her?'

I said cautiously: 'Yes. I met Mitch. Several times.'

'Mitch? Was that what they called her? Her name was Michele.'

'I know. Alan called her Mitch.'

'Quite likely.' He nodded to himself as if he had already thought of it. 'Do you know why she was named Michele?'

I said sarcastically: 'Because her parents liked it?'

'Obviously.' Now he was irritated. 'But why a French name? I'll tell you. Because she was half French.'

I had known that. But now I was thinking clearly. And something in his voice had alerted me.

'What do you mean, Charles – she *was* half French?'

He said: 'Oh, my dear boy. I should have realised you wouldn't know. She's dead, of course. That's the whole point of our conversation.'

Colour and form; voice and perfume; unexplained chemistry and magic. Mitch was not dead. Mitch could not be dead. I wished I had not come here, and had never met Charles Le Page and had never written the Kennedy biography and had died on the Anzio beachhead. It would have been all right if the little pigeon hole had never been opened. But now it was not all right.

I said mechanically: 'I didn't know. And why is it the point of our conversation?'

'Because you're going to tell her story, m'boy. That's what it's all about. Hundreds of men and a few women are sitting down at this moment, writing their war memoirs. It's going to be big publishing business in all the years to come. How I did my bit to win the war. The public wants that: the glamour and the pain all over again. Britain won the war and has lost everything since. We still have rationing – food, clothes, petrol; we have building regulations which mean you can't have a new house, we have currency restrictions which mean you can't go abroad or drum up capital for a new business, we're short of electricity and coal and goods in the shops, we have crippling taxes, and we have a god-forsaken government which glories in being ascetic and shepherding the masses in poverty from cradle to grave, all in the sacred name of Socialism. The people need escape, and they're turning to books which tell them that even if they're not winning the peace, they certainly won the war. And yours is going to be one of the greatest, because it will give them not a hero but a heroine, and one who did something few others even dreamed about.'

'What did she do?' I heard the words as if someone else had voiced them.

He said: 'She stepped out of an aeroplane over the southern slopes of the Alpes de Haute Provence. She was one of a small group sent to help the Resistance prepare for the Allied invasion of the South of France in August 1944. And she disappeared. Somewhere down there, she died. And that's your story. Why, rather than how. I don't want a spy story. I want to know about a woman who did something extraordinary, something that would terrify the rest of us just in contemplation. You'll never find out what happened to her, and in our terms it doesn't matter. It's the rest of her life which matters. Where she came from, and what drove her to do such an incredible thing.'

I said: 'I can't imagine.' I was remembering her, with her fair hair and luminous eyes and her laughter, and the feel of her hands, and it was real. The present was a dream, a small nightmare distorted by Le Page's face and smooth voice which told me things I didn't want to know; the past was all that mattered, because I would understand it. I had been there.

'You'll have to imagine,' he said. 'That's the right word – imagination. It will be like a detective story. Her father's still alive. I can tell you where to find him. After that you'll be on your own – except for the remarkably good fortune that you actually met her. I want a drama. I want flesh on the bones of the story. Immerse yourself in it. Seek her out, write the conversations she might have had, cloak the facts with conflict and pleasure and real people. Write it as if it were fiction; but it will be real-life fiction, all true except for details which won't make anything into a lie yet which will give the truth a life and reality to capture and overwhelm the reader.' He was waving his big hands now, completely taken over by his vision and the extravagence of his language. 'She is the ultimate heroine, the stuff of which the greatest fiction is made. But she lived, and that will lift the story above any fiction. Don't write it as a conventional biography. Dramatise it, humanise it, imagine the bits you can't discover and use them to illuminate her. And you, the writer, are part of the story. See yourself from the outside, remember the little conversations you had with her and adapt them to other circumstances and other people so that they all live alongside her . . .' He collapsed back into his chair, face flushed, eyes shining, a trickle of sweat along his jaw; delighted with himself, exhausted by himself, fascinated by his own rhetoric.

I gave him time to recover, because at that moment I did not want to talk. And then it was over because he had said it all. So I promised to consider it. He said: 'You must do it. It's made for you.' He could never know how accurately and intimately it was made for me, and how difficult it would be because of that.

*

A couple of days later I rang his office and spoke to Anne Henshaw-Reid.

'Have lunch with me,' I said. 'I want to talk about Charles's proposition. He says you know more about it than he does. But don't tell him. I want to talk with you, not listen while he talks to both of us.'

She said in her cool voice: 'All right. As long as you promise not to tell him afterwards.'

I promised.

*

It took forty-five minutes to walk from my flat in Chelsea, catch a tube to the embankment station below Charing Cross, and then walk through the gardens to the Savoy, climb the steps which lead up beside the Coal Hole pub into the Strand, and then cross into Maiden Lane close to Covent Garden. Rules Restaurant was, and is, one of my in-town favourites, and rather more expensive than I usually chose for an ordinary interview lunch. But I thought Anne Henshaw-Reid was not ordinary. Her presence had a subtle impact – on me, at least

– and I wanted to know why Le Page had not suggested that I should talk with her, since she seemed to have started the whole thing. I also wanted to know what he had meant when he had described her as being 'fearfully well connected', and how she had come to work for SOE during the war.

I thought of these things as I travelled in for our appointment; and knew there was another reason for talking with her, the possibility that she had known Mitch. For the long-closed memory box had been opened, and it was quite beyond my power to close it again.

She wore a severe black suit superbly and seemed pleased to see me. We talked about the weather and the traffic and Britain's parlous economic plight while we were shown to a table in one of the small curved alcoves opposite the bar, and decided to risk the venison with a bottle of Margaux, and I said: 'What do you think of Charles's proposition? Is there a book in it?'

'That will depend on you,' she said, and it was a gentle challenge. She spoke beautifully, yet without affectation.

'No. I can research the story, if I decide to take it on. But there has to be a story worth telling. Do you think there is?'

'I don't know. But you will take it on.'

'Will I?' I stared.

'You wouldn't have asked me to meet you if you hadn't intended to.'

I said: 'I might just have thought your company would be pleasant.' I was being careful, for she wore a wedding ring: something I had not noticed in Le Page's office.

'Perhaps.' She shrugged, and it was an attractive gesture. 'But I don't think so. After you talked with Charles he told me you would accept. He said you were intrigued by it.'

'Just interested,' I lied. 'Not least because he offered me an advance before I started. But I'm sure you know that.'

'Of course. It's a measure of his regard for you.'

'Do you like working for him?' I threw the question away

as the waiter brought the wine and, when I nodded, began to open the bottle.

She watched his quick hands and said: 'Mr Cameron, if I didn't it's unlikely that I would tell you.'

'My name is Neil, as you well know,' I said. 'Why did you tell him about Mitch?'

For the first time she smiled, and I liked it.

'Neil,' she said. 'All right.' She paused as the waiter poured a little of the wine. I sampled it, approved, and watched as our glasses were half filled. Then she added: 'I told him about Michele Tamworth because she was the only woman I knew who did a parachute drop over there. There were others, but I didn't meet them. And they were very few.'

I picked up my glass, studied it, then said: 'Here's to you.' She smiled again, said 'Thank you, that's kind,' and we drank before I said: 'Did you know her well?'

'No. In that business it wasn't sensible. And people were rarely around for long. They went away for – training.'

'Hampshire and Scotland,' I said, just to demonstrate that I knew a little about it. 'But one doesn't talk about these things. Even now, according to Charles. Did you like her?' I was sure I sounded suitably casual.

'Yes. We were in similar personal situations, which drew us together.' She spoke very quietly now, and I looked down at her left hand. She saw the glance. 'That's right. My husband was killed too. He was in the *Hood*.'

'I'm sorry.' I meant it. The *Hood* was a battle cruiser which blew up when the guns of the *Bismarck* sent a shell into her magazine. Fifteen hundred men died within seconds; only three survived. It was one of the Navy's greatest tragedies.

Two waiters arrived with our venison and the trimmings. We allowed the ceremony to distract us, and when it was over she had dismissed her memories and said: 'But I didn't know much about her, except the things in her records.'

'Which told you what?'

She said: 'You don't make long speeches, do you?'

'I ask questions. I try to make other people talk.'

I thought I saw disappointment in her eyes. Blue eyes, very clear. Perhaps Le Page was wrong; perhaps she was a little curious about Neil Cameron the man as well as about Neil Cameron the writer. As if she knew she had lowered her guard a little she said quickly: 'It's all still supposed to be confidential. But I'll be editing your book so I suppose I'll have the chance to make sure you don't offend the moghuls.' Cool again; brisk and impersonal. 'She was born in France of a British father and a French mother. She was educated partly here and partly there. She married Alan Tamworth in 1941. I don't remember much more than that.'

'Parents?'

'Her mother was dead. She'd lost contact with her father.'

'Did that worry her?'

'I don't know.' She was trying to remember. 'There was nothing about it in her records. I asked her once about her family and she just said, "There's no one". Thinking back, I felt she was being defensive. But it wasn't my business.'

'Charles says he knows where her father is. Do you?'

'I do now. He told me.'

'Who told him?'

The smile again. It wasn't just her mouth; it was in her eyes, too. 'I don't know. He conducts everything on a "need to know" basis: like the security services. Perhaps it's habit or just because he likes to be dramatic. Or maybe there's another reason. He had contacts with the intelligence services during the war. Mostly Five.' She meant MI5 which deals with home security. 'He still has friends there somewhere.'

'So after you told him about Mitch and suggested there might be material for a book, he went off and talked to a contact?'

'Yes. Someone told him more than I knew.'

'Who's his friend?'

She reached for her glass, drank a little, and studied me over the rim. 'You're quite extraordinary. You ask questions like a machine gun. It leaves the feeling that once you've learned everything you'll discard me as just another used-up contact. Will you?'

This time she had deliberately lowered her guard, and wanted me to see it. She put down her glass and a waiter materialised and refilled it. I waited until he had gone before I said: 'No. Unless you want me to. And at this moment I hope you won't. Promise me that we'll have at least one more lunch before you decide.'

Her laugh was cool, collected, disciplined; part of her character. 'I promise.'

I moved my glass towards her and said: 'Here's to the next lunch. Or dinner if you feel it might be worth the risk.' She responded, our glasses touched, and now her eyes were openly studying me.

'Did you know her very well?'

'No. The time was too short,' I said briskly. 'Who is Charles's contact at the MoD?'

'I don't know. I told you – he doesn't talk freely.'

For some reason I didn't believe her. I said: 'You don't know – or you don't think it's wise to tell me?'

'I don't know.' She was coolness itself, but still I didn't believe her. Maybe it wasn't significant; just her instinctive reluctance to name names after working for an élite and highly secretive organisation.

I said: 'It doesn't matter. I'll find out. I want to talk to him if he knows things about her. How did she get into the clutches of SOE?'

'I don't know that either.' She was still resentful.

'She didn't just walk up to the front door and say "I want to be an agent, please". She wouldn't have known where the front door was. Did you work in Baker Street?' Orchard Court in Baker Street was one of the two London centres from which SOE operations were controlled.

'Yes.' She showed no surprise that I knew about it.

'It must have been a rather special place.'

'It was. There was an extraordinary atmosphere.' She was thawing a little now. 'The people made it; and knowing the sort of work they were doing.'

'Was that where you met Mitch?'

'Yes.'

'Some one must have brought her there. Who was it?'

Suddenly, to my surprise, she reached across the table and put her hand over mine.

'Please. Don't ask questions like that. You know the rules. I can't tell you who people were. Don't be angry.'

I looked down at her hand, then up into her eyes. At that moment I could not have been angry if I had tried. So I said: 'All right. But don't get excited if I ask the wrong questions. What was she like when she came there: tough and hard and rarin' to go, or scared?'

She let her hand linger for just another moment before she moved it and said: 'She was quiet and calm, as if she had made up her mind about something. I liked her. She was so – so competent, and in control.'

Mitch, quiet and calm and in control. The Mitch I had known had not been quite like that; not all the time, anyway. I said: 'Someone brought her there. Someone made the initial contact, or maybe she with him. Perhaps she was looking for something, after Alan's death. Revenge. Was that it?'

'Revenge?' She stared, as if she had not thought of it before. 'Perhaps. She didn't talk about any of it. If she wanted revenge she didn't tell me.' Then she hesitated, thinking. 'But she might have been capable of it.'

I nodded. I knew that Mitch had already shown enough resource and courage to make many other things possible. She would have been capable of revenge. It looked as if someone in SOE had given her the opportunity. Perhaps a contact of Alan's, when he began to fly those Lysanders on the moonlit nights, ghosting into French fields to pick up unnamed Resistance workers who needed to report directly to London or who had been blown to the Gestapo and were on the run.

But still it was not easy to imagine her deliberately seeking the colossal risks which were run by agents dropped 'over there'. By the middle of the war we all knew the excesses of which the Gestapo was capable. It was astonishing that there were ever any volunteers.

Anne said: 'How much do you remember of her? You were remembering then, weren't you?' She was bringing me back to the present, and to herself.

I dragged myself into 1947 and Rules Restaurant where Dickens himself had lunched. Looking around now, I imagined the place had changed little in all the time since. I said: 'Yes. I was remembering. But not very clearly.' I thought about Dickens because I didn't want to tell her about Mitch.

'How long did you know her?' Gentle questioning, in contrast with mine.

'A few weeks,' I said vaguely. 'And I didn't ask too many questions about her life. There were – I guess there were other things to talk about. What did Charles mean about you being well connected?'

She was startled. 'He's always saying silly things.'

'Tell me how well connected you are. I've always been wary of people with double-barrelled names. But I could be persuaded to make an exception in your case.'

She frowned at me, trying to decide if I was serious; then, suddenly, we were both laughing.

'Oh, you fool! What do names matter? Mine was Henshaw, and when I married Tony I didn't want to lose it. Someone once traced the family back to the early Tudors. So we amalgamated names as part of the deal.'

'And what about being well connected? I don't think Charles was talking about the Tudors.'

'He was talking about a relative who has a title and a lot of money. One of Charles's ponderous jokes.'

'And what about your old friends in SOE?'

That startled her. She shook her head quickly.

'I haven't any. No real friends.'

'Yes you have. A man, probably. What's his name?'

'No.' Again she shook her head. 'If I gave you a name you'd ferret him out and there'd be a hell of a row – to no purpose. Forget it. There's nothing there.'

I said: 'I'll put that on ice. Tell me where Mitch's father lives.'

'Cambridge.' She searched her handbag until she found a piece of paper. 'There. Is that where you start?'

'No. I started with you. And we still have a lot to talk about. Where do you live?'

She studied me, openly taking in my face and the hair which, as Charles Le Page had said, was beginning to grey at the temples.

'I like your style, Neil Cameron,' she said softly. 'I live in Hampstead with my mother. And you?'

'I live in Chelsea with somebody else's cat. And I'll cook you a primitive meal there tomorrow night, if you'll risk it. I'll even promise to return you intact to your maternal home afterwards, if you insist.'

'I insist,' she said in her cool voice. 'And I accept.'

'I like your style too,' I said. There was a little wine left and I poured it. We drank in silence, looking at each other.

Yet it was a diversion. Half an hour later she had gone, and I was wandering towards Trafalgar Square, remembering her face and her dark hair and the way a strand of it always seemed to want to fall across her forehead; and finding that the image blurred into a four-year-old memory and another voice and fair hair and chemistry I could not explain but which I had loved and feared; and the air raid sirens were sounding and the night was alive with savage noise and light and refugees finding shelter. She had cried a little; and I would never forget.

I had wanted to forget; and had come close to doing so, or at least to pushing the memories so far away that I could pretend they were not there. Perhaps it would have been better left like that; but now I could not turn away from it. Now I had to know everything there was to know, right back to the beginning, and build it into a monument: not to please Le Page and his company or to earn money, but to purge my own soul.

Anne had more to tell, even if she did not realise it; and there might be incidental enjoyment for us both during the telling. Le Page had more to say, and there was his unnamed friend who knew a lot. Others, too, would contribute; they would be identified along the way. But first there was a man in Cambridge, because he had seen things all others had forgotten.

It had to start with his story.

PETER

1917–1932

1

The sun shone on the nightmare. The skeletons of trees threw tortured shadows across the churned land. Pitted roads and tracks drew uncertain lines on either side of the dark, wandering Somme. And carved across it all were the trenches where there was death and man's ultimate degradation.

But the sky's blue dome was beautiful: gentle, stretching beyond imagination, offering unlimited freedom and solace for the adventurous spirit. Men died in that blue expanse; yet to live in it even for only a little time was an experience to treasure for all the time that was left.

Captain Peter Armstrong always felt that about flying, even though there was sometimes fear when an Albatross locked on to his tail or dropped on him unseen out of the sun. No one knew about that, of course. He guessed they all felt it; but to confess to it was unthinkable. And there was a little less now, for the new Sopwith Camels were incredibly manoeuvrable and could out-turn an Albatross.

He was up this morning over the brown land and the trenches, testing his aircraft after engine trouble. Now, at 5000 feet, a droning speck to those who sweated in the earth below, he opened the throttle and put the nose down for a last loop before returning: down, building up speed, 100, 120, 140, then back with the stick and up, the horizon gone and everything blue for ever, and over until the world came back above his head and began to turn towards him. He closed the throttle, ruddering to keep her straight as the power came off, and pulled her tight out of the dive, his mouth wide in a grin of pleasure beneath his goggles. Then, picking up the power again, he headed for base behind Arras, seeing the straight line of the desolate road from Bapaume across no-man's-land towards Cambrai, a road strewn with the debris of war, broken by shell holes, swept by murderous machine gun fire.

He watched for landmarks, losing height, finding the field with its cluster of grey buildings along one side, turning steeply over trees and dropping in to a near-perfect three-point landing on the rough turf. He taxied over to the hangars, closed the throttle and switched off; then sat in the cockpit, enjoying the silence and the thought that after two more days there would be a week's leave, a train to Paris, then south to the little town of Montargis and Marie-Claire. A week with Marie. He felt his excitement even now, in the stark, functional cockpit of the Camel.

A mechanic ran towards him: the man who had worked on his engine early in the morning.

'Is she OK, sir?' Shouted, anxious words from twenty yards away.

Peter took off his goggles and gloves, swung his legs clear of the cockpit and slid from the fuselage to the ground. He moved easily, with the confidence of an athlete.

'Absolutely, Dalton. Like a bird. You've done a good job.'

'Thank you, sir.' The man was pleased, not only by the praise but because he was proud of his work. 'I'll have another look at it, just to make sure.'

'Excellent.' Peter strode away towards the mess hut alongside the hangars. He was tall and long-legged, and moved as if he was conscious that someone, anyone, might be watching him. He ran up the mess steps, through the door, and greeted Major Stewart Munro-Frazer.

'Hullo. Been up on a test flip. Anything doing?' Peter was one of the few officers below the CO's rank who dared to omit the 'sir' when he addressed the fiery little Scot.

'Cover for a recce at noon,' Munro-Frazer barked. It was his normal manner of speaking. He always wore leggings which he tapped repeatedly with a leather-covered cane. His junior officers spread the rumour that he slept with it beside his pillow. 'Robinson's unwell, damn him. I want you to lead the squadron. My office at eleven-thirty. I'll give you the details.' He looked sharply at his flight commander. 'When are you going on leave?' He was clearly thinking of the unfortunate Robinson's indisposition.

'The end of the week.'

'Where to? Paris?' Words like pistol shots.

'Montargis. To see Marie-Claire. Staying at the family chateau. It'll be an interesting week.'

'I'm sure.' A hard stare. 'Wealthy family, I believe you said. Hope you get in some good shooting.'

'I'm taking a gun. Hoping for the best, you know.'

'Good.' Munro-Frazer snapped out the word. 'My office. Eleven-thirty prompt.' He marched away.

On the other side of the mess lounge a figure stirred from an old armchair which had come from a nearby farmhouse wrecked by a German shell. Peter saw the movement and nodded in greeting.

'Hullo, Hugo. What are you doing here?'

Captain Hugo Thoresen was an intelligence officer from Brigade Headquarters. He was a little shorter than Peter, strongly built with a square jaw and permanently narrowed, compelling eyes. He was regarded with caution by some of the officers, for it was rumoured that in addition to his liaison function with RFC units, he had some undefined security briefing. Besides, it was said, he was only half British: his father was a Dane, and one could never be sure where one stood with some of these Continentals.

'Came to have a word with your esteemed CO,' he said. His English was perfect, but the hint of an accent betrayed the Nordic half of his parentage. 'Today's operation, and a few other things.' He extended a hand and Peter shook it warmly. Unlike some of his fellows he liked Hugo. 'I gather you're off to see your beautiful lady.'

'A whole week. Must have a break some time.' Peter

grinned. Hugo had met Marie-Claire when he had joined them at a Paris night-club party in the spring.

'Spot of shooting, I heard you say. I envy you. Haven't enjoyed a good day with a gun for some time.'

The hint was obvious, and Peter said: 'If you can get a few days leave, why don't you join us? Overnight, perhaps. Marie would be pleased to see you. A chance to meet her old man. He's quite a character.'

'That's very civil of you. But you can hardly invite your own guest to someone else's party.' Thoresen's courtesy was no more than that, and he waited for Peter's objection.

'It's not a party. Just a personal visit to my elegant French lady. She'd love to see you. Try to arrange it.'

Thoresen nodded. His smile, as usual, was no more than a slight widening of his hard mouth, and did not reach his eyes.

'I will. Just a couple of days, maybe. I'll find my way, if I get the chance. Thank you.'

They talked on, about the war and Thoresen's last visit to the front line and the squadron's fortunes and losses, until eleven-thirty when Peter sauntered into the Major's office and said: 'Let's hear the good news, then.' He saw the glint in Munro-Frazer's sharp eyes and added, 'Sir,' but it was no more than a gesture. No one else in the squadron could have survived as he did.

At noon he briefed his pilots. They gathered round him, in front of his aeroplane, attentive. He was not only one of the best pilots; his courage and his leadership were proven, and the ribbon of the Military Cross demonstrated it. He said: 'Jerry is up to something. A recce squadron is going to take a long look. We have to look after them. This is our sector.' He unrolled a map and held it against the propeller of his Camel, pointing. Behind the pilots Munro-Frazer watched, Hugo Thoresen beside him. Peter ignored them, concentrating on his instruction. Then the pilots scattered to their machines, climbing in, signalling to their mechanics who swung the propellers. The aerodrome was awash with harsh noise. Peter checked his watch, raised a hand and opened the throttle, taxiing out in front of the squadron, glimpsing the Major and the Captain who were distant spectators.

Dust clouds rose as the eleven other aircraft followed him in line astern, engines snarling. They bumped across the grass, gaining speed, tails up; then rose, wings swaying, climbing away. The sky was still blue, but cumulus clouds towered now in the east, and Peter banked steeply, setting course for them, watching the squadron form up on either side in three groups of four.

On the ground Hugo Thoresen said: 'Have your chaps seen the Von Richtofen Circus in this sector? I hear he's moving this way.'

Munro-Frazer tapped his leggings.

'They've seen nothing. Where did you get that information?'

'Just something I heard.'

The Major said sharply: 'Why didn't you warn Armstrong?'

'No point in spreading ugly rumours.' Thoresen's narrowed eyes watched the receding specks of the aircraft against the distant cloud mass. Then he turned. 'Time for a drink before lunch?'

*

Snow mountains towered, split by canyons with rounded walls, valleys below precipices: threatening cloud masses drifting out of Germany towards the Flanders plain. As the twelve aircraft climbed, the pilots saw the thunderhead spreading flat and heavy from the side of one of the mountains.

Below them stretched the green and brown map of the land, and now the zig-zag of the trenches split by the north-south line of the Canal du Nord, and the first shadow of the clouds, sharp-outlined across the haggard remains of a wood. Flashes, too, from behind the lines on both sides, and smoke curling; then the dirty cottonwool of anti-aircraft shells exploding below the squadron, around the scattered dots of other aircraft flying low; the reconnaissance aircraft which the Camels had been sent to protect. They flew on towards the clouds at twelve thousand feet, searching the sky, until a Very light curled up from the leader's aircraft. Wings tilted against the last of the sunlight and eyes strained to see what Armstrong had seen as they turned; down towards a group of half-a-dozen moving crosses a mile below, crosses which materialised into other aircraft, themselves bearing crosses in the too-familiar black shape: Albatrosses, grey and lean. As the Camels fell towards them Peter Armstrong rocked his wings, the signal which meant 'Pick your own targets'.

As they closed to within five hundred yards of the enemy a pilot out on the left wing of the loose formation remembered his training. His eyes were riveted on a grey aeroplane he had selected as his personal target; yet a corner of his mind was repeating a word to him, over and over, until it penetrated his excitement and he heard it: sun. Then the phrase: watch for the Hun in the sun. For a fleeting second he looked upwards and saw something red coming out of the eye-searing glare close to the clouds which now towered over him. His head jerked round and he saw a second red aircraft behind the first and he pulled his stick back and to the right and ruddered frantically, breaking formation, not so much in fear but as the only means he had in that frantic second to attract the attention of his leader. Peter saw him go and thought Christ, the bloody coward; then realised that if he was running away he would have gone down to the left, not spiralling up to the right. He twisted in his cockpit, saw a red shape three hundred yards above, and went into a frantic corkscrew. The rest of the squadron saw him and knew what it meant even if they had not seen the half-dozen aircraft dropping like hawks from the edge of the great cloud above. In an instant the hunters had become the hunted and the machine guns chattered. Peter dragged his stick back and began a desperate climb. Fabric shredded from his port wing as bullets stitched a row of holes across it.

Then he saw his attackers clearly: red Fokker triplanes. And his heart jumped, for red Fokker triplanes meant the Richtofen Circus, and the Red Baron was supposed to be operating to the north, over Ypres and Lille. He spiralled upwards against the face of the cloud wall which was now grey instead of white, then saw a flash and knew it was lightning. Immediately rain hit him, the Camel shuddered under the impact, and he was into the cloud and grey swirling oblivion.

It was the end of the fight, for although he turned back west at full throttle, minutes seemed to pass before he broke out of the moving cloud mass and the rain squall which surrounded it, and there were no other aircraft in sight. He flew back, thinking about Von Richtofen operating in the sector, and his own mistake in attacking Albatross scouts without keeping a constant watch on the sun.

At the squadron's base six of the aircraft had landed. His arrival made it seven. Then they waited, but none of the others came back. Von Richtofen's attack had been devastating.

He was late for dinner that night. Hugo Thoresen had gone, the mess was quiet, and there were five empty chairs. He did not enjoy the meal.

*

Marie-Claire Philomene Mascarella de Lattre was twenty-seven years old, the only daughter of Philippe Charles Mascarella de Lattre and his late wife Anne-Marie, with family records tracing to many years before the French Revolution and into medieval Italian history. She was dark and good-looking, with a pleasing disposition spoiled only by a touch of hypochondria, and had remained single only because her father had decided many years before that his daughter should restore the family's ailing fortunes by marrying both wealth and a title – a combination which unfortunately had not materialised among her suitors. Now he prepared to look generously upon the handsome British officer who appeared to be courting her, for although de Lattre was a little vague about Peter Armstrong's precise financial state and prospects, he was at least an officer with a decoration for gallantry, he belonged to the flamboyant band of aviators who seemed to hold the future of the world at their daring fingertips, and he presented himself with a panache and a polish which augured well for his future. Besides, Marie-Claire herself had become impatient with her father's conservatism and was showing signs of rebellion which made him uneasy, for at sixty-nine years old he did not take kindly to suggestions that the world was changing and that the young generation should have greater authority over its affairs.

Now he welcomed Peter to his considerable family home despite the handicap that neither spoke the other's language. Marie-Claire, whose English was excellent, had to play the interpreter and did not always trouble to translate precisely what was said, for she was increasingly impatient with restrictions with which her father tried to surround her. 'I am in imminent danger of neither rape nor seduction,' she had told him – an observation which itself concerned him. At the time Peter was unaware of these domestic subtleties, but he knew he was being scrutinised closely. Indeed, de Lattre's stare made him uncomfortable, for the older man was an imposing figure with a steel-straight back, a hawk-like nose, eyes deep-set in a thin, haughty face, and grey hair combed straight back from his high forehead. He was impeccably dressed, as always, with a stiff collar and dark tie, a suit which appeared to have come from his tailors only that morning, and highly polished shoes. He was master of his estate and looked it.

The chateau was a fifteenth-century fortified manor house with twenty-eight rooms within its four-feet-thick walls and a water supply which depended wholly upon a well in its kitchen garden. It was the heart of 2000 acres of farmland most of which was tenanted to share croppers whose affairs were governed rigorously by François Boisy, steward and personal assistant in all matters to the owner. Peter liked him, for he sensed humour beneath his gruff exterior, but again language was an unassailable barrier for them both.

On his first evening at the chateau he dined with the family in some degree of splendour, with servants in constant attendance, and it was not until eleven o'clock, when the summer night had fallen on the flat lands stretching on either side of the river, that he was able to suggest that he and Marie-Claire should have a brief stroll around the still-warm garden, and so engineered time alone with her.

In the garden they held hands, he kissed her passionately, and she pressed herself against him and ruffled his short fair hair with a hand which kept his face close to hers.

'It's been so long,' she whispered. 'I thought you would never come. Promise that you won't leave me for a moment – not even to go shooting with Papa.'

'I promise,' he said, and then remembered Hugo Thoresen and added reluctantly: 'There might be just one occasion when I'll have to shoot for a half-day. I saw Hugo last week and he virtually asked if he could call for a few hours during my leave. I know he's hoping for a chance to shoot with your father.'

'Well, let them go shooting,' she said. 'I'd rather you caressed me than that wretched gun of yours.' She kissed him again, and he felt the tip of her tongue and resolved that Hugo could do what the hell he liked but that he, Peter, was going to stay right here.

Two days later Thoresen telephoned from the local railway station and de Lattre sent a servant in the family Peugeot to collect him. When he arrived he bowed low over Marie-Claire's hand and addressed her and her father in fluent French, and continued to do so until Peter said quietly: 'If you don't mind, old boy, I'd prefer that we spoke English sometimes. I don't understand their language too well. If you use French I'd appreciate the occasional translation for my benefit.'

Thoresen surveyed him.

45

'I'd forgotten,' he said. 'It's very fortunate for you that Marie-Claire speaks English so well.' He did not trouble to lower his voice and for an instant Peter was annoyed. Then he dismissed the feeling and said simply: 'Thanks. It would help.'

The next morning Thoresen went shooting with de Lattre and Boisy, and Peter went with them because his host clearly expected him to do so. Marie-Claire was not pleased and produced one of her headaches at lunch time, but when Thoresen sought her out upon their return she responded to his flattery, appearing to forgive him for taking Peter away much more readily than she forgave Peter for going.

It was in the course of their quiet conversation that Thoresen suddenly took her hand and said urgently: 'This is the first time I've been able to talk to you alone, and we may not have long. Don't commit yourself to him, Marie-Claire. Give yourself time to know me. I promise you will never regret it. Let me come back to see you when he's not here.'

She had not expected it, and stepped back in surprise.

'My dear Hugo, you are a startling man. I'm deeply fond of Peter, and you must know it. I can't make promises like that to you.'

He reached for her hand again, and pulled her quickly towards him.

'You can if you want to. I'm beginning to love you, Marie-Claire. Give me a chance to show it.'

He was still holding her close, his eyes intent on hers, when the door opened.

Captain Peter Armstrong had not gained his reputation in the Royal Flying Corps only by being a good pilot; and he reacted to Thoresen as quickly as he might have reacted to a marauding Fokker or Albatross – four long strides, a hand on Thoresen's shoulder to swing him round, and an explosive short-arm jab deep into his solar plexus. Thoresen went backwards across the room, doubling, momentarily almost

46

paralysed, while Marie-Claire let out a short sharp scream and grabbed Peter's sleeve to prevent him going after the other man.

'Peter – don't.' She was staring at him in astonishment; and excitement, too, for it was the first time two men had fought over her and she was aware of a curious thrill mingled with her alarm. 'Papa would be furious –'

She checked, for Thoresen was rising slowly to his feet and his expression thrust aside concern about her father's reaction to the quarrel. But Marie-Claire did not lack courage, and she broke away from Peter, planted herself firmly in front of Thoresen, stared into the blazing slits of his eyes, and snapped: 'Keep your temper, Hugo. There'll be no fighting here if you value my friendship. You're both guests in my father's house and you'll behave properly. Stop this ridiculous business and shake hands.' She looked over her shoulder. 'Peter, come here. Shake hands with Hugo and forget it.'

For long seconds the two men stared at each other, the girl keeping them apart. Neither spoke, so Marie-Claire seized their right hands and pulled them together.

'Shake hands,' she said, and the authority in her voice surprised them both.

Finally Peter nodded.

'All right. I've made my point. The matter's ended as far as I'm concerned.'

Thoresen said nothing. But his narrowed eyes never left Peter's as he allowed the girl to bring their hands together. Their clasp was hard and brief; then Marie-Claire took each by an arm and turned them towards the door.

'It's lunch time,' she said firmly. 'Now come with me, and don't give Papa any hint of a difference between you.'

She led them from the room, smiling brightly at them both, but the doorway was too narrow for the three of them and she had to let them go.

As they followed her into the grand central hall of the

chateau, Thoresen hissed: 'You'll regret that for the rest of your life.'

Peter looked at him coldly.

'Not as much as you will if you touch her again.'

They went on, following the girl, side by side and looking straight ahead, shoulders squared and coincidentally in step, across the hall and into the dining room where their host greeted them with sherry. They were respectful to him, courteous to Marie-Claire, and polite to each other throughout the meal. Then Thoresen announced that he must leave and within half an hour was saying his farewells, bowing low over Marie-Claire's fingers, shaking hands cordially with de Lattre, and nodding brusquely to Peter as he climbed into the Peugeot to be driven to the station.

As the car disappeared down the curving chestnut-lined avenue which led to the road, de Lattre scratched his grey hair reflectively and said: 'A charming man. One to be treated warily, perhaps. But I'd like to see more of him. A gentleman, without doubt.' Tact persuaded Marie-Claire not to translate the comment for Peter's benefit. But the sentiment was obvious and did not please him.

Later in the afternoon they escaped from the house and sat in the garden for a long time, talking; as a result of which Peter was satisfied that the incident with Thoresen was no fault of Marie's and she became even more fascinated by the memory of his dramatic physical response to Thoresen's overture. So in the early evening it was easy for them to walk out to the summer house which was conveniently concealed from the chateau windows by a large willow, and embrace with increasing passion until she said: 'Peter – this is becoming very intimate.' She drew back from him, adjusting her dress which he had pulled away from her shoulder. 'We could so easily be disturbed here.'

He knew it was not a rebuke, for her eyes were bright, her breathing had been deep and fast, her tongue had been fire against his; and the time for pretence had past. He said huskily:

'Marie, my love, I want you.' It was the first time he had dared to say anything like that to her.

He reached for her again, and she hesitated just long enough to whisper: 'Not here, darling. It's too public in spite of that tree.' Then she was in his arms again, and he pulled her down beside him. The rough wooden seat was hard but neither noticed that. His hands cupped her breasts, caressing, and her own fingers explored him eagerly. Once she whispered, 'No – not here,' but it was a forlorn protest for she had already lost control. She seized his hand, guiding it against the smooth silk of her dress, along her thighs, murmuring, 'Please, please,' against his lips, then throwing her head back, arching her neck and staring up at him with wide eyes and dilating pupils and moaning, 'Oh dear God, dear God, dear God,' then shuddering against him, screwing up her eyes now and gasping again and again until she was quiet and he felt the sweat running down his back and was astonished that he had remained almost passive throughout her surrender.

It took her a long time to regain sufficient composure to return to the house. And before they did she whispered to him: 'I know you want me. And I want you. Come to my room tonight. Give Papa an hour. He'll be asleep then. And his room is a long way from yours and mine.'

He was sufficiently aroused not to care about the risks of discovery, and some time after midnight he tip-toed along the darkened corridor and discovered the door of her room ajar. He pushed it open, slipped inside, and found the curtains drawn back and moonlight flooding across the bed where she lay waiting for him.

It was five in the morning when he left her; and five the next morning, and the one after that.

They parted at the end of the week swearing undying love, and he returned to his squadron privately vowing that he would fly more cautiously, even though he had a score to settle with the Richtofen Circus.

He survived the next eight weeks, shot down four red

49

Fokker triplanes and two Albatrosses and neither heard nor saw anything of Hugo Thoresen. At first he wrote to Marie-Claire almost every day; but by the third week he managed only three letters, then two in the next, then one, and finally none at all. Hers came frequently, although because the postal service to the Front was erratic sometimes three or four arrived at a time and he had to study the postmarks so that he opened them in the correct order. Then, in the seventh week, her letters stopped, and he wondered if her ardour was cooling in step with his. For nine days he heard nothing; until there came the letter which changed his life.

She wrote simply: 'My darling. You must have wondered why I have not written. It was because I had to be sure that what I have to tell you was correct. Now I am certain it is. I suppose it was inevitable and that we must have been mad. But it was a delicious madness. Darling, I'm pregnant. I have your child inside me. Please, please come back to me. I couldn't bear it if you didn't. You gave me your promise. I have absolute faith in you. And I love you for ever. Marie.'

He read the letter three times, sat on his bed. Then, when the cold sweat had dried and he had had a stiff whisky from the bottle he always kept in his locker, he said aloud: 'Damn, damn and damn. You bloody fool.' He stared down at the letter and knew he had never really intended to marry her, even at the height of their passion. But now . . .

That evening he confided his problem to a fellow officer who said: 'My word, old chap, that's difficult. But you'll have to do the honourable thing, you know. Not much option. I mean, she'll be in a hell of a state if you back out now. And what if she wrote to the CO? He'd tear you into little pieces if he knew what you'd been up to – and smaller ones still if he thought you wouldn't marry her. Anyway, she sounds a smashing girl. And with a fair bit of family money, which can't be a bad thing. If I were you I'd go straight back there and jump into bed with her again.'

He knew his advisor was right. So the next day he telephoned his promises, the wedding was arranged, and four weeks later Marie-Claire became Mrs Peter Armstrong.

Six months afterwards a daughter was born to them in the grey-walled chateau. They named her Michele Marie.

2

On either side of the chateau's main doors were wide stone-framed leaded windows; and on either side of those rose great round turrets with narrow windows and arrow slits which betrayed the turbulence of the times in which the house was built. The slits had been glazed long ago to keep the draughts away, and on a day in October 1920 provided secret opportunities for the servants to watch the crowd gathering on the great carriage drive which stretched across the front of the house.

The occasion was one of the grandest at the chateau for many years: the first opportunity since 1914 for de Lattre to host a shoot in the style to which he and his family had been accustomed in by-gone times.

It had all begun the previous day when the weekend's house guests had arrived. Several had brought maids who were found rooms in the nearby estate cottages. Then, in the evening, there were more guests – those who lived near enough not to need accommodation. They came in great clattering cars and in horse-drawn carriages, to attend the dinner which de Lattre hosted as the preface to the following day's sport.

The day began with breakfast in the hall: croissants of various flavours, pastries, buns and cakes, jams and honeys, cold meats and cheeses, with unlimited coffee constantly freshly made. But there was no alcohol, for de Lattre would not permit it for men who were to handle guns; and he presided over it all, elegant in his expensive tweeds, bright-eyed and quick-tongued as he strode from group to group, welcoming, joking curtly, bowing to the ladies.

Then, under a hazy autumn sun, the men filed out through

the double doors and gathered on the drive where a selection of carriages waited to take them to the heath and forest area of the estate where Boisy declared the sport would be best; leaving the ladies in the accomplished care of Marie-Claire.

And among them went Peter Armstrong; blue-uniformed now, for the Royal Air Force had succeeded the khaki-clad Royal Flying Corps as the air arm of Britain's rapidly declining military might. He was there because de Lattre had insisted that he should be presented to the family's most distinguished acquaintances: although he did not know that de Lattre had confided to his daughter: 'I'm particularly anxious that he should meet certain people. I have an unhappy feeling that once he leaves the protection of his uniform he will need friends in the right places.'

Her father's concern did not surprise Marie-Claire. Marriage to Peter had produced little evidence to support his previously-vague references to a well-to-do landed family somewhere in the Yorkshire dales. He had relatives there; that was clear from letters. But in time she began to suspect that the only land they possessed was a few score acres of wind-blown hillside plus a little in-bye in the valley bottom to support the ewes when they came down to lamb. She only found out later that his parents were poor farmers whose son had been taken from them by a better-off childless uncle and educated expensively at private schools from which he had, to everyone's surprise, qualified for Cambridge; and from where he had been sent down in 1915 for persistently neglecting his studies in favour of ale and the ladies of the town.

He had then joined the army, and his impeccable speech and elegant manner had swiftly marked him out as officer material. He was fascinated by flying, and it was not long before he had worked his way into the newly-formed Royal Flying Corps, which brought out his ultimate attribute – undeniable courage which, allied to an exceptional instinct for the fundamentals of flight in the flimsy craft which provided his entry to air warfare, led to two years of distinguished active service. Remarkably in an arena where the casualty rate was devastating, he emerged unscathed and now, married to Marie-Claire, felt that the problems of earning a living in the chilly post-war climate were perhaps less pressing than he might otherwise have expected.

He sauntered towards his father-in-law, followed by the loader allocated to him from among the estate workers, waved a casual farewell to his watching wife and prepared for the day's sport.

As the first birds arrived he shot sparingly and well; then as more pheasants rose and crowded the air across the line he was fast and accurate, taxing his loader to the limit, and demonstrating a skill and courtesy to his fellow guns which led, later, to a number of quiet comments in his favour as guests moved around the vast buffet table in the chateau's hall. Peter passed among them, Marie-Claire at his side as interpreter, their little daughter standing with a servant on the fringe of it all. He was taller than most of the guests, and a number of the women glanced at him admiringly. Now and then he caught their eyes, and only the boldest were able to hold his inviting gaze across the crowd. But although his presence was noted by many, none expressed to de Lattre an interest in his future – not least, the old man realised, because of Peter's obvious indifference to the need to utter even one word of French. As long as his wife was with him he conversed through her with ease and charm; if she moved away he became aloof, making no attempt to communicate with others.

At one point de Lattre paused beside his steward and confidant and said quietly: 'I see you are watching my son-in-law, Boisy. He has done well today. But it is a pity he does not try to speak our language.'

Boisy, with the assurance of the trusted senior servant, murmured: 'He doesn't want to, sir. He clearly doesn't see his future in France.' And he did not trouble to hide his disapproval. He knew that Marie-Claire's marriage had been important to the family for two reasons: the natural concern of a father that his daughter should marry into a comfortable as well as a happy life, and the estate's need for an injection of new blood and new money. And Boisy was aware that the second consideration was of increasing concern to de Lattre. The estate itself did not pay for the upkeep of the chateau, and many of the tenants' cottages and buildings were in need of repair. The steward knew little of the family's financial affairs beyond the boundaries of the estate, but he was aware that they depended heavily upon investments in Paris and London and that both had suffered severely as a result of the war. De Lattre had once confided in him that he had hoped his daughter would achieve two things for the family – an heir and a fresh financial impetus. Now she had given birth to a daughter, whom de Lattre did not consider to provide the best solution to the succession problem, and she had taken a husband whose polish was beginning to appear somewhat superficial.

François Boisy was concerned about all this, for he had worked for the de Lattre family all his adult life and had a deep affection for the old man. He was fond of Marie-Claire, too, for he had watched her grow from childhood; indeed once he had cherished secret, unhappy dreams that, although he was fifteen years her senior, she might one day forget his humble background and respond to confessions of love and worship which he repeatedly rehearsed in the confines of the small house he occupied next to the chateau's home farm. Time had dimmed the hope until it had been finally extinguished, but he remained anxious for her welfare and happiness; and, in consequence, critical of her husband.

Across the room he saw Peter edge through the crowd towards the little girl who stood beside a black-skirted maid and watched the people with obvious boredom. Peter stooped and lifted the child up, sitting her on his arm, talking to her. She laughed at him, trying to pull his hair, and he tickled her face and then playfully pulled her hair in return. She put her arms around his neck, pressing close to him and whispering in his car, and he turned and carried her among the crowd to the luncheon table where he selected a snack for her, talking to her all the time and making her laugh.

Boisy approved. Perhaps the de Lattre fortunes would have to look elsewhere for their salvation; but at least Peter Armstrong was a good father.

His eyes sought out Marie-Claire, deep in conversation with a group of guests; and for some reason he could not define his mind qualified the previous thought with a tentative, curious question: a good father, but a good husband too?

Boisy, standing alone, found himself shaking his head; then checked the slight movement, for he realised Peter was looking at him across the heads of the people. For an instant he met the questioning gaze; then turned away, wondering what coincidence had drawn their eyes to each other at that moment.

3

●━━●

The winds were blowing; not hard as they sometimes did, but enough to whip sand into the air and compel men to narrow their eyes against it. The desert had greened after the winter rains, and the shepherds and camel Bedouins had ranged out across the stony emptiness which stretched away from the edge of the Euphrates plain towards the Iraqi-Arabian border, searching for new grazing.

And beyond the border the Moslem fanatics gathered, war banners furled but ready, camels watered and horses rested; waiting for the signal to attack the wandering tribes of Iraq.

Peter Armstrong knew they must be out there somewhere, for the pattern was established. That was why he was there, in the heat and dust at the RAF station just outside Basra, standing now beside a big wooden-framed notice which told those who passed the gates of the camp that London was 3,432 miles to the west and Baghdad 247 miles to the north.

It was 1924 and he had been in Iraq for a year as part of the small RAF force charged under the war-end Treaty of Versailles with keeping the peace between Iraq's King Feisal and Arabia's Ibn Saud; and more particularly with protecting the desert tribes against the murderous raiders who had once been Ibn Saud's shock troops. Now they were beyond his control as they swept periodically out of the Arabian vastness to steal the flocks and camels of the Iraqi shepherds and kill as many of the tribesmen as they could find.

Peter had little personal sympathy with either side, although he was sorry for the shepherds who had no hope of defending themselves against the thousand-strong bands of bloodthirsty raiders lurking safely in Arabia until they were ready to strike. Much more important to him at the moment were his own prospects, for he was still a Flight Lieutenant and knew he had little hope of further promotion. The RAF was being decimated by the politicians back in London and he would be fortunate even to retain his commission if the cuts went on. If he had known how to earn a living as a civilian he would have resigned two years before, in frustration; but he had no formal qualifications and no skills except those of a pilot.

He turned away from the giant milestone towards the long, low administrative buildings, his cap pulled over his eyes against the searing sun. He walked slowly, the back of his shirt dark-stained with sweat. Dust swirled in a sudden miniature coil in front of him, waist-high, moving as he moved. He watched it, hating it. Maybe there were worse places; but not many. He wrote letters twice a month: one each to Marie-Claire and Michele. It was easier to write to Michele than to his wife, because she was interested in anything, everything, with the naive, appealing curiosity of a six-year-old. She wrote to him, too: pages of childish scrawl about school and her friends and where she had been and what she would do when he came home. Her photograph was on the locker at his bedside; Marie-Claire's, as well, but it was Michele's he looked at more often, wondering how she was changing, feeling that precious time was passing, escaping. Marie-Claire had the child all to herself and he resented that, and the service which imprisoned him so far away.

He swore softly as he watched the dust swirl away towards the airfield.

In the mess he called for a drink but had hardly tasted it when Sanderson came in and said quietly: 'Come to my office, Peter. Bring your glass if you like.'

He followed the Squadron Leader over to the block next to the mess. Sanderson said: 'There's trouble. One of Feisal's agents came out of the desert yesterday. Ibn Saud's lunatics are massing. Our tribes are scattered all over the desert. There'll be a massacre. But that's not all.'

Peter sipped his cold lemonade, enjoying it.

'It's enough. What else?'

'Politics,' said Sanderson. He was short and sharp-featured, and his voice was as clipped as his brief moustache. 'Britain has been leaning on Ibn Saud. He won't admit he can't control his tribesmen. But he has agreed to join us in a peace initiative. He's going to put pressure on them from behind, and we're sending an emissary to meet them from the front – right out there in the desert.'

'That sounds like fun.' Peter raised his eyebrows. 'Why are you telling me?'

'Because the whole squadron may be involved. The tribes are expected to move up to the border tonight and our emissary will cross to meet them at dawn tomorrow. He'll try to talk peace with them. But he'll also tell them that if they attack he'll whistle up the RAF. And that means us.'

'So it's stand-by tomorrow. Have you told anybody else?'

'I only got the signal from Baghdad two hours ago.'

Peter drained his glass, set it down on the desk and scowled at it. Then he looked up at Sanderson.

'I've been in uniform a long time,' he said. 'It's taught me many things. Not least that conversations like this always have a purpose. Am I leading the squadron tomorrow? Or is there something else?'

'I'm leading the squadron tomorrow – if it has to take off,' Sanderson said. 'You have a special job. Someone has to fly the emissary out to the border. And you know the area better than most.'

Peter stared; then whistled between his teeth.

'So that's it. Thank you for nothing. Where am I going?'

Sanderson turned to a map on the wall and pointed to an area a hundred miles north of the Kuwait border.

'That's where the Saudis are gathering. I can give you a map reference – to within twenty miles one way or another.'

'Do they know we're coming?'

'They're bound to know Ibn Saud wants to stop the raid. They also ought to know that the British are involved and that we're trying to contact them.'

'How will they react, then?' Peter asked. 'Usually if they see one of our aircraft they fire on it – which isn't much of a hazard as long as we're airborne. But I'm going to have to put this emissary chap on the ground. What are his chances?'

Sanderson shrugged. He gave the impression that he was not particularly concerned about the emissary.

'In his place I wouldn't be very happy. But I suppose he's some sort of expert on the Bedouin. And there'll be killings all over the desert if we just sit back and do nothing. It's risky, though.'

'Not least for me,' Peter said grimly. 'Because I'll be on the ground with him. When does he get here?'

'He's coming down from Baghdad on the train this afternoon – be here in time for dinner. You'll have plenty of time to talk to him.'

He spent the next hour in the hangars, watching mechanics checking over his two-seater Bristol. It was a clumsy aeroplane to fly after the Camel scouts on which he had finished the war. But it was strong and sturdy and stood up to the tough desert conditions well. He decided he definitely did not like the thought of landing on the Arabian side of the border close to a thousand Bedouin religious fanatics with war banners unfurled.

He was in the mess bar when the emissary arrived. The small room was crowded and for several seconds he could not see the visitor clearly, except that he wore an expensive cream silk and mohair suit and a trim beard and moustache. It was only when he turned that Peter saw him full face and thought: Christ Almighty, I don't believe it.

The emissary was Hugo Thoresen.

Sanderson brought him towards the bar, picking up a beer for him from one of the Arab waiters, guiding him towards

Peter who stood, erect and stiff-faced, contemplating the perversity of coincidence.

Thoresen did not look directly at him until they were almost face-to-face. Then he stopped, as startled as Peter had been seconds before and unable to conceal it.

Sanderson said: 'Flight Lieutenant Peter Armstrong. He will be your pilot tomorrow. Peter, meet Mr Hugo Thoresen.'

Peter took a long breath and said quietly: 'Hullo, Hugo. This is a surprise.' He extended a hand.

Thoresen's deep-set eyes were narrowed, as always, and difficult to read. He accepted Peter's handshake briefly.

'Surprise indeed. I had no idea you were here. Still less that you'd been briefed to fly me.' His voice was deep, curt, and just short of hostile.

Sanderson stared from one to the other.

'You know each other? How remarkable.'

'Remarkable indeed.' Peter had recovered his composure. If he was to be stuck with Thoresen he might as well make the best of it. 'Hugo and I met during the war.' To Thoresen he said: 'In civvies, I see. Must say I expected the army to be doing this job. Do tell me what you're up to these days.'

'Diplomatic Service,' Thoresen said abruptly. 'Middle East postings of one sort and another for the last couple of years. I speak enough of the local lingos now to be able to talk to the Bedouin. That's why I'm here.'

'It's a useful starting point,' Peter said. He was considering Thoresen as a diplomat and decided the story did not fit. The Diplomatic Corps, maybe; but it had to be a cover. Clearly Thoresen was flying high. He added: 'A lot of water has passed under our respective bridges since France. Plenty to talk about tonight, before we consider what we do in the morning.' He was trying to be friendly.

Thoresen sampled his beer, then set the glass on the bar.

'I'm sure there are things to talk about,' he said. 'But we've an early start in the morning. I suggest we have our drink, sit down for a few minutes with your Commanding Officer –' he nodded formally to Sanderson '– to consider tomorrow, then enjoy our meal and have an early night. And I don't suppose the last few years are really worth discussing, for either of us.'

Peter eyed him. He thought: you superior swine, you still think you're the cleverest man you ever met. Let's see how you like this one. He said: 'As you will. There's one thing worth mentioning now, though. When we put down in the desert tomorrow, I can't keep the engine ticking over while you do your diplomacy thing. It would over-heat. But if I stop it, you'll have to swing the prop when we take off again. And the Bristol engine is a handful. We usually still use the old-fashioned three-man team here. Have you ever swung a prop?'

Thoresen's cold gaze did not waver. His fingers stroked one side of his short dark beard.

'I've done many things,' he said easily. 'Just to set your mind at rest, I'll start your aeroplane in the morning, when we take off from here.' He reached for his beer and finished it. 'If you're ready, Squadron Leader,' he said to Sanderson, 'we'll go into your office and I'll tell you what will happen tomorrow.'

*

The stars were bright and close, as they always are above the desert. The wind had died during the night and the Bristol throbbed comfortably westwards through the last of the darkness. Behind, the horizon was already clear before the approaching day.

The two men huddled in the open cockpits, flying suit collars turned up, helmets close about their heads. The desert dawn was cold.

Peter concentrated on his navigation, using a torch now and then to check air speed and compass, and glancing occasionally at the stars. Nothing else was needed, other than his chart. He had a revolver in the holster at his waist, another in his flying suit pocket, and a box of grenades concealed behind his seat. He had not mentioned the grenades to Thoresen; that was a surprise he would keep to himself until they were needed.

As his torch beam flickered across the instruments it settled for a moment on a photograph clipped to the panel. Fair hair, and dark eyes which seemed to watch him. He never flew without her picture. Thoresen had seen it in the hangar lights that morning before, as good as his word, he had swung the Bristol's propellor for a first-time start.

'Your daughter?' he had inquired crisply.

'Yes. Taken last year. She was five then.' He had passed the picture to Thoresen proudly.

'Pretty. Very pretty.' Thoresen had held it up to the lights. 'She'll grow up into a beautiful lady. Perhaps I may meet her one day.'

Peter had nodded without comment as he had fitted the photograph into its slot on the instrument panel. The apparent cordiality had surprised him, for the previous evening's desultory table talk had been more curt than friendly.

One thing had emerged, though: before his Middle East travels Thoresen had spent a number of short holidays at the de Lattre chateau, shooting with his host and François Boisy. Peter had known nothing of that – either, he now reflected, because Marie-Claire's father had not mentioned it in his letters or, more likely, because she had not translated references to it when she had read the letters to Peter. Nor had anything been said on his own rare visits, and suddenly he was uncomfortably aware that that could only have been because his wife had told de Lattre that the subject should not be discussed.

But he could give Thoresen no hint of that, so he had said, just for effect: 'I knew you'd been there a few times. In fact once – can't just remember when – we missed you by only a few days.'

'Indeed?' Thoresen had not sounded disappointed. 'Did

you manage to get there often, before they sent you out to this God-forsaken place?'

'As often as leaves allowed,' Peter had lied. He certainly would not admit that the cost of the journey down to central France had prohibited some of the visits Marie-Claire would have liked to make. They lived in a little semi-detached house near Northolt, Peter's last home base, and his Flight Lieutenant's pay had been hard pressed to support the domestic scene on top of his own service social life, the full details of which were not always known to his wife. So holidays in France were forfeited, although de Lattre sometimes sent train tickets for Marie-Claire and Michele when Peter had no leave available. He had never objected, for such occasions left him free to enjoy other, secret friendships; and he was glad to think of Michele going back to the chateau, for it was a magic place in her child's eyes. She had been brought up to speak English and French equally, and although she sometimes confused words and phrases in the two languages, she was effectively bilingual and totally at ease in her grandfather's great house and the little village nearby. François Boisy was devoted to her and spent hours teaching her to ride one of the ponies in the chateau stables, or taking her to watch work on the estate farms and for picnics on the banks of the river while Marie-Claire talked with her father.

Sanderson had tried to brighten the coldly courteous conversations during the dinner, but found it hard work; so much so that he had said quietly to Peter at the end of it: 'Am I misreading, or do you and our visitor dislike each other?'

Peter had raised an eyebrow and murmured sarcastically: 'Like each other? We're lifelong friends.'

'Do you want to tell me the story?'

'It's simple. We had a slight physical difference over a lady. I won – both the encounter and the lady. He doesn't seem to have forgotten. It won't interfere with what we have to do tomorrow, if that's worrying you.'

'I'm sure,' Sanderson had said. But Peter had been aware of his frown as they had parted.

Now he dismissed the memory. They had reached the border area, and the yellow disc of the sun slid up into the eastern sky behind them and flooded the barren land with pale golden light in that abrupt transition which is the desert's hallmark. Peter climbed to eight thousand feet to get a wider view, and within minutes glimpsed a grey shadow stretching across the desert floor: a half mile wide rectangle with uncertain edges. He raised a gloved hand into Thoresen's line of sight and pointed, turning his head and seeing the other's brief acknowledgement, then dropping his port wings and turning in a slow, descending spiral against the hazy bowl of the sky.

He came down half a mile from the Bedouin encampment, holding minimum flying speed in a low pass across the ground, studying the surface for boulders or the tell-tale signs of soft sand before he settled into an approach. He had landed on the desert many times, and this proved no more difficult than most. His wheels touched, bounced once, then ran, jarring. He held the tail up for as long as he could, until the last vestige of lift had gone and he pulled the stick back. When they stopped he gunned the engine, turning and taxiing back to his touch-down point so that they could use the same stretch of land for take-off. Finally he swung the aircraft so that the rear cockpit's Vickers gun covered the direction of the Bedouin camp, and switched off.

When he turned, Thoresen had already heaved himself up out of the cockpit and was taking off his helmet. He nodded curtly to Peter, then dropped to the ground. Peter sat on the fuselage at the back of his cockpit, watching the line of tents in the distance; seeing camels tethered, then horses; looking for the first sign of men.

Thoresen had taken with him a Union Jack on a short stick, and now held it aloft as he began to walk towards the camp. He walked steadily, unhurriedly, as if it were an early morning stroll. Peter had to admit to admiration, for Thoresen must have known as well as he that there was always the chance that one of the more fanatical tribesman would fire on him as he got closer.

But no shots split the desert silence, and the man in the khaki drill suit and flying coat walked on, passing from the barren desert floor to the sparse newly-greened pasture surrounding the water hole which was the heart of the camp. He held his flag above his head, and now brandished in his other hand a roll of parchment which was his peace document.

He was within a hundred yards of the nearest tents when three men appeared, long cloaks wrapped around them; tiny figures from Peter's viewpoint, but not so tiny that he could not see the rifles in their hands. The visitor reached them and they stood together; then walked into the encampment. Faintly, Peter heard a horse whinny, but nothing else. He thought suddenly: what the hell do I do if I hear a shot and Thoresen doesn't come back? Do I just take off without him? He shrugged to himself. There would be no alternative.

Half an hour passed before he again saw movement at the edge of the encampment. The sun was hot, although nothing to compare with the temperatures that would come later in the day. He knew that in a little while the camp would become difficult to see as the heat haze rose from the barren land. But he could see well enough now, as horses were led into view and Thoresen walked with the group of men who led them, long robes and head dresses shifting in the wind. Then Thoresen mounted a horse, and several men swung into other saddles alongside him.

Peter watched them come. At a distance the Bedouin thobe looked dramatic, even glamorous; although he knew that at close quarters it would be revealed as a dirty, ragged and smelly garment. The group cantered easily towards him, dust swirling behind the hooves, Thoresen pale beside the dark-skinned men surrounding him.

Then, beyond them, along the dark edge of the encampment, men appeared. Some led horses; a few, camels. All seemed to carry rifles; although that was unremarkable, for the rifle was the Bedouin's constant companion. They seemed to move warily, watchfully; several hundred dark-robed men emerging from the far-off lines of tents as if they were stalking the small group of horsemen who rode unhurriedly towards the solitary aeroplane.

Peter glanced at the Vickers gun behind him. He would have liked to have been nearer to it, but it was too late; a movement towards the gun could destroy whatever delicate balance had been achieved by Thoresen.

He could see the approaching riders clearly now. Thoresen looked at ease. He was talking to the Bedouin by his side. The man was listening carefully, his dark craggy face and deep-set eyes immobile and guarded within the frame of the kaffiya about his head. His thobe billowed out around his horse's quarters, like a sail flapping in slow motion. And behind, the long line of men moved closer, dark stealthy spectators stirring the dust, the sound of their coming silenced by the vastness of the desert.

The horses rattled the stony surface as they trotted. Thirty yards away they stopped and Thoresen dismounted. He went straight round to the front of the Bristol and Peter, interpreting the signal, slid into the cockpit, flicked switches, and raised his hand. Thoresen grasped the tip of the propeller blade, reaching and balancing carefully, then swung it down and round and the Bristol rocked as the gearing grated and the engine caught first time. Thoresen walked easily around the wing and across to the rear cockpit. He nodded to Peter and shouted: 'Okay. Off you go.'

Against the din of the Bristol's engine as Peter eased the throttle lever forward, neither heard the shot. But as Thoresen slid down into the cockpit both heard the smack of the bullet as it tore through the canvas fuselage behind them.

Peter slammed the lever all the way forward. The riders who had come with Thoresen had not moved; so the shot had come from the dark, shifting line of men who were now less than three hundred yards away. The Bristol lurched forward, a great cloud of dust lifting around it, half concealing it; then more bullets slammed into it and through it, and Peter twisted and shouted back at Thoresen: 'The Vickers – give 'em a burst –'

The Bristol was accelerating now, bumping over stones. Peter looked back, but Thoresen was low in his cockpit, making no attempt to man the gun. He saw canvas shred away from the lower wing on his right, close to the nearest strut, and knew they had been hit again.

Then he was hit himself, somewhere below the left knee. The impact twisted him sideways, slammed his leg against the cockpit side, jerked his foot clear of the rudder bar. The Bristol swayed as involuntarily he applied too much right rudder. Then he grabbed his left knee and lifted the leg, pushing his foot back against the pedal. At the same time he felt lift under the wings and eased the stick back, and the Bristol came away from the ground, crabbing but gaining height. Something clanged in front: a bullet glancing off the engine cowling. He was flying along the line of tribesmen, a slow lumbering target, so he banked steeply away, feeling agony surge up through his leg, aware of wetness around the calf and ankle. Christ, he thought – Jerry couldn't do this in two years, now a tribe of bloody desert savages has put one into me. He swore wildly, putting the Bristol down as low as he dared, flying directly away from the Bedouin line, getting to hell out of it as fast as possible.

And then he saw the photograph, and the eager, laughing face obliterated by blood splashed over it. He reached forward, trying to wipe it away, but it smeared; and suddenly a great surge of anger swept through him. They had desecrated her, spoiled her, and he was running away. Like hell he was. Not after they had done that. He lifted the Bristol, throttle wide, turning. A quick glance at his left leg. Blood on his trousers. A lot of blood. He held the Bristol in a climbing turn, groped in his pocket for a handkerchief, steadied the stick with his forearm and tied the handkerchief in a tight roll just below his knee, pulling the knot hard. He looked sideways and saw the ranks of the Bedouin in the distance as he swung the Bristol's nose around the horizon. He did not even glance back towards Thoresen; if he had been hit that was his hard luck. Those bloody Bedouin had put one into him and had fouled her picture, and they were bloody well going to pay, by God they'd pay. His leg hurt like hell but he was controlling the rudder bar. If he didn't lose too much blood he could fly this thing. He was coming back now towards the tribesmen. Even at a distance he could see their rifles glinting against the brown desert. Some were kneeling, others standing behind them, all aiming. He put the nose down, flogging the engine, lining up on the nearest of the thiyab-clad ranks through the sight over the single gun on the Bristol's engine cowling; then squeezing the trigger and zig-zagging so that his fire covered as wide an area as possible. Once he looked back. Thoresen should have been up in his cockpit, hammering at them over the side with the Vickers. But he was not. He was shouting, although Peter heard nothing. Shouting obscenities: that was clear in his face which was distorted in fury. He was waving an arm. Peter banked suddenly, steeply, and gravity thrust Thoresen down into his seat. The Bristol came round full circle, low down over the desert, a hundred feet, fifty, thirty, and they were back among the scattering Bedouin, dipping until the undercarriage was scarcely above the robes and dark faces and waving rifles as Peter snatched a genade from behind his seat, pulled the pin, and tossed the heavy metal egg over the side. Then he did the same thing again and again, without looking to see the result, rolling to come back because he had one grenade left, seeing robed figures running and many lying on the ground, swearing because now his leg was throbbing and there was a searing pain running down to his ankle. He clamped his jaw tight, lifted the aircraft's nose, and turned away to the east.

Not once on the flight back did he look round at Thoresen.

He sat hunched, sweating; then shivering. His left foot was numb and he knew he would have to use one hand to push and pull his leg so that he could operate the rudder for landing. As they sighted the base he began to feel sick, and as he came in on the downwind leg a wave of dizziness confused him for a moment. He began to swear aloud, concentrating on the words, shouting them, cursing Bedouin and the RAF and Thoresen and himself, anything to keep his mind intact, turning steeply into his final approach, pushing his useless leg. And all the time looking at the blood-streaked photograph until he stopped swearing and talked to her, promising her that he would get down in one piece, that he would come home again. The Bristol was drifting, crabbing, and he only straightened it at the last moment as he put it down hard, felt it bounce then settle, dropping the tail quickly. He tried to hold it straight but his leg would not work and the aircraft swerved to the right, raising dust clouds. Somehow he got it straight again and then stopped it. In the silence he said to the picture: 'There, I told you I'd do it. I promised you.' His voice sobbed in his throat.

When the ground crew got to him he was sitting in the cockpit, his head down, his face twisted in pain, snarling up at Thoresen: 'Why? Why did I do it? Because they bloody well put one into me – because they shot up an RAF plane – Christ, keep away from me, you bloody yellow bastard – you should have been working the Vickers –'

Thoresen did not go with him to the station hospital. Instead he went to see the Station Commander and said: 'I don't care how good his war record was. He's wrecked the whole peace initiative. I know we were fired on. But it's not the wild elements which matter. It's the leaders. And they were talking. Then that stupid idiot machine-gunned them, and threw grenades at them. He probably killed a hundred or more. He's ruined months of careful negotiation. They'll never listen to Ibn Saud again if he tries to talk peace with Feisal.'

The Station Commander said: 'I'll interview him, of course.

But don't forget that he was wounded. You're lucky he could fly you back.'

'I was unlucky to have an irresponsible, hot-tempered pilot who might have been good in the war but is obviously a menace in peacetime,' Thoresen snapped back. His narrowed eyes glittered. 'I can tell you that my masters will be looking for heads to roll.'

4

● — ●

François Boisy said: 'There are some crows on the edge of the wood. Let's see if we can get any of them. They're cruel. They peck out the eyes of lambs.'

He was walking across rough pasture with Michele. She was twelve years old, tall for her age, with long hair and fine features. Under her arm she carried a lightweight 28-bore shotgun; a small gun beside the big 12-bore in Boisy's hands, but the right weight for a child taking her first field lessons.

She walked proudly beside the steward. He was her great friend at the chateau, always finding new things to teach her when she came there on holiday. She wished her father could spend as much time with her at home as Boisy spent when she came to the chateau, but she knew he was always very busy and had to be away a lot. She glanced up at Boisy and said: 'I've been looking forward to this. Daddy has often told me about shooting with you. He says you're a very good shot and know everything about the country.'

'He's a better shot than I am,' Boisy said. 'He's one of the best shots I've seen.'

'I wish I could go shooting with Daddy sometimes,' she said. 'But he never has time to teach me.'

'Never mind. I'll teach you now. Let's walk quietly along the edge of the wood. And remember the lesson we had yesterday, in the field behind the big barn. This will be just the same, only the targets will be moving.'

She walked ahead of him, with the exaggerated stealth of a child for whom reality is still a game. And for a moment he felt sorry for her. She should have been with other children.

He thought she must be lonely, sentenced so often to adult company. He knew she had school friends in England; but he also knew that Marie-Claire had few friends of her own and leaned heavily on her young daughter for companionship. Boisy thought that most children in those circumstances would have been subdued and stilted, or precocious. But Michele was fresh and eager, with an attractive blending of adult dignity and childish charm. She was sensitive, too; full of the need to right the wrongs she saw about her, like shooting crows because they blinded lambs.

He followed her beside the wood, watching her as she sought her targets; and wondered what the world held for her. Certainly, by the time she was adult there would be little left for her here, he thought.

Presently, in one of the big rooms of the chateau, Marie-Claire heard the first gunshots.

'Michele enjoys herself so much,' she said. 'And François is kind to her.'

De Lattre nodded his gaunt grey head.

'We're lucky to have him. He's a great strength to us. I'm too old to know how to handle things now. He takes more and more of the responsibility.' It was a confession he found painful.

Marie-Claire said quietly: 'How serious have things become?'

'We have four hundred acres left, some of that land will have to go soon, and the house is running away with what money remains.' His voice was sad and spiritless.

She glanced quickly around the lofty room, with its embossed ceiling, its great marble fireplace and heavy old-fashioned furniture, and its threadbare carpet. The house exhibited every sign of neglect. Only three servants were there now, and all but nine or ten of the rooms were shut off. The most valuable furniture had been sold, and some of the pictures, too. The de Lattre fortune had almost disappeared.

'How long do you think you can keep François?'

De Lattre looked weary. 'He will be the last to go.' Then his thin face smiled. 'But I can't imagine we will sink as far as that. He belongs to this place nearly as much as we do. My greatest regret in all of it is that I can no longer afford to pay the fare for you and Michele to come here often. I wish Peter had been able to earn more money for you.'

Several gunshots echoed across the fields in quick succession, providing a distraction which Marie-Claire welcomed. She did not want to talk too much about Peter. Since he had had to resign his RAF commission they had had a difficult time and she had not told her father much about it. Nor had she told him about her strained personal relations with her husband, or that she had twice asked him if there was another woman somewhere, and had not believed him when he had denied it. It had taken all the courage she could muster to put the question, for she knew there could be only one reason for his increasingly transparent excuses for absences from the house. Once he had been able to blame service commitments with some conviction. But after that was over he had found new reasons to be away, even while he had been unemployed. Now his work took him away for weeks at a time, and she knew as certainly as if he had told her that he would still stay away if his job allowed him to come home.

Only Michele drew him back sometimes. He loved her deeply, Marie-Claire knew. When he came home he brought her dresses and toys, and talked with her solemnly about childish things, and told her long stories which she loved. And then he had promised that as a twelfth birthday present he would take her for a flight in an aeroplane and she was wildly excited about it. He was a little late, for her birthday had been several weeks before; but he had promised her and he rarely broke a promise to Michele. Perhaps when they got home from this holiday he would turn up again.

Her father was saying vaguely: 'I've never really understood what he does these days.'

She dragged her mind back to the great living room and its

shabby furniture, and her dignified, ageing father. 'He's a pilot, like he's always been,' she said. 'For all those years when he was in uniform he flew fighters and bombers. Now he – he flies civil aircraft. You know – passengers. People are getting very interested in flying. It's quite a good job, really.'

*

Three lorries trundled down the road, each towing a trailer. Cautiously they turned through a gateway into a long field and edged into a line beside the high hedge bordering one end of it.

Each carried, in red lettering which filled the side panels, the legend 'FLY HIGH – BRITAIN'S BIGGEST AIR SHOW' and then the words 'Daring Stunts to Thrill You. Plus Your Chance of a Flight.'

The Fly High Air Circus had arrived at a farm two miles from Kenilworth. And already the two-man publicity team had plastered the area with posters urging the public to see The Greatest Flying Show in Britain, and to find out for themselves what flying was like. Five Bob for a Flip, screamed the notices. See Kenilworth From the Air – The Thrill of a Lifetime. A van topped with a giant horn loudspeaker toured the town and surrounding villages, bellowing the same message, and now the posters would go up around the flying field too.

Over it all presided Charlie Feldman – 'Chuck', inevitably, for he was American. He was part owner of Fly High, and its driving force. He wore a check shirt, riding breeches and cowboy boots, and harangued his team constantly from the flap of the ridge tent which was his office. A pilot himself, he was also tough and ruthless, and fully capable of settling arguments with his fists if the need arose – although it rarely did, for instant dismissal was his first disciplinary weapon. With unemployment at an all-time peak in 1930 he needed little else to encourage maximum effort.

75

Then, at noon, the town had its first glimpse of the week's spectacle as five biplanes arrived from the Fly High base at Hendon and dived, rolled and looped over the streets before heading out for the airfield, sideslipping in to land one after the other. They needed plenty of ground space, for only the single Avro Avian had brakes. It came down smoothly, the pilot taxiing up the field towards the line of tents. Two crewmen ran out, grabbed the wingtips and slewed the Avian round, then darted away to manoeuvre the first of the four Avro 504Ks to land. The Avian pilot pushed off his helmet, eased himself from the cockpit, and looked around.

The Fly High Barnstormers had arrived.

From his tent Chuck Feldman strode into view, grinning widely. 'Hey, Pete, that's great timing – right on the button.' He held up an arm and tapped his watch enthusiastically.

Peter Armstrong waved back.

'The schedule says twelve-thirty – we arrive at twelve-thirty. How are things?'

'Great. Just great. Grab a coffee. Then we'll talk the day's programme through.' He turned back towards his tent; then paused, watching critically as a 504 bounced across the turf. Suddenly he was excited, shouting: 'Look at that guy. Too fast, too damn' fast. Waited till he was half way along the field before he put her down. Who is it? Craddock?' He cupped his hands to his mouth and bellowed to an apprentice: 'Nick – grab her – swing her – swing her.' The apprentice leapt into action, sprinting towards the approaching aircraft's port wing, running alongside, tugging furiously until the 504 came round in a circle.

Peter said: 'What's all the fuss? He wouldn't have hit anything.'

'I know that and you know that,' Feldman retorted. 'But I'll lay you a buck to nothing that for one crazy second he didn't know. He left his touch-down late. I'll talk to the guy. C'mon.'

Peter unzipped his oil-stained leather jacket as he followed Feldman to the tent, looking around the camp carefully.

Barnstormers lived a nomadic life during the season, and the lie of the land, the shelter of hedges and the layout of tents were important for their comfort. He ducked under the flap of Feldman's tent, slung his jacket into a corner, and perched on a folding wooden chair as the American poured strong coffee and said: 'If the weather holds we'll make a fortune here. Like we did at Bradford. How d'you fancy another Bradford, eh?'

Peter nodded approval. He fancied another Bradford, where the people had come in their thousands through the week and the sun had shone all the time. He needed another Bradford, too, because the weather had been unkind during some of the earlier shows. Feldman paid his ground crews a wage, but pilots worked on commission only: a lot of people meant a lot of money, but if the crowds were thin Feldman's cunning pay structure could mean there was nothing left for the men who provided the entertainment – and who risked their lives sometimes in the old aeroplanes which were all the circus could afford. It was the same for Peter as for the others, even though he was billed as the star of the show and netted an extra ten per cent as reward. So the size of the crowd was important.

They talked over the programme, then Peter stood up. 'I'll check my tent. But there's just one little personal thing, Chuck.'

'Go right ahead, right ahead.' Feldman waved a hand expansively. 'Anything I can do for you, Pete, I will.' His grin was fixed on his face, and suddenly his eyes were bright and hard and wary.

'You know I live in these parts,' Peter said. 'I'd like to call home for a few hours. And I want to bring my daughter back and give her a quick flip. I promised her that as a birthday present. She won't get in the way.'

Feldman's grin widened. He did not mind what Peter Armstrong wanted, as long as it was not more money.

'Sure, Pete, sure. Whatever you say. It'll be great to welcome the little lady – see how her father pays the rent, eh?' His laugh was short and sharp. 'How old did you say she was?'

'It's her twelfth birthday present. She's very excited about it.'

'That's OK. Give her a real long one – over the town – anywhere you like. When she gets here, you bring her right to this tent and I'll tell her what a great guy her father is. OK? You be sure to bring her here. I'll find her a birthday present. Sure I will – help her to remember her big day, eh?' He slapped Peter's shoulder as he ducked out of the tent.

That afternoon they went through the show routine, the pilots using the occasion to get to know local landmarks and wind peculiarities, until it was time for the finale, introduced by the booming voice of Chuck Feldman over the loudspeakers as 'the greatest and most daring exhibition of stunt flying you'll ever see, by one of Britain's war heroes, Peter Armstrong, who fought the Von Richtofen Circus over Flanders, won the Military Cross, held the ranks of Captain in the RFC and Flight Lieutenant in the RAF, and was wounded fighting savage tribesmen in the Arabian desert'.

It was, quite simply, Peter's cue to risk his life as he rolled, looped and dived at dangerously low altitudes, bounced the Avian across the turf on one wheel, picked up coloured streamers with an undercarriage hook, and subjected the aircraft to stall turns and gravity thrust for which it was never designed.

Immediately he landed, ground crew and pilots were amongst the crowd offering five-shilling flights, and soon the 504s were cruising around the countryside, nervous passengers clutching the cockpit sides then being bullied into quick exits to make room for the next customers, for every minute wasted was money lost and Feldman was always near at hand to calculate it. If passengers were allowed to dawdle, or refuelling was less than a panic procedure, he harangued the culprit afterwards in his harsh voice, ensuring that others were around to learn the lesson at the same time.

Peter had to wait for three days before rain prevented flying. Then he drove his battered Morris Cowley to Stratford-upon-Avon and the little village where Marie-Claire and Michele now lived in a terraced cottage. They had not heard from him for a month, but his wife greeted him loyally and Michele danced around him when he told her he had acquired a tent for them both alongside his own at the airfield, and that tomorrow he would give her the birthday flight.

The sun shone the next day and he said to Feldman: 'My daughter's here, and my wife. You remember I promised the girl a flight?'

The American scratched his head and frowned.

'Sure. I remember something. But it had better wait. I don't want you outa my sight till I know everything's AOK for this afternoon's show.'

Peter knew what that meant. Once the customers started to arrive he would be working non-stop until dusk and it was too dark to fly. He looked across the field and saw Michele in her blue dress and with her long hair swept by the breeze, and said, as if it were of little consequence: 'So the child doesn't get her birthday present. But I'm going to bring her over here – introduce her to you. You said you wanted that. Remember?'

Feldman stared at him, eyes narrowed. Then he snapped, 'Sure, you do that, Pete,' and watched as his star pilot strode away across the field, calling to the child. She ran to him, and then a slim, quietly dressed woman with dark hair and a pretty face came out of a tent. Peter spoke to them both, pointing back towards Feldman; then the three of them came towards him.

The American watched them come, and the way the girl held on to her father's hand and the excitement in her face, and muttered to himself: 'You bastard, Pete. You're setting me up.' Then he turned back into his tent, picked up the butt of a cigar from the boxwood desk, and was lighting it when Peter lifted the flap and said: 'Chuck, meet Marie-Claire and Michele.'

He went outside then, cigar trailing blue smoke, shook his visitors enthusiastically by the hand, and boomed: 'It's great to meet you, Marie-Claire. Pete talks about you all the time.' He flashed a knowing glance at Peter, then turned to the child. 'And this is Michele. Hi, Michele. You got a great guy for a father, I'll tell you. Best pilot there is. You must be proud, real proud.'

Michele looked at him. Her excitement was controlled now. The breeze blew a strand of hair across her face and she flicked it aside. The gesture was unpretentious, yet curiously sophisticated.

'I'm very proud, Mr Feldman,' she said. 'I'm proud to be here, as well. And to meet you.' Her voice held a child's charm, yet beneath it was the confidence of an adult.

Feldman stared, startled without knowing why. For an instant he thought: I've been set up, all right. Then he was surprised to feel his resentment fading, and suddenly found himself grinning at the further thought: Aw, what the hell? The kid's great.

He said: 'It's great to meet you, honey. Your father tells me you just had a birthday. Well, I'm real glad to hear that. Now you stay here. I'll be right back.' He twisted on the heel of his cowboy boots and walked away with long, fast strides towards one of the circus vehicles; disappeared inside, then came out holding a leather flying jacket, unzipping it as he came back to them. He held it out.

'If you're going to fly, you'll have to dress properly. This may be a bit too big, and it ain't quite new. But it's warm. You put it on now. And when you come back, you keep it. Call it a birthday present from old Chuck, eh?'

She took it from him, turning it, inspecting it, as if she could scarcely believe what she saw. It was brown, with a small grey fur collar and fur cuffs. There were stains and scuff marks on it, but to her that made it all the more romantic and exciting. She looked at him with bright eyes and said: 'It's marvellous. And it's mine – I may keep it?' She reached up quickly, put an arm around his shoulder, and kissed him on the cheek, whispering: 'Thank you, Mr Feldman, thank you. I shall keep it all my life. Oh, thank you.' And she kissed him again.

Feldman, not usually given to embarrassment, looked down at her and grinned his wide grin to cover his momentary confusion.

'That's OK, honey. I'm glad you like it.' Then he recovered, took the jacket from her and held it out. 'C'mon. Let me help you put it on.' He winked at Peter and Marie-Claire. 'She'll be the best-dressed kid on the field. I'll find her a helmet. Then you get into that kite and give her the thrill of her life, Pete.'

He found a leather helmet for her, and goggles, and supervised as she put them on, turning to Marie-Claire as he helped her to adjust the helmet and asking: 'You don't mind me doing this for her, Marie-Claire? Sure you don't mind?'

Marie-Claire shook her head. She was clearly delighted.

'Of course not. You're very kind. She's been looking forward to this for weeks.'

'Then we gotta make it a great day,' said Feldman enthusiastically. He patted the girl on the head. 'Now you get out there and let your father show you how gently he can fly that Avian.' He looked at Peter. 'Gently, I said, Pete. None of your crazy stunts, now. And that's an order.'

Peter, who had stood back in silent surprise throughout the American's expansive reaction to Michele, said easily: 'How else, Chuck? She's going to enjoy every minute.' He took her hand. 'Ready? Happy about it?'

She nodded, hair waving across her shoulders below the helmet. Her eyes shone as she looked up at him.

'Oh yes, Daddy. And you don't need to make it too gentle. I want to know what it really feels like to fly.' She hesitated, then added mischievously: 'As long as you don't make me feel sick.'

They all laughed, and Marie-Claire and Feldman watched as father and daughter walked away across the rough turf to the silver-and-blue Avian with the words FLY HIGH painted in red along the sides of the fuselage.

Beside the aircraft, Peter helped Michele into the rear cockpit and tightened the safety strap around her waist. Then he said seriously: 'I know you're going to enjoy this. But if you want me to turn back, just hold up your hand. I've a little mirror fixed there' – he pointed – 'so that I can see my passenger. And I'll be watching. Ready?'

She looked at him from within the high sides of the cockpit like a child seeing wonderland and nodded repeatedly.

'I'm ready. And I won't want you to turn back. Not if you fly all day.'

He grinned, then climbed into the front cockpit, signalled to a mechanic who swung the propeller and listened to the song of the engine. He checked his mirror and saw her flushed, excited face and watched her pull the goggles over her eyes; and for the first time in all his years of flying he felt a small doubt gnaw at his chest. Flying was dangerous; and he was taking his own daughter with him, into danger. He had not thought about that, when he had promised her the flight. He had only wanted to please her. And she had been pleased beyond words, not only to fly but – he knew – to fly with her father.

He glanced down into the cockpit, at the photograph clipped to a strut below the simple instrument panel. She had not been able to see that when she had climbed into the rear cockpit. When they landed he would show it to her, so that she would know she always flew with him. He hoped that would please her, too.

He opened the throttle and the little biplane bumped forward, turning towards the open field. He wondered what she really thought of him, now that the glamour of uniform had gone. He had come down a few steps in the world, from an Air Force officer and pilot to a barnstormer in a cheap-jack air circus flying clapped-out planes for a rough-tongued, tight-fisted American crowd-pusher. That had been Thoresen's doing. To hell with Thoresen. Peter had never known what had gone into the report on the Bedouin incident: only that three months later, when he was still grounded by his damaged leg, he had been told that 'higher authority' had found his conduct irresponsible, that it had had serious consequences for Arab-British relations, and that by the end of the year he would be expected to resign his commission. 'Regard it as part of the cut-backs,' they said.

He held the throttle wide and lifted the tail as the Avian picked up speed, snatching a quick glance at the mirror and Michele's face, small and round within the helmet, her eyes hidden behind the goggles but her mouth wide, laughing. Thank God he had not had to tell her the truth. Just part of the cut-backs; that was the story. No mention of the incident, or Thoresen, or the report. He had told Marie-Claire, but they had promised each other they would never tell Michele. She did not have to know that her father had been thrown out in disgrace. His record showed that he had resigned. That was all anyone had to know. Only Feldman knew what had happened at Basra. One night, after too much whisky, he had told the American, who had said: 'The Goddamsonofabitch. I hope he gets what's coming to him. One day he will, sure as hell. You wait and see.'

He dipped his wings in a salute as he came over the tree tops. Wait and see? He would have to wait forever and beyond. Thoresen had had his revenge.

*

Three days later the Avian took off again, followed by the 504s. The trucks had already left, on their way to a field near Southampton and another barnstorming show. When the aircraft landed Chuck Feldman shouted: 'You guys – come over here – I wanna talk.' They came, stained trousers and leathers, scarves flying over open-necked shirts, hands oil-stained and grimy; sauntering across the field. They were the only men who did not run when Feldman shouted orders.

He said: 'That show up in Warwickshire' – he pronounced it with a clipped pause between syllables as War-wick-shire – 'was OK, but not sharp enough. I saw some of the crowd talking while you were flying. That ain't good. They shouldn't have breath for talking when you're up there. So we need new tricks. Maybe one of you flies a plane like crazy – pretend you ain't flown before – scare the hell outa them. And we'll work out a dogfight between Pete and one of you other guys – fit you up with dummy guns firing blanks. Let Pete show what it was like in the war, eh? Work on it, willya? If we don't get new ideas we'll be outa jobs. OK?'

He dismissed them with a wave of a hand, but Peter turned back as the others moved out of earshot and said casually: 'I've got a friend lives in Southampton, Chuck. You don't need me to sleep on the field, do you?'

The skin crinkled around Feldman's eyes.

'Sure I don't need you sleeping here,' he said. 'You go see your friend.' He looked at Peter critically, then added: 'And I hope you ain't too proud of yourself. If I had a wife and daughter like you got up there in War-wick-shire I guess I'd be proud to keep away from friends.'

He dragged half a cigar from his shirt pocket and strode away, lighting it and trailing smoke.

*

Two more years passed before Peter's friends could no longer be ignored by Marie-Claire. The girl in Southampton gave it away by writing to him at his home because he had stopped visiting her and she was angry, and for the first time Marie-Claire deliberately opened a letter addressed to Peter.

After that she made inquiries: until she tracked him down to a semi-detached house on the outskirts of Bristol where he was sharing a bed with the wife of a ship's captain who was at that moment sailing westwards across the Atlantic.

He made no attempt to excuse himself. He said he would accept divorce and would try to support Michele through the rest of her schooling, provided Chuck Feldman could hold his little company together as long as that.

It had been as civilised as such things could be. 'You'll have to go,' she had said. 'I can't live with you any more.' No tears, although he guessed she would cry a lot later. If he could have felt ashamed it might have been easier for her; but it had been going on for so long, with so many, that he did not care much.

Except for Michele.

No excuses. Marie-Claire had told her that Daddy was going away to live with someone else. He might come back to see her now and then, but that would be all. And she never spoke to him about it. At fourteen she was no longer a child, yet not enough of a woman to know what to say. Once he had tried to explain, to excuse himself, but she had walked away, out of the room, and the words had choked him.

Now he had packed his belongings. He had said goodbye to them both: stiff words from a script he had prepared carefully but had not learned very well. 'I'll come back to see you,' he said to Michele. But she had just stared at him, and he knew he would be forever haunted by the proud hostility and the contempt on a face which seemed so much older than her years.

He drove along the road without looking back; then stopped around a corner where they could not see him, and covered his face with both hands and wept, whispering her name again and again and again.

ANNE

---◆●◆---

1947

1

There was nothing else he could tell. He was a lonely man, prematurely aged, living on his memories; and his memories of Michele ended on that day in 1932. He had never attempted to find her, and did not know what had happened to her until I went to see him.

At first I thought he would refuse to talk to me. I was a stranger on his doorstep, telling him that I was researching for a biographical tribute to his daughter; and when he stared, uncomprehending, and I told him she was dead, he held on to the door frame for a moment and closed his eyes. Then he said, 'I'm sorry, I don't want to talk to you,' but I persuaded him to hear what I planned to do, and when he learned that I had known Michele he began to ask me what she had been like then, ten years after his last glimpse of her, and if she had married and what her husband had been like; and he was hooked.

He was around fifty-seven and looked much older, with his thin grey hair and lined face. There must have been many more girls in Peter Armstrong's life after he and Marie-Claire parted, and a lot of alcohol too, I guessed, through long late nights without enough food.

He had worked for Chuck Feldman for another two years before the American had surrendered to persistent take-over offers from the giant Alan Cobham Air Circus. Feldman had joined Cobham as an airfield manager, but there had been no room for Peter. He had touted a living as a freelance pilot for a time, then had combined that with selling second-hand cars. For a year he was unemployed, then opened a newsagent's shop in Cambridge which made just enough money to enable him to put in the requisite minimum flying hours each year at the local aero club and keep his pilot's licence. So when the war started, although he was forty-nine he was able to get a job with Vickers-Armstrong as a ferry pilot, mostly flying staid personnel transport aircraft between the various Vickers factories. He had dreams of being promoted to their team of test pilots but he was too old and had to watch from the tarmac as the Spitfires, Wellingtons and Lancasters were flight tested. But he met many of the Air Transport Auxiliary pilots who ferried tested and repaired aircraft from the factories to the squadrons.

We were in our third, and last, long question-and-answer session when he began to talk about those days. I had almost lost interest, because I could see little useful material emerging from his war memories, until he said: 'A lot of the ATA pilots came and went from Castle Bromwich. I often used to see them. That was how I met up with Chuck again.'

'Chuck Feldman? He was still in this country?'

'Oh yes.' He felt for a cigarette: his tenth or twelfth of the afternoon. 'He went back to the States, but couldn't settle. He tried to join the American Eagle squadron in the RAF – you know, long before America came into the war – but he was too old. So he joined the ATA instead, ferrying Hudsons across the Atlantic. That must have been hairy.' For an instant the old adventure light gleamed in his far-away eyes and his lined face creased further as he grinned. 'I met him in the crew room at Castle Bromwich early in 1943. He'd come to pick up a Lanc we'd had in for repair. We met face-to-face in the doorway. Just like that.'

Then he stopped talking and drew hard on his cigarette. His eyes were dull again, and the skin crinkled around them so that I could hardly see them; but I knew he had remembered something and was wondering if he should tell me. We were sitting in the lounge of the little house he had on the outskirts of Cambridge, and to give him time I walked through to the kitchen to make some fresh coffee. When I came back he was relaxing in his chair, a newly lighted cigarette between his fingers, staring at the ceiling. I poured coffee, pushed a cup towards him, and waited.

At last he said: 'Chuck had met her.'

I stopped stirring sugar into my cup.

'Her? You mean Michele?'

'Yes.' Still staring at the ceiling. 'In some club in London. A couple of months before. Strange, wasn't it? The coincidence, I mean.'

'Was it a once-only meeting? Or did he see her again?'

He drew in smoke and exhaled it, then looked down at the coffee cup, noticing it for the first time, and said: 'Thanks.' He tasted the coffee. 'He only saw her once. He arranged to meet her again, but she didn't turn up. But that was the war, wasn't it? It happened all the time.' He drank more coffee, then said quickly, as if it were a confession: 'I asked him to contact the club, to see if they knew where she was.'

'You wanted to find her?'

'Yes.' More cigarette smoke. 'I wondered if we could – make it up. It was a forlorn hope.' He reached for his cup, cradling it in his hands as if he needed to warm them. 'Anyway, I never heard from him again. So I suppose he didn't find her. Or she told him she didn't want to know me.'

He was looking at me; then, when our eyes met, he turned away and stared out of the window. The memory was hurting. He had come close to her, after nearly ten years; and then had lost her again. And he was afraid that she had rejected him.

I said: 'You never heard from him? Do you know what might have happened to him?'

He dragged his gaze away from the window.

'What might – oh, you mean Chuck? No idea. Probably went back to the States after the war. If he survived. Some of those ATA people didn't.'

That was all I got out of him. But he had given me an idea.

Anne Henshaw-Reid was becoming something of a habit. I rang her and invited her for dinner. She came to the flat to sample my version of Steak Diane and a bottle of the best Medoc I had been able to find, and I told her about Chuck Feldman and Michele in London.

'I've got to find him,' I said. 'Even if he's in America. He might have had only five minutes with her. Or they might have talked for hours.'

'Or he might be dead,' she said solemnly. 'Peter Armstrong was right. There were casualties in the ATA. Remember Amy Mollison?'

'I know. But most of them came through. And Chuck sounds as if he was a survivor.'

The last of the day was fading outside. I leaned over and turned on a table lamp. Her hair shone in the soft light. She said cautiously: 'I've an old contact at the MoD who might be able to arrange access to ATA records. They would give us his home address up to whenever he left the service. May I follow it up for you?'

I liked her use of the plural. She was beginning to feel an involvement which went beyond that of a publisher's editor; and I was beginning to hope that the involvement was with me rather than just the book. Rather formally I said: 'Thank you. That's kind. Don't let it be a lot of trouble, though.'

She smiled the cool smile behind which she so often sheltered. 'I won't let it give me more trouble than I think it's worth.' Then the smile drifted away and she was warm and closer to me. 'Let me help you, when I can. I'd like to.'

My habitual and infernal flippancy prodded me and I said: 'Do you say that to all your authors?'

As soon as the words were out I knew they were a mistake. The hurt showed in her eyes, and then the professional detachment came between us like a sheet of glass. I could see, but I could no longer touch.

'It's our job to be helpful,' she said distantly. 'But perhaps

I'd better leave it to you. I'll arrange the access. You follow it up.'

I stared down at my plate, wondering what wretched quirk of character prompted such stupidity.

'Sorry,' I said. 'That rather spoiled the steak, didn't it?'

'The steak was delicious.' She raised her eyebrows, as if she had not understood. 'You're a very good cook.'

'A good cook, and a poor conversationalist.' I was suddenly terribly anxious to make amends. She had reached towards me, and my inane humour had rebuffed her. I groped for a way out and couldn't find one, and there was an embarrassing silence until she said: 'I don't think so. Forget it, anyway. Apart from Chuck Feldman, what's the next move?' She asked as if she did not really care.

I said mechanically: 'François Boisy. If neither the war nor age have killed him. Peter Armstrong told me that Michele and her mother went to live in France a couple of years after the divorce. So Boisy would know what happened next. I'm going to Paris next week. I'll hire a car and drive down the N7 to Montargis and try to find him.'

'Didn't she tell you anything about those years, when you met her during the war?'

'I don't remember,' I said defensively. 'What about you? You knew her, too.'

Very quietly she said: 'I can't think of anything now. I'll try when I get home. But I had the feeling you didn't want much help.'

I grasped the straw.

'Don't torment me. I made a silly joke, in bad taste. That's all it was.' I reached for her hand across the table because I needed to touch her.

She was still, her eyes bright and searching in the low lamp light. Her fingers were warm under mine, and she did not draw them away.

'Then I'll say it again,' she said softly. 'The thing I said before your – your joke. Let me help you, because I'd like to.'

93

I stood up then, still holding her hand, and moved round the little table, guiding her to her feet. The room was quiet; it had never been so quiet. She came, unresisting, her head back a little and her eyes big and dark as I kissed her. I did not try to hold her, except her hand, and she had not reached for me; we just stood, bodies touching but not demanding, lips together, then as if at a signal parting slightly in the hint of experiment.

And all the time her eyes were wide and asking questions of mine: questions no one had asked since Michele.

When it was over she whispered: 'Why did it take so long?' But I didn't know the answer, except that I was a little afraid of her and I couldn't explain it, so I let her turn away and she sat down at the table again and pushed her fingers through her hair as if it needed disciplining, and took a long breath before she said: 'Don't talk about the book any more. Talk about you. Things I don't know. Which means everything. What happened to your marriage?'

'It ended. Though I didn't know you even knew there'd been one.' I was playing for time, calming myself.

'Charles told me. But I'd have known anyway.'

I sat down, staring at her.

'How?'

'Something about you. You're wary of women. You're not a shy man; just the opposite. So there had to be another reason. It scarred you. What went wrong?'

I shrugged. I had never made a secret of it.

'Just another war casualty. Probably we'd still have been together if it hadn't been for Hitler. But she couldn't wait. It's boring.'

We talked on like that; feeling our way, neither of us committing. I couldn't understand it. I should have been all over her now, breathing heavily; and she should have been responding, wondering how long it would be before I tried to get her into my bedroom and what she would do when I did.

I never did try to get her into the bedroom; not that night, anyway. We sat there long after the darkness came in the street outside, asking questions and giving careful answers and reminiscing and never mentioning the book again or how she might help, until it was time for her to go. Then we kissed again, and this time we did hold each other and I knew she wanted what I wanted but we were both afraid of it, and of ourselves. It was too soon.

We walked down the mews hand in hand and along King's Road until we found a cruising cab. As she got in I kissed her, quickly. And all the way back to the flat I could see her eyes looking into my mind.

*

François Boisy had a lot to tell; but not everything, because he had not shared the end of the next phase in Michele's life. At one point I thought there would be a gap which could be bridged only by my imagination; until, long after Boisy, I found the link I sought, reluctant but incontrovertible. So in the end, although I had to fill in some of the missing pieces later, the picture was completed. In the beginning, though, its substance came from my journey into France in the spring of 1947.

Montargis is a small town on the slopes of a wide river valley. In the summer the river is reduced to little more than a series of streams running through shingle and it is possible to walk across if you are not particular about getting your shoes wet. But now the water was wide when I drove over the bridge into the centre of the town.

It took me some time to find the de Lattre chateau. That had to be my starting point because if François Boisy was still living I had no idea where else he might be. I tried several shops with my less-than-perfect- French, but no one seemed to have heard of the family. So I went to the town hall, and a pretty girl said: 'Oh yes, I know the place. Someone still lives there, I think. But it's tumbling down. I'll show you on the map.'

Half an hour later I drove my hired Citroën between two great ivy covered sandstone gateposts and into a wide dirt drive lined with old chestnuts, beeches and overgrown bushes which half-hid neglected grassland beyond. The drive was all of two hundred yards long and ended with a flourishing bend through the trees which effectively concealed the detail of the house until the visitor was close to it.

Then I sat in the car and stared. It looked immense: all grey stone, turreted at the front corners, with three stories and lines of windows. Tumbling down, the clerk at the Hotel de Ville had said. She was right. The walls were flaking and chipped, several of the upper windows were boarded inside broken glass, moss grew in crevices and cracks and hung from the gutters, and a long drainpipe was broken with a section missing.

I left the car and walked over the carriage drive, covered now with tufts of grass and weed which hid what was left of the gravel, and looked at the battered front door. There was neither bell nor knocker, so I hammered on it with the heel of my hand; repeatedly, until at last I heard shuffling footsteps and a bolt being withdrawn.

The door creaked as it swung open.

FRANCOIS

1937–1940

1

The old man was dying, and Michele was walking in the great walled garden with Paul Laval. Their arms were around each others' waists and every now and then they paused and kissed. François Boisy thought it was wrong.

She should have had more respect for her grandfather. But perhaps he had been dying for too long; too long for youth to contain itself in sombre tension and suspended grief; certainly too long for Michele to contain herself, for she had never been able to do that easily.

He watched from a window, hidden by the thick stone mullion. He was not really spying; he had glimpsed the couple in the garden and had watched more in regret than curiosity. He thought Paul Laval was a playboy, a young and unappealing adventurer.

But then perhaps Michele was an adventurer too. The way she looked at Laval, and the way she kissed him. She knew men. The steward was sure of that. He saw it in her eyes and the curve of her mouth and her walk. She knew more about men than, in François Boisy's view, any girl of nineteen should.

It seemed a long time since she had come to live at the chateau. For two years Marie-Claire had struggled after her marriage had broken. Peter had kept his promise about supporting Michele. But then he had lost his job with the air circus and de Lattre had told his daughter to come back to France and settle at the old family home. At least there was enough money there to keep them.

Enough. But only just. Two thousand acres had shrunk to a thousand, then to four hundred, and now to two hundred as the investments failed, the debts mounted, and the old man became older in mind as well as in body. The house was crumbling around them with shabby furniture standing on threadbare carpets, many of the rooms closed, pictures and valuables sold, and only one servant left – apart from Boisy, who was now effectively the estate's master.

He had been out walking what was left of it, yesterday. Michele had been with him, a 16-bore shotgun on her arm, looking for crows. She had always hated crows, ever since he had told her they pecked out the eyes of living lambs in the spring. Boisy remembered her at twelve, asking him to teach her to shoot. She had been a good pupil. In the following years, when she had come to live at the chateau, she had spent a lot of time with him, learning how the remains of the estate were farmed, how the books were kept, how the last of the woodland was managed. Boisy treated her as he treated everyone else, with gruff candour and little humour; an impatient, even intolerant façade which disguised only thinly his devotion to her wishes. She was Marie-Claire's daughter and for him that was enough. She was mercurial and wilful, and often he did not understand her; but she had a mobile, expressive face and eyes which sparkled with sudden enthusiasms, and she laughed easily. She listened carefully when he told her things, and usually heeded his advice, which flattered him. And she was even more beautiful than Marie-Claire had been when he had laboured through his lost, secret obsession so long ago.

But now she was changing.

It had happened since she went away to Switzerland. She must go to finishing school, the old man had said, watching her with his dimming eyes; and he sold another two hundred acres of land to pay for it. He would have liked her to go to university but it would have been a waste of money because she did not want to go, and in any case she did not have the academic flare. So he sent her to a finishing school near Berne for a year.

When she went away she was a girl, thought François

sentimentally; now, three quarters through her year, she was a woman. Was she really only nine months older? And what had happened to her in that time, to change her?

Perhaps he was getting old; but at fifty-five he did not think so. Perhaps he was out of touch with youth. A bachelor could not be expected to understand. But he could remember his own youth, and he did not feel out of touch. So, silently, he just felt a little sad, because the innocent girl had grown so suddenly away from them all.

He was still standing by the window when Marie-Claire came into the room. He glanced round, but did not move. She walked over to him and said: 'You're very intent, and very serious, François. What are you looking at?'

'Your daughter. She is with her friend.' He nodded towards the garden. It was his habit to be forthright.

'And you don't like him.' She looked over his shoulder in time to see Michele swing round on Laval's arm, confront him, and then kiss him, pressing herself momentarily against him. 'We should not be watching. It isn't fair.'

He turned away from the window.

'I know. But since I am as concerned for her as you, there's no harm.'

She watched the couple embrace, then part to resume their stroll.

'Does he concern you so much?'

He shrugged, and pushed a hand through his thick, greying hair.

'He is out for what he can get. A young man with more money than conscience. You know what I think – you've asked me before.'

She said: 'You're the only one I can talk to. Father lives in his own private world, and it's getting more and more distant. You're our prop. And soon you'll be the most important person here.'

His weather-hardened face creased into a rare smile.

'No, Marie-Claire. You are the important one. And she –'

he nodded towards the window '– is more important still, because she has all her life to live. That's why I worry.'

She squeezed his arm affectionately. His tweed jacket was harsh under her fingers.

'You'll be the most important because the less money there is, the more we need you to tell us what to do. We'll be helpless without you.'

He knew she was right. Marie-Claire had never been totally worldly. Until Peter Armstrong had arrived she had been protected by money, privilege and convention. Then she seemed to have drifted through the ensuing years, never becoming involved with other service wives, rarely making close friends outside. She had built her small world about her daughter, and he hesitated to think what might have happened to them if they had not been able to return to France after the marriage had ended.

But Michele was different. She was so much like her father; too much, he thought sometimes. She was spectacular on a horse, jumping hedges and fences with her hair flying and with an ability to stay in the saddle which owed more to instinct than to finesse and classic technique. She was uncommonly good with a shotgun and a small-bore rifle, she skied and skated at dangerous speeds and, most extraordinary of all to the steward, she rode a 250cc motorcycle.

Until a year ago she had done it all with the unselfconscious and innocent charm of reckless youth. But now the innocence had gone, and the wilful woman emerging from the pretty chrysalis had the grace of a cat which had not learned to understand danger, and a hint of sensuality which could come only from experience.

François Boisy considered the thought, then shrugged. He was being melodramatic, attributing to her more than she possessed. Yet he still thought he was not too distant from the truth, although in spite of the trust and respect which existed between them even he could not discuss such things with the daughter of his employer. He had to conceal his anxieties.

They both turned at the sound of tapping on the tiled mosaic floor of the corridor beyond the room. They knew it was the old man's stick. Then the door creaked open.

He was eighty-nine years old, and looked much older; a walking skeleton inside his beautifully tailored clothes which sagged from his thin stooping shoulders. His eyes were dull and sunken, wisps of white hair straggled across his scalp, and the skin hanging on his cheekbones was the oddly smooth, almost transparent creamy-white which sometimes is the mark of coming death for the very old.

He said, in the croak which now passed for a voice: 'The news. I heard the news on the wireless. Hitler's been speaking. About Austria again. All one people, he said. He'll invade. Then there'll be war. Like last time. A million and a half Frenchmen. All dead.'

Marie-Claire went to him and guided him to a chair.

'Don't worry, Papa. He won't invade. And even if he does, it doesn't mean there'll be war. Austria's far away.'

'Sarajevo was far away,' the gaunt face crackled. 'We couldn't stop him. France is too soft. Too many pleasures. And communists. Eating our will. I don't want to see it.' A tear ran down one cheek. He did not seem to notice. 'It will be the end of us here. Remember I told you.'

Boisy said gruffly: 'You won't see it, sir. Neither will the rest of us. Because it won't happen. Now, what would you like for lunch?'

A shaking hand waved him away.

'Nothing. Can't eat today. Where's the girl? Where's Michele?'

'In the garden, with Paul,' Marie-Claire said. 'Do you want to see her?'

'See her? I can't see anything.' The dim eyes stared. 'But bring her. I want to ask her something. And it's private. Send the boy away. I don't like him. He won't bring her happiness. And you stay away. Both of you. It's private.'

Marie-Claire and the steward exchanged glances. She

raised her eyes momentarily in a gesture of despair, then said: 'All right. I'll see if I can find her.'

Boisy said: 'I'll tell her. You stay with him.' He went out of the room, down the long tiled corridor, through another door and across a great conservatory with glass partly obscured by moss and with weeds scattered among the pavings, and out into the garden.

Five minutes later Michele came quietly into the room where the old man sat. Her fair once-long hair was shorter now, collar-length and framing her fine-boned face with soft waves. She was tall, with high young breasts modelled by a silk blouse, and with hips slender and supple within a close-fitting skirt. Anyone who had met the handsome Peter Armstrong would have known this was his daughter.

She looked at her mother questioningly, and Marie-Claire said: 'Grandpapa wants to talk to you.' She nodded at the skeletal figure in the chair.

'Private,' the old man croaked. 'Private. I want to talk to her alone.' He waved a dismissive hand and Marie-Claire shrugged, looked helplessly at her daughter, and went out of the room.

Philippe de Lattre waited until he heard the door close, then crooked a bony finger. His teeth showed as his thin lips disappeared in what once would have been a smile.

'Sit down with me. You haven't told me about La Croix. Your school. Do you still enjoy it?'

'Some of it.' She perched on the edge of a hard chair, watching him curiously. 'Some of the things we learn are interesting. But when they try to turn us into elegant ladies they're rather boring, because they're not really elegant themselves.' Her laughter was quick and low and musical.

He clawed at the arm of the chair with long fingers, pulling himself forward. He was like an old, weak vulture, crouching.

'What about your social life? Are you meeting the right people? People who do you credit? Who are as good as yourself?' His voice dropped conspiratorially.

'Oh, yes. That's part of the course. Have you forgotten?'

He waved an impatient hand.

'No, no. I remember. But your private social life. Do you still go to the embassies? Have you met our ambassador again? It's most important that you meet the right people. You must marry well. The family needs that. Marry well. Yes?' He cocked his head on one side, peering at her.

She said: 'I don't know about marrying, Grandpapa. But I've been to the French, the British and the German embassies. To receptions and parties. And I've met the French and British ambassadors. They're both charming.'

His head tilted again, and the fingers gripped the chair. He tried to whisper, but the sound was still a croak.

'Are you being properly escorted? Does my friend treat you well, and escort you fully, and introduce you to the right people? That's important.'

His eyes stared at her, but she was just a shadow to him and he could not see the faint flush which coloured her cheeks.

'Oh, yes. He invites me to the parties. And escorts me. He's – very attentive.' Her voice was low, and cautious.

'Good.' The old man eased back in his chair. He had made the effort to talk, and was suddenly weary. 'It's a secret. Never forget. My special arrangement for you. Never tell. No one understands how important it is.' He leaned his head against the chair. 'Now bring your mother. I think I'll go to my room.' His hand gestured, the fingers clutching at the air.

She stood up, watching him anxiously, then walked softly to the door and opened it; and found herself facing François Boisy whose bright, shrewd eyes stared at her from the dim corridor.

'I thought I should come to see if you needed me.' His voice was low, rough-edged. 'I know he can be difficult sometimes.' He glanced over her shoulder into the room.

She said: 'I didn't hear you. He says he wants to go to his room. Will you go with him?'

He nodded. 'I'll help him.'

'Thanks. I'll tell mother.' She went quickly away along the corridor, her heels clicking.

Just for a moment the steward turned to watch her go. He thought she was quite beautiful enough to be vulnerable, at only nineteen. And he did not like what he had heard as he had stood briefly outside the door.

Yet there were still things he could not bring himself to say to the daughter of his employer, no matter how much he thought he should.

*

'He could go tomorrow,' the doctor said. 'But his heart is still strong and his respiration is no worse. So I would guess at one or two weeks, three at the most.'

It was the most definite forecast they had had.

Afterwards François Boisy said: 'I think we should telephone Michele at La Croix. She should be warned that it is now very close. We must make sure she can come to the funeral.'

So Marie-Claire tried to contact her daughter at Berne, but there was a delay on the line which the operator said would not be cleared that night, and the next morning she had a meeting with the family's lawyers, so she asked François to make the call.

When he asked for Michele he was told she was attending a lecture by a visiting American film director. So he spoke to Madame Anna Veni, the school's First Mistress, and said: 'The news will not shock her. She knows her grandfather has not long to live. But she should be warned that he is worsening and that we may ask her to come home within the next week or two.'

Madame Veni assured him that she would make all arrangements for Michele's journey when it became necessary. She was a friendly woman, ready to talk, and because François was still worried by the hushed conversation he had overheard between the old man and his grand-daughter, he said: 'Madame, as the family's steward I have to accept greater responsibility at this difficult time. So that I may reassure Michele's mother, tell me if you are satisfied that she is happy and progressing well.'

'But of course she is happy,' Madame Veni said. 'All our students are happy. She is one of our bright stars.'

'Does she still have the advantage of attendance at certain embassy events?' François asked. He was not used to conversational subtleties and felt uncomfortable.

'Indeed. It is a wonderful advantage. So socially instructive, and so useful that she should meet well-connected and distinguished people under formal circumstances. It's a valuable part of her education. She is envied by her fellow students.'

The steward took a long breath and asked: 'You are satisfied that she is properly escorted on these occasions, Madame?'

'My dear sir, of course I am satisfied.' Madame Veni was shocked. 'She is impeccably escorted. Indeed, there is a function tomorrow evening, and I had a personal telephone call yesterday from her grandfather's great friend, extending an invitation to her. As always, he will escort her personally and be responsible for her safety until she returns in the morning.'

'Her grandfather's great friend?' François tried to sound only momentarily forgetful.

'Of course.' The voice was impatient. 'As Monsieur de Lattre's steward you must surely know Monsieur Thoresen.'

'Oh yes, Madame. I know him.' François said quickly. 'Monsieur de Lattre has so many friends. Of course. Monsieur Thoresen.'

'He is an important person at the British Embassy,' Madame Veni said proudly. 'I am unsure of his title, but he is most influential.'

François allowed the conversation to drift on before concluding it pleasantly. But when he had replaced the telephone he stood for a long time looking at it. He remembered Thoresen as a one-time regular visitor to the chateau and had shot many times with de Lattre and his guest. A hard-eyed man, professionally ruthless, François judged; but also a man of great charm and sophistication. Handsome, too, and probably aware of it. But they had not seen him since Marie-Claire and Michele had returned to the chateau to live there, and François had overheard enough of other people's conversations to know that Marie-Claire did not like her father's bearded shooting companion. There was, instinct told him, something he did not know about the family's relationships with Thoresen. And now he remembered the subtle changes in Michele's manner since she had gone to Berne, and the hint of sensuality in her movements and the way she looked at men; and he remembered, too, Madame Veni's comment about Thoresen being responsible for Michele's safety 'until she returns in the morning'.

He thought about it for the rest of the day until Marie-Claire returned from her meeting. By then he had decided that there were some things which duty demanded he should discuss with the daughter of his employer, and he met her in the great hall and said: 'I must talk with you. On a very confidential matter. I am greatly concerned.'

*

Madame Veni was short and wide-hipped, and spoke beautifully in French, German and English. She was the daughter of a French count and a German actress, and ran one of Switzerland's most distinguished schools specialising in preparing the daughters of the wealthy for an impressive entry into the adult social world. She was normally brimming with confidence and prim humour; but now her plain face had paled and her eyes widened in disbelief.

'But Madame Armstrong,' she said plaintively, 'I had a long personal telephone call from Monsieur de Lattre soon after

Michele came here. He was most anxious that she should be able to take advantage of Monsieur Thoresen's extensive Diplomatic Corps contacts. He gave me explicit authority to allow her to be escorted by Monsieur Thoresen; and I must say he has always impressed me as being a true gentleman of great courtesy.'

Marie-Claire, who had travelled as quickly as possible to Berne with François Boisy at her side, was tight-lipped. 'No blame attaches to you, Madame,' she said curtly. 'My father has become old and his judgement has suffered. It may be, indeed, that there is no reason for concern. But we must make sure. How long ago did Michele leave for the embassy reception?'

'An hour.' Madame Veni looked as if she was about to weep. 'But I cannot believe there is anything wrong. He is such a gentleman. He treats her as – as a father.' She clutched despairingly at the edge of her desk.

'We shall see. Do you have Monsieur Thoresen's address?'

'Only the British Embassy. I have had no need to know his private residence.'

'And the embassy won't reveal the private address of a diplomat,' François Boisy said. 'We'll have to find another way.'

Madame Veni pulled herself together. She said grimly: 'We'll search her room. There may be notes, or letters.' She stood up and marched to the office door, gesturing for them to follow her.

There was a note: a single piece of paper in the bedside locker in Michele's tiny room. An address, a telephone number, and the letter H. Marie-Claire put it in her handbag and said: 'We'll come back in the morning, Madame.'

It was evening now, and by the time their taxi had reached the address, the daylight had almost gone. The house was on the edge of the town, a tall villa with a wide hanging shingled roof, bright shutters and no lights in the windows. François left Marie-Claire in the taxi and knocked on the door, but there was no response. He returned and said: 'Let's go back to the hotel and eat. If there's an embassy reception it won't be over for a while. And if they're somewhere else they'll probably be out late.'

They ate dinner largely in silence, enclosed by their own unhappy thoughts, until Marie-Claire said nervously: 'I'm glad you came. I don't know what's going to happen, but it might be unpleasant. I don't think I could face it on my own.'

He shrugged. He was solid, dependable, and confident; a man who had assiduously polished his exterior but whose peasant background was never far beneath his rugged surface. He accepted responsibility without assumption.

'My place is where you want me to be. If there is unpleasantness, don't worry. You look after your daughter. I'll deal with Thoresen.'

An hour later they were outside Thoresen's house again. It was still in darkness, so they parked nearby where they could see it, and waited. The taxi driver was curious but they waved his questions aside and after a time he settled with his head against the side window and began to doze.

It was after eleven when a car stopped outside the house; Marie-Claire reached for the door handle but François touched her arm.

'No. Give them time.'

They saw Thoresen clearly in the street lights, his beard neatly trimmed, his evening suit and black cloak immaculate. He held the taxi's door open, Michele stepped into view, and Marie-Claire's breath hissed between her teeth.

The girl wore pale blue silk: an elegant, low-necked full length gown beneath a fur jacket. Even at a distance and with only street lamp illumination, Marie-Claire knew she had seen neither garment before. She watched, aching with tension, as Thoresen paid off the taxi, then offered his arm. Michele took it, pulling herself close to him as they walked up to the house door, laughing at something he said, looking up into his eyes. Oh dear God, Marie-Claire thought, they're lovers. But she did not move as the couple went into the house and closed the door. Lights came on in a ground floor window; then, after several minutes, in a bedroom window as well. Marie-Claire clutched at the door handle again, but once more François whispered, 'Wait,' and they watched as, soon afterwards, the bedroom light went out.

A quarter of an hour passed in silence punctuated only by the soft snoring of the taxi driver. Then the downstairs light went out and, almost immediately, the bedroom light was turned on again. This time François said: 'Now. Let's go.'

They walked quietly along the road and up to the door. The sound of the knocker echoed through the house. They waited, then heard a scraping sound above their heads as a window was pushed open.

'What do you want?' Thoresen's voice. He spoke French. In Berne it could equally have been German.

François held Marie-Claire back in the shadow of the small porch roof above the door and called: 'May we use a telephone? There's been an accident. We want an ambulance. Please help us.'

A short silence; then: 'All right. I'm coming.' The window closed.

Seconds later the hall beyond the door was illuminated, bolts were withdrawn, and the door pulled wide. Thoresen, still wearing his evening shirt and white tie but without his coat, stared out into the darkness. Marie-Claire thought he looked like the devil with his carefully shaped beard; handsome, with dark hair greying and those narrowed eyes she remembered.

She stepped into the light and said: 'Hullo, Hugo. It's been a long time. But I'd have known you anywhere.'

Shock registered. For an instant he tightened his grip on the door as if to slam it. François responded quickly, thrusting out a leg and bracing his stout shoe against the bottom of the door. But Thoresen did not move; except, slowly, to straighten his shoulders and to grow taller as he did so.

'Marie-Claire. You astound me. And escorted by your good steward, I see. How may I help you?'

She did not hesitate, and he knew that without physical violence he could not stop her; so he allowed her to walk past him into the dark-panelled hall with its tiled floor and staircase ascending on one side. But his wide shoulders were a barrier to François until Marie-Claire said: 'He comes too, Hugo. Otherwise we go to the embassy and complain that you have abused an old man's trust in order to seduce a girl.'

Thoresen shrugged and stepped aside. Mockery raised his dark eyebrows.

'How melodramatic,' he murmured. 'Clearly you have allowed your imagination to run riot. Before you make fools of yourselves, we'd better talk.' He surveyed Boisy with apparent distaste, then closed the door behind him. 'We'll go into the sitting room.' He gestured with exaggerated courtesy along the hallway.

Marie-Claire said: 'I'm going upstairs to find Michele.'

'You won't go upstairs.' The cultured voice was a whip-crack now, and Thoresen moved to block her way. 'You'll talk to me –'

'Hugo – what is it – who's there?' They looked up. Michele was at the top of the stairs, pulling a housecoat close around her slender body. Then her hand flew to her mouth and her eyes widened.

Thoresen snapped over his shoulder: 'Leave this to me. Stay there.'

'No, Hugo. You will leave it to me.' Marie-Claire's voice cut through his now. Her confidence astonished François. She looked up at Michele. 'Come down. You need to hear what I'm going to say.'

The girl stared, confused then suddenly defiant. She tied the belt of her housecoat, gathered the skirt in one hand, and walked slowly, carefully, and very deliberately down the stairs, saying: 'I'll hear nothing. What do you want? You're interfering. I'm grown up – or had you forgotten?' She reached the foot of the stairs, her face flushed with embarrassment and anger, clutching her skirt, the curled fingers revealing a big diamond and emerald ring. Marie-Claire noted it, and the expensive satin housecoat.

'I'm not here to quarrel with you,' she said, 'because you don't know what you're doing. You don't know this man as I do. It's time you did.'

Thoresen retorted: 'She knows me better than you ever did, by a thousand times.' He looked across at Michele, his dark eyes compelling, and held out his hand. Without hesitation she pushed past François and went to him, slipping her arm through his, standing close to him, her face proud. She said: 'I love him. One day we'll be married. Our ages don't matter. We love each other. I don't want to hear anything else.'

François's quick glance at Marie-Claire said 'Let me speak'. He breathed in hard, his thick chest expanding. And in the confines of the hallway his voice boomed.

'Like it or not, you'll hear what Marie-Claire has to say.' He levelled a finger at Thoresen. 'Or I'll go straight to the embassy and complain that you've used your position to corrupt a young girl. When the story's out it will finish your career.' He swung on Michele. 'And if you interrupt I'll go to the police and report that you're in moral danger. The Berne police are unusually particular about things like that. Now be silent and listen.'

The violence in his voice startled them and Marie-Claire came in quickly: 'I'm going to give you facts. You think you know this man, Michele. But do you know he was responsible for your father's dismissal from the Royal Air Force? That's right. Dismissal. Hugo Thoresen condemned him in a report of an operation in which your father was his pilot and was wounded. He did it because of a quarrel, seven years before, over me. I rejected him and your father hit him. He swore he would have revenge. And all through the years he kept visiting the chateau, flattering your grandfather, waiting for his chance. That's the man you say you want to marry.' .

The girl stared at her, still clutching Thoresen's arm; stared as if she had not understood. Thoresen said smoothly, disparagingly: 'What a remarkable distortion. Peter Armstrong was guilty of wrecking a delicate political situation. He was grossly irresponsible and clearly unfit to continue his service.' But Michele did not seem to hear him. She looked at her mother, then at François Boisy's grim and rugged face, then back at Marie-Claire.

In a small, strained voice she said: 'Do you swear to me that every word of that is true?'

'Your father hurt me terribly,' Marie-Claire said. 'Do you think I would protest that he was mistreated if it were not so?' Thoresen started to speak but her voice lashed at him. 'But there's more. If a man could nurse a grievance for so long, could he not go further? Maybe he took his chance for the ultimate revenge when your grandfather unwisely thrust him towards you. Maybe he decided that because he had been unable to have the mother, he would have the daughter.'

They were statues in the hallway, for seconds. Then Thoresen snapped: 'That's damned nonsense. You're as irresponsible as your wretched husband –'

But he broke off as Michele wrenched her hand away from his arm. She held it out to Marie-Claire, as if trying to touch her, yet not moving, and whispered: 'Don't lie to me. Promise you would never lie to me.'

'I didn't come here to lie,' Marie-Claire said. 'I came to tell you the truth about the man who pretends to be your lover.'

It exploded then. Thoresen moved, raising his arm, fury suddenly distorting his face, and François shouldered Marie-Claire aside and roared: 'If you touch her I'll kill you.' He was six inches shorter than Thoresen, but he was heavy and strong and the jabbing punch which Thoresen threw at him seemed to glance off his shoulder, unnoticed. Then Michele screamed, and the shrill sound cut between them.

'No – stop it –'

In the frozen moment she faced Thoresen, close to him, wide eyes searching his face.

'Deny it, Hugo. Tell me it's lies. Deny it now. Not part of it. All of it.' A whisper, but loud and clear in the stillness.

Thoresen's dark eyes focussed on her. He snapped: 'Lies? Of course it's lies. I would not have had your mother if she'd offered herself.'

Then she hit him: a sweeping, slashing back-handed blow across his face with all the strength of her arm. The sound was like wood splitting, the force of it jerked his head sideways, and she lashed her hand back in the opposite direction against the other side of his face, her fingers leaving red weals. Then she turned, pushed between Marie-Claire and François, running, lifting her skirts as she clattered up the stairs on her high heels, calling back hysterically: 'Don't let him come near me. Wait for me.'

Thoresen started to move, but François blocked his way with Marie-Claire close behind. For seconds he hesitated; then his face, still carrying the marks of Michele's fury, assumed its habitual superiority in the line of his mouth and the lift of his eyebrows. He took a long breath and said smoothly: 'You may have her back, Marie-Claire. One day she will decide what your interference has cost her. I could have offered her the world. Her impact amongst Europe's sophisticates has already been greatly to her credit – and not a little to mine, if I may say so. With further education at my hands she would have been fit to mix with kings and presidents.'

François growled: 'You wanted her for your own gratification. A beautiful girl on your arm, with other men of your age envying you and whispering about you.'

Thoresen shrugged elegantly. 'My dear Boisy, I would not expect you to understand.' He gestured with a quick turn of his head towards the stairs. 'She asked you to wait, so you have my permission to do so. But forgive me if I do not share your vigil.'

He turned and strode along the hallway to a door at the far end, opened it, and was gone.

They waited for tense minutes, looking at each other occasionally but not speaking, listening to movement in the room above, until Michele appeared at the head of the stairs. She wore a plain brown coat and scarf and carried a small suitcase. She had removed almost all trace of make-up from her face, which was pale and carefully expressionless. She came down the stairs, her eyes fixed on her mother.

'I've left behind everything he gave me,' she said. 'The clothes and the jewellery. It must all be worth a great deal of money.'

Then, without looking round for a sign of Thoresen, she walked erect and proud and sad to the door and out into the night.

Marie-Claire telephoned Madame Veni the next morning and told her that Michele did not wish to complete her year's course and that everything relating to Thoresen should be forgotten. Then they returned to Montargis. For a week Michele spent most of her time in her room, or riding across what was left of the estate. She was neither resentful nor angry, but seemed to withdraw amongst her secret thoughts and memories, except when she visited her grandfather as he lay in his room. She did that twice a day, staying for an hour or more each time, talking quietly to him, listening as he croaked at her, comforting him. She was with him one afternoon when he raised himself suddenly on his elbows, looked at her with wide eyes which, incredibly, were no longer dull, and rasped: 'War. There's going to be another war. Don't let them catch you. Remember. Never let them catch you. I don't want to see it.' Then he lay back, his eyes dulled, and he died.

Except for the curious villagers, not many people came to the funeral service, for Philippe de Lattre's friends had all gone before him and there were few left who remembered the days of glory when dinners were served in the great hall to thirty or forty guests by white-gloved servants, and the shooting parties roamed the estate, and the stables were crowded with fine horses, and the farms were productive. It was all over quickly and quietly, and the family went back to the chateau and wondered what there would be in the future.

The day after the funeral Michele came down to breakfast and said to Marie-Claire: 'It's time I contributed. I'm going to find work. If I can start a career, that would be even better. And don't worry about me. I'm not ashamed of what happened. I was very angry, but that's gone now. So is Paul Laval and everyone I knew before. It's all forgotten. Will you forget it too, please?'

They stood beside the breakfast table and clung to each other in reconciliation, and Marie-Claire wept a little, but Michele was dry-eyed and confident; until the postman delivered a small packet which contained the diamond and emerald ring she had left in Hugo Thoresen's bedroom. With it was a note which said: 'You might as well have this as a souvenir. There's no one else I particularly want to give it to.' It was signed simply with his initial. And just for a few seconds tears ran down her cheeks, because she was shocked by it.

Then she was angry, and showed it to her mother and said: 'He's still trying to keep a hold on me. Well, I'll show him he can't. I'm going to send it back.'

But Marie-Claire shook her head.

'Keep it,' she said. 'There's no way we can calculate how much it cost us when your father had to leave the Air Force. Hugo Thoresen owes us all more than he can ever repay. Have it valued and insured. It's worth a lot of money. One day you might need it. Call it a small repayment from a very guilty man.'

*

After Philippe de Lattre's death, the financial problems of the estate became even more apparent, with taxation debts accumulating, the great house decaying, and only a small income from investments and the last farm to set against either. The taxation liability had to be settled quickly, so François put all the land on the market except for ten acres around the house.

Marie-Claire left him to deal with the accountants and the lawyers, and thus, only weeks later, it was he who called a meeting in the great hall, where he had set out papers in neat piles on a table.

He said: 'I've finished the calculations. The picture is worse than we had imagined. There's only one possible outcome. You must close the chateau. Perhaps you might wish to sell it, if you can find a buyer, although it needs a lot of money to restore it.'

Mother and daughter looked at each other. They had talked about the possibility already. Eventually Marie-Claire said: 'If there's no alternative, we must do it. We can move to Cambrai.'

The last of their properties was a small detached house just outside Cambrai in France's north-east corner. It had been tenanted for years but the last tenant had left months before and the house had been empty since. Its running costs would be a fraction of those required for the upkeep of the chateau.

'Do you want to put this place on the market?' François asked. The sadness showed in his eyes.

'What else? It will cost us money just to keep it standing closed and shuttered. And once we leave, we'll never be able to come back. I hate to say it, but we have no choice.' She hesitated, then added: 'But if we go to Cambrai, I hope you'll come with us, François. You are still part of the family, even though there are now only two of us left. And the house is big enough for you to have your own rooms.'

The steward stared, unable to conceal his surprise and embarrassment. He said roughly: 'I can find somewhere here, around the village. And a job of some sort. Don't worry about me.'

It was Michele who settled it. She said: 'You'll find it easier to get work around Cambrai or Arras. And we don't worry about you. We worry about ourselves. We both need a man's help.' She did not add that if she married one day and went away, Marie-Claire especially would need a man's help, for in spite of the competence with which she had confronted Hugo Thoresen, she remained singularly unable to deal with most of life's routine hazards on her own. But François Boisy knew what she meant, and finally nodded.

'I'll come,' he said. 'I've been with the de Lattres all my adult life. If you still want me, I'll stay with you.'

So in the spring of 1938 the shutters were closed for the last time, much of the furniture was sold and the remainder stored in upstairs rooms, and they left the chateau's affairs in the hands of a Paris estate agent.

But by now Germany had annexed Austria and was hurling abuse at Czechoslovakia, and Europe shivered in the winds of impending war. So no one wanted to buy a crumbling chateau which needed a small fortune to restore it to reasonable standards, and the old building remained empty while Marie-Claire and her daughter settled in their quiet house in the north-east. Michele became a receptionist in the director's office of a local textile factory and was soon promoted to become his personal assistant; François obtained work as the manager of a farm in the absence of the owner who had emigrated to French Canada; and Marie-Claire became the housekeeper for them both and let time drift by in a haze of faint disappointment.

They were still there when the British and French governments handed Czechoslovakia to the Germans, and war fever mounted through into 1939 and the German invasion of Poland.

Only then did Marie-Claire seem to realise that they were living in the heart of the land which had been devastated twenty years before, over which Peter Armstrong had fought his battles with the Albatrosses and the red Fokkers, and across which the German armies had marched.

2

They would never forget the day; sitting, cold with apprehension in the living room, hearing the clinical radio voice cataloguing the end of their world.

It had started just as the daylight came. Madame Challon who lived alone in the next house hammered on the door. They found her standing on the step in an old dressing gown with her hair in curlers, tears streaming down her cheeks in the cold light, sobbing, 'God save us, oh God save us, it's happened, they've invaded, the Germans are coming.'

They took her inside and turned on the radio and it was true, the Germans were coming into Holland and into Belgium and worse, into the Ardennes and that was France. Airfields were being attacked and guns were shelling and tanks rumbled out of the east, and all their nightmares were real.

They must eat because they might never eat again. They snatched breakfast together and did not taste it. Marie-Claire burned her mouth because the coffee was hot but hardly noticed until long after it was done. It was the 10th of May, 1940, and the uneasy, unreal war which had slept fitfully through the winter had woken without warning and was roaring towards them.

The radio voice said the Luftwaffe had attacked Dutch and Belgian airfields at dawn, that the German army was across the frontiers, and paratroopers were falling out of the sky to capture bridges. Heavy casualties were being inflicted on the invaders, it said; but somehow they did not believe that. Madame Challon went back to her house, still weeping. They listened to the radio and went out to talk to other neighbours and the rumours began to fly.

Marie-Claire was calm but a little vague, as if she had not quite grasped the enormity of it. Michele was calm too, and hardly spoke, while François went up to the attic and oiled his 12-bore and his .22 rifle which he had brought from the old house, and checked his supply of cartridges before he went to the farm four miles away, promising to return if the news became worse. Then, later than usual, Michele went to her office in Cambrai, leaving her mother to listen to the radio reports.

It was not until evening that the confusion began to assume a dreadful pattern. In Holland, Arnhem and Nijmegen were taken by the Germans, securing for them vital bridges; Rotterdam airfield had been captured by paratroopers; and worst of all for the French, panzers were crossing the Meuse near Sedan. But French army statements were reassuring, and Marie-Claire nodded approvingly as she heard confident reports of units moving forward to hold the enemy.

The next day was Saturday and the rumours were worse. A dozen tanks rumbled past on the road outside the house, shaking the ornaments, and there was a lot of air activity, but it was all French and British. Later a big army unit swept through in lorries, and Michele went into Cambrai to buy extra food and found the shelves almost empty and people scurrying, heads down and grim. She came home in time to hear the radio report widespread German bombing in Belgium and then a German claim that troops had crossed the Albert canal which had been regarded as a major obstacle to invaders. On Sunday François heard a noise in the attic and found Michele sitting cross-legged on the floor, loading and unloading the .22 after hearing about paratroopers bringing panic to Belgian towns. Somehow he was startled, although he had been her teacher.

'Would you use that? It wouldn't be like shooting rabbits and foxes.'

'I know.' Stark and unemotional.

'All three allied armies are moving up to meet them. They'll be stopped in a few days, a long way from here.'

'They're not a long way from here now. If they can cross the Albert canal and the Meuse they can cross anything.' She unloaded the rifle and stood up, looking at him. He thought she was older than yesterday; much older. 'Which do you want – the .22 or the 12-bore?'

Choose your weapon. And fight side by side with me. That was when it hit him; the totality of it. It was no longer a man's war. It was everybody's war. A war for beautiful girls as well as for soldiers and farm managers.

'If it comes to that – you can choose.'

'The .22. It's lighter. If I can hit rabbits with it, I can hit Germans.'

They climbed out of the attic, down the narrow ladder. Then she said quietly: 'When I went to Cambrai I bought trousers for myself. And for mother. I haven't told her yet.'

'Why did you buy them? I've never seen you in trousers.'

'So that I can look like a man if I need to. Soldiers rape women.'

*

They began to talk about leaving when they heard that the panzers were sweeping across the Ardennes and had reached Montcornet which was only 90 kilometres away and well to the south, and heard the rumours that another tank column was crossing the Belgian border into France directly east of Cambrai and less than 70 kilometres distant. It would have to bridge the River Sambre before it could reach them, but all the time the radio reported that rivers and canals were being crossed.

Then they heard that Holland had surrendered and that the roads were crowded with thousands of refugees. And in the afternoon they saw the first of the long columns of frightened, weary people trekking past with their handcarts and horses and riding bicycles.

'We ought to leave,' François said. 'I think we should go back to Montargis.'

Michele said: 'I've already packed. One big suitcase each. That's all the car will take, with a few boxes.' She looked at François. 'And the guns.'

Marie-Claire stared from one to the other.

'But what will happen to the house? And all our furniture?' It was a plaintive protest against the inevitable. She was frightened, because the situation had become so much worse so very quickly, in spite of the French army's optimistic bulletins.

'If they get as far as this, I won't care about the house. I'll only care that we're not here.' Michele opened a school book of maps. 'Have you looked at this? There are tanks heading straight for us, and another lot coming up from the south. We could be trapped here, unless we go now.'

François pointed. 'We should go south-west, to Amiens. Then we'll be moving away from them. But we'll still be getting nearer to Paris.'

They left before dawn on the 16th, their small Peugeot crammed, the two women wearing the trousers Michele had bought. They had spent the night going round the house, making final choices to take this or leave that. Michele took few small possessions, but was careful to slip two things into her shoulder bag: Hugo Thoresen's ring and her British passport. She took the ring because it was valuable and in the last few hours she had realised how little money they had available to them and how much they might need; and she took the passport secretly, not knowing why but feeling she wanted it with her. She held dual nationality – something her father had arranged when she was a child – and now she was happier to know that her claim to be British was in her bag.

They drove along the Bapaume road and found it crowded with refugees. Many were sleeping in fields and under hedges, but others were travelling on through the darkness. Most were walking, pushing laden carts; some were riding bicycles unsteadily, with bundles roped to their backs; but there were many cars and lorries on the road, piled high with boxes and mattresses. They drove slowly and carefully into the first of the daylight, huddled in the car, not daring to ask each other where the Germans might be on this new day but knowing they could not be far away.

At about nine o'clock they found the road blocked with shouting, confused people and stationary vehicles. Michele whispered, more to herself than the others, 'We should have left yesterday, I knew we should,' as they edged forward. An old woman stumbled against the side of the car under the weight of a huge bundle across her shoulders. She leered through the windows and yelled: 'Bastards – riding in a bloody car – why don't you walk like the rest?' François said: 'Take no notice. She probably shouts like that at every car.' They crawled on, still hearing the woman's shrill voice, until they could move no further.

Then they saw the cause of the blockage: a unit of the French army, armoured cars and several light tanks, coming up the road towards them. An officer was standing up in the leading car, shouting orders. Refugees milled around, hurling abuse. Soldiers climbed down from the vehicles and began to force a way through the crowd, rifles held above their heads, ordering lorries and cars on to the grass verge, marshalling people. The crowd behind surged forward and a soldier struck out at a civilian who swore at him in Flemish. Several other men began to fight the soldiers; French against Belgian, fear prodding the refugees, anger spurring the men in uniform.

It stopped when the officer in the armoured car took out his pistol and fired it twice into the air. A woman screamed somewhere and the dozen brawling men separated. The armoured car moved forward, the officer shouting and waving his arms, and the crowd scattered, climbing over fences into fields, trying to get out of the way. The car was like the bow of a ship in a heavy rolling sea, the people dividing before it and surging along its sides. François drove on to grass and the armoured vehicles edged past one by one, the tank tracks churning the macadam road surface. A man climbed on to the running board of the Peugeot as an army truck came close and his boots scraped the door. The car rocked as people pushed against it. But no one was talking or shouting now; just sullen, frightened faces through the glass.

Then the convoy had gone and the great column of people trudged on and the vehicles threaded clumsily between them.

They reached Bapaume and saw that most of the shops were closed and many of the house windows shuttered. Police stood in groups at street corners, but did not interfere. People had been crowding through the little town all the previous day. There was no point in trying to sort out the obstructions.

On the Albert side of Bapaume the road widened and François was able to pick up speed, driving between the columns of people, following a battered truck to which four men and three women clung, their belongings piled high. But presently they became aware that only the vehicles were moving. The people crowding the roadsides with their carts and bundles had all stopped, facing east, heads up, eyes staring. François switched off the engine, letting the car coast; and then they heard the explosions.

Five kilometres away, ten, even twenty: they could not tell. Guns or bombs. Guns probably; somehow it sounded like guns. The air seemed to vibrate. One heavy explosion shook the ground. That might have been a bomb. François muttered, 'Dear God, they're not far away,' and restarted the engine, accelerating, overhauling the battered truck.

They were close behind it and its bulk hid from them the approaching army patrol car which came round a corner very fast, headlights on and horn blowing. People scattered and the driver of the truck swerved and stamped on his brakes. The vehicle rocked and two of the women who hung on to its sides were thrown off. They hit the road, rolling over, and François braked hard to avoid one of them, pulling out into the path of the unseen patrol car.

The crash stunned their senses. A mudguard was torn off the Peugeot and one front wheel buckled beneath it, fracturing the stub axle. The car bounced off the army vehicle, turning sideways and sliding into the back of the truck which had stopped. Someone fell off the truck on to the bonnet of the car, sprawling and scraping. Then everything was still, in the frozen moment which follows impact; until Marie-Claire began to moan softly, sitting amidst the jumble of luggage on the Peugeot's back seat, covering her face. But she was unhurt, and Michele and François pushed open the doors and struggled out to help the two women who lay in the road.

And again they heard the distant guns.

Half an hour later the car had been abandoned and they joined the mass of refugees on foot, struggling with suit-cases too heavy to carry for long, leaving boxes of precious possessions in the car, minds numbed by the scale of their disaster.

But Michele took the .22 and Francois carried the 12-bore, with a handful of cartridges each. And the rumble of the guns was closer.

At midday the sun forced through the overcast sky and the temperature rose. They stopped to eat bread and cold meat and cheese which Marie-Claire had packed carefully the night before, sitting on their cases in a farm gateway, watching the unbroken stream of people trudging past; not speaking, weary already, with aching minds asking how far they would get before tanks appeared across the fields and what would happen to them then.

At first they were hardly conscious of the aircraft engines coming up out of the east, gradually drowning the sound of guns. François stood up, shading his eyes, staring. There were two of them, low down. He did not know what they were, until the shuffling crowd stopped to look and a voice shouted 'Stukas' and the word was repeated, growing in volume, edged with hysteria; then submerged by screams as they heard the machine guns.

The two aircraft came down the road in echelon over the countless people, flying slowly at less than two hundred feet. François saw the small bombs beneath the cranked wings, and one of them fall, and yelled, 'Lie down, oh God, lie down,' as he pushed Marie-Claire to the ground and tried to throw himself on top of her. But she rolled away towards the roadside ditch, half rising as she went. Michele screamed, 'Mother – get down –' but the words were lost as a bomb exploded somewhere and smoke billowed as people sprawled and screamed and ran, falling over each other. The aircraft engines roared directly overhead and machine guns rattled and there was an explosion which crushed hearing and breathing and senses. Something bounced off François's back. He twisted and saw it was an arm, tattered. Then he saw Marie-Claire kneeling, face contorted, blood spreading in patches across her chest, hands clutching the air; until she rolled over, legs kicking in trousers Michele had bought for her. He scrambled towards her and Michele screamed just once.

She was dead before they reached her and held her as if the contact would bring her back, raising her head and Michele saying 'No, no, no,' and all around people were dead and dying and mutilated and crying out. The aircraft disappeared but they could hear the engines and they were not going away. A man wearing a blue woollen jacket lay face down, finger ends clawing at the road, but he had no legs, just awful bloody torn flesh and shattered bone. A woman hugged the unrecognisable remains of a small child, her face a mask of blood with eyes staring out of it. People crawled over each other in agony, belief crushed from them, and the survivors stood up and one of the aircraft was circling and someone screeched: 'He's coming back, the swine's coming back.'

Then François saw Michele scrambling, reaching for one of the cases then tearing at the string which tied the .22 rifle to it, grabbing cartridges from her pocket and feeding them into the five-shot magazine. He tried to call, 'No, don't do it,' but Marie-Claire's bloody body was still against him and horror gagged him as he watched, unbelieving.

She was on her knees now, turning her head to the sound of the aircraft then seeing it low across the fields, coming back towards the road and the people. She crouched against the hedge, the rifle to her shoulder, following the aircraft round. It was coming in diagonally, not directly towards her, and she could see it clearly. She waited until it was close before she fired, then followed up with two more shots, then the last two, working the bolt fast, and the wings tilted against the bright sky and the aircraft rose, turning away, and Michele was searching for more cartridges but this time the aircraft was not coming back and she stood up, watching it go.

François saw her, with the rifle across her body, and the tears welled up inside him as he clutched Marie-Claire and his voice said: 'Peter Armstrong, she is your daughter, and if you could know you would be proud.' But no one heard him because of the sounds of suffering and death all around.

They had no tools, but graves had to be dug, so François trudged across a field to a farm and came back with two spades. They dug into the side of the ditch to make a place for Marie-Claire, not deep but enough to hide the dreadful-ness. Then Michele helped him to lay her there, and not once did she say a word. They covered her, and gave their spades to someone else in the confusion, just holding them out until a man took them; then François said quietly: 'Come with me to the farm. Bring your case.'

They struggled through the hedge and across the fields to the farm buildings, François heaving two cases along, leaving the horror behind in the bright sun. He led her to an open barn and pointed.

Propped against straw were three bicycles.

'There's no one here. They must have left, in a car or something. We'll take two of those.'

Michele said distantly: 'I hit that plane. I know I hit it twice.'

Then she wept, standing in the barn and covering her face with grimy fingers, her mother's blood on her coat. He reached for her, an arm about her shoulders to comfort her, but she shrugged him off. 'No. That will make it worse. Just leave me.' So he turned away and within minutes she had regained control, wiping her face with streaks of dirt from her hands.

'I'm all right. Let's decide what we have to take. We can't cycle with the cases.' Flat voiced, hard; a stranger to him.

It took them fifteen minutes. Then they tied one lightly-laden case to François's back with string and wire they found in the barn, made a cloth bundle to tie on Michele's back, tied the guns to the bicycle frames, and rode down the farm lane.

They cycled for hours without stopping, not quickly but steadily, seeing countless lorries rumble by in the opposite direction towing guns and crowded with troops; all the time passing refugees, sometimes a dozen, sometimes thirty, sometimes many more in a long column. Cars and lorries overtook them. Once a driver sounded his horn repeatedly when the road was blocked by people and they saw a man throw a stone through the windscreen, then others seize the car and try to turn it over before the driver managed to accelerate away.

Michele said: 'Animals. It's turned us into animals, fighting each other. The Germans will win while we're fighting each other.' It was the first time she had spoken since they had left the farm.

Then, at dusk, she spoke again. 'I can't go much further without a rest.' She sounded ashamed.

They found another farm and paid the old woman in the house a few francs to let them sleep in a barn. They ate the last of Marie-Claire's bread and cheese, and drank water from the farm pump. After that they washed as well as they could and the old woman brought hot coffee to them. They thanked her and asked if she had heard any guns, but she was deaf and had heard nothing. Then they lay in the straw on the barn floor, a few feet apart, and drifted into restless sleep, their legs and backs aching and their buttocks sore from the saddles.

At four o'clock Michele woke and shook François.

'Come on. If we start now the roads will be quieter.'

They climbed astride their bicycles and pedalled away, forcing their stiff legs up and down.

In the afternoon they reached the outskirts of Amiens, hungry and desperately tired, cycling slowly through the flat market garden area north-east of the town. There were fewer refugees now. François was leading, and he turned into a lane which led across a drainage channel bridge to one of the little houses.

A man answered their knock. He was big and shabby, sixty years old, and suspicious until François said: 'Will you sell us some food? Anything. We'll pay you. And have you heard where the Germans are, please?'

The man shook his head and said roughly: 'I won't sell you food. We've had dozens like you today. All begging. I gave them some vegetables and sent them away. None of them offered to pay. You did. That makes you different. Come in.'

He took them into the kitchen and his wife warmed beans and potatoes and gave them an apple flan and coffee. While they ate the man said: 'The Germans are in Peronne, with tanks. They'll be here tomorrow unless the army can stop them. That's the rumour, anyway.'

Peronne was forty kilometres away, the land was flat and the roads were narrow but good; so they got back on their bicycles and rode away, trying to conserve their strength but pedalling hard.

Amiens was quiet; unnaturally quiet. They crossed a canal bridge, seeing a few people hurrying among the buildings on either side of the Boulevard d'Alsace Lorraine. A lorry trundled ahead of them and turned down a side street. Beyond the roofs the great bulk of the Notre-Dame Cathedral rose, its spire soaring. That had been their landmark for the last hour. There was a wooden barrier across the entrance to the Gare du Nord and a sign, 'Military Traffic Only'. A crowd of forty or fifty stood around it. Some of the men were shouting that the trains should be kept running because that was their last chance to escape. Beyond there were parked cars. A man was running and a woman stood in a doorway, weeping. Then Michele saw a baker's shop and bought two baguettes – all the shop had left. They pushed the bread into the bundle on her back and pedalled on until they reached the Rue de Paris and turned south onto it.

A signpost said Paris was 131 kilometres away.

Then they saw the troops, more than they had seen throughout the past two days; countless men and countless lorries standing along the side of the road. Many of the lorries were commandeered civilian vehicles with the names of their former owners still painted on the sides. There were field guns, scout cars and armoured cars. As they cycled along the lines of men and vehicles they looked at the troops and saw grim faces staring back at them. Then whistles blew and the men clambered up into their lorries and the convoy bellowed into life.

They rode for another hour, then stopped for a rest, propping their bicycles against a tree at the edge of a small wood which came right up to the road, sitting on the grass.

They were there when they heard engines; several vehicles, a different sound from the lorry noises they had heard before, beyond the field alongside the wood. They stood up to look and saw an armoured car, two light tanks and an armoured troop carrier with a dozen or more soldiers on it, travelling at high speed along a narrow lane. And they knew immediately that they were neither French nor British.

'Into the wood. Quickly.' François grabbed Michele's arm. They heaved their bicycles and their luggage through a bedraggled hedge and in among the trees, dropped them into the undergrowth, and picked their way into the wood. The engines were louder. They peered through the trees and saw the four vehicles coming up the narrow lane which joined the Paris road close to the edge of the wood. The men on the troop carrier sat in two rows, facing each other. Their helmets were the German shape.

'A patrol,' François muttered. 'A probe, sent out in front of the main advance to report back by radio.'

'I wonder how far in front they are.' Michele looked at him. 'We left the guns with the bicycles. Better get them.'

'No.' He shook his head emphatically. 'We can't fight an armoured patrol. If they see us it'll be better if we're unarmed.' But Michelle spat out: 'Like mother was, and all those other people? I'm going to get the guns.'

She started to move away, but François clamped a hand around her wrist. She winced and jerked her arm, but he held on.

'I'm not going to let you commit suicide. Those are trained soldiers. If we fire on them they'll kill us within seconds.'

Her face flushed and she tried to stare him out, defiantly; but his fingers were tight around her wrist and his jaw jutted and he was more powerful than she, so she shrugged and he let her go. She massaged the wrist where he had hurt her and whispered through tight lips: 'They'll kill us anyway if they see us.'

They pressed against a tree trunk and watched the patrol. It reached the Paris road and stopped. The men in the troop carrier had turned and were facing outwards now, rifles levelled. They were two hundred metres away but clearly visible. An officer standing in the armoured car shouted something and pointed towards the wood. To Michele and François it looked as if he was pointing directly at them. Then the armoured car turned on to the road, towards them, and François hissed: 'Oh dear God, they're going to use the wood for shelter.'

He reached for Michele's hand and they retreated among the trees. The wood was a mixture of old oak, beech and birch, with a lot of neglected undergrowth, but it was not dense enough to conceal someone within fifty metres unless they lay down. They struggled back, picking their way through brambles and branches which tore at their clothes and scratched their hands and faces. The engines were closer and through the trees they glimpsed one of the tanks in the field alongside the wood, and the troop carrier behind it. They began to run then, stumbling over the rough ground.

Until the shooting started.

It came from in front of them; and the Germans were behind. They stopped, wide-eyed, listening in the silence which followed the first burst of fire. Then there were more shots and a bullet whined through the trees close by, and they dropped face down into the undergrowth.

'Achtung – dort drüben!' Then the crump of high explosives, one, two, three in quick succession. Engines bellowed raucously and a tank opened fire, the hammer-crack of the gun merging with the scream of a shell through the trees and the explosion somewhere beyond, then a second. Small-arms fire rattled and Michele covered her head with her arms because it was very close. More shouts, unrecognisable words in the din, and acrid cordite fumes. François looked sideways through the undergrowth and saw a column of earth spout high and a flash and swirling smoke. Then a vehicle crashed into the wood a hundred metres away, engine roaring until a succession of explosions submerged it and a machine gun crackled and bullets whined through leaves and branches and thudded into tree trunks.

It went on through hell's eternity yet could only have lasted minutes before a silence more intense than anything they had known. Michele stirred and François hissed: 'Lie still. Play dead.' Then there was movement, careful shuffling steps in the wood, and suddenly engines erupted and more explosions, guns banging and shells hammering senses into momentary oblivion and the earth shaking and the engines receding, racing, and a machine gun blasted short bursts of fire close by.

Then silence again, except for the engines, distant now; until there were more shuffling footsteps, clear and close, a voice muttering and the words emerging, taking form as the footsteps stopped.

'Two of 'em – there.' Silence. 'Bloody hell – civvies. Dead.'
English words.

Without moving Michele whispered in the same language:
'Oh thank God. British. Thank God.' She turned her head
slowly. Two khaki-clad soldiers stared down at her, rifles
pointing. One said: 'Christ. It's a woman.'

Very slowly she rolled on to her side, facing them.

'I'm British.' She had to make an effort to speak the language
after so long. She said it again, louder. 'Oh thank God it's
you. I thought it was the Germans.'

'Bloody hell,' one of the soldiers said. 'You're British? What
the hell are you doing here?' But the rifles still pointed.

'Let me get up, please.' One of the men nodded and she
pushed herself to her knees, turning to François. He moved
cautiously, looking at the soldiers; then said in his own
language: 'They are. They're British. Really British.' His voice
was low, and remarkably steady.

'Who's he?' One of the soldiers moved his rifle, covering
François.

'I'm English. He's French.' Michele came to her feet, very
slowly. 'We were trying to get away before the Germans came.
We ran into the wood when we saw their tanks. Then the
shooting started.'

One of the soldiers relaxed, rifle barrel dropping. But
the other was rigid. He said: 'You got an identity card, or
something?'

She nodded, again and again. 'Yes. A passport. In my bag.'
Oddly, her shoulder bag was still hanging on her arm. She
offered it to the soldier. He said: 'Show me.'

She opened the bag, rummaged, and held out her British
passport. He took it at arm's length, stared at it, opened it.
Then he grinned.

'Sorry, miss. We're a bit – tensed up. After that bit of fun.'
He lowered his rifle and gave her the passport. 'You were
lucky. You must have been right between us. And you're not
hurt?'

She shook her head. 'We're all right. Only scared.' She looked at François. 'You are all right, aren't you?'

'Just scratched.' He looked at blood running down one hand. 'A branch. It's nothing.'

Michele translated, adding: 'He doesn't speak much English. But he knows enough to understand what we're saying.'

A voice shouted nearby, the undergrowth crackled, and more men came through the tress, staring at them. The soldier who had looked at the passport raised his voice.

'Have the bastards gone?'

'One tank and the troop carrier.' One of the newcomers pointed, grinning through dirt streaked across his face. 'The rest are over there.'

They all turned. Through the trees smoke was rising, dark and oily, from a tank. The turret was torn open, like a twisted can. They could see more men in khaki uniforms, moving cautiously. The man with the dirt on his face said: 'Watcha got here, then? Civvies?'

'Yes. And the lass is British. How's that for a surprise?'

They looked, startled. One said: 'Bloody hell – what are you doing here?' Then the man with dirt on his face shouted: 'Hey – Sarge – come over here. Look what we found.'

After that it was easy. The sergeant took them to the field and they saw men lying, a dozen or more, all in German uniforms. One was groaning and a soldier was bending over him. Further along the wood the armoured car was on its side against a tree, two men hanging from it. Then the sergeant took them to a young lieutenant and they told their story, and everyone marvelled that they had been in the centre of the battle and had survived. The lieutenant said: 'We've been watching them for the last ten minutes, getting closer. We just waited behind the wood until they were within range. We couldn't believe it when they stopped. They were sitting ducks.' He put his arm around Michele's shoulders and gave her a squeeze. 'And an Englishwoman, in the middle of this lot? That's something we didn't expect.' He grinned down at her. 'Don't worry. We'll look after you. But we'll have to be quick about it because we don't know how far away the main Jerry force is.'

He took them round the wood to where three army lorries were drawn up in the trees. Men were wheeling a light field gun round to attach it to one of the lorries. A big armoured car was nearby and a soldier sat on it, wearing earphones. When he saw the lieutenant he called: 'Sir – a message for you.'

The lieutenant went to the car and talked to the soldier. They studied a map. Then the sergeant joined them and they stood close together, debating, before the lieutenant spoke to another soldier who jogged away across the field towards the Paris road.

He came back to Michele and François and said: 'Can't hang around here, I'm afraid. But I've sent a man to stop the first vehicle heading towards Beauvais. Passenger trains were still running there this morning. So you'll probably be all right if we can get you as far as that.'

They collected their suitcase and bundle from the edge of the wood, untied their guns and slung them from their shoulders, ignoring the stares of the soldiers when they saw the way Michele handled her rifle. Then the soldier standing in the road stopped a lorry and the lieutenant took them to it.

'Translate for me. Tell him this is army business and he must take you to Beauvais.'

The lorry driver stared down warily; listened to Michele, then shrugged and gestured to the nearside of his cab. They climbed in, squeezing close together on to the seat beside the driver. The lieutenant stood back and saluted and they waved their thanks.

An hour later they were in Beauvais and caught the last train of the day to Paris, still carrying their guns.

3

Mice and dampness were the biggest problems. The mice were everywhere, and the damp chilled rooms and corridors. A window had been broken on the ground floor, someone had been living rough in what had been the main kitchen, and the wind and rain of the winters had funnelled inside.

They set about cleaning it up, recruiting helpers from the village. Then some of the furniture which had been left upstairs was used to give the great hall a semblance of comfort. There were still plenty of logs in the old storehouse, so big fires blazed every day even though there was summer outside. Sleeping was difficult at first because the mattresses which had been left behind were covered in mould; so they bought cushions and blankets and made two bedrooms as comfortable as they could.

But all the time they listened to the radio and its grim catalogue, starting with the capture of Amiens and with it the heart-tripping realisation that they had been only forty-eight hours ahead of the German tanks. They wondered what had happened to the young lieutenant who had helped them, and the soldier who had inspected Michele's passport, and the one with soil on his face. Could they have survived with their single gun and their puny rifles and mortars against the onslaught of the Panzers?

Then a day later they heard that those same Panzers had reached the coast beyond Abbeville and that the bulk of the British army and a huge segment of the French had been cut off; and then within days that the Belgian army had surrendered.

After that, and worst of all, came the first reports of the evacuation of the trapped British army from Dunkirk, and that a hundred thousand French soldiers had gone as well. The whole of north-east France was under German occupation and the remnants of the French army were regrouping to defend Paris.

That was when Michele went into a room she had rarely seen since the initial cleaning of the house in their first exhausting week: her grandfather's bedroom; the room in which she had sat with him when he had died.

She was wandering along the north corridor, her footsteps echoing on the tiles, and went into the room because she wanted to look out on to the ruined garden where she had once spent long hours on the lawns between colourful flower beds.

The bare boards creaked and she smelled the dampness which still lingered through so much of the house. She leaned on the window-sill and felt the sun through the dirty glass, and a great depression surged through her. She could not go on living here, in this great mausoleum of memories, with only François as her companion. She loved him as a favourite uncle; but he did not belong to her world. And in any case she had to find work and there was none worth-while in Montargis.

What was her world, anyway? Chaos and fear, with death not far behind. She tried not to think of her mother, up there on that northern roadside with German boots tramping by. What was Cambrai like now, and her little office in the factory which had swung over so quickly to producing army uniforms when the war had started, and the men and women who worked there? And the house where she had lived when the chateau had been abandoned? Seized by the invaders, used as billets for uncaring soldiers?

She turned her back to the window and tried to remember the room as it was, and the gaunt old man in the wide bed. And she heard his voice again, an echo in a corner of her memory. 'Don't let them catch you.' A croak, the last before he faded into whatever lay beyond his suffering. 'Don't let them catch you.' The words whispered through her mind.

And then she knew. The British had gone, the Belgians had surrendered, the French were in disarray, the country was demoralised. The German net lay from Abbeville south and east to Neufchatel and beyond. How long before it spread west to smother all the Channel ports, and Paris itself; and then little Montargis?

Don't let them catch you.

She would not.

François was on the carriage drive, scything through a weed forest. She said: 'I'm sorry. I can't stay. There may still be a chance to get out. I'm going to try. Do you want to try with me?'

No. He was French and he would stay in France. And he did not want her to go alone so he argued with her through the afternoon. But the old man's death rattle was loud in her memory, and she would not let them catch her; so she talked on the telephone with the family lawyers in Paris, then told him: 'I'm going tomorrow. This house is mine now, and you may live in it for as long as you like. There's no money left, so you'll have to make do as best you can when it needs repair. But it won't all fall down at once, and you can make a home in some of the rooms. I've instructed the lawyers.'

She left at dawn the next day, in a taxi to Montargis then on the first train to Paris. It was the 7th of June and the German army was moving west along the coast towards Le Havre and inland against the desperate remnants of the French army.

She would try to get to the coast and find a ship leaving one of the ports. She had more than enough money to pay, and there was always the ring in her bag.

But there was one last hope of help, or at least information and guidance. She walked along the Rue du Faubourg, trim in a grey skirt and blue blouse and jacket, her hair neat and shining in the sun, through the tense scattering of people and the traffic crowding in the narrow street, and turned through the arch which led to the British Embassy. A barrier was down and she showed her passport to the uniformed guard. He spoke briefly on a telephone and let her pass into the square courtyard where cars were parked and steps led up on the right to the elegant entrance of what had once been one of the grandest houses in Paris.

Inside it was cool and calm. A receptionist listened patiently to her request. She was middle-aged and showed no anxiety. Michele waited, sitting in a leather armchair in a window overlooking the secluded courtyard, until a man came down the stairs which curved into the reception hall from above.

'I'm John Bower.' He was around forty, quiet and competent and comforting. His handshake was firm, and that was comforting, too. 'I'm afraid things are a little difficult here. We have to make many unexpected arrangements. But I'll try to help. You want to get to the coast?'

'Yes. I want to try to get back to England. Is there any chance?'

'No one can be certain. But ships are sailing from Cherbourg, and Le Havre is still open although we have no real information about shipping there. There's been some bombing. Cherbourg will be your safest bet. What will you do if you can't make it?'

'Try to come back.' She shrugged. 'It's better than sitting at home in Montargis, waiting and wondering.'

He did not try to conceal his admiration.

'You're very courageous, to do it on your own. If you wait a few minutes I'll ring Cherbourg and see what the situation is.'

She sat there, looking out into the courtyard, seeing her mother's grave on the distant roadside, hearing screams; and then the echoes of the great house and the old rasping voice saying don't let them catch you, and footsteps on the tiled floor of the reception hall coming from the wide corridor beyond the stairs. The footsteps checked and she glanced round; then came slowly to her feet.

The eyes were still dark and narrowed, the beard still neat, and Hugo Thoresen said: 'How unexpected. Quite extraordinary.'

Instinctively she took a step away, and he noticed it.

'Hugo. I – I had not thought you might be here.'

'Of course not.' He was entirely at ease. It was just a surprise meeting of old friends. 'And may I ask why you are here? Is someone taking care of you?'

'Yes.' She was recovering; aloof and defensive. 'I'm going back to England. I came for advice.'

He eyed her. His face betrayed nothing except faint curiosity.

'Advice? You'll need more than that. Do you know exactly how you're going to do it?'

'No. I'll find out as I go.'

Again the steady gaze; unreadable now. Then he turned to the receptionist. 'I'm taking Miss Armstrong to my office.' And to Michele: 'Come.' He moved away, without waiting for her response.

He had taken a dozen steps before she stirred. Then she found herself following him.

Beyond the foot of the wide stairs the reception hall narrowed; beyond again was a corridor. He used a security key to open a door and went through it without glancing back to see if she was with him.

The room was small, furnished with an ornate walnut desk, two chairs and a big metal cabinet. The cabinet doors were open and papers were piled on the desk and chairs. He gestured.

'We're getting ready to leave. Now tell me what you're trying to do.'

She stood stiffly, her back to the door.

'Get away. Before the Germans come. A man named John Bower is ringing Cherbourg to see if ships are still sailing.'

He nodded, content with his superior knowledge.

'They are. And from Le Havre, although the Germans are only forty miles away. But you haven't a hope. For every place on a boat there are a hundred people. Money is changing hands, ten thousand francs at a time. And that doesn't guarantee anything. It just gets you onto the docks. Bribery isn't a disease. It's a business. The French excel at it, in times of stress. Their entrepreneurial instincts continue to surprise me. Don't waste your time. Or risk yourself. Go home.'

She said: 'Thank you for the advice. I shall still try.'

He raised his eyebrows.

'And what does your mother think? And Boisy, your faithful guardian?'

'Don't mock me.' Her voice was ice-edged. 'Mother is dead. Killed by the Germans. François prefers to stay. I've nothing to stay for. And I have a British passport.'

He stared at her, calculating.

'So you have. I'd forgotten. I'm sorry about your mother.' His eyes narrowed so that she could not read them. 'You are remarkable. But then you always were. And you are British. So since you are determined to hazard yourself, we must do our best for you.' He waved one hand towards the mass of papers. 'I've another hour's work, deciding on priorities for destruction if it becomes necessary – as I'm sure it will. Then I shall leave myself. I have been instructed to return. I shall take you with me.'

She pressed her back against the door.

'No. I don't want your help.' She forced herself to add, 'Thank you.'

'Thanks are not required,' he retorted. 'And while you may not want my help, you unquestionably need it. You may wait here until I'm ready.'

Behind her there was a sharp knock. She moved away from the door and Bower pushed it open. He looked questioningly at Thoresen.

'Everything's under control, John. Miss Armstrong and I

are old friends. A remarkable coincidence. I'll look after her myself.'

Bower's anxiety showed.

'Things are difficult, Hugo. I've telephoned. There's bombing at Le Havre and chaos at Cherbourg.'

'I know.' Smooth and unexcited. 'But I have to leave myself, as you are aware. I'll take her with me.'

'Ah. That's good news.' Bower looked at Michele. 'You must be very pleased about that, Miss Armstrong. You couldn't be in better hands. I'm really quite relieved. I confess I was about to advise you not to go. We're rather under pressure, as you'll understand. So I'll leave you. And good luck. Even with Hugo's help you may need just a little of that.' He smiled encouragingly as he went out. He left the impression that he had been discussing a minor difficulty.

'I'm not going with you, Hugo.' She said it quietly, decisively. 'There's nothing else to say. Now kindly allow me to leave here.'

'I'll do not such thing.' He was indifferent to her protest. He had made a decision. There was no room for argument. 'You'll stay until I'm ready to leave.' He picked up papers and began to sort them.

'Don't give me orders.' Anger flushed her face. 'I can look after myself.' She turned, picked up her small bag, and reached for the door handle.

He moved quickly then, surprising her. His hand closed over hers on the handle, pulling it away. He stood close to her, and suddenly his eyes were no longer difficult to read. Instinctively she recoiled from them, but he held her wrist tightly.

'You little fool. What the hell do you think this is? A game? You'll still be on the dockside of wherever you get to – if you get there – when the Germans come. And looking like that' – his eyes raked her slender figure from legs to shoulders – 'the first group of soldiers you meet will have you inside the nearest army lorry with your skirt over your head. Is that what you want?' The violence in his voice had the impact of a blow and she twisted her arm away from him, trying to free herself, her teeth clamped against the pain of his grip.

'Stop it. Let me go –'

Then he hit her, across the face; not hard, but sharply enough to sting and shock her into silence. He pulled her roughly forward so that his face was close to hers.

'What are you afraid of? Me? You must be mad. I'm not after your body again. But because I remember it I don't want the bloody Germans to get their hands on it. I'm offering you the only chance you've got to get to England. Call it something I owe you. Call it anything you like. But for God's sake stop bleating like a silly schoolgirl and let me get you out of hell before the gates close.'

Then he let her go and turned back to the desk, reaching again for his papers.

And she was still, except for the fingers of one hand massaging her wrist and arm. Still and silent, watching him, hating him, yet unable to leave him.

Presently she felt the side of her face where he had slapped her. But only her dignity was hurt now. Gradually her breathing steadied, and when the flush had faded from her cheeks she was pale. And she knew she was frightened. For the first time since she had climbed into the lorry on the Paris road outside Amiens, and the young lieutenant had saluted her, she knew she was truly afraid. She had felt her skirt smothering her face and iron hands holding her down and men ripping the clothes from her body and their hot breath and sweat and had heard their grunting and jeering, and there was no alternative but to go with him. Before the gates closed.

For a long time she watched him. He ignored her, sorting papers, shovelling them rapidly into piles, opening files, throwing them on the floor first to this side, then to that.

Then, abruptly, he pivoted on his heel.

'Stay right here. I'll be back in five minutes. Then we go.'

He was back in less than five minutes. Another man was with him, tense and quick-eyed.

'Burn those on the left. And for Christ's sake make sure they're burned. The rest don't matter.' He jerked his head at Michele. 'Come on.'

The man glanced at her curiously as she followed Thoresen out, wordless; down the corridor into the big reception hall. He spoke to the pale receptionist and the uniformed security guard at her side, and scribbled his name on something. The guard released one of the big doors and he strode through, without checking that she was still with him. In the courtyard he pointed to a black Citroën.

'That one. Put your bag on the back seat.'

She did so. Another case was already there. She climbed in and he slid behind the wheel, starting the engine before he had closed the door. The guard at the barrier saluted. Then they were in the street, behind an army lorry, heading west.

'Are we going all the way by car?' Her voice was stilted; artificial.

'Yes. The trains are chaotic. God alone knows how long they'll be able to keep a passenger service running. And we need flexibility.'

They overtook the army lorry in the narrow street, accelerating.

Every vehicle in Paris seemed to be on the roads. Avenue de Friedland was jammed with cars, vans and lorries, many piled with boxes and cases. Thoresen was impassive, showing no impatience, looking straight ahead. But he lost no opportunity to squeeze between traffic, millimetres only to spare, or to take to the pavement to get around a blockage. They reached the giant Arc de Triomphe roundabout and he joined the mêlée quickly and surely, threading between vehicles, ignoring the wrath of other drivers, emerging on the other side fast down the centre of the road, headlights flashing. The junction with the Peripherique was the centre of a massive traffic jam and it took several minutes to find a way through. Then they were over it and he resorted to side streets, twisting between vehicles, once bumping down a narrow alley between high walls, crossing a pedestrian square and rejoining the street beyond. They went through Nanterre like that, and headed out towards St Germain.

Presently, as the traffic thinned, she said: 'What do you do at the embassy? You seem to have a lot of authority.' A hesitation; then with a tinge of bitterness: 'But I suppose you did in Berne too.'

He glanced at her, as if surprised; as if he had forgotten he was not alone in the car.

'I am a civil servant.' Dismissive; don't ask questions like that, without needing to use the words. He jumped a light, accelerating sharply. 'But the authority is ended. My job now is to get back to London.'

'Will Paris be captured?' She had to travel with him and now was determined to make the journey as normal as possible. They could not go on for ever in silence.

'Yes.' No emotion. 'A week, perhaps. There'll be no fighting in the streets. The Government will try to save it from that. You know what happened to Rotterdam when the bombers were sent in.'

'You think France is beaten, don't you?'

'France has neither the means nor the will to fight on. And you know it.'

She was staring through the windscreen, hardly seeing the traffic; calm, taking her cue from him, showing that she could be equally detached.

'And us. What are our chances? Tell me the truth.'

'Fifty-fifty. It depends how fast the Germans move, whether the French army surrenders in separate units or fights on until there's a central order, on how quickly we drive and the direction of the German advance. And ultimately on certain of my friends.' He paused, looking at her briefly. 'What happened to your mother? I'd like to know.'

She marshalled the words, taking her time; then, flat and

hard: 'We were among the refugees, between Cambrai and Amiens. German planes bombed and machine gunned us. It was murder. Deliberate. Sadistic.'

He nodded understanding. A single brief movement.

'There was some of that. Probably still is. All part of spreading terror and blocking roads. I'm sorry. In spite of what she said about me, I was fond of her.' No emotion. Just a simple statement, like reading from a paper.

She looked away, out of the nearside window.

They were driving fast through traffic, tyres squealing on corners, making good time across the river and through St Germain then out beyond into the suburbs. After a long time she said: 'This is the N13. The road to Cherbourg. Is that where we're going? Not Le Havre?'

He lifted his hands momentarily from the steering wheel, palms uppermost. They were pale and well manicured; but she had noticed that about his hands a long time ago, in another world.

'We have no choice – unless we go to Brest. My last information was that the Germans were moving fast towards the Seine. Advanced units could be across the river any time. If we go for Le Havre we not only run the risk of finding it at a standstill, or even in German hands, but more immediately of encountering a German armoured unit on this side of the river. So it's Cherbourg; at least for the time being.'

An hour later they reached Evreux and he stopped at a garage. They would allow him only fifteen litres of petrol. When he went into the little office to pay he stayed for ten minutes and she could see him holding a telephone. Then he came back.

'Cherbourg. We'll be all right if we can get there tonight. The Germans are moving fast and there's no reliable news of how far they've got. But from now on we'll be driving directly away from them, and this car is faster than tanks.' He said it without humour or excitement. It was just a routine report.

Later they passed through a village and he stopped to buy

bread, cheese and a bottle of red wine. He handed them to her and said: 'Give me something to eat while I drive.'

She broke the bread into pieces, trying to make a sandwich he could hold in one hand, bracing herself against the movement of the car as it swayed through corners. She handed the bread and cheese to him and he took it without comment.

Presently, distantly, she said: 'I'm sorry I behaved foolishly at the embassy. I should have been grateful. I am, now. Please remember that, if anything goes wrong.'

For the first time since their shock meeting that morning, he smiled: a brief widening of his mouth.

'You're a British citizen. I'm –' a fractional hesitation '– a representative of His Majesty's Government. I decided you were my responsibility.'

'Doing your duty.' A hint of sarcasm.

'Of course.' He held out his hand for the wine bottle, steadied the car, and took a quick drink. Then, on a straight stretch of road he changed gear and overtook several slower vehicles before he added: 'Your mother was wrong. It wasn't revenge.'

She stared at the label on the wine bottle. Beaujolais, 1937. The same year. Berne, and her humiliation. She took a long breath.

'Opportunism,' she said calmly; then added, 'and part of my education.'

He looked straight ahead, driving very fast into the bright western sky.

After that she dozed for a long time, until they reached Caen. He gave no sign that he had noticed she was awake so she said nothing, eventually sleeping again on the run north up the peninsular.

As they neared Cherbourg they passed army traffic for the first time for more than two hours. It slowed them, and the light was fading when they came into the town, threading among vehicles along the straight Avenue de Paris and on northwards towards the Gare Maritime.

At the main gates a security guard stopped them. Behind him stood two soldiers, rifles on their shoulders. Behind the soldiers was an army lorry towing a mobile anti-aircraft gun. There were sailors, too, from the naval base away to their left. Thoresen stopped, got out, spoke to the guard, and went with him into an office block. He was away for half an hour. All the time traffic passed through the gates in both directions; but many incoming cars were turned away. One of the soldiers unslung his rifle when a driver shouted and began to shake his fist. The soldier was young and wary, but his gun was steady and the driver got back into his car and drove away.

Then Thoresen came back, dark-coated and dark-bearded in the dusk and the lights over the dock gates. As he settled in the car he said curtly: 'There's still some shipping movement. But everyone is very nervous and under pressure. There's a small merchantman tied up at the transatlantic terminal, with limited accommodation. They're hoping to get it away before dawn, for Plymouth. But they've been letting people through the gates all day and there's a big crowd down there. We'll have a look.'

The guard raised the barrier and they drove through and between lines of dock buildings, out towards the moles where the big ships moored. But there were no big ships; just a single-funnelled cargo vessel of no more than five thousand tons, a general carrier with two cranes on her decking. She looked as if she might have had a dozen passenger cabins. And the dockside was packed with people, several hundred, spilling away from the ship, all watching for movement around the gangway. There was no way through for the car and Thoresen parked it against a wall.

They got out. Michele eased an aching back and looked around. They had passed the passenger terminal building. Somehow Thoresen must have had permission for that. Now they could have boarded the merchantman; except for the press of people.

They could see along the side of the ship, and an officer

coming down the gangway and speaking to two policeman at its foot. The policemen beckoned towards the fringe of the crowd and half a dozen people carrying bags and bundles walked forward.

Immediately the crowd erupted. Shouting first, then a surge of movement. The half-dozen were overwhelmed, disappearing in the swaying mass. The two policemen drew their truncheons, struggling. Then sailors appeared on the deck and the gangway shifted, a small crane lifting it away from the ground. The crowd's shouting changed to an ugly howl. More policemen came running, truncheons waving.

Michele shouted against the noise: 'They shouldn't have allowed all these people to get as far as this.'

Thoresen shouted back: 'There's no control. Most of them will have bribed their way here. Unless the army moves in there'll be a riot.' He gripped her arm, his fingers hurting her. 'Come on. We'll never get near that ship. And if we did the crowd would lynch us. If the master's any sense he won't lower the gangway again. Keep close to me.'

He led the way back to the car, forcing their way through the shifting edge of the angry crowd; then reversed away from the quay, back around the buildings, into the shadow of a deserted crane.

'We'll let it calm down. Get some sleep. Later I'll check.'

They slept side by side in the dockside darkness, heads against the car windows. The night was warm and the day had been long and tense, and Michele drifted away into oblivion without knowing if Thoresen slept for long. When she awoke the dawn was a faint line against the sky's blackness, and he was no longer there.

When he reappeared he carried two cups of coffee, slid into the car and said: 'The ship sailed without passengers. Troops have cleared the crowd back through the terminal building. The authorities are trying to get some sort of order into things. There's another ship due this morning and they've asked for a cross-Channel ferry to be sent from Jersey. But there are more people arriving all the time. If we join the mob there's no guarantee we'll get away in spite of my special passes.'

She sipped her coffee. It was hot and sweet and alerted her quickly. She felt calm, almost detached, as if they were discussing someone else's future.

'So what do we do? I'm not going to back off now. I'll get to one of those ships if I have to swim for it.'

He studied her in the half-light. Around his neat beard his jaw and cheeks were noticeably unshaven.

'You were always a stubborn lady.' Quiet, and slightly amused; telling her that he understood her far better than she understood herself.

Suddenly she rebelled and rapped: 'Don't talk down to me. Don't give me the father-figure image. That was how you started – remember? Until you got so close to me that I thought I was in love with you and I was in your bed before I knew what had happened. Well, I'm older now. Very much older. So don't be condescending. If you want to back out just tell me, and I'll find my own way. Or if you want to ditch me, just tell me that. I won't make a scene.'

He stared; startled by her quick anger then withdrawing behind his habitual screen of superiority.

'You sound as if you want to ditch me.' Indifferent now; a token rebuke. 'You will please yourself, of course. And I must say I admire your courage, even if it's foolish. But you will do rather better if you stay with me.'

'And do what? Come on, Hugo. Spell it out. My life's at risk as well as yours. I want to know.'

He shrugged, finishing his coffee and setting the empty cup in the footwell below the steering wheel. 'You will know as much as I'm prepared to tell you,' he said brusquely. 'I shall shortly go into the passenger terminal and wash and shave. Then I shall find breakfast and spend the day having a look at the town. This evening I shall drive out of Cherbourg to a certain place and a certain meeting with others. I have sent and received messages while you have been asleep, with the kind assistance of the French naval authorities. I am satisfied that the outcome has a good chance of ensuring my safe passage to England. If you want to join me, you are welcome to do so. Unless you prefer to swim after the ships which may or may not arrive here today.'

She struggled to control her anger, and to face the unavoidable conclusion that she had to stay with him. 'I'm sorry I flared,' she said stiffly. 'But you are infuriating. You were like that in the past – never telling me anything of importance until the last moment. I think you enjoyed worrying me, then solving my problems by revealing that they no longer existed because you were a jump ahead. Of course I'll come with you, if you still want me to. I've trusted you so far. I have to go through with it now.'

He opened the car door.

'You may thank me when we're back in England,' he said sarcastically. 'Now I'm going to wash. If you care to come with me I'll show you facilities you may wish to use yourself.'

Without a word, she took her bag from the back seat of the car and followed him through the dawn light to the passenger terminal. Just once he looked round, and thought he saw tears glistening on her cheeks. But he could not be sure, and when he looked at her again there was no sign of them.

Later he left her in the car again and went away on one of his mysterious errands before returning and driving away from the docks and into the town. They had breakfast at a small café, and then he drove to the shopping area where he said: 'I have no interest in these things, but if you want to walk around and look, I'll be content to follow you.'

After that they sat at a pavement café and drank coffee until it was lunch time, their conversation spasmodic and cool; and after lunch they went back to the car where he settled without a word and went to sleep. She walked off again to the shops but soon became tired and returned to the car and dozed herself.

Early in the evening they had a light meal, and then drove

out towards the west. And not once did he refer to the arrangements he had made or what might happen.

It was eight o'clock when they passed through Les Pieux and drove on along a narrow track towards the sand dunes which broke up the rocky coastline. He left the track and turned across a flat, sandy plateau raised above the beach. When he stopped he took a map from his pocket and studied it closely, then nodded at a private thought as he consulted his watch.

'We have half an hour to wait. Let's walk down to the beach before the sun disappears. It could be quite romantic.' But the sarcasm which tinged his voice ensured that she did not misunderstand him.

They strolled in silence. The sea was calm and dark against the dying sun and the red-rimmed clouds scattered through haze along the western skyline. Sometimes she looked at him, waiting for him to tell her something, but refusing to give him the satisfaction of declining to answer her questions. He pointed to cormorants, black on scattered rocks, and a hawk circling a low headland, and flotsam scattered along the sand; chatting idly, easily, in a peace which seemed to deny the nightmare edging inexorably towards them. Then he turned back and she followed him up the winding path to the car and watched him take binoculars from beneath a seat.

He checked his watch again, turning the face so that he could see in the last rays of the sun. Then he leaned on the car and raised the glasses to his eyes and, very slowly, began to pan them across the horizon. She waited, breathless, seeing her suspicions confirmed, knowing that he was looking for a ship; a ship which would not call at Cherbourg where the angry, desperate passengers crowded hopelessly: a ship for which he had made his own unmentionable arrangements.

A breeze rustled over the thin, spiky beach grasses, chill at the ending of the day, and she shivered. Behind, the land was dark. But there was still light low in the western sky beyond the beach and the flat, grey sea; enough light to outline a ship.

Then he was still, steadying the glasses, concentrating. She stared, straining her eyes, seeing nothing except gold-tipped clouds and haze which hid the rim of the sea. He watched for minutes, and the anger surged in her again that he should treat her as a child who would not understand the strange world of adults like Hugo Thoresen; but she suppressed it because she was fascinated, and also because she was afraid to quarrel with him now.

Presently he opened the sloping lid of the luggage boot and took out a large torch. She thought it was the biggest torch she had ever seen; like a miniature searchlight. He studied the sea with his glasses again, laid a pencil along the roof of the car as a marker, then carefully lined his torch along it.

Then he began to signal.

She did not understand the morse code, so could only watch and wonder. He seemed to be repeating a pattern of long and short stabs of light. When he stopped he watched the horizon through the binoculars.

And she saw the answer: a bright pin head of light, flickering. She was surprised how close it seemed.

When he responded with his torch there was one brief further signal from the sea and he lowered the glasses, satisfied.

She could restrain herself no longer. Very quietly she said: 'Don't you think it's time you had the courtesy to tell me something.'

He raised his eyebrows in the dimness, feigning surprise.

'Of course. Why not – now I have something to tell you? You must understand that until this moment I could not be sure that the things I had hoped for would actually happen.'

'What things, Hugo?' Still quiet; still struggling to be patient.

'That we should be picked up from this beach by a ship,' he said coolly. 'A little inconvenient activity by the Germans could have spoiled things for us. But now I think everything will be all right. Get your bag. We're going back to the beach.'

He picked up his own bag and the big torch and led the way down the winding path, through the rustling grasses, to the dim, chill sand. The water's edge was a hundred yards away and he strolled towards it as if time was of no consequence. She felt the shingle cold beneath her thin shoes, and the breeze cold off the sea which sucked and lapped in small, long straight waves she could hardly see.

When they reached the water he levelled the torch and flashed its beam. Seconds later came the response: four quick stabs of light. He said: 'Excellent. They'll be here in ten minutes. They've already launched their boat. I'm surprised we haven't heard the ship's engines. She can't be far off.'

She thought it was time for another question, and said: 'What sort of a ship?'

He looked down at her, surprised in the growing darkness.

'Of course. I didn't tell you. We shall be in good hands. She's a Royal Navy frigate which, conveniently, happened to be in St Helier.'

She stared, holding her breath for a moment. Then she took a step towards him, the sand clinging to her shoes.

'Hugo. What *are* you? What *is* your job with the Government?'

He said easily: 'I told you. I'm a civil servant.'

She glanced once out across the sea, but saw nothing.

'Does the Government always send warships to rescue civil servants?'

'Probably not. It depends on many things.'

She turned back to him, searching his face in the gloom.

'They must think it's very important that they get you home: or that the Germans don't get you. Is that it?'

'I did not have time to question their motives,' he said. 'Let's say I have friends in the right places. And you should not complain.'

She shook her head, and the very last light of the day glinted in her hair as it moved.

'I don't. I'm very fortunate. I'm only now realizing how

fortunate. Are you going to tell me what you do – who you work for?'

He said: 'Yes. I work for the Government. And I'm a fixer. I arrange things. I have arranged that you and I shall return home in relative comfort and a good deal of safety. That should be enough for both of us.'

He stepped away from her, raised his torch again, and flashed it. Almost immediately the reply came, and now its source was close. They listened to the splash and slow rhythm of the waves, and a seabird calling, and the shingle shifting beneath the moving water; and the regular ripple of oars somewhere out there, faint then clear, positive, and movement on the black water and a bright light which did not flash but remained on them, outlining them. The boat was visible now, and scraped its keel on the long slope of the beach, and two men climbed over the side and dropped into the shallow water, wading towards them.

One said, in a clear, cultivated voice: 'Mr Hugo Thoresen? I'm Lieutenant David Winter. I'm delighted to meet you.'

He reached them, holding out his hand to clasp Thoresen's. But his eyes were on Michele in the torchlight.

Thoresen said: 'I'm glad to see you here, Mr Winter. May I present Miss Michele Armstrong, with whose family I have been acquainted for very many years? She will be accompanying me back to England. I'm afraid I didn't have time to include that information in my signals.'

The Lieutenant nodded. He stood, the water lapping around the ankles of his seaboots, and saluted Michele.

'It will be our pleasure to have you aboard, Miss Armstrong.' He looked at her, and her skirt blowing in the night wind, and added: 'If you will permit me, I'll carry you to the boat. The sea is rather wet tonight.'

PART TWO

ALAN

━━━◆━◆━━━

1941–1943

1

On 27th of April 1937, at the ancient parish church of Nantwich in the county of Cheshire, Neil Gordon Cameron was married to Joan Nancy Pritchard. He was a twenty-five year old journalist working for the News Chronicle in Manchester; she was two years younger and a nurse at a Manchester city hospital. They had known each other for three years and the world was a beautiful place.

Five miles away on that same afternoon, Alan Geoffrey Tamworth, in his last year as a modern history student at Manchester University, twisted clear of clutching hands to score a try for his college in a rugby match with a team from Liverpool University. He was twenty-two, tall and strong, and delighted with his jinking, swerving run which had assured victory for his side. For him, too, at that moment the world was a beautiful place.

He had never heard of Neil Cameron, who had never heard of Alan Tamworth. And neither had heard of a girl named Michele who lived in a decaying chateau close to the Ouanne River in France and who was as beautiful as that April day.

Ten years? Ten thousand, and in another world. In May 1947 I sat in the window of a Leicester Square steakhouse which had risen from the rubble of a bombed building, watching the evening sun through the great trees, and wondered about time and fate, and life and death; and, had there been no war, if I would still have been married to Joan, and who Alan and Michele would have married because it would not have been each other, and where I would have been now because it would not have been here with Anne, listening to her telling me that she had tracked down Charlie Feldman while I wondered how long it would be before we went to bed together, because I knew we would.

'He lives just outside Bristol,' she said. 'The ATA records gave his last known address, and I rang the local post office who said there's someone named Feldman there now. It has to be him.'

I dragged myself away from the disturbing vision of Anne in other circumstances.

'We're lucky. He could have been anywhere in America.'

'Why is it so important to find him? He only met her twice, and the first time she was a child.'

'We don't know what happened in 1942,' I said. 'We only know what Peter Armstrong knows. Chuck Feldman could colour a lot of things.'

She was watching me curiously.

'I think this is very strange. People are telling you intimate things. I can't imagine Peter Armstrong wanting to see details of his love life in print. Yet he told you, knowing you're researching for a book.'

'He's a lonely man who needs someone to be interested in him. I gave him a chance to expose his soul and I think he felt better for it. Especially when I told him what had happened to Michele. He'd always hoped that one day she might seek him out and forgive him. Then I turned up and broke his dream. He just wanted to talk then.'

'Will it hurt him, to see it all in a book?'

'It depends what I write. I don't know what's going into the book. I'm just writing everything down, everything I know or can guess, using my imagination a little when I have to, leaving gaps I hope I can fill later when I've tracked down someone else.'

She said: 'You're getting involved with these people. You care about them. You worry about what they did, and why.'

'That's what Charles wanted.' I couldn't tell her I had gone much too far ever to turn back. And that the most difficult part was to come; the part where I would have to write about myself. How much of that would I use in the final version? Nothing, perhaps. I could write Michele's story without any of it. But there would be a private manuscript. There had to be, now. Like Peter Armstrong, I needed to confess, and to learn about myself from that confession; even if nobody else read it. Just to see the words would help. There was no feeling of guilt. They were both dead, so it didn't matter. Except to me. And the scars were still deep and painful. I had to resurrect it all and set it down.

She was saying: 'I think you're getting more involved than Charles expected.'

A rebuke? I stared at her. More than Charles expected – or more than Anne expected? How much had I given away in these little meetings which were becoming less and less casual?

'He should be glad,' I said. 'Maybe it's a bigger story than he realized. I know a lot about Alan Tamworth. I did a radio story on him once, remember. But I need to know more about the others. I need to find Thoresen especially. If he's still alive.'

'What do you know about him now?' I thought Thoresen fascinated her, too.

'Not enough. I'll get the rest, somehow.'

She said quietly: 'You're very confident. You believe in yourself, don't you?' It was a tribute.

I shook my head. 'I don't believe in anything except luck – good and bad. Sometimes I can cope, sometimes I can't. But there's no belief in that. Just the fortunate possession of certain attributes and the unfortunate lack of others.'

'No.' She squeezed my fingers, then traced lines along them, studying them. 'That won't do. Complex people can't get by with simple philosophies like that. And you're very complex.'

'I'm simple,' I said. 'And right now I'm simply enjoying your company. Let's get for a walk. Down to the river.'

We had finished our meal, so we went outside and wandered through to Trafalgar Square and then on round Charing Cross to Villiers Street which led to the Embankment. We walked hand-in-hand, enjoying that little intimacy, and I remembered the very first time I had walked down that narrow street holding a woman's hand.

My wife's hand.

We arrived in London just before Christmas 1937, eight months married and me starting a new job with the BBC. I was going to be a radio journalist and I was excited about it; more excited than Joan who had not wanted to leave the north where her parents lived. But I didn't pay much attention to that. She would get used to it. She had already found a new job at St Thomas's hospital. We rented a flat off the Edgware Road and I settled down to mastering the transition from the written to the spoken word, to learning microphone techniques, programme production, and how to adapt to the strange, suffocating yet undeniably stimulating atmosphere of the prejudiced, ingenious, self-satisfied monolith called the British Broadcasting Corporation.

But Joan did not get used to being away from the north. We were happy enough together and she was popular with our friends, for she was vivacious and pretty with her dark hair and elfin face; but she could not adapt to the cut and thrust of London and feeling that while you were a part of it you could never belong to it because its special quality was not its size but its enthusiasm and that existed only in the minds of its millions. So as the certainty of war grew, she talked of the dangers of bombing and the merits of the open Cheshire fields, and I knew it was an excuse she hoped I would accept for myself.

But I could not do that because by now I had been absorbed into the confusion, the conflict and the dream, and there was talk in the BBC of adventure: of men who would go off to war not as soldiers but as reporters, with the clumsy recording equipment which was all we had then but which would still enable the fortunate few to bring the sights, the sounds and the smell of war back to the firesides of those left at home. So when the war came we agreed that she should go back to her parents' home and that I would take every chance I had to join her there, even if for only a night at a time.

It was our first step towards disaster.

I was not chosen initially as a war correspondent: that privilege went to men who were already nationally-known broadcasters. It became their task to persuade by example the sceptical military high commands who did not believe there was a need to provide the public with day-by-day eye witness reports. War, said the generals, was a soldier's job: civilians would be told what had happened when the soldiers were ready, just like the last time.

But this was not like the last time; and after the first few months the politicians over-rode military conservatism as the gravity of the task facing Britain and France became apparent, and decided that the mammoth effort which was required of civilians as much as armed forces could be better stimulated if people knew what was happening to the men in uniform.

I volunteered for the army a month after the war started; but before my number came up I ran for a train on Euston station, fell over somebody's kitbag, and broke my left leg just below the knee. It took a long time to heal and kept me out of uniform until the summer of 1940 by which time the BBC had persuaded Whitehall that it needed many more correspondents and recording engineers on permanent attachment to the armed forces, and I got my chance.

Meanwhile Joan, working in a hospital near Macclesfield, showed signs of resentment that, although nominally still a civilian, I could not get home more often. I sailed on coastal convoys, flew on a mine-laying operation along the Dutch coast, watched a Guards' armoured unit being formed and trained on Salisbury Plain, endured winter weeks in a Hebridean outpost and terrifying nights with the fire-fighters in the London Blitz; yet although she heard my voice in radio news bulletins describing what I had seen and felt, she did not seem to take my commitment seriously.

Yet somehow the significance of it did not seem to dawn on me until, after I had been away for several weeks, my father-in-law took me out for a drink specifically to warn me that he thought my marriage was in danger. He was a pleasant, good-natured man for whom I had developed a lot of respect. But we both found it difficult to communicate once he had told me awkwardly that he thought his daughter had become sexually starved to the point of needing satisfaction and that if I could not provide it he feared she might find someone else who would.

Perhaps it should not have been a surprise. In bed Joan was exciting and totally exhausting; and made no secret to me that she found my absences a strain. Later I tried to talk to her about it, but she became uncharacteristically reticent, and for the first time I felt we were losing our ability to communicate and understand.

Then, within weeks, I was sent to Gibraltar and from there to Egypt and along the North African coastal strip for a three-months' stint with the advancing British and Commonwealth army. When I came back it was without warning and I flew into Manchester and turned up on Joan's parents' doorstep unannounced at eight o'clock in the evening.

When we went to bed that night she tried hard but it was obviously a sham and I knew somebody else had been there, probably that same day. So I asked her outright, without anger or even excitement. I think the shock of it made her confess that there was a doctor at the hospital who had become her lover and that I was right about that very day.

She wept as she told me, but I thought her tears were

prompted less by regret than fear of my reaction. And I just sat there in bed and looked at her, stupidly, telling myself that I should have expected it, wanting to salvage something and then feeling there was nothing left to salvage. At last she whimpered: 'I suppose you want a divorce.'

I heard my voice saying: 'I don't know. Do you want to marry him?'

'He's married.' A hopeless little sound. Suddenly she saw what she had started.

'Then decide if you want to save his marriage,' I said. I lay down with my back to her. 'I don't want to talk about it tonight. Wait until the morning.'

I lay awake until the daylight came. Then I drifted into sleep until I woke, exhausted, around nine o'clock. She was working that day and had gone. I wondered what she would tell her doctor, and if they would have it again before she came home.

She came back at the end of her shift, pale and tense. We made polite conversation because her parents were there, but her father knew something was wrong; I could tell. That evening we went to a pub, just to get away from them, and I said: 'Well, did you tell him?'

She nodded miserably.

'What did he say?'

She gulped. 'He doesn't want to leave his wife.'

'What did you expect?' I said. 'I suppose he said he loved you. They all do. It's obligatory. Only fools believe it. He wanted to screw you and you let him. It's as simple as that.'

She flinched, then shook her head. 'I wanted it first. He was just – willing. I'm sorry. You started something in me. Now I can't stop for long.' She looked at me across the little round pub table, confused. 'Why don't you hit me, or something?'

I stared. That had not occurred to me. Whatever else I did to her, it would not be that. I looked at her drawn face and round, panicking eyes. 'What about today. Have you had it today?'

She shook her head several times, her hair jerking on her shoulders.

'No. Oh God, no. I just – told him – you knew. He was scared. Now I won't go near him again.' She started to bite a finger nail. 'What are you going to do?'

'Have another drink,' I said.

My leave was not enjoyable, yet we parted still married, still talking to each other, still trying to convince her father there was nothing wrong, but with a kind of hopelessness. On the night before I left she turned to me in bed, and I took her suddenly, savagely, as if it were revenge and I wanted to give her more than she could ever hope to get from any other man and make her cry out for me to stop, but she didn't.

I came back within a week and she assured me that she had kept away from her doctor and I believed her; and it went on like that for several months until I forced myself to stop thinking about it. But I knew it could not last for long and when I was sent back to North Africa I did not even ask her to promise she would try to control herself. It was the end, and we both knew it.

I lived with that through the grit and the dust of the desert as the newly formed Eighth Army surged across Egypt to relieve the famous Tobruk garrison after its eight-month siege, and then fought on into Libya. In spite of the speed of the advance and the heavy fighting along the way, I got a number of despatches back to Cairo, and several pointless, artificial letters from Joan caught up with me when I stopped for what I thought was a well-earned rest in Benghazi. Then Rommel struck back. Within three days there was headlong retreat with the BBC's intrepid Neil Cameron in the temporary care of the 4th Indian Division. We got to Gazala, ran into a fast-moving Panzer unit, and poor Ron Parkinson who had been my recording engineer for four months was killed in the scout car beside me. If he had been driving and I had been the passenger, I would have been the one left buried in that arid waste beneath a pile of stones.

I stayed in the hell-hole called Tobruk until early May when I received a letter from Joan telling me she could not wait any longer and was leaving her parents' home to live with someone she euphemistically called a friend. The letter was dated two months before. I was still getting used to that when Rommel's long-expected attack started and the great tank battle of Knightsbridge, south of Tobruk, left the Allied forces in total defeat and was the start of the long, bitter trek back to El Alamein, a mere sixty miles from Cairo. Twice I came within minutes of capture, and in retrospect know that at the time I hardly cared: there didn't seem to be much to go home to. But each time the troops dragged me out of trouble and I was still in one piece and still sending stories back to London when the Allies' last line of defence was established in a bid to save the Suez Canal and the whole of North Africa.

That was when I was recalled, and lost the chance to report on the battle of Alamein and the Allies' ultimate victory in North Africa. Instead I was thrown head first into a skirmish of a different kind.

It was sordid and dull. She had left her doctor to spend time with a major from a nearby army camp; then had found comfort with a junior executive at a Manchester engineering factory making parts for aero engines; a young man said to be unfit for military service but clearly fit for service of another kind. She was living with him when I got there, yet I didn't even feel I wanted to see him. I suppose by then I just wanted the whole thing ended. But he was an unpleasant character who tried to stop me talking to her, so I took him by the collar, pushed him up against a wall and broke his nose and two of his ribs. It cost me a twenty pound fine for common assault and a delay in the start of divorce proceedings. But Joan and I were polite to each other, and I almost felt sorry for a girl who needed a man so badly that she had had to have three in action while I had been away.

The rest of the year and the first half of 1943 seemed to drift away, ordinary and lonely after the dangers and discomforts and companionships of the desert; until the Director of War Reporting sent for me and said: 'There's something special coming up. If you don't want it, say "No" – it's strictly a volunteer job.'

'Try me,' I said. At that moment I would have volunteered for anything, except perhaps the Far East, which nobody fancied.

'It's a seat on a big bombing raid. I know it's been done before. But there are new bomber control methods which make our raids much more accurate, and the RAF wants the public to know that we're getting better and better results, especially as the casualties get higher.'

My heart was jumping a bit. RAF bomber losses were heavy these days. I had flown operationally once, but that had been an easy one. This would be different.

I said, playing for time: 'Why me? Jobs like that usually go to the famous names.'

'Keep working at it,' he said. 'You might be the next Dimbleby. And this job could help. We don't want it only for home consumption. If it's good, it could go to America. Churchill is still trying to persuade the Yanks that night bombing is the best bet for them as well as for us. Something really special could get a lot of attention. And the word is that they'll find a really special target for it.'

I took a deep breath and said: 'All right. You sold it. But I don't just want eight hours sat in a Lancaster over Germany. I want to spend a month on it. Get to know the crew. Live and work with them, watch them go off on earlier raids and talk to them when they come back, go drinking with them, meet their girl friends, become part of them so that they accept me and ignore the recorder.'

He grinned. 'You just got yourself a job. The RAF says it'll pick a top crew – bags of experience, good personalities, an Aussie or two so that we can send something down under, maybe a Canadian. Go away and think about it.'

'I thought,' I said. 'When do we start?'

I didn't know what I was starting.

2

•—•—•

The great maintenance hangar echoed with voices; hollow, confused sounds bouncing off the metal walls and high roof. Three hundred or more men had strolled in and stood in groups: pilots here, navigators there, bomb aimers and air gunners and wireless operators also separating themselves, instinctively. There were no orders that they should do that; but they had trained in those groups, and still sought the comfort of familiar faces and familiar brevets on their tunics.

But today would change all that. They formed ranks loosely but still keeping their groups intact: Sergeants and Pilot Officers, even a few Flight Sergeants and Flying Officers alongside each other. Then they were brought to attention and dressed to the right, straightening their lines, suddenly disciplined.

The Chief Ground Instructor jumped up on to a table so that he could be seen.

'At ease, gentlemen,' he said curtly, and watched them relax. 'You know why you're here. It's crewing up day. From now on you fly as complete operational units. Those of you who go on to heavies will be joined later by a flight engineer and an extra gunner. But at the moment we're looking for five-man crews. Sort yourselves out.' He dropped down from the table, pulled a pipe from his pocket, and began to stoke it as he walked briskly from the hangar.

The ranks wavered. Slowly the talk swelled. Sort yourselves out. Get yourselves into groups – pilot, navigator, bomb-aimer/gunner, wireless operator, tail gunner. No one knew anyone in another group, unless it was by chance. Nevertheless, sort yourself out. Find four other men to fly with, to fight with, to die with. Even at this stage they knew the losses were mounting. What did the rumours say – fifteen ops then, on average, you got the chop? What had started as a great adventure for which they had all volunteered was rapidly assuming different, sobering proportions.

Pilot Officer Alan Tamworth reminded himself that the pilot was always the captain of an aircraft, irrespective of rank. So far he had been a newly commissioned pupil pilot, doing as the instructors told him. Now he had to be the boss – once he had found a crew. But how? Appearances meant nothing, except that an untidy man probably had an untidy mind and that was not to be recommended. Maybe the calm collected ones were the best bet; but then maybe not – in a fight you needed fast response and naked aggression; from a gunner at least.

He looked at the air gunners. Bright, quick eyes looked back. Five feet nothing, sharp features and a grin. He took a tentative step; so did the Grin.

'Hullo. I can shoot straight. You want a good tail-end Charlie?' London. A quick talker. Sergeant.

'That's what I need. I'm Alan Tamworth.'

'Mick Silver – sir.' He threw away the courtesy. Once they were a crew he would never need to use it. 'Everyone calls me Goldie. Shows how perverse people are.'

They shook hands. Alan said: 'Know anybody else who's as good as you and me?'

The grin again. 'No one's as good as you and me, skipper. But I know a wireless-op who's nearly as good.'

'Grab him,' Alan said. Suddenly he felt better.

Who mattered most? The navigator. He got you there; more importantly, he got you back. The navigator group was disappearing in the mêlée. Several stood talking to pilots. He had missed the best. Come on, don't be stupid, how can anyone tell just by looking at them? He moved towards a group of three. They were glancing around, warily. No one wanted to be left uncrewed at the end of the morning. Usually only the quiet, shy ones were left. A full crew of quiet, shy ones was nobody's idea of fun. One of the navigators caught his stare. Australia flash, sergeant, good looking, tall and serious but with a strange sparkle in his eyes.

'Hi, skip. I can find the second street lamp on the left in the Unter den Linden; as long as somebody can drive me there.'

Alan stuck out his hand. 'Alan Tamworth. I can drive you there.'

'Chris Coltrane. It's a deal.'

Goldie came back with a sergeant wireless operator, unsmiling, intelligent, incredibly thin. 'Bob Galway,' Goldie said. 'Don't let him fool you. He can sink a pint in four seconds with a following wind.'

They stood together, starting conversation, where are you from, how was the course, anybody married? Bob Galway was, Goldie was running away from a girl who thought she was pregnant. There was still a bomb-aimer/front gunner to find; a combination of icy nerves and quick reflexes. Alan said: 'Hang around. I'll be back.' He wandered away, searching. Two bomb aimers stood talking. How the hell could he go up to them and ask one and not the other? Which one, the sergeant or the PO? The sergeant solved it by waving to someone, then edging away to talk. The PO pulled out a pipe and began to fill it. He looked at ease, almost indifferent to the hubbub around. Left a bit, left, hold it, steady, steady, bombs gone. He looked steady.

'Alan Tamworth. You want to risk your neck with me?'

Steady eyes, studying his face.

'How the hell do I know?' A glance down to inspect the tobacco in the pipe. 'Like a marriage market, isn't it? Dip in and take your chance. Sure, I'll fly with you. I'm Philip Martin.' He condensed the first name to Flip.

They shook hands. Alan liked the hard grip. And he had a crew.

A week later they flew together for the first time, trundling around the training circuits in a twin-engined Wellington, working hard, quipping, insulting; names with personalities now, fears and fads and obsessions, quick humour or, like Bob Galway, no humour at all.

Christ Coltrane was the driving force: the first to the bar, the first to find a girl, the first to the aircraft and the first to start a rowdy party. Someone called him Digger and he said: 'Don't call me that. Stand in a bar and shout "What'll you have, Digger?" and you'll be trampled in the rush.' Goldie said he acted like a greedy dog, always hungry for something, anything; so they called him Dingo, all except Galway who never used nicknames.

But it was Flip Martin with whom Alan felt most at ease: not because they were commissioned and that separated them from the others in the mess, but because of his extraordinary calm. Whatever the problem, the hairy moment, he either had the answer or the right word to scale it down to size. He was the steadying influence, the reliable counsellor, the one everybody turned to for advice: even Alan himself.

And so they came to know each other, and went to war together.

*

By the time the dust had settled it was obvious that the whole building had been blown into the street. Two other buildings were on fire nearby and the flames lit up the tumble of stone and brick and steel girders. Above, jagged walls stood on either side in stark silhouette against the flickering glow of the tortured darkness. London had been like that through most of the winter; only this time Alan Tamworth and Chris Coltrane were in the middle of it.

They had had forty-eight hour passes after completing fifteen operational flights and had come to London for what Dingo had forecast would be a raving weekend. That Saturday night they had spent four hours and far too much money in one of the underground night clubs which kept going in spite of Goering's Blitz, and at one in the morning escaped from the girls who had been their dancing companions and who were clearly going to cost them a lot more money if their acquaintance was prolonged, to start the long walk back to a crumbling flat in Kensington which Alan had borrowed from an old university friend who was away doing something mysterious in a Sheffield arms factory.

Just after they left the sirens wailed across the city, then the guns opened up in the distance, the searchlights probed the darkness, and the unsynchronised rhythm of Heinkel engines echoed in the black sky as the bombs began to fall. First they were away to the south, but then the raid moved like a tide across the Thames and the West End and suddenly the two airmen sprawled on their faces in the deserted street as a stick of bombs straddled buildings close ahead of them.

When they picked themselves up they could see the great mound of rubble in the light of a flaring gas main fire a hundred yards away. The aircraft engines still rumbled overhead and there were more explosions further away, lights flashing and flames reaching, and Dingo said: 'Christ – so this is what it's like.' He looked at Alan. 'I reckon we'd better see if we can help, Skip.'

By the time they got there the wardens were out, and one tried to turn them back until Dingo snapped, 'Don't be bloody silly, mate,' and they clambered past him, looking around, searching for somebody who might need extra hands. Fire engine and ambulance bells pealed, and they followed two steel-helmeted rescue workers up the shifting debris. A nearby building was blazing and the flames outlined them in ghastly wavering gold and red.

They worked for unknown time, their uniforms which had been so smart an hour before now torn and filthy, their hands bleeding as they grabbed masonry and heaved it aside in the search for survivors. They helped rescue teams carry away four mutilated bodies then joined an attempt to reach a man they could see in somebody else's torchlight. He was in uniform.

'He's RAF,' Alan said; and they increased their efforts to lift away timbers and stones.

When they got him out they thought he was not badly hurt except for a gash across his head. An ambulance crew passed a stretcher across the rubble and they lifted him onto it. He was a sergeant pilot, and he stirred and tried to raise himself. Alan held his shoulders and said: 'Take it easy. You'll be okay now.' The sergeant said something Alan could not understand as they steadied the stretcher and struggled down towards the waiting ambulance. The sergeant stirred again, rolling sideways, and in the light of the flames Alan saw his shoulder flash.

He said to Dingo: 'He's French.' The sergeant was trying to tell them something and Dingo bent over him, then looked up and shrugged. 'He's talking French,' he shouted above the noise of an ambulance bell nearby.

They got him to the door of the ambulance and a woman's voice said: 'Let me see if I can understand him.'

She climbed down from the driving seat of the vehicle, neat in her uniform, steel helmet pushed to the back of her head, fair hair curling from under it. As they pushed the stretcher into the ambulance she went inside with it, bending over the man. He was mumbling and she crouched beside him. Alan and Dingo looked at each other. The French was rapid, fluent. Dingo muttered: 'Would'ya believe it – a sheila talking French as if it was her own language, in the middle of this nightmare.'

She came back to them. 'He's rambling. I can't make sense of it. Better get him to the first aid post quickly. Do you want to come?'

Alan looked at the man on the stretcher. French or not, he was RAF. 'All right. We'll see him as far as the hospital.'

She said: 'The two of you can squeeze into the front.'

Behind them the ambulance doors clanged as one of the crew went inside and pulled them closed after him. They scrambled into the front passenger seat, the woman hauled herself up behind the wheel, started the engine and let in the clutch.

'Hold on.' She raised her voice above the engine noise; then set the alarm bell going and accelerated. They grabbed for handholds as the vehicle swayed through a corner, hearing the tyres squealing. In the dim interior they could hardly see their driver, except for the steel helmet pushed far back from her forehead and her hands winding the big steering wheel and changing gear.

Then she leaned across and shouted to Alan who was nearest: 'We'll skip the first aid post. He may have a fractured skull. Straight to the hospital would be better.'

Within minutes the ambulance bumped into the hospital yard, and she reversed fast and straight up to the ramp, then twisted in her seat and disappeared through the door. They heard her calling to a porter and by the time they had scrambled out the vehicle doors were open and the stretcher was being transferred to a trolley. She called over her shoulder: 'Come on in. We'll make sure he's all right.'

The casualty reception area was crowded and no one took notice of them. The stretcher was being wheeled through curtains and the ambulance driver went with it. They waited outside; then she came back and said: 'Is he a friend of yours?'

'No. We just helped to dig him out.'

They were both looking at her in the subdued lighting of the hospital hallway. She dragged the steel helmet off her head and shook her hair. 'God, I feel a mess,' she said, then starred at them critically. 'But not as much of a mess as you two look.' She saw the blood on their hands. Some of it had been transferred to Dingo's face. 'You're not hurt, are you?'

'Hurt? No – a few cuts, that's all.' It was Alan. Dingo muttered: 'Hell's bells, talk about an angel of mercy.' He grinned through the grime on his face; then he and Alan stared at each other's uniforms and he ejaculated: 'Christ, we are in a mess.'

178

Alan looked down at his own torn trousers and jacket.

'It's all right for you – I have to pay for mine.'

'Serves you right for getting a commission.'

Then they forgot their own appearances and turned to the girl who stood between them. Her face was dirt-streaked and her hair had a layer of dust across it and her uniform was dirty, but her features and her eyes and her slender figure had them both holding their breath for a moment, until Alan said: 'I suppose it would be good manners if we introduced ourselves, even if we're too filthy to shake hands. At least I'd like to know the name of the fastest ambulance driver in London.' He nodded towards Dingo. 'He's Chris Coltrane. I'm Alan Tamworth.'

She held out both her hands, one to each of them.

'Your hands are no dirtier than mine. Hullo Alan, Chris. I'm Michele Armstrong.'

*

Four weeks went by before he had another chance to get to London. Then he telephoned her and they met in the bar of the Piccadilly Hotel and she said: 'By yourself? I thought you might have brought your Australian friend.'

He looked at her keenly.

'I got away when he wasn't looking. Disappointed?'

'He seemed like good company,' she said. 'But I'm sure you are too.'

They talked over their drinks and afterwards through a meal, and he told her where he came from and how many operations he still had to do before he ended his tour and what a marvellous crew he had, and never mentioned that several times they had come back with pieces trailing from their Wellington and once he had been sure they would not get back at all. Then it was her turn, and she told him how it was that she could speak to the French sergeant in his own language, and that she had escaped from France with only hours to spare, but she was vague about the details and did not mention Hugo Thoresen.

He said: 'You just came here – with nothing, and no one? No money, or relatives?'

'It was either that or stay and take whatever was coming. I couldn't face that. But I brought something with me. A ring, which was worth a lot of money. I sold it. That helped me to start.'

'And why ambulance driving?'

'Why not? I had to earn a living. And do something useful.'

'It's hairy,' he said. 'Really dangerous, night after night in the Blitz.'

She said quietly: 'So is flying aeroplanes.'

He looked surprised, pretending he had not thought about that; then grinned and said: 'Too serious. I know a club, off Dean Street. A cellar with a three-piece band and a dance floor as big as this table. I have to be back by six in the morning which means the last train out tonight. But that still give us two or three hours.'

She looked pleased. 'All right. Let's try it.'

By club standards it was too early for a crowd, but they liked that as they sat at their little corner table, then danced, holding each other lightly, not too close but close enough to show they were interested. Once when they went back to their table he said: 'Where do you live?'

'In half a flat in Ealing. A couple of rooms and the use of a crummy kitchen and bathroom.'

'Half a flat? Who has the other half?'

She looked surprised, mischief in her eyes.

'Is that important?'

He gave her a cigarette. 'It might be. I'm just wondering what sort of company you keep.'

She accepted his light. 'It's the ambulance service sector controller.' She said it as if it were a confession.

His eyes never left hers. In the dim lighting they were almost black, but shining. 'What's his name?'

She took shelter behind her glass, as if she needed time. Then she said: 'Phyllis.'

He relaxed. 'Good. I thought you were going to say Philip.'

'Would it have made any difference?' She was openly teasing him now.

His eyes narrowed. He was pretending to be angry, but she knew he was not.

'I would have been furious. I am, anyway, because you gave me a bad moment. Do you enjoy tormenting men?'

She said: 'I haven't known many men well enough for that.'

'After all those years in France? What about the Latin lovers we hear so much about? Don't tell me it's all French propaganda.'

She played with her glass. Suddenly she was serious.

'I only had one French boy friend. He would have been a Latin lover if he'd had his way, but I would never quite let him. There was someone else. He wasn't French. And he taught me a lot about men. In the end, some things I'd rather not have known. But he paid his debt. He helped me to escape from France.' She looked up at him, surprised by herself. 'Sorry, Alan. You don't want to hear about that. You tricked me into – remembering.'

The band began a slow sentimental number. They both knew the lyric. *That old black magic has me in its spell, that old black magic that you weave so well.* He took her hand and they walked onto the little dance floor. This time he held her close and said: 'Where is he now? Did he escape with you?'

She nodded, her hair brushing his face.

'Yes. But I don't know where he is. I haven't seen him since the day we landed.'

'Because you don't want to?'

'I shall never want to.'

'Do you want to tell me?'

'One day I might.'

She was warm and comforting against him. They danced

as if they had always been together like that. *Those icy fingers up and down my spine, that same old witchcraft when your eyes meet mine.* She looked up at him and whispered: 'Tell me the truth. You're not married, are you?'

'No. I'll take you to meet my parents if you like, just to prove it.'

She shook her head against his shoulder. 'I believe you. But some people aren't like that. Not these days.'

'We are. You're going to let me see you again, aren't you? As soon as I can get leave of some sort?'

'Yes, please. I'll try to arrange something too, so that I'm free.'

'Out of London, if we can. Away from the Blitz.'

Other couples were on the floor now, crowding them. They were very close. *Down and down I go, round and round I go, in a spin, loving the spin I'm in.* His lips brushed her hair. She moved her head so that she could see his face. 'I didn't think it would be like this, Alan. Not quite like this.' So quietly that he hardly heard her.

'I thought it might be. If I was very, very lucky. That's why I didn't bring Dingo.' He saw the question in her eyes. 'That's what we call Chris. Everyone has a nickname. It's a RAF obsession.'

'What do they call you?'

'Nothing unusual. Skipper, or Skip. Most bomber pilots get that. It's a sort of – discipline.'

She put her face against his shoulder for a moment, then looked up at him again. 'I'll call you Skip. When no one else can hear.' Then she added quickly: 'I like Alan. But Skipper suits you. You're a hard man, I think, behind the smile.'

'Hard?' He shook his head. 'Obstinate, maybe. But not with you. I know when I'm beaten.'

Later they came out of their dark, smokey, music-filled cellar and walked arm in arm and close together into Regent Street and round to the Piccadilly Tube where they picked their way amongst the hundreds of people who slept every night on the platforms and she went with him to St Pancras where he had to catch his train to Huntington.

On the platform he took her chin between his thumb and forefinger and kissed her once, lightly, on the forehead.

'Goodnight, Mitch. I'll ring you as often as I can. And we'll fix something for that leave. If you'll still want to, by then.'

She whispered: 'I'll want to. However long it takes.'

*

When it came he telephoned to tell her the date and ask if she would like to go to a riverside hotel at Henley. She hesitated, then said: 'I'd love to. But I have to say this. So there aren't any misunderstandings. It's separate rooms, Skip. Do you mind?'

He said: 'I've already phoned the hotel and checked that they have – separate rooms. I didn't think of anything else.'

'I didn't imagine you would. But I had to say it.' He could hear the relief in her voice.

*

Six days seemed like three. Walking beside the river, feeding the swans, rowing lazily for hours, sitting through evenings in a pub garden which sloped down to the water, toasting each other across candle-light at a table; a dream, wondering, contented. By the end they felt as if they had known each other for a year, it was so easy; and knew they could not let it end.

But at night they could hear the German raiders over London, and the guns. Fires glowed low in the sky; there were ambulances down there amongst the exploding bombs, and the RAF sent Wellingtons out to Germany and not all of them came back. Tomorrow did not belong to their six-day world; only today was real and had to be kept forever in case that was all there was left. So on the last day he stopped in front of a jeweller's window in the town and said: 'If I were to say I loved you and wanted to marry you, and you were to say yes, which ring would you want me to buy for you – now?'

She stood for what seemed to him an eternity, her fingers locked into his, her eyes searching his face as if she was trying to memorise every line; then whispered: 'If you were to say you wanted to marry me, I would say yes, and I wouldn't need a ring to seal it because I love you too.'

So he kissed her there in the street and they did not even know that people were staring. That night they had their last dinner of the holiday and the candle flames gleamed in the ring he had bought. It was a thousand times more beautiful than Hugo Thoresen's ring had ever been, for this was no fantasy.

*

They had to wait until the end of his tour before they could marry, because when he went back to his squadron there were raids night after night, and when the crews were not flying they were on stand-by until it was too late to use the time; and every day he telephoned her and every night she prayed for him as she drove through the streets of hell in her ambulance and he flew out to Germany in the mounting fury of revenge for London and Coventry and Birmingham and Southampton and all the rest. Most of the time he went to the Ruhr, and he liked that best because that was where the biggest arms factories were, and the coal mines and the railway centres, and Germany could be hurt most. But the thought of Mitch in the burning streets of London filled him with anger, and he always made sure that even if Flip Martin could not identify their targets clearly, his bombs went down into the middle of the holocaust so that the Germans would learn what the British already knew about war in the night.

But then it was the last flight of their tour, and it was nearly the last flight of all time because one engine was put out of action by a night fighter over the Dutch coast before Goldie drove him off. Dingo said the rear gunner's language would have been enough, if the German pilot could have heard it. They came across the North Sea, lower and lower, and were down to two thousand feet by the time they crossed the coast of Suffolk. So they diverted and put down at Wattisham, and only found out when the Wellington slewed on touchdown that one tyre had been shredded by bullets. They ploughed off the runway onto grass and the undercarriage collapsed, but they were still in one piece when the wrecked aircraft stopped moving. They scrambled out as quickly as they could, afraid of fire, then stood in a group as rescue vehicles surrounded them, letting relief flood into them.

Flip Martin, in what was voted the understatement of the tour, felt for his pipe and tobacco, without which he never flew, and said: 'I think we have been remarkably lucky.'

Then Chris Coltrane pulled off his helmet and scowled at Alan.

'I always thought you were a lousy driver, Skipper. That was a bloody rough landing.'

Then, suddenly, they were laughing, slapping each other on the shoulders, near to hysteria because an hour before they had thought they were going to die and now they were alive and it was over, at least for a time. And as they climbed into a truck they all looked back at the black silhouette of the wrecked Wellington on the wet dawn grass, and Alan said: 'She was a good kite. I'm sorry we bent her in the end.'

The next afternoon they went on leave; and two days later all came together again for Alan's marriage to Michele in York where his parents lived. The ceremony was in a chapel in the great Minster, there was a riotous reception in a city centre hotel, and a late departure for the newly married couple on their way to a rented cottage in the Lake District. They only got as far as Harrogate that night, and as they stood on either side of the double bed in their room Michele said: 'Hi, Skip. You want to know something?'

He nodded. 'Tell me.'

'I love you.'

And then they threw themselves together on the bed, fully clothed, clinging, laughing, kissing, unable to believe their happiness.

3

• — •

'Sure I remember her,' Chuck Feldman said. 'In the RAF Club in Piccadilly, right there in the centre of dear old London.'

He was grey-haired now, in 1947, and married to the widow of a former fellow-ATA pilot who had disappeared over the Atlantic. He lived just outside Bristol and had an administrative job at the big Filton airfield.

'Tell you one thing, son. They were great days. Wouldn't've missed them for a fortune. This country sure took a hammering. It was a privilege to be here and see you folks come through it.'

His cowboy boots had gone, but he still wore a check shirt and a string tie, and still waved his hands expansively to emphasize his enthusiasms.

'How did you meet her?'

'I didn't,' he told me. 'She met me. Right there in the bar of the club. I'd gone there with some RAF guys after I'd flown a Spit into Biggin Hill and had to kick my heels for a coupla days waiting for another kite to fly out.' He grinned and stuffed a cigar into the corner of his wide mouth. 'You can see what I'm like, son. I make a lotta noise. Never been in a bar yet when folk didn't know old Chuck was around. So there I was with the only bottle of rye left in the place, and arguing about flying some goddam kite with this guy who'd signed me in, when I saw this dame giving me the eye. I'll tell you, I straightened. I thought "Chuck, this is it, boy, you made it at last – and what a peach to make it with".' He grinned at the memory, struck a match and puffed a cloud of smoke around his head.

I said, to humour him: 'You thought it was a pick-up?'

'Sure did, son. I was old enough to need that sorta flattery. Still more nowadays, I guess.' He ruffled his wiry grey thatch. 'So I just gave her the come-on and waited. And sure enough, within a minute she was there. Oh boy, I sure thought I had it made.' He inspected the cigar critically, then stuck it between his teeth.

'What did she say?'

'Remember it like it was yesterday. She said, "You have to be Charlie Feldman," and I just stared, 'cos that wasn't what I'd expected. So I said, "Yeah, sure, I'm Chuck Feldman," and she said, "You won't remember me because I've changed a bit, but I'm Michele, Peter Armstrong's daughter". Hell, I couldn't believe it. She had changed – and how. From just a kid with thin legs and straight up and down to the sorta dame you dream about when you haven't had a woman for a long time. Face and hair and figure – boy, she was flying high. So we just got together and I introduced her to the guys I was with and I was real proud to do that, I'll tell you, real proud.'

'Was she by herself?'

'By herself – a dame like that? You're crazy.' He grinned, his cigar jutting. 'She had half a dozen RAF guys with her. And one was her husband. Bomber pilot. Name of –' he searched his memory, scowling '– name of Alan something. Alan – that's right.'

'Tamworth,' I said. 'Lancaster pilot. DFC.'

His cigar swivelled across his mouth.

'Hey – you knew him? Well, how about that. Yeah, Alan Tamworth. He was a great guy. Didn't make a lotta noise. But great. And there was some Australian with him – funny name – Dingo. Like the Aussie wild dog. Just been commissioned. They were celebrating. And a bomb aimer – forget his name. Those three guys had flown all over Germany. Don't know how many raids. More guts than I had, I'll tell you. So we just talked. They were fresh off a conversion onto Lancasters and I'd flown Lancs, so it was great to swop notes.'

'Did she say anything about herself? What she was doing – apart from being married to Alan?'

He wrinkled his forehead.

'Don't recall much. Hell of a lot of talk about flying. They were great guys.' His eyes lit up. 'Sure I remember. She'd been driving ambulances in London. Imagine it? A dame like that, driving a blood wagon in the Blitz? But there'd been something about her when she was a kid. Confidence. The sorta kid you remember. Then she'd moved outa London when she married. Still driving ambulances, but up in Lincolnshire somewhere, near his base.'

'Scorton,' I said. 'Or it was after he'd done his Lancaster course.'

He stared. 'I didn't know that.' Then he added accusingly: 'You don't need to ask questions. You know it all.'

'Only some of it.' I shook my head. 'But I do know Peter Armstrong.'

He sat up, spilling cigar ash.

'You mean you know him now? You know where he is?'

'He lives in Cambridge. I was with him a few weeks ago.'

He puffed a cloud of smoke, excited.

'Hey, that's great. I often wondered about that guy. Best pilot I ever met. Biggest womaniser, too. I'm no prude, but I felt sorry for his wife. She threw him out, didn't she? Yeah, I remember. But that don't mean I didn't think he was a great guy. And you know something? I met him during the war – two or three months after I met Michele. Just like that.' He slammed a fist into the palm of his other hand.

I played innocent. 'You did? Tell me.'

'One of those crazy things, son. Though maybe not so crazy. I was in and out of factory airfields like a blue-assed fly. And he worked for Vickers. Must've been odds even that we'd meet one day. There he was, sure – coming out of the crew room at Castle Bromwich. Bang, in the doorway. We just stood and stared. Then danced around like a coupla kids. The other guys thought we were nuts. That was a helluva day.'

'Did you tell him you'd met Michele?' I was still pretending I didn't know anything.

'Sure.' He chewed the cigar, reflecting. 'He was real sad, then. Hadn't seen her since she was a kid. Didn't know where she was – in France or England. Marie-Claire neither. You know what happened to Marie-Claire? I'll tell you. Some goddam sonofabitch in a Stuka killed her. Michele told me. I had to tell him that. It hit him real hard, son. After all that time, and all those goddam women, it still hit him hard. But it was the girl he wanted to see again. I guess he really loved her. But he was afraid she wouldn't want to see him. So I said I'd go back to the club where I'd met her and try to find out where her husband was. I did, too, but no one knew.'

I said: 'If he'd listened to the radio in the summer of '43 he would have heard her husband's name. I broadcast about him. He could have traced him through the BBC.'

Feldman chewed his cigar, inspected it and grimaced. Then he looked at me from under his eyebrows.

'Something you maybe don't know,' he said. 'He would never have tried to find her. Maybe he never heard the broadcasts. But if he had, he'd have been scared to make a move. I had to be the go-between – find out if she ever wanted to see him again. He was scared outa his pants that she'd reject him. That woulda been the worst thing that coulda happened to him. He was terrified she'd think he was going to sponge on her. You know what I mean? The poor old man trying to lean on his long-lost daughter. No – whatever else, that wasn't Pete. He had to know she wanted to see him before he showed himself. He was a pretty sad guy. And I never saw him again. Piled a Mosquito up in a fog landing. Didn't fly for a year – broke a few bones. Never went near Castle Bromwich again. Forgot about him, I guess – we were all so goddam busy. But now – where did you say he is?'

'Cambridge. I can give you his address.'

He leaned forward, groping in a pocket, pulling out a diary and a pencil.

'You do that, son. I'll go see the guy. Maybe give him a lift, hey? Must be a helluva thing, to find out your daughter's dead. Killed by those bastards. It sure got to me, when you told me; and I was just a guy who met her a coupla times. Now you do something for me.' He levelled a finger. 'When your book's published, you let me know about it. I'll buy it. I'll be the proudest guy in the world to show it around, and say I knew her.'

He meant it. But I knew he was wrong. Because whatever Chuck Feldman felt, his pride wouldn't be a thousandth part of mine. Or his sadness.

4

Scorton. Four-engined Lancaster bombers flew from there. It was a big station, luxurious by some standards, with permanent buildings and good concrete runways. On a day early in July in 1943 I walked up to the guard on the main gate and presented my credentials. Ten minutes later I was escorted to the station adjutant's office.

'I'd been warned about you.' He was being pleasant. 'We've chosen a crew. Good characters, outstanding record, interesting backgrounds. You'll find they're a pretty cool lot, but they're looking forward to meeting you even if they may not show it at first. They know what you're going to do, and they'll do everything they can to help.'

That was a relief. I was afraid a battle-hardened bomber crew might have been sceptical of a war correspondent who had flown on only one operation before – and that a mine-laying job when no one fired a single gun. Tramping the North African desert and dodging Rommel's Panzers was no substitute in the eyes of the RAF for running the flak gauntlet over Berlin, and I knew it.

I need not have worried. The adjutant showed me to the billet I would use for as long as the job took, and then led me into the officers' mess at lunchtime for introductions.

The first thing I noticed about Alan Tamworth was his eyes. Friendly, and rock-steady. They looked at you and through you when he spoke. He was tall and strong-shouldered, quiet and quick-humoured – and in a crisis level-tempered too, I learned later. Fifty-three operational flights, including one to

Hamburg the night before, must have left their mark, but he did not show it.

Nor did Chris 'Dingo' Coltrane or Philip 'Flip' Martin; or, when I joined them in the Sergeants' Mess later, Mick 'Goldie' Silver or Bob Galway. Or perhaps I was just not sensitive enough to see it, at that moment.

But it takes seven men to fly a Lancaster, so I also met Andrew 'Andy' Douglas, who manned the mid-upper turret, an ex-motor mechanic, a dour Scot, and the youngster of the crew at nineteen years old; and the Canadian flight engineer Frank 'Cap' Kappa who, it was said, had more money than all the rest of the squadron put together because his father owned an oil well and ten thousand acres in Alberta.

By the time we had talked and they had realized that, whatever else, I was not the complete idiot they had feared, outside the rain was falling steadily from thick dark clouds, and the prospect of operations that night receded steadily through the afternoon. At five in the evening they were stood down, Alan went to see his wife at a nearby pub where he lived with her when he was off station, Dingo went off for a date with his latest sheila, and I had a meal with Flip Martin then several beers with the other four which gave me a chance to learn something about them.

The next morning the clouds were high and Alan said: 'I know you're not going to make your trip for two or three weeks, until we get one to the Big City or somewhere else a bit special, but you'd better find out what a Lanc feels like. We've been cleared to take you up for an hour.'

So they kitted me out, gave me a lecture on using a parachute, and we climbed into a truck for the run to the airfield and the waiting aircraft.

It was the first time I had been close to a Lancaster. Matt black for night flying, over a hundred feet of wing and seventy of fuselage, thirty tons of metal towering over me on great wheels, nose rearing ahead of the four engines against the sky.

It was the most forbidding and exciting war machine I had ever seen.

We climbed up a short ladder through a door on the starboard side, behind the wings, and Alan pointed to the left and said: 'That's the way Goldie goes. To the rear turret. Once he's in there we know he can't go far astray.' Then we went forward, past the Elsan toilet which was pointed out to me with proper ceremony; past the mid-upper turret which hung down from above so that we had to duck under it; then up onto a higher floor level because we were now on top of the bomb bay and had to stoop as we squeezed past the rest bed (Dingo's special property, he told me solemnly, because of the demands his sheila made on him), then a scramble over the main spar which linked the wings across the width of the fuselage, to the wireless operator's seat beneath the astrodome and the navigator's curtained compartment. After that it was a squeeze through to the cockpit where Alan sat on the left and Cap had a bench seat alongside and a footrest which Flip had to push aside to get down into the nose. There he lay on a cushioned hatch when he was being a bomb aimer and stood up to grasp the triggers when he needed to operate the twin Browning machine guns in the nose turret. It was all starkly functional and claustrophic between the spars and the sharp-edged metal panels and the instruments and the ammunition runways. They had rigged a small perch for me between the navigator and wireless operator, and I wondered what it would feel like on the home leg of a seven-hour trip over Germany.

Alan said: 'Come and stand behind Cap while we go through the checks.' Then he started a chant which Kappa repeated or qualified for minutes as they ensured that the Lancaster was fit to fly. After that the engines were started one at a time; then there were more checks before he released the brakes and we moved away from dispersals, the engines hammering in my unaccustomed ears. I had understood hardly anything and realized that I would have to do a lot of homework before the real thing.

Then we were turning on to the end of the runway, and the concrete stretched ahead of us for ever and Alan chanted more checks about throttles, trim and flaps; until he looked over his shoulder at me and said: 'It's against the rules but you can stand there if you like, as long as you hold on – or go back to your seat.'

I said I would stand, so that I could see the ground twenty feet below and the discs of the propellors as Alan opened the throttles. Power surged through the aircraft and we started the take-off, accelerating hard. I felt the tail come up, and then the runway fell away beneath us and I was flying in a Lancaster. I forgot about being a war correspondent and that I might die and surrendered to the sheer thrill of it as the nose pointed towards the clouds, the engine note changed as Alan throttled back a little and we climbed away from Scorton and the world.

The clouds were not as high as I had thought. Suddenly we were under them and then a great grey envelope folded around us and the earth was gone. The Lancaster vibrated as we churned on, and Kappa turned to me and said something. I shrugged because I could not hear him, and he leaned across and grabbed the swinging lead which dangled from my headset and plugged it into a socket. His voice said in my ears: 'A couple of minutes of this, and we'll be above it.' He pointed to the button on the mouthpiece which hung loose from my helmet because we were not on oxygen, and I pressed it.

'Okay,' I said. 'I could do with some sunshine.'

He grinned back. 'There's plenty where we're going.'

Suddenly I felt a glow. I was being accepted. And I wanted nothing more than that at this moment.

It was getting lighter beyond the moisture rivulets which ran across the perspex windscreen. Then with startling suddenness we were out of it and the sun was blinding on the whitest white I had ever seen. The blue stretched above in a great dome, brilliant, and Alan held the Lancaster down so that we skimmed the cloud tops in an exciting rush over ridges and shallow valleys with wisps of free cloud flashing past at two hundred miles an hour and the great engines snarling sound and power on either side of us.

We were up for forty-five minutes. I was shown the rudiments of control, the meaning of the instruments, the navigation equipment and charts, the radio set, the bomb sight and the turrets. I lay in the nose, looking down through the perspex dome which was all that separated me from a fall into eternity; I went back to the tail turret and Goldie extracted himself so that I could sit in his place while he showed me how he worked the four guns. They were kind and patient and good humoured and I felt an honoured guest in their strange and private world.

When we landed and the great black Lancaster had come to rest, the silence was like a smothering blanket for seconds. We clambered down the ladder and took off our helmets and without a thought for my meagre expenses allowance I said: 'Thanks for the initiation. The first night you can get off the station, the party's on me. Girls as well.'

That was how I met Michele.

*

For reasons best known to Bomber Command, the Scorton squadrons were not on operations that night, so we all met at the bar of a pub on the northern outskirts of Lincoln, and since I was there only with their blessing I had invited the flight commander who was a Squadron Leader, and the squadron leader who was a Wing Commander – bomber idiosyncracies which I never explored – and the adjutant who had arranged it all. There were five ladies of whom three were wives and two were not, and the bar was crowded with men and women in blue uniforms and in civilian clothes. Alan came in late with a girl beside him and pushed through the crowd and said: 'Michele – this is Neil.'

Her hair was fair; not blonde, but light and touched with

pale gold and waving across her forehead and curling across the collar of her dress. Her face would have been a triangle except that her mouth was wide and full of laughter; and her eyes shone in the bar lights as she extended a hand and said: 'Hullo, Neil. You have my sympathy – trying to turn this lot into public heroes.'

They jeered, embarrassed, and I said: 'Don't get it wrong. This is warts and all. "Tell it like it is," my lords and masters said.' And they jeered again, seizing the pints which appeared along the bar.

Dingo's girl was the prettiest, the Wing Commander's wife was the most sophisticated and glamorous, and I didn't remember the other girls for long. But I remembered Michele because she talked easily and was relaxed and her voice was musical. Somehow we found ourselves together at the end of the bar while Alan was talking to the Wing Commander and she said: 'Are you looking forward to all this – or is it a chore?'

I stared. 'A chore? It's an honour. And I'm excited about it – in spite of being scared.'

'You're not scared,' she said. 'You've been in the desert.'

'How did you know that?'

'Alan told me. He didn't want to do this thing with you, until they told him you'd been all the way from Tobruk to Benghazi and back to Alamein. Then he changed his mind.'

'That was kind of him. I don't think it qualifies me.'

'He did. How long were you there?'

'A few months. How long have you and Alan been married?'

'Two years. Are you married?'

It didn't hurt any more. I shook my head.

'No. I was. But we don't talk about that.' I grinned to show I didn't care. 'Where did you live before Alan?'

'London,' she said. 'I drove ambulances. I still do, but it's not quite so hairy here. Before that I lived in France, until the Germans chased me out.'

'Do you speak French?'

'It's my other language. Sometimes I confuse the two.'

'I envy you,' I said. 'I'd love to be able to think in another language. Will you want to go back, after the war?'

She shrugged, an attractive movement of her shoulders. 'To visit. But we'll live here.' Absolute confidence that there would be a time after the war for them both. I wondered if she had to keep convincing herself; if she knew that the average aircrew only managed ten or twelve operations before they were shot down, whereas Alan had completed over fifty. Were the odds stacking up against him? Or were the risks encapsulated totally in each flight, so that you faced it all again and again, every night the same as the last, with the same degree of risk? What could it be like, when friends disappeared and new ones came to take their places until they disappeared as well, two or three aircraft at a time, each with seven men you knew and drank beer with and who had wives and girl friends like this one talking to me with her quick eyes and her assurance? And what could it be like for her to hear the massed Merlin engines at night and know he was up there and going away and the guns were waiting for him? Tonight he was with her, leaning on the bar and laughing with his beer tankard in his hand, and they would go back to their room and their secrets. But tomorrow night the bar would be quiet and she would be alone and their secrets would only be in her mind, with her prayers. If the men who flew in the Lancasters were brave, the women who waited had a special courage known only to those who are left behind to hope and to wonder.

Yet in that she was no different to the rest. So why was she different? Why, at the end of the evening when my party was over and I was back in my small room at Scorton, was she the one I remembered, and whose face came back to me without conscious recall and whose voice ran through my mind until there was grey dawn beyond the curtained windows?

*

'Take it from this side. My right profile is better.' Dingo grinned into the camera from the confines of the curtained navigator's compartment. Behind him Galway said solemnly: 'Better than what – your arse?' The photographer scratched his head and snapped in feigned exasperation: 'If I don't get more co-operation we'll still be taking these when the big op starts.'

It had been going on all morning as we tried to get a satisfactory set of pictures of Alan and his crew looking as if they were working. The tone had been set by Goldie who wanted to be photographed sat on the Elsan, and Dingo had already secured for his private collection a picture of himself stretched on the rest bed clutching a large and lewd drawing of a naked girl. The RAF photographer worked well in the confined spaces, but his less-than-helpful subjects were determined to turn the occasion into a farce. They knew that the pictures were a necessary part of the whole exercise and would be used after the raid to dramatize the publicity for my broadcasts. So they used humour to camouflage their embarrassment, for none of them welcomed the thought of being the butt of jokes from other crews. Nonetheless they were under orders, and after a couple of hours the patient photographer announced that, in spite of everything, he had got what he wanted.

I was photographed with them and enjoyed the hilarity until I caught the thoughtful Martin in a solemn moment and said quietly, 'Sorry if it's a bore, Flip,' and he looked at me with his steady eyes and murmured: 'I'll be happier when I see them in the papers.'

That was the needle. The pictures would be released after we came back. And in the last week three Scorton Lancasters and twenty-one men had not come back.

I looked up at grey clouds sweeping in from the west, heard sudden rain pattering on the perspex around Alan's cockpit, and hoped the deteriorating weather meant there would be no operations that night.

We climbed out of the aircraft and drifted back to the mess for lunch, with Dingo and Goldie still throwing grinning insults at everyone. But now the jokes were not quite so funny; to me, at least.

At four o'clock flying was cancelled, and we scraped up enough money for a night in Lincoln. Andy Douglas and Bob Galway opted out, but Dingo arranged to meet his girl at the hotel we had chosen for a meal and, of course, Alan took Michele with us.

He treated her like the rest. 'Hey, Mitch – your round this time.' She drank beer with us, and sometimes her eyes caught mine, and she sat next to me at the table and said: 'Tell me about Egypt. Did you see the pyramids?'

'Yes. And got fleeced by the guides.'

'Was it worth it?'

'M-m. I'd like to have gone back, with time to explore by myself. But the guides won't let you near without an escort if they can help it. It's all incredible. Dusty and dramatic, if you have the right imagination. It must have been extraordinary for the explorers, the real archæologists who opened up the tombs. They're the most interesting part – more than the pyramids, once you've got used to the sheer size of them.'

'I'd love to see them.' She said it dreamily; sadly, as if she thought she never would.

'After the war – you never know.' I reached across the table for something and my hand brushed her arm. It was like a small electric shock, and I thought she felt it too, so I was careful it didn't happen again. 'Where did you live in France?'

'Cambrai, for a time. Before that, Montargis. A little town south of Paris. Lovely. But I don't suppose it is now.' She looked at me quickly, as if she felt I would understand that she was just a little homesick for the time that had gone.

'Tell me.'

She shook her head, and her hair shone as she moved. 'There's not much to tell. Childhood memories are the best.

It all fell to pieces, even before the war started. I was glad to leave it. There wasn't much of the old time left.'

Dingo dug me in the ribs with his elbow. The interruption startled me. 'Don't monopolise the lady. Australia's bigger than France – and Egypt.' He grinned.

Somehow I was surprised that he should have heard us. It had seemed such a private conversation. I said: 'And noisier, if its ambassadors are any guide.'

'Noisy – me?' He feigned offence. 'It's reaction. You should see the outback. Not a sound for a thousand miles.' He jabbed a finger towards Alan across the table. 'Hey, Skip – next time we're on ops put a few extra cans of petrol in the old kite and I'll take you there. It's more interesting than Cologne.'

The banter absorbed us and took up the rest of the meal, until Goldie dug in his pockets and said loudly as the waitress passed: 'Anybody got any money? I'm skint.'

Kappa was the first to pick it up. 'Money? I thought this was your party. I've only got a couple of bucks.' His Canadian drawl drifted across the dining room and the waitress turned her head. Dingo dragged out a wallet, inspected it, and pronounced: 'One pound ten and a squashed rabbit's foot. It's got to be your party, Goldie.'

'Come on, don't take the mickey.' Goldie looked uneasy. He pretended to notice the waitress for the first time and whispered loudly: 'Hey, if you lot ain't got enough cash, we're in trouble. How're we going to pay?'

Alan said, in his quiet, cultured voice: 'We're all right. Mitch is the chancellor. She always has plenty.' He looked at his wife expectantly and she pretended confusion, clutching her handbag, shaking her head. 'I didn't bring enough for this.' She looked at me as if asking to be rescued, and I saw the secret laughter in her eyes and said: 'This is embarrassing. Alan told me I was his guest. I didn't bring a cheque book. I can put a quid in the pool, though.'

'Bring it out, sport. Let's see how much we can muster.' Dingo dug into his wallet and threw two notes on the table.

We all added something, taking care that the total fell woefully short of requirements and making a lot of noise which attracted the attention of other diners until, suddenly, we fell silent like guilty children as the head waiter materialized, brandished a piece of paper and said starchily: 'You wanted the bill, sir?' He addressed Alan, presumably because of his rank.

'The bill?' Alan looked surprised. 'Did we want the bill?' He turned to Dingo for advice and the Australian took the bill, scowled at it, and said: 'Hell's bells, we'll need a bank loan to pay this.' He passed it to Goldie who beckoned the head waiter and said cheerfully: 'If we pay half, how much washing up do we have to do to clear the rest?'

The head waiter, who was clearly not open to barter, said: 'I'm sorry.' He glanced at the sergeant's stripes on Goldie's arm and carefully omitted the customary 'Sir'. 'I doubt if that will be acceptable to the manager.'

Kappa drawled: 'Then go and ask him if he'll make us a present of it.'

Around the dining room conversation had virtually stopped. Heads were turned, some faces were hostile, some embarrassed, a few obviously amused. The head waiter marched away and Alan said quietly: 'Give me the bill.'

Goldie did so, Alan took the necessary number of notes from his wallet and put them on a plate, the pool of money in the centre of the table was scooped away, and by the time the waiter returned with the manager we were sitting back, smoking and chatting.

The manager loomed over us and said loudly: 'I understand you are unable to pay your bill.' He was a large, grey-haired man with a florid face.

Alan completed his conversation with Kappa before he turned. He was the picture of affronted dignity.

'Unable to pay? Are you trying to be insulting?'

The manager loomed even larger.

'My head waiter informs me that you told him you were unable to pay. You even asked if you could wash up.'

Alan shook his head. He said, as if dealing with an unpleasant disciplinary matter on the station: 'I'm afraid you have not conducted adequate inquiries. No one told your waiter we were unable to pay. You should ensure you are properly informed before you make allegations. The reference to washing up was merely an expression of my tail gunner's preference – he would rather do that than the next op. I don't blame him. Here's your bill, and the money. In the circumstances you will not expect a gratuity, of course.'

The whole room watched as the manager took the money, counted it, flushed and said: 'I apologize, sir. There has been a misunderstanding.' Alan said mercilessly: 'As an officer in the Royal Air Force, I resent your insinuations. So does my wife and my crew, and so does our companion who is a distinguished war correspondent with the BBC. Elsewhere, I might even have expected some recompense. But I doubt if you will extend that courtesy.'

He turned back to Kappa and resumed his previous conversation. We followed his lead, and Dingo and Goldie muttered loudly about insults from people who didn't know what the war was all about. The manager and the waiter hesitated in momentary confusion then marched away, red-faced, watched by the other diners.

They stood outside the dining room. I could see them through the glass doors, arguing. Michele whispered to me: 'I hope that didn't embarrass you. It's the third time the boys have done it. Let's see if it works.'

I had realized that the whole thing had a well-drilled air about it, but now I stared at her.

'If it works? What do you mean?'

She was very close to me. Her perfume drifted and her eyes were bright and I was aware of her as I had been earlier in the evening.

'Wait and see. Look – the manager's coming back.'

He was no longer red-faced, but pale and hard-mouthed. He moved briskly between the tables, steeling himself for an unpleasant moment, until he stood beside Alan, but the skipper ignored him until he cleared his throat and said: 'Excuse me, sir.'

Alan glanced up. He said stiffly: 'You've brought the change? Good.'

The manager placed the bill and three notes on the table at Alan's elbow.

'I apologize for this unfortunate misunderstanding,' he said unhappily. 'My head waiter obviously made a serious mistake. In the circumstances I hope you will accept a reduction in your bill – as a measure of my regret.'

Alan stared down at the notes as if he found them distasteful. Then he nodded curtly.

'Since you offer it, I will. My crew will appreciate it.' He turned to Martin and said: 'We must have another look at that bombsight, Flip.'

The manager walked away, almost on tip-toe, as Martin responded. Beyond the glass doors he talked again with the head waiter, and Alan leaned across the table, picked up the money, and said: 'A dignified exit, ladies and gentlemen, if you please.'

So we left, watched by the two dozen or so diners who remained. Goldie was last through the door, and before it closed he turned, faced the watchers, grinned and bowed.

There was a lot of laughter behind us as we went.

*

By now the whole station knew why I was there and that we were waiting for a big operation. Galway had opened a book, taking bets on the target and the duration of the flight. Berlin was the favourite and was soon odds-on, even though raids on the Big City were few in the summer because of the short nights: until the night after our dinner when Berlin was the target and I was not included.

Now I was beginning to understand the tensions with which

the aircrew lived, because it was not until the afternoon of each day that I knew I would not be flying that night. Every morning I found myself pausing, just for a mite of a second, to wonder if this would be the day; and then to ask if I would be alive at the same time tomorrow. Every time I pushed it away, angry with myself; but the next day it happened again, until I came to expect it. And twice I spent part of each night in the operations room, waiting for the Lancasters to return, watching them marked up on the board, and aware of a stab of anguish when one was recorded as 'missing'.

Most of the time there was no escape for the crew. Even if the aircraft had not exploded, getting out of a blazing, out-of-control Lancaster in one piece, complete with parachute, required a lot of luck as well as agility.

And that was not the end of the peril. There were unpleasant stories about aircrew who came down in target areas being beaten to death, or hanged from lamp posts in the streets, or thrown alive into blazing buildings.

Alan Tamworth and four of his crew had faced all that fifty-five times; the other two had been with them for twenty-five of those flights. It was not surprising that their parties were noisy and that they sought relief by tormenting hotel managers and playing childish practical jokes on each other.

Tonight was their sixth trip to the Big City in their current tour of thirty operations. I was allowed to sit with them through the briefing: the roll call, the intelligence officer's description of the target, how it would be indicated by the new pathfinders with ground and air flares of different colours, what the defences were expected to be like; then the meterological officer's survey of the weather; the navigation leader's briefing and the time-check as watches were synchronized; the bombing leader's up-date on the load each aircraft was carrying and how it would be dropped, the signal leader's short speech to wireless operators, the gunnery leader's reminder to air gunners of the latest enemy techniques; the flying control officer's description of take-off patterns, diversionary airfields available for returning damaged aircraft, and the ultimate landing procedures; and finally the Station Commander's words of encouragement.

After that I joined Alan and the crew for their meal. There was less joking than usual; more sarcasm and cynicism and silences; until we had finished and I said casually, 'Good luck, have a good trip, see you in the morning.' Then I kept out of the way. Take off would start an hour or so later and they didn't want hangers-on as their private tensions mounted.

Later I wandered out towards the watch-tower. The long summer evening was still not over, and buildings and aircraft were clearly visible in the last daylight. Above, the high thin cloud which had covered Lincolnshire all day was still there, and a half moon somewhere above it. Only the crews would see that, as they climbed through the cloud after take off.

The first crew bus was leaving the locker room, turning on to the perimeter track towards dispersals and the dark outlines of the Lancasters; shielded headlights gleaming yellow. Another was loading, men climbing aboard laden with parachutes, life-jackets, ration boxes and navigation bags, joking roughly with the WAAF driver. I had seen it all before; but tonight's trip was the first really long one since I had arrived at Scorton. And a big one, too. The Intelligence Officer had told us that seven hundred aircraft would be flying that night.

I wished this had been my raid. To get it over with; and to be with the boys. I knew now that I was terrified that they would die while I was still on the ground waiting for some mysterious higher authority to decide which trip would be mine. Before morning I could see the carefully chalked 'Missing' against them on the operations room board, and the last hours would tick away while we waited to hear if they had landed at a satellite airfield or been picked up by Air-Sea Rescue off the coast. And when there was no longer any hope the squadron commander would go to see Michele in her little room a mile down the road, and I would pack up and leave Scorton, and the world would be empty.

An engine was turning across at dispersals. It banged and stuttered, settled into harsh roar; then another awoke, overtaken by a third, and the sound spread and swelled into a heavy droning as exhausts flickered down the lines of Lancasters. A small Austin saloon passed me and stopped below the watch-tower. I saw it silhouetted against the pale western horizon, and the pennant on the bonnet. The Station Commander watched most of the departures from there, with the handful of men and women who were the airfield's eyes and ears.

The first aircraft was moving. Amber perimeter track lights glowed and engine notes rose as pilots steered their great chariots in clumsy procession towards the red light on top of the airfield controller's caravan: two parallel lines of bombers, noses high against the last of the day, converging on the main runway.

Then the controller's light turned to green and the first aircraft turned onto the runway, engines bellowing, and moved away down the flarepath, gathering speed, a black shadow bearing seven crouching men against the sky; followed before it was airborne by another, until the whole fleet was away in a great roaring wave of sound which numbed the mind and blotted out the thoughts about where they were going and why and how many would return.

In the strange, forlorn silence which always followed an operational take-off, I walked slowly away and back to my room, threw off my greatcoat and lay on my bed, staring up at the ceiling, fighting depression.

Presently I got up, pulled out my typewriter, and began to write down my impressions of the night. The work occupied my mind and I began to feel better. This was why I was here: to record, to interpret, to react; so that other people would know what it was like for the men who had chosen to fight Nazi Germany so dangerously and dramatically, and how the tools of their hellish trade were being improved.

After an hour or so I went along to the mess. Only a dozen

people were there – non-flyers and two or three newcomers not yet allocated to crews. I nodded to those I knew and settled in a corner with my notebook and a beer, scribbling random thoughts. A corner of my mind said be positive, they'll be back, tomorrow night could be your big one, make sure you can do your job as well as they'll do theirs.

I didn't notice the steward until he said: 'Excuse me, sir.' He was tall and thin and sad, hovering behind my chair like an old, hook-nosed black and white parrot. 'Telephone for you.'

I nodded, drank the last of my beer, and went out into the corridor. There were two telephones, one with the receiver off the hook. I picked it up and said: 'Neil Cameron.'

She said: 'I hope I'm not disturbing you. It's Michele.'

Two minutes later I was driving my little car down the road to the pub where she and Alan had their room, because she had told me she needed to talk to someone and hoped I might not be too busy.

It was a small two-storey place with exposed beams and dark furniture. The bar was busy, but only four other people were in the little lounge and she sat by herself in a corner with big eyes and hair reflecting the indifferent lights. I said, 'Hullo,' and looked at the empty table. 'Not drinking?'

'Waiting for you.' She smiled briefly. 'Whisky, please. I think they have some.' You could never be sure.

I went out to the bar and came back with two large Bells and a jug of water. I held the jug, questioning. She shook her head. 'I'll live dangerously tonight.' It was meant as a joke, but somehow didn't quite make it. So I sat down and raised my glass. 'Here's to you.' She nodded but did not respond. Instead she said: 'This is a terrible impertinence, asking you to come here. You don't mind, do you?'

'A little time in your company is a privilege.'

'You always know what to say.' The smile again; protective. 'May I smoke?' She knew I didn't.

'Of course.'

She took a packet from her handbag, extracted a cigarette and found a lighter. She held the lighter in both hands and inhaled quickly, saw me watching her and said: 'I'm sorry. I'm a bit tense tonight. They're on a big one, aren't they?'

I nodded. Even now, so long after take off, those who knew were still not supposed to talk about it.

She said: 'I heard them go. I can always hear them. But then I got – a feeling. Usually when they're away I get together with Molly Packard. You know – "A" Flight commander's wife. They have a little house down the road. But she's away with a sick mother, or something. It's strange. I've often been by myself. It doesn't usually bother me.'

'But tonight it did.' I thought of myself on the airfield, and the depression.

She nodded: 'Yes. I stayed upstairs until I couldn't stand it any longer. I came down then, but the landlord and his wife were busy. There was no one here I knew. I just needed to talk to someone. I thought you might – understand.' She was pleading; her eyes and her voice and the way she smoked her cigarette.

It shocked me. Michele with her laughter, buying her round of drinks and joining in the jokes. Strong and resilient. Not tonight, though.

'Some of it,' I said. 'And I'm a good tryer. Have you had a meal?'

'I ate something.'

'But not much. How about a sandwich? And some coffee?'

She was silent for seconds, looking at me. Then: 'All right. If you'll have something with me.'

'I can always eat,' I said. I went out to the bar, persuaded the landlord, and came back. 'Now stop worrying. You've seen it all before. This one's no different.'

'Is it Berlin?' She whispered it. I suddenly thought she dreaded Berlin.

'Yes. But he's been there before. A lot of times. And with these new navigation aids it's a piece of cake.'

She shook her head, suddenly angry.

'It's never a piece of cake. And especially Berlin. That's the worst. How can you say that?'

'Because if I don't we'll drive each other up the wall,' I said sharply. 'That's why the boys are always cheerful. They know the score, Mitch, just like you do.' I stopped. She was looking at me curiously, no longer angry. 'Sorry. That's Alan's name for you. I shouldn't have used it.'

'You can use it. I'd like you to.' Quietly.

'He might not.'

'He won't mind. Sorry I jumped down your throat. It's just that – they've had two close calls going to Berlin. One of them got Alan his DFC. I'm afraid of Berlin. Tonight I thought I'd had a – a premonition. The more I thought about it, the more I felt sure. I started to panic a bit. That's when I rang you. You're closer to them than anyone, except me.'

I thought about the operations board and my own picture of someone writing 'Missing' against their aircraft, and my stomach tightened.

'We all get feelings like that, sometimes. They don't mean anything – except that we're tensed up. Forget it. He'll be back in the morning, and then you'll wonder what all the fuss was about.'

The landlord came in with sandwiches and put plates in front of us. He looked at me curiously, went back for the coffee, set it on the table, and said to her: 'Is that all right, Mrs Tamworth? We're a bit short tonight, I'm afraid.'

She smiled up at him. 'It's fine, thank you. Neither of us has eaten much. It's very welcome.'

He went out, looking back at me, and I said: 'Want to bet that he finds a way to tell Alan you've been entertaining a man in a strange uniform?'

She laughed, quickly and musically; like the Mitch I knew.

'No takers. He's sure to. He watches over me like a guardian. Don't worry. I'll tell him first.' She stubbed out her forgotten cigarette and reached for a sandwich. 'I think I'm hungry.' She looked at me quickly. 'Thanks to you.'

'Tell me how you met him,' I said. 'Tell me the love story.'

'In the middle of an air raid.' She elaborated, filling in the details; then about their holiday and how quickly they had made up their minds. She said: 'If I'd been told I would marry someone I'd known for so little time, I'd have laughed at it. But it seemed so right. And it still is.' She frowned, hesitating; then added: 'I think I was lonely. Perhaps that helped to push me.'

'Most people would be lonely, arriving in the middle of a war, no relatives, no friends. You're a brave lady, Mitch.' This time she didn't seem to notice I had used Alan's name, and it felt right. 'How did you get out of France?'

'I was lucky. I was with someone from the British Embassy in Paris. A man my father knew in the first war. He was getting out, too. He was something in Intelligence and had a lot of influence. He drove us to Cherbourg and the Navy sent a frigate to pick him up. I just tagged along.'

'They sent a frigate? He must have been important. Who was he?'

'I've forgotten.' She said it with an odd, quirky smile which told me a lot. 'That's enough about me. Tell me something about yourself.'

'Did your important friend help you after you'd reached this country?'

'No.' She shook her head emphatically. 'I told you. I've forgotten him. And I didn't need help. I lived in a hostel for a while, then started driving ambulances. That earned me enough to live on. Finally Alan came along. And here I am. Now what about you? What happened to your marriage – or is that not my business?'

'No secret,' I said. 'She was a sexy lady who couldn't wait for me to come home. It doesn't bother me any more.'

She poured coffee, raised her eyebrows as she held the milk jug and I nodded. She added a little from it, then passed the cup. I took it quickly and put it on the table, keeping my eyes on it as if I was afraid I might spill it. I knew she was looking at me, so I concentrated on choosing a sandwich.

'I'm sorry,' she said quietly. 'Even if it doesn't bother you now.'

I glanced up. Her face held nothing except polite concern.

'I was for a time. But now I think the whole thing was a mistake. So maybe it happened for the best.'

'Do you have parents?'

'Yes. In Cheshire. I don't see them often. We write sometimes. Are your parents in France?'

'No. My mother is dead. She was French. I don't know where my father is. The family broke up a long time ago.'

'Don't you want to find him?'

She thought about it for seconds before she said: 'He hurt my mother terribly. He hurt me, too. But it was a long time ago. I suppose it's possible to forgive. But it's difficult to find out.'

The conversation had become stilted. I wondered if it was because of her parents, or because of something else. I thought I should not be there.

Yet I could not have refused. And now the tension in her had eased and she had pushed her visions of Alan away. Other things had taken her attention, and she had wanted that when she had sent her cry for help. Come and talk to me, distract me, make me think about something else, anything except him and where he is now and the fear, the awful searching fear.

We talked on, about her father, and the chateau near Montargis, and my time with the BBC and what North Africa was like, until the coffee pot was empty and the sandwiches had gone and we had had another whisky to say goodnight and Alan was somewhere in the flak and the searchlights and among the night fighters and she said: 'You've been a good friend. Thank you.'

I stood up. The other two couples who had been in the lounge had gone a long time ago.

'He'll be okay. Stop worrying.'

She looked at her watch. She was quite calm.

'I heard them take off. More than three and a half hours ago. They'll be there now. Right over the target.'

I said: 'Four more ops to go. Then all this will be behind you. Concentrate on that.'

She walked with me to the door.

'One of those is yours.'

'So?' I shrugged deliberately. 'A job of work for me, a job of work for them. We're all a lot safer than those fellers in North Africa or Burma with a rifle and bayonet.'

She nodded. Her expression was carefully bright.

'I suppose so. Thank you for coming. I hope it hasn't been a bore.'

I said: 'It's been one of the nice things that have happened to me.'

We stood, just for a second, looking at each other, and I saw a flicker of apprehension in her eyes and turned away quickly in case she saw it in mine too.

Then I turned back, disciplined again.

'Let the landlord know you'll be getting a phone call in the wee small hours. It'll be me, telling you he's back. Will you hear it?'

She whispered: 'You really are a good friend. I'll hear it.'

'Don't watch me go,' I said. 'It's chilly outside.'

I went quickly, calling, 'Goodnight' to the landlord who was washing glasses, and closing the door quietly.

I drove back to the station, holding the steering wheel tightly, wondering what was happening to me.

For a time I lay on my bed, fully clothed, alternatively dozing and thinking about Michele and trying not to think about Alan and his crew. Thinking about Michele produced nothing except a growing conviction that my imagination had become unhinged. I was irresponsible, traitorous, lusting after another man's wife, conjuring responses where none existed. The sooner this job was over, the better. In the meantime I would behave with meticulous propriety. I drifted in and out of sleep plagued with visions of Alan discovering me holding Michele, kissing her, caressing her in their bedroom; and of Michele alternately welcoming and rejecting me, coaxing and condemning . . .

Presently I pushed it all away and wandered down to the operations room, checking the schedule against the clock and the maps, working out where the returning bomber stream should be. I went into the mess hall and drank coffee; then to the watch-tower and climbed the stone steps.

No one took any notice. They were used to me by now, accepting that I was gathering background information for my eventual broadcasts. It was just after 3.30 a.m., and the interior of the watch-tower was a small, warm world insulated from the black airfield by its subdued, shielded lights and wide windows. Two WAAFs, a Flight Sergeant and the flying control officer lounged there, drinking tea, smoking and reading; waiting.

It seemed a long time before one of the WAAFs straightened, adjusted her headphones and said to the flying control officer: 'I've got Easy Two, sir. Loud and clear.' Lancaster coded E2 was on its way in across flat East Anglia, heading for the landing beacon: the first of the Scorton aircraft to return.

I listened to their calm instruction. After Easy Two came Jig, then Able One and Two in quick succession; then others, until a dozen aircraft had been picked up, identified, and stacked at different heights in slowly descending squares. I wanted to go outside to hear the first sound of the engines, but I was afraid I would miss the WAAF's response to Charlie Two, the Lancaster carrying Alan and his crew. I stood against a wall with a dry mouth and a heart thumping in my chest, listening to the comfortable, friendly voices in the tower, watching the flickering radar screens, hoping and telling myself that premonitions were for the superstitious, and I was not superstitious.

The FCO caught my eye and I said: 'What's the usual spread of arrival times from a Berlin raid?'

'An hour.' He shrugged. 'Sometimes more. There are often one or two which land somewhere else. You never know until daylight. Worried about your boys?'

'I have a special interest. I'll be glad to see them back.'

He nodded in the low light. 'Of course. Plenty of time yet.'

Easy Two was coming in and the runway lights were on. Then it was a procession, engines filling the faint dawn, and others were calling up for landing orders.

We had twenty or more either landed or stacked when the WAAF said: 'Repeat call sign, please,' pressing one hand against her headphones. Then she nodded. 'You're very faint, Charlie Two. But I hear you.' As she read out height and course instructions the FCO winked and I let out a long slow breath that I seemed to have bottled up in my aching chest for half an hour.

Fifteen minutes later he nodded towards the windows.

'They're on finals. Next to land.'

I said, 'Thanks,' and went out of the tower, closing the door quietly, and walked quickly down the stone steps. A Lancaster came in, landing lights clear, engines throttled back, settling, and others moved in distant silhouetted procession along the perimeter track to dispersals. The air was filled with the booming snarl of engines. I waited, watching up-wind, listening.

Then I saw her lights against the sky.

She came in steadily, slowly, correctly, touching down quite early, tyres squealing. I could see her shape in the landing lights. Her engines died to a tick-over and I heard her brakes, a harsh thin sound against the background of the Merlins as she went past the tower, down the runway, then almost disappearing as she reached the point where Alan would swing her away on to the perimeter track.

I turned and walked away, striding out, the dawn wind about my ears. I felt taller, lighter on my feet.

Five minutes later I was in the mess. I picked up a telephone and dialled.

Her voice said: 'Hullo?' A small, careful sound.

'You can go back to bed and sleep well,' I said. 'He's landed.'

*

The wind brought rain the next afternoon, not only to Lincolnshire but to wide areas of England and Northern Europe. Great banks of cloud built up over Germany, bombing operations were cancelled and crews allowed to stand down and take thirty-six-hour passes which had been accumulating. And I was summoned to London for a conference of available war reporters, so I said to Alan: 'If you and the boys would like a quick tour of the BBC, I can fix it.'

They were all pleased by that, and Alan said: 'May Mitch come? She has friends she hasn't seen for a long time – she could look them up while she's there.'

That was after he had said to me privately: 'Thanks for holding her hand, Neil. I guess it's getting her down more than she admits.'

It was all fixed for the following day. But then came a hole in the foul weather, the Scampton squadrons were put on stand-by, and the BBC tour had to be cancelled. But Alan said: 'Mitch still wants to see her friends. She can stay with her old flat-mate. Any chance of a walk round the studios for her? It's a shame she should miss it.'

So I said yes, because there was no alterntive; and because I wanted her company.

We caught a midday train from Lincoln and the journey passed in pleasant conversation. But I was careful not to look at her too often, and felt her own reluctance to let her eyes hold mine. In London we said goodbye casually and I went to my conference. Then, early in the evening, I met her in Langham Place and we started our tour. It took a long time, because she talked animatedly with everyone we met and watched from a seat beside the studio producer as the nine o'clock news – the day's main bulletin – was read by Alvar Liddell, the man whose voice had become almost a national symbol.

By the time we had finished, the hole in the weather had widened in a band across France and south-east England. We stood outside the studios and I said: 'The sky's clearing just in time for us.' So we set out for her friend's flat, easy in each other's company, still laughing at the evening's jokes.

Perhaps forty-eight hours' bad weather had lulled the defences, because we heard the wail of the sirens only seconds before the anti-aircraft guns opened up. But London had not had a big raid for many weeks and I was not apprehensive.

'Let's walk on. We can soon find a shelter if we need to.'

As we went we listened to the guns, firing from the other side of dockland, with searchlights fingering the scattered clouds. Not close enough to worry about, I thought; until there were engines beating overhead, a thin eerie whistle and a massive explosion within a few hundred yards of us.

She had been through it all before and was flat on her face in the shelter of a wall before I was, arms over her head.

The bomb lit up the night with a great searing flash and the ground shivered as the explosion hammered around us. Then we scrambled to our feet and I grabbed her arm.

'Over there – the church – run.'

It was a ruin, but great stone archways stood against the night and the flame-red flashes, and they were much better than a wall in an open street. We climbed over a broken fence, across scattered masonry and under the nearest arch as another bomb exploded and the air vibrated. Instinctively we covered our ears, crouching together against the stones.

Across the street an incendiary bomb spluttered, then another, flaring. They lit up an alcove behind us, the remains of the vestibule, with a great stone across it forming a roof. We backed into it as the first of a stick of bombs fell nearby, whistling down; then another, and I pushed her against the stones in our small darkened corner and held her tightly, trying to shield her. The earth rocked and the night seemed to collapse about us in stupifying, mind-stopping noise and flashing light. The masonry shielded us from the blast as another bomb battered our senses, but the fear was real and exposed our souls and I heard my voice shouting 'Oh Christ Almighty', and she made a little whimpering sound against me, so quietly and yet I heard it against the rolling, jarring thunder and the crack of the explosions.

Then it eased, roaring away, and we were still pressed together, crouching, holding on to each other until we pushed ourselves upright. There were no more bombs, but the guns were firing continuously, one battery in the park not far away, and shrapnel rattled and bounced off the ruins around us. She stayed close to me, her face against my shoulder and her hair across my eyes, and the fear subsided and all I knew was that we were alive and she was there.

Somewhere there was a fire and the glow flickered into our sanctuary. She pulled back, not her body, just her head, looking around then up at me, and I could see her wide eyes and the reflection of the darting flames in them and they were very close and neither of us moved until she whispered: 'Neil. Oh, dear God.' Then she put her face against my shoulder again and I kissed her hair and she knew I had done it but did not try to move. The fire was crackling and there was an ambulance bell in the distance. Muffled, her voice said: 'I was scared then. More than I've ever been.' I nodded, holding on to her. 'So was I.'

More guns and more shrapnel, and she shivered, still holding, but we both knew it was a pretence: the danger had gone as long as we stayed under cover until the guns stopped. I kissed her again, on the forehead, and she raised her face so that she could see mine, and our eyes locked and this time neither of us tried to break the spell until I said: 'This is the last thing I wanted. No. That's not true. But I never wanted it to show.'

I held her by the shoulders and she whispered: 'Neither did

I. But we both knew. Right from the start. Something –
strange. But it mustn't show again. Please don't let it show
again.'

I said: 'It never will.' And felt indescribably sad.

But it was out now. We had touched, and confessed, and
that made it so much worse because there was no pretence to
shelter us. Don't let it show again. She was Alan's wife. That
was her world. So what had she known, and why? I had said
nothing. Two brief contacts, passing and gone. People did
that all the time and felt nothing. People looked at each other
and saw nothing. But we had spoken in silence and had heard,
and had pushed it away until fear had released it. Reaction?
No, it had been there already. For both of us.

Alan's wife.

I let my hands slide down from her shoulders, along her
coat to her sleeves. For seconds our fingers locked. Then it
was broken.

'I'm sorry. I never meant you to know.'

Guns banging, but distant now, and fire reflecting on cold
stones. No more aircraft engines. Her eyes, her compelling,
questioning eyes, in the flickering dark. Then her hands
covered her face and I knew she was crying. I reached out
and my fingers touched her hair. She stood still, hiding in her
hands.

'Tomorrow it will be different. Away from here. Back in
the real world.' I heard the words as if it were someone else.
Lying.

But it would be locked away. And we would never let it out
again.

She drew her fingers down her face. Red light flickered on
her cheeks. They were wet and shining. But she was proud.

The guns had stopped. Ambulances, fire engines, shouting.
But no guns, no bombs. It was past.

'Come on,' I said. 'It's safe now.'

We clambered across the stones, back to the street and the
fires. A hundred yards away a building was down, a great pile

of masonry, smoking. No way through. Firemen reeling out hoses, running. We went the other way, side by side, not touching.

*

Maximum fuel load. WAAF tractor drivers towing out the long lines of bomb trolleys to the silent aircraft under the summer sky. Cookies – 4000-pounders – among the thousand pounders. No incendiaries.

A big one. And special.

The squadron commander sent for me. Tall and black-moustached, three rings on his battledress, a DSO and a DFC below his brevet.

'Yours is tonight,' he said.

I felt detached, as if I was watching someone else consigned to hell and I didn't care very much about them. After so much waiting it was unreal.

'Where to?'

'I can't tell you. But it's different, and important. Something to make it all worthwhile.'

I hoped he was right.

'Does Flight Lieutenant Tamworth know?'

'Yes. And so do the engineers who have to fit that infernal machine of yours into the Lanc. They're working on it now.'

I wandered outside. I had not seen Alan since Michele and I had returned from London at the weekend. I did not want to see him. Guilt would be written across my face and he would see it.

He was in the mess, and he grinned when I came in.

'Hullo. Heard the good news?'

He did not see it. No anger, or contempt. He didn't know. There was nothing for him to know.

'Yes. Just seen the Wing Co. Where do you think we're going?'

'No idea. But there's a flap on. Something big.'

'I'd better go and check the recorder. It would be a shame if the gremlins got into it, after all.'

By the time I got out to dispersals my equipment had been installed, squeezed into a corner against the main spar, the infamous main spar which made getting about a Lancaster so difficult. The fitters turned the power on and I went through the checks. Everything worked. How it would perform at 20,000 feet with the flak rocking us and Alan corkscrewing away from a fighter, was another matter. But Dimbleby and one or two others had done it, so why shouldn't I?

Back in my room I gathered my notes. I underscored words and phrases, memorising afresh. Once we got back there would be no time to spare. If the raid was important the first news of it would be on the morning bulletins and my initial piece would be wanted in London as quickly as a train could get it there. Then there would be the full recording to edit, the reports live to mike in the nine o'clock news that night, the drafts for America and Australia and Canada; and the publicity interviews for the press.

Plenty to prepare. And to take my mind off it now.

Briefing was at four o'clock. Early. Must be a long one. But that wasn't news – we already knew about the maximum fuel load. Everyone was there. Every aircraft at Scorton would be airborne that night. The map on the platform was covered. That was unusual. Then in they came and we all stood up: the Station Commander, the Squadron Commanders, the nav and bombing leaders and all the rest. The senior Intelligence Officer came in last and stood at the side of the platform while the preliminaries were chanted, looking thoughtful.

Then he said: 'This is a big one, gentlemen. And very important. Recce aircraft have been checking on reports we've received from the underground. Their photographs have proved that our intelligence is good. The Germans are experimenting with revolutionary aircraft. It's your job to destroy their work – for all our sakes.' He dragged aside the cloth covering the map and pointed. 'There. That's where it's happening. A hundred miles north of Berlin on an island off Germany's Baltic coast. Peenemunde. A major experimental station. Tonight you're going to hit it so hard that it will take the Nazis months to recover.'

On the other side of the room a BBC engineer was recording the briefing. Like the rest of us, he would remain in a sort of no-man's-land from now until long after the bombers took off. Security would be even tighter than usual. He would record the whole briefing, then the censors would delete the sensitive parts: which would mean three quarters of it. But we would probably only want ninety seconds, just to get the atmosphere.

Peenemunde. I had never heard of it. And it was a long, long way.

Alan was two rows in front of me. I could see his dark head. Handsome. Listening intently. The man whose wife I coveted. And tonight I would fly with him, and interview him, and he would help me, and my life would depend on his skill and courage. It must never show again, she had said. And I had promised. The hardest promise I would ever make.

The Intelligence Officer was saying: 'There are big hangars which are essentially factories. There are administrative buildings where German scientists and engineers are working and domestic quarters where they're living. And there's the airfield itself. The targets have been divided amongst the attacking force. Ours is the airfield. We're bombing in moonlight and from ten thousand feet for greatest accuracy.'

Ten thousand. I heard the intakes of breath. Half the usual height. Just where the flak would be most deadly.

I could see Bob Galway, writing something. I wondered what there was for a wireless operator to scribble down at this point in the briefing. He must have felt my stare and glanced round, his thin face hollowed and gaunt. Then he winked, a grin touching his mouth, and suddenly I knew he was working out the profits on the bets he had taken. If it had been Berlin he would have been in debt for the rest of the year. But it was

Peenemunde and no one had heard of it, and the humourless Galway would have enough money to take us out for the biggest binge of all time when we got back.

When we got back. This was a six or seven hour flight to one of the most important military targets in Germany. And in moonlight. When we got back? God help us. Some of us would not get back.

'Six hundred aircraft will take part,' the Intelligence Officer said, 'of which forty Mosquitoes in the first wave will divert to attack Berlin, to confuse the enemy.'

But the enemy would not be confused for long. If they could not bring their full defensive forces to bear on our way out, they certainly would on our way back. The planners would regard that as a minor victory. Better to lose a bomber after it had attacked than before.

As long as you were not flying in it.

Six hundred aircraft. Recent losses had been heavy as German defences became more sophisticated. The pattern said that tonight we would probably lose forty, maybe more if Peenemunde was as heavily defended as its importance warranted.

Snap out of it. This is your one and only. Alan and Dingo and the other three of his original crew had done this fifty-six times. Cap and Andy had done it twenty-six. How do you think they feel?

Scared. More scared than I felt? I was afraid of the unknown. It was not unknown to them. That ought to make it worse. Yet I could see them, scattered among the crowd in this corner of the briefing room, concentrating, exchanging quick grins when the IO cracked a joke, making notes. Just like all the rest. Smoking. That was the only sign. They all smoked too much. And the dark shadows under the eyes and the over-quick responses.

Snap out of it. This is a job. You'll get back. Alan will get you back. Fifty-six ops. He's one of the untouchables. One of those who can always feel that it only happens to somebody else.

That's what they all feel. Otherwise they couldn't do it.

Pathfinders, master bombers, target indicators in the air and on the ground. I was expected to tell the Great British Public about all those. I focussed on the Intelligence Officer and began to make my own notes about heights and code colours for flares, and listened closely to the navigation leader's detail of the course as he pointed to the red ribbon pinned across the map and talked of turning points, timings, routes in and out. The fear drifted away, pushed into the background as my mind became fully occupied.

It went on, through the bombing patterns, what each aircraft was carrying in its ten thousand-pound bomb load, and the fuse settings; on to radio frequencies and call signs and radio silence areas, the enemy's newest night fighters, and finally the routine stuff about take-off and return.

Then we crowded together and walked out. Alan was beside me, and I realized I must have been in the middle of my secret little nightmare when take-off times were detailed. I asked him.

'Nine thirty. Meal at seven thirty. Didn't you hear?'

'Must have been dreaming.' I wondered where Michele was now.

Aircrew scheduled for the night's operations got bacon and eggs. No one else was allowed eggs, and sometimes did not get bacon either. It was my second full aircrew meal, and I remembered enjoying the first. Somehow this one did not taste so good.

Afterwards I went back to my room and turned on the radio. Today the Americans had bombed the ball-bearing works at Schweinfurt, the biggest raid yet by the American air force and the deepest daylight penetration into Germany. Air battles all the way there and back. Forty known losses, others still missing. God, Germany would be like a hornet's nest. Waiting for us.

I began to sort through my notes. I was not supposed to take them with me, in case we were shot down and something survived which might tell the enemy things they did not know. But I scribbled a few things in a small notebook as last-minute reminders, slid the rest into a file alongside my typewriter, and surveyed the room.

The awful thought burrowed into my mind that I might not see it again; that tomorrow some stranger would be here, sorting through the notes and my clothes.

In the locker rooms conversation was less casual than usual as we kitted out, then lumbered to the crew busses carrying lifejackets and parachutes. The WAAF driver was rough on the clutch and Goldie said: 'She drives like you fly, Skip – and to hell with the machinery.' But the joke fell flat.

We crowded out, passing parachutes and ration boxes and the rest, under the line of Lancasters in the fading daylight. I followed my crew down to the ladder which reached up to the open door in the side of Charlie Two's fuselage. Charlie Two. She was Alan's favourite. Some Lancasters were better than others, in performance or handling. In Dingo's language, Charlie Two was a beaut. We crowded round the ladder. Goldie went up first. Alan was behind me, last. I glanced at him and he said: 'I'm always last. It's our tradition.' Or superstition.

I wanted to bend down and touch the ground with my hands. In case I never touched it again. I said: 'Tradition's important.' And went up the ladder.

It was 9.40 p.m. by my watch when Alan eased the throttles and the Lancaster rolled forward to join the long, clumsy procession on the winding perimeter track heading towards the take-off marshalling point.

There we waited, watching the black shape of the aircraft ahead of us, the four Merlin engines idling out there against the incoming night.

Alan said: 'Checks, Cap. Throttles?'

Frank Kappa at his side read gauges and touched levers as he went through the drill.

'Throttles on twelve hundred.'

'Trims?'

'Aileron and elevator neutral.'

'Supercharger?'

'Medium.'

'Pitch?'

'Fine and locked.'

'Flaps?'

'Twenty degrees down. Okay.'

'Gills?'

'Rad shutters auto, intake cold.'

'Fuel?'

'Tanks checked, cocks and boosters on, cross feed off. Right tank selected.'

Then, as they went through the last of their chant about hydraulics and gyros, the green light showed and the aircraft ahead bellowed into life and moved forward. Alan edged the starboard outer throttle, ruddered left, twitched the brake lever, and turned thirty tons of Lancaster smoothly into line with the runway; waited, holding her on the brakes; then saw the green light again.

Now it was our turn.

*

We climbed to ten thousand feet and saw the moon brilliant on scattered cloud tops. In the mid-upper turret Andy Douglas said: 'Hell, they didn't tell us it'd be as bright as this.' I knew he was thinking about night fighters.

For a time I stood behind Alan's armour-plated seat-back, listening to the spasmodic exchanges over the intercom. We seemed to be all alone in the vast black night dome, a tiny speck crawling across the invisible earth as we climbed steadily towards the first marshalling point for the main bomber stream. Fear had gone now, driven away by the fascination and novelty, the feeling that we were cocooned in a great metal monster, away from the world and its dangers.

We were over the North Sea. I read 16,000 feet on the altimeter and Alan jerked his thumb to show me two other aircraft silhouetted by the moon. Then we altered course to Dingo's direction, heading for Denmark, and I went back to my cramped corner by the main spar, switched on the equipment and cut my first recording.

It was as much a trial as anything, but it went well and I did two or three minutes on the take-off and the start of the flight. Then I took the microphone forward, asked Dingo for our course details and recorded his reply, and went on to Alan with a couple of routine questions, just for atmosphere.

He played his part well, saying: 'We feel as if we're on our own, but there are six hundred aircraft up here, converging on our target. We must have kept a few people awake as we climbed up across the towns and villages towards the coast. And we'll be waking up some more down there in Denmark now.' And I got an unbidden picture of Michele in the bedroom I had never seen, listening to the engines.

I said: 'Could your wife have been one of those?'

He looked sideways at me, as if the question had surprised him, then nodded. 'I expect so. She can usually hear us go.'

We reached 20,000 feet, the height at which we would fly to the target, and settled at a steady 240 miles an hour ground speed with only 180 on the air speed indicator because of a following wind and the thin air at our operating height.

I was looking over Dingo's shoulder in the navigator's corner when my earphones said: 'Pilot to BBC. Come up front and fly this thing for me.'

Dingo's head twisted. His oxygen mask hid his expression as he pressed his mike button.

'Hell's bells, Skip – you been on the grog or something?'

'Pilot to navigator. Less of the lip, please.'

Dingo gave me a push and jerked his thumb. His wink was an enormous distortion of his eyes.

When I got to the cockpit Cap had moved out of the way and Alan said: 'Thought you might like to know what it feels like. As long as you don't record it. Don't worry, I've set the auto pilot for the hand-over.' And he extracted himself from the pilot's seat, transferred his intercom lead to the socket beside the engineer's bench, and I slid in behind to take his place, plugging in my own lead.

'Okay, now you've got her,' Alan said. He leaned over and released the auto pilot control, and I held a Lancaster bomber on course with my own hands and feet.

Gently he moved the control wheel, a little left, a little right, then said: 'Now you do it.' I did, and felt the great black wings shift. Then I put the nose down a few degrees, then up again, and he said: 'Easy, isn't it?' And settled back in Cap's seat and, in the dim cockpit, folded his arms.

If we lived through tonight, this was something I would never forget.

It lasted for ten minutes, to the accompaniment of occasional jokes from Dingo and Goldie, until I pressed my mike button and said: 'BBC to crew. I don't know what all the fuss is about. It's so boring. I think I'll have a nap, if Dingo'll get off the rest bed. Wake me when things get interesting.'

Alan reset the auto pilot, I made my way for him, Frank Kappa squeezed back into his seat, and normality was restored as Dingo gave a course, height and airspeed check.

Just one hundred and ten minutes after take off we were over the Danish coast and Flip Martin's voice said from the nose: 'Bomb aimer to Skipper. Yellow marker flares ahead on track.' Dingo chipped in: 'Nav to pilot. Right on time, too.'

This was one of the year's new developments: the course for the main bomber stream marked at certain turning points by pathfinder bombers which had preceded us. Crews were still distrustful, fearing that the flares would guide the night fighters, but it was a development which had become a standard feature of operations.

We passed over the flares, changed course, and went on our way, still with no sign of the defences; until tail winds pushed us ahead of our schedule and Alan had to throttle back. We were in the second wave to attack and had to hold off until exactly the right time because, with so many aircraft attacking a small target, there was a real risk of collision unless flight plans were carefully followed.

Indicator flares from one of the pathfinders twinkled on Rugen Island, north-west of Peenemunde, Dingo gave final course instructions, and in clear air under the bright moon we began our run in to the target, now marked ahead by red flares, explosions from the first wave of the attack, and ringed by the sparkle of flak. Out there, somewhere above us, the master bomber was circling, instructing us, marshalling his forces.

I talked my way through it, describing what I saw, recording every second; and all the time hearing in my earphones the unseen master bomber's crisp advice and encouragement, Alan's calm voice checking and rechecking, and Flip Martin guiding him as if it were an easy exercise.

The flak was light – the attack must have taken the Germans by surprise – but there were fighters about now. I saw two of them in the brilliant moonlight, close to us, but they disappeared. I saw two Lancasters go down, too: flames streaming, smoke curling. One exploded in the air, a red spreading flash against the flames below and the moon above. And still Flip's steady voice guided us and we cruised on as if all else was on a glass screen and only we were real, until Charlie Two lurched and he said 'Bombs gone.' Then the aircraft turned steeply on to the course that would take us away from the target, and two miles down the tilting wing I saw Peenemunde and the flames twinkling and explosions rocketing in the moonlight.

Flip said: 'Bomb aimer to Skipper. I reckon those were bang on. Couldn't have been better.'

'Well done, everybody. Now watch out. Every night fighter in Germany is heading this way.' Easy and matter-of-fact. He could have been talking to Mitch about friends calling.

Less than five minutes later the fighters found us.

A warning light flashed on Alan's instrument panel, indicating a following aircraft, and almost immediately Goldie said sharply: 'Tail-end to pilot. We have company. Four o'clock low and climbing.'

'Okay. Eyes skimmed, everybody. They hunt in pairs.'

I picked up my lip microphone and began to talk, getting it on to the disc, knowing that if Alan began to throw the Lancaster about there would be no hope of recording. Then Andy snapped: 'Mid-upper to pilot. Fighter seven o'clock low, climbing,' and Goldie's voice, sharpened: 'Tail-end to pilot. Stand by to corkscrew starboard . . . stand by . . . corkscrew starboard . . . go.'

The Lancaster rolled to the right, nose down, straightened, then pulled to the left, climbing, throttles wide, steadied and dropped to the right again. I kept on talking, hoping the recorder would stand the vibration and the roll angles. Andy was shouting something, then his guns fired a short burst and our next turn was steeper and Goldie's four-gun turret was firing.

Then we were hit, cannon shells exploding somewhere down the fuselage, the aircraft shuddering. I held on with both hands against a vertical bank which suddenly, violently, twisted the other way and Flip Martin said: 'Christ, he nearly hit us – nearly took the nose off.' Then for me in my dark corner everything became a confusion of swaying, surging movement, gunfire from at least two of our turrets, rapid exchanges between the gunners as they passsed information and Alan reacted to it, and more cannon strikes. Recording was impossible and I concentrated on memory until my earphones said: 'Pilot to BBC. Cap's been hit. Come up here and help him to the rest bed if you can.'

Still flat calm, totally in control.

'Okay, Skipper. On my way.'

We seemed to be climbing steeply and I fought my way up the fuselage, then hung on, bracing myself, head down as Alan went into a diving corkscrew. When we steadied I bumped past Galway and Dingo and heaved myself into the cockpit.

Frank Kappa was leaning forward, holding his left arm against his body, blood on the torn sleeve of his flying jacket. Alan said: 'Take his mask off. We're below ten thousand.' I did, and in the dim instrument lighting saw his face, crumpled with pain.

Mercifully we seemed to have eluded the German fighters, and it took two or three minutes of steady flight and the help of Bob Galway to get Cap back to the rest bed. There we cut his jacket sleeve away, tied a rough tourniquet around his upper arm above a gaping, bloody gash, and Galway gave him a morphine shot. Then I struggled back to the cockpit, put on Cap's helmet with its built-in-earphones and mike, and said: 'He'll be okay, I think. Bob's watching him for a few minutes.'

There was no reply, and I saw Alan looking out along the port wing. There was a vibration running through the airframe and his hands were moving on the airscrew pitch and throttle levers. Then he said: 'Pilot to crew. The port outer's been hit. I'm closing it down. We're on three from now on. Keep watching for the fighters.'

As calm as ever. Routine stuff. I marvelled.

The fighters never found us again. But the flak did, as Dingo said cheerfully: 'According to my reckoning we should be nowhere near guns. Somebody's been moving 'em around.' I sat on the engineer's bench and watched white and yellow lights bursting ahead of us. Then one exploded close in, dead ahead, and Alan shouted: 'Duck – duck!' and I put my head down and heard shrapnel rattling on the aircraft's skin and Flip's voice: 'That was close – right down the gun barrels.' Another flak burst somewhere just below rocked us and I knew we had been hit again. But we were flying straight and level now, so I went back to my corner, set up the equipment, and cut another two-minute commentary, all the time hearing Alan, Dingo, Flip and Bob discussing our course, fuel resources, and the state of the aircraft.

Then I went forward, trailing a mike cable, and said to Alan: 'Have you time to talk?'

'Sure. Go ahead.'

I said into the mike: 'What are our problems, Skipper?'

He took the mike from me.

'Nothing we can't handle. One engine was damaged by the fighters and I've shut it down. But now we've dropped our bombs and used half our fuel we're not heavily laden and we can manage on three. For a time we weren't sure of our whereabouts because of the evasive action we had to take, but we've sorted that out, I think. We're cruising at 130 miles an hour groundspeed against a headwind and holding 7000 feet. She's sluggish to fly, and I think our aileron controls are damaged – those are the controls to the wings which help us to bank and turn – but as long as we don't meet any more fighters we'll be okay.'

He grinned at me as he returned the mike. If he was afraid, he didn't show it. He was the skipper, and he was in control. I went back to my corner, adding my own observations to the recording: 'That's how the pilot sees it. But I know he's under-stating the situation. We're flying in a badly damaged aircraft and we're still three hundred miles from home. There's a long way to go.' I hoped I sounded as calm as he did.

An hour later the battered aileron controls became stiffer and the Lancaster more difficult to fly. We were over the Danish coast when Dingo gave us a new course, Charlie Two lurched sickeningly as Alan wrestled with the controls, and I got the feeling that we would not get back. I recorded something, but it seemed a waste of time; I felt no one would ever hear it. Even Dingo had stopped wise-cracking, and we had not heard from Goldie in the rear turret for half-an-hour.

Mitch would be asleep now; if she had been able to sleep. Maybe she was sitting up, fighting another premonition, waiting for the returning engines overhead. I edged back to Cap's seat. Alan ignored me, concentrating on the controls. He held the wheel with both hands and his head moved steadily from side to side as he looked into the darkness and then across the instrument panel. He never stopped looking. That was something I had noticed about him from the beginning. He seemed to miss nothing, to understand everything he saw.

'Pilot to crew. We're down to 6000. Keep your fingers crossed.'

We did, all the way from the Danish coast, out across the North Sea, with our height dropping to 5000 feet, and Bob Galway said: 'Wireless op to Skipper. I've got troubles of my own. I'm receiving okay, but the transmitter's U/S.'

'Okay, Bob. There are worse things.' Like one dead engine, reducing lift dragging us down, damaged ailerons, and the injured Frank Kappa. Flip had been back to look at him and reported that he was only half conscious and still bleeding, and that there was a sharpnel wound in his chest as well as the big one in his arm.

We flew on westwards, until Charlie Two lurched and my heart jumped as a wing dropped; until Alan said: 'Pilot to crew. She's temperamental.' And after another lifetime, Dingo's voice: 'Nav here. Should be over the Lincolnshire coast in two minutes.'

'Thanks, Dingo. Stand by, Bob, with the day's colours, in case a fighter picks us up.' Every night the Very signal colours were changed so that returning bombers could identify themselves and German intruders could not. Getting it wrong could be fatal.

I went back to get another short commentary on the disc. I did not have to ask Alan what the problems were. Normally we would pick up the landing beam ten minutes from base, identify ourselves, join the circuit at 2000 feet and let Control talk us down until we switched our downward identification lights on, lined up with the runway funnel lights and came in on final approach. But we could not transmit, so we could not tell Control we were there and needed help. But Galway could hear Control's transmissions and said: 'Wireless op. Sounds as if things are quiet down there. No other aircraft about at the moment.'

'They'll all be back and in the sack by now,' growled Dingo.

We were down to 3000 feet, not from choice, and sinking steadily. Gingerly Alan put the under-carriage down. Everything worked and he grinned at me. Suddenly I felt he was glad to have someone sitting there, no matter how useless. Just to be able to communicate satisfaction; or alarm.

No flaps, Alan said. Something must have been hit. He tried three times. No use. That meant a long shallow approach, a high landing speed, and everything depending on the brakes. As long as they were not damaged too.

He tried a turn, and Charlie Two sagged and crabbed. Aileron control was obviously minimal. He tried to use engine torque to drag us round, but it would only work one way. At 2000 feet we saw the landing beam, where it should have been. Another tentative turn, and a lot of wallowing. The moon had nearly gone, and the blackness was relieved only by a faint light coming up out of the east.

'Pilot to crew. Aileron control is worse, there are no flaps, we won't know about brakes till we need them, and oil pressure's dropping fast in the port inner.' Hell, that was new. If that one went we would only have the starboard engines left. Could a Lancaster fly on two engines, both on the same side – and no ailerons? 'We'd better reduce the odds. Stand by to bale out. I repeat, stand by to bale out.'

I looked at him. He saw my head movement and nodded, emphasizing his instruction.

'What are you going to do, Skip?' Quiet and easy, from Flip in the nose.

'Get Cap down in one piece, if I can. But the rest of you had better go. Stand by until I give the order.'

Silence for seconds; just the engine roar, no longer heard because it had been there for so long.

'Nav to Skip. Another problem. My intercom's U/S. I can't hear you.'

'Tail to pilot. Are you talking? My earphones are dead. Can't hear a thing.'

'Flip here. What did you say you're going to do, Alan? I didn't hear your reply.'

'Andy to crew. Is the skipper okay? I'm not receiving him.'

'Bob here. It's not just that I can't transmit. I can't hear the skipper on intercom.'

Another silence. Alan was looking at me. I stared out through the screens at the night, then glanced at him, tapped my headset, and shrugged.

Alan thumbed his mike switch. 'I'll have the lot of you court marshalled when we get back. You're crazy.'

I went on staring at nothing, thinking that in ten minutes I might be dead.

Alan tried another turn, then throttled back, feeling for the stall, experimenting. He corrected the course, dropping lower. Dingo said: 'Counting on my fingers, Skip, I reckon base is one mile dead ahead.'

Twenty seconds later we flashed our call sign on the downward identification light, repeating it, repeating it; then adding SOS twice for good measure; and saw a green Very light float up some way to our right.

'You're a lousy navigator, Dingo. Three hundred yards off course.'

'Don't be stupid. They moved the runway, just to confuse us.'

'Well, in case they move it again, everybody belt up. Strap Cap into the bunk, Bob. You use his seat, Neil. Usual crash drill if things start to fall apart. And if there's a fire, get Cap out first.'

The runway lights were on now, and we cruised slowly past, down to a thousand feet. Charlie Two was vibrating badly. I kept looking at the black shape of the port inner engine, but it was still going. Alan opened the starboard throttles and rolled into a turn to port, but it was clumsy and I felt my stomach rise as if we had hit an air pocket. More throttle and she steadied, turning slowly through 180 degrees. I read 800 feet on the altimeter. Then we were parallel with the runway lights again, much further away, and we lumbered on into the night. Alan feathered the airscrew on the sick engine and reduced its revs. But it was still doing a bit of the work as we came to the end of the downwind leg and began the final 180-degree turn.

I saw 600 feet registered and felt the great battered airframe crabbing. Alan was struggling with the controls, using his body weight to boost the strength of arms and legs which by now must have been aching badly. He had pushed his helmet back a little and the reflection of the instrument lighting shone faintly on his forehead.

Then the runway lights glowed ahead, a long way ahead it seemed. I looked at the altimeter again. 400 feet and going down: too quickly, and Alan pushed the starboard throttles, countering the swing with right rudder. The left wing dropped and it seemed a long time before the damaged ailerons responded to the wheel. Alan helped the left wing up with more power from the sick engine on that side, and miraculously we were lined up with the runway and down to 200 feet.

At the last moment she lurched and crabbed again, but somehow he picked her up and we came over the airfield boundary flat and very low. He dragged the throttle levers back and when we touched the tyres squealed and we didn't bounce even a foot as he held the wheel hard against his chest and grabbed for the brakes.

For a sickening two seconds nothing happened. Then they worked and we felt our headlong progress checked, checked again after a moment's surge, until we rumbled down between the runway lights, straight, controlled, seeing fire engines and an ambulance pacing us out there on the dark perimeter track, waiting for the pile-up that never came.

Alan even tried to reach dispersals. But as he turned off the runway Charlie Two staggered as a tyre burst and dragged round in half a circle before, at last, she stopped and Alan cut the switches and the engines shuddered as they died and we all sat still in the silence.

Then Flip Martin said: 'Bloody good show, Skipper.' But no one else spoke for long seconds, and I saw Alan lean his head against the armour behind his seat and, just for a moment, close his eyes.

He's back, Mitch. He's brought us all back. And I couldn't take you from him if you asked me to, and I know you never will.

*

I slept on the train to London, wrote the last of my initial script in a studio, supervised the assembly of my recordings and argued with the censor – a calm, understanding Squadron Leader with whom it was difficult to quarrel – and went on the air at six o'clock that night. Then I had two hours' sleep and we put out a twenty-minute programme after the nine o'clock news.

After that I slept for nine hours without stirring, then spent two days assembling more material for overseas transmission, a special package for America, and did several ten-minute talks for feature programmes using on-the-spot recordings to recreate the drama. Everyone seemed to be pleased with it all, there were newspaper interviews with Alan and the crew, and a week after the flight I had a telephone call from the Station Commander inviting me to go back the next day.

I did, to meet again the men with whom I had lived a lifetime in seven hours. They were preparing for leave after their last operation of the tour the night before.

Frank Kappa was cheerful in hospital and talked enthusiastically about getting back on to operations in three months' time. But even if he did, it would not be with the same crew. This was dispersal day: leave, then new work training others or whatever else the RAF decided for them.

Alan said: 'Let's keep in touch. After the war we'll get

together again. But come and say goodbye to Mitch before you go.'

I stood in the quiet lounge of the pub where they had lived for four months and she said: 'We'll see you again one day. Please write sometimes. And take care. You've become a very good friend.'

'That's been my privilege.' I held her shoulders and kissed her once, lightly, on the cheek. As I drew back her eyes looked into my mind and momentarily her teeth caught her lower lip.

I shook hands with Alan. 'Thanks aren't enough, Skipper. I'll never forget.'

They watched me go, side by side, holding hands. I knew I would never see them again.

It mustn't show. Don't let it show.

It didn't.

THORESEN

---◆◆◆---

1947

1

•—•

Peter had been with me for an hour and was already half way through his fourth cigarette. We sat in a corner of the Cumberland Hotel's lounge at Marble Arch. He had telephoned: no food, he had said; just coffee and a talk.

I welcomed it. Maybe there was something he had forgotten to tell me. Anything would help. I was depressed, first because I didn't know where to turn next, and then because reviving all my dusty memories of Mitch and setting them down explicitly had left me exhausted. I knew so much more about her now than when our lives had crossed so briefly in 1943: Peter, François Boisy, Chuck Feldman, had painted subtle colours across a picture which previously had been just an outline drawing around one small, brilliantly etched, sadly remembered corner. And there was Alan, too; the man whose skill and courage and unfailing courtesy had ruled out for all time any possibility that I might hazard his happiness. Re-reading the old notes, listening again to my old recordings still hoarded in the BBC library, and then deliberately weaving it all into a reconstruction of my memories, had been even more difficult than I had expected. They were dead, and even after the years I felt the loss aching in me.

But there was more, for I had seen in their mirror an image of myself, and had not liked it. I had broken no rules, committed no offence, betrayed no friends; but the question had been asked in my mind, and for fleeting moments I had wanted to yield to it. That she would probably not have wanted to yield with me was immaterial. I had exposed my secret soul and found it wanting. I was only a step removed from Peter Armstrong's follies.

I watched his face now, and saw the likeness. That was another reason I welcomed this moment: he was a living link.

He had smartened himself up for our meeting: a well-pressed grey suit and his hair trimmed. His eyes were brighter, too, and his manner that of a man refreshed after a long sleep.

He said: 'I've thought a lot about you. I don't know how much of what I've told you will appear in your book. There are some things I wouldn't like to see. I hope you'll be kind.' He studied me curiously. 'Strange – I still don't know you well. But I feel you're sympathetic enough to treat me reasonably. And, I hope, to do something for me.'

'I don't know what I'll write,' I said. 'Not least because at this moment I've reached a dead end. But I'm not looking for victims to crucify. What could I do?'

'I never imagined she might be dead,' he said distantly. 'I'd always dreamed I might find her again. You know – a miracle. It was a dreadful shock when you told me what had happened. Now – do you know where she's buried?'

'I don't know anything about what happened at the end. Somebody does, somewhere. But I still have to find out who, and then what.'

He stared across the busy, plushly-furnished lounge, but he was seeing another place, another time, and the child of that time.

'When you know, will you tell me, please?' He stubbed out his cigarette, concentrating on it. 'If she has a grave, and someone tells you where it is, let me know.'

He was quiet and calm. And suddenly I knew what had happened to him. He had spent so long hoping, and yet afraid to pursue his hope because he had feared rejection at the end, that it had sapped his spirit and his life had sagged and broken under the weight of it. Now there was no hope, and once the awful impact had been absorbed it had released him from his bondage. The fear of rejection had gone, for now there was no one to reject him. He was disciplined again.

'You want to see it?'

He nodded, focussing on me.

'Yes. Very much.'

'So do I.'

He calculated, still watching me, trying to read me.

'Maybe we could go together.' A hesitation before the confession. 'It's odd. I used to travel so much. But I haven't been abroad for twenty years. And I don't speak French. I suppose I'm a bit – afraid of it. But tell me if you'd rather not.'

I poured some coffee, watched the bubbles circling, and imagined a hillside under the Mediterranean sun, and lines of graves, and hers lost among them and neglected. Was it like that?

'I don't speak French very well. But enough to keep the two of us out of trouble. It's a deal, Peter. If I find out, we'll both go.'

He relaxed, relieved. He said, 'Thank you,' and hid behind the business of lighting another cigarette.

I said: 'It might take a long time. I've only one small link with what happened in the last few months. And we're up against the Intelligence services, which are not noted for talking freely.'

He dragged smoke down, and his mouth tightened.

'It's horrible. That they should send a woman to do a job like that.'

'She was as much French as she was English,' I said. 'There were countless French women in the Resistance move-ment.'

He shook his head, suddenly angry.

'It wasn't the same. They sent her there. They didn't have to do that.' He looked down at his cigarette. 'It was my fault, anyway. If things had been different, years and years before, she wouldn't have been in that position.'

I said sharply: 'Lots of families split up. And the war killed millions. We're all just pawns, struggling along as best we may. None of us is perfect. Don't blame yourself. Blame –' I groped '– blame Hugo Thoresen, if you like. If he hadn't had you pushed out of the RAF, things could easily have been different.'

'No.' He combed fingers through his grey hair. 'I was off the rails before then. Maybe there would still have been a chance, though, if it hadn't been for him.' He looked hard at me. 'He turned out to be a swine, didn't he?'

I wondered how he would describe Thoresen if I told him about Berne. But I was not ready to do that. Until I did he would never appreciate the man's impact on his family. His shadow had lain across all their lives.

'You never know, when you meet someone, what influence they may have on you in the future,' he said. He leaned back, thinking. 'I guess I'd have reacted differently if I could have known, that first time I saw him.'

'When was it?'

'A briefing just before an offensive – 1916. He was there in the background. He didn't seem to do anything, except listen. And look at people. Some of the others were suspicious of him. But that was because he was half Danish.' He grinned, and suddenly there was a hint of old enthusiasms in the curve of his mouth and the brightness of his eyes. 'Not British, old boy, you know,' he mocked. 'The army was like that, then. He was a loner. I talked with him at first out of curiosity. I wanted to know more about him.'

'Did he ever tell you much?'

'He never told anybody much, about anything. He was something in Intelligence. Not quite what he seemed to be. But entertaining. Very well educated, of course.'

'Where?'

'I forget. High grade public school in England, then English and Danish universities. But it wasn't only that. His family background gave him the edge. His father was a diplomat.

Hugo saw a lot of the international high life as he grew up.'

'And his mother?'

'Oh, very wealthy. Family money out of textiles a generation before, then shrewdly invested. No rags-to-riches-to-rags in three generations there. They're still big in the City now. You've heard of the Henshaws. His Lordship and Sir James must be nephews, or something.'

I stared at him. Just sat, and stared. And felt the depression lifting.

*

She was warm and eager, and her hair sometimes reflected the low bedside light as she moved her head, and her tongue sent fire through me. It was not the first time she had been into my bed, for we had come to know each other very well; but this was different, special, as if the other times had been only tentative explorations and the ultimate revelation had been hidden until now.

I let my mind bury itself in her passion, because I did not want to think, at this sublime moment, about what I had to do.

I had left Peter, gone straight to a telephone, and asked her to have dinner with me. But the restaurant had been crowded and people were too close to permit the questions I had to ask, and in the taxi she had said: 'I want you, Neil. Oh God, I want you.'

So the questions were still unasked and it was one o'clock in the morning and we were locked together for the second time and we both cried out and then her tears came. How strange that she wept in ecstasy. I've always done that, she said, I can't help it; and that night she had wept three times because it had started in the living room when we had caressed as soon as we had closed the door of the flat.

But now it was over and she curled against me, our breathing deep and hard and our bodies damp where they touched and her forehead shining in the light when I opened my eyes to look at her. And I still had to ask the questions.

We slept for a while; then I got up, found a dressing gown, and made coffee while she went into the little bathroom for a quick shower. When I brought in the coffee she was standing tall and slender and naked, looking at me; then laughed and said: 'If you're going to be modest, I'd better be the same.' So I found pyjamas for her and she slipped into them and sat cross-legged on the bed.

Much later she brought up the subject of my research and I took a long breath and said: 'When Hugo first told you the Michele story, did you see it as a potential book or was that his suggestion?'

It was intended to shock her, for I knew that was the only way to break down the barrier; and it did. She stared at me, her dark eyes big and unfathomable, a lock of her hair falling across her forehead. Then she whispered: 'What are you talking about?'

'You and your cousin,' I said. 'Or is he a second cousin? Probably. Anne Henshaw, who married Lieutenant Anthony Reid and became Anne Henshaw-Reid; and Hugo Thoresen, whose mother was a Henshaw and married a successful Danish diplomat. Was she your mother's sister, or cousin? It doesn't matter. Was he the one who recruited you into SOE work from the Wrens? It would be logical. The intelligence Services work very much on personal recommendation and connection.'

She was still staring at me; then swivelled round on the bed and sat upright, her bare feet on the floor.

'Did you have to bring that up now?' She was hating me.

I remembered her in the bed and the way she had struggled to get closer to me when we were already part of each other; and then I remembered that she had lied to me, not once but several times, and that Charles Le Page had lied to me and that had probably been by arrangement with her; and I said: 'Sorry if it seems inappropriate. But we were talking about the book. And you once told me you like my style. This is just part of it.'

She stood up and began to move about the room, picking up her clothes, looking at them.

'I'm going. Please call a taxi for me.'

'He suggested the book, didn't he? He told you about the marvellous girl who had gone down over France on a parachute to join the Resistance and what a superb operator she was until the Gestapo caught her, and what a great book it would make. That was Hugo, wasn't it? Where is he now, Anne? I want to talk to him.'

She wrenched off my pyjama top and began to disentangle her bra, turning her back to me as if she couldn't bear that I should see the breasts I had caressed such a little time ago.

I said: 'Did he tell you she'd been his mistress? Did he tell you he had seduced her when she was nineteen years old, that he had betrayed her grandfather's trust and had used his diplomatic privileges as a weapon to flatter her and spoil her and get her into his bed?'

She had stopped wrestling with the bra. She stood still, holding it, her back straight and smooth and white in the bedside light, the pyjama trousers low on the curve of her hips. Then, without turning, she whispered: 'I don't know what you're talking about.'

'Of course you don't. He wouldn't have told you. And he wouldn't have expected that the author you chose for the job would ever find out. It was buried in his past. But not far enough. Like some of his other tricks, starting with his revenge on Peter Armstrong after their quarrel over Michele's mother. A long history of trickery and concealment, Anne. Where is he now? I want him.'

'I don't know.' Faintly.

'Yes you do. He's still in one of the Intelligence departments. Six, I expect. He was with the SIS before the war, wasn't he? Then he would move into either Seven or Nine, either Resistance or linking with the escape routes. That's how he

247

came to get his claws on Mitch again. Now I expect he's back in Six. Stop trying to protect him. He's not worth it. He sent her to her death. There was more to it than you ever knew.'

Very slowly she turned. Still holding her bra. Still naked to the waist. Incredulity creased lines between her eyebrows. Then the tears glistened in her eyes and she wiped them away angrily and whispered: 'You didn't have to do this now. Not when I'm so – so vulnerable.' Then she covered her eyes, and let me put my arms around her and hold her close. I felt wretched, but it had been the only way.

Presently she said: 'It's not true. He wouldn't do things like that.' But her voice said she knew it was true.

'Who thought up the story about Charles getting information from his old friend at the War Office?' I asked. 'It fooled me right down the line. Hugo's idea, I guess.' She didn't argue, and I knew I was right. But she drew away from me and sat on the bed, pulling the pyjama coat around her shoulders, staring at the floor. I said, 'I'll make more coffee,' and padded into the kitchen.

When I came back she was still on the bed. She did not look at me until I held a cup out to her. Then she took it and raised her eyes. She was hurt and she was ashamed, and the two emotions chased through her and bruised her.

'You're cruel.' She whispered it. 'I wouldn't have believed you could be cruel. Right at the beginning I asked if you would discard me when you'd got all the information you wanted. Now I know you will.'

'No.' I sat down beside her. 'It just had to be this way. If I'd waited until tomorrow you'd have stuck to the story he'd told you to tell. You promised him, didn't you? That you'd never let me know where it came from? And Charles went along with it because he thought it sounded like a good story. It is. The best any of us will ever hear. But there was one thing Hugo couldn't have known – that Mitch and I had a special relationship.' Her head jerked up, her eyes rounding. 'No. It never went as far as that. But something strange

248

happened when we met, and we both knew what it meant, so when I started to research the story I went much further, much deeper, than your dear cousin could have expected. Is he a cousin, by the way?'

'Yes. Second cousin.' Her voice was small and miserable. 'And you're right. All the things you've said. I'm sorry. I – I couldn't have guessed that you and I would – find our own special relationship. Once I was into it, I couldn't get out – without betraying him.'

'He wasn't worth the sacrifice,' I said. 'Now – I want him. Where is he?'

*

I would have known him anywhere, from Boisy's description; even Peter's, from all those years before. Older and greyer, maybe; but handsome still, with the small, neatly trimmed beard outlining his mouth and jaw, and the hair a little longer than the fashion but perfectly cut. He was in the American Bar at the Savoy, where Anne had told me he sometimes went around six in the evening. I had been there every night for the past week, looking for him.

He was talking to the barman. I stood beside him and asked for a large Scotch on the rocks. As the barman turned away I said quietly, without looking at him: 'Mr Hugo Thoresen. It's taken me a long time to find you.'

The barman poured whisky over ice and put the glass down in front of me. I looked sideways at Thoresen and said: 'Would you care to join me? It could be interesting.'

He did not move. I'll swear his mouth did not move either, as he said: 'That is most courteous. I'm drinking Campari.'

I guestured to the barman. When he was out of earshot I said: 'We have a mutual friend. Your delightful second cousin Anne.'

He watched the barman as if it were important to do so.

When the drink came to him he picked up the glass, inspected it, and raised it fractionally. 'Your good health, sir. I didn't catch your name.'

I acknowledged and tasted the whisky. 'Neil Cameron. The author commissioned to write a book about Michele Tamworth, formerly Michele Armstrong, the daughter of Peter Armstrong and Marie-Claire Philomene Mascarella de Lattre with whom, on a day in 1917, you suggested you were in love and thereby started a chain of events which have led to this meeting.'

He digested it, without a flicker of expression, staring, unblinking.

'I understood you were thorough in your research, Mr Cameron. There is a vacant table in the far corner, a little away from the ears of others. Shall we occupy it?'

Without waiting for my response he walked easily away; then settled, adjusting the creases in his trousers.

I joined him and said: 'So you knew about me.'

'Of course.' He inclined his head. 'It was in my interests to know who had been chosen for this fascinating assignment. I trust, sir, in view of your name, that you are of impeccable Scottish ancestry, even though you carry no trace of the accent?'

'Impeccable,' I said. 'Even though English born. As impeccable as your own separate Danish and English lineage. Shall I tell you how I knew about that?'

He shrugged. His eyes were half-concealed beneath narrow lids.

'If it would amuse you to do so.'

'I find little in the situation to amuse me, but much to interest me. I learned that your mother was a Henshaw – which in turn led to my further inquiries of Anne Henshaw-Reid – from Peter Armstrong.'

The eyelids lifted fractionally.

'Armstrong? How extraordinary. If I had given him any thought in the last twenty years – which I have not – it would

250

have been to imagine that he had died, probably from alcoholic poisoning.'

'He's alive and well, and he has told me a great deal about you,' I said. 'So have others. François Boisy, for example. I know about Berne, and the way you used the confidence of Philippe de Lattre, which you had so carefully cultivated, as a route to seduction. That was a shameful episode in your life.'

His eyes were bright now; hard and bright and calculating. But his face was immobile.

'You take a great risk, sir, speaking to me in that manner.' Soft-voiced, but diamond-sharp at the edges. 'If your disreputable business is blackmail, you greatly over-estimate your situation.'

'It is exactly that,' I said. 'But I don't want money. I want information. You started this, Thoresen. You talked your misguided cousin into submitting an idea to her employer; an idea centred on the girl she had once met when she worked for the Special Operations Executive, an organization in which you played no small part. You wanted to see Michele's story in print, for the greater satisfaction of your own secret spirit. But you didn't know that when my name emerged from her husband's records, it was that of a man who had his own secret reasons for delving far deeper into the story than you or anyone else might have expected. A conventional biography would have sketched briefly over her French–English childhood and would then have concentrated on her war-time life, the tragic death of her husband while he was helping the French Resistance, her desire for revenge, and her ultimate sacrifice. Was that what haunted you – her death, and your own responsibility for it? You sent her there, didn't you? You chose her, you groomed her, just as you groomed her for high society in 1937 and took your own satisfaction on the way. How did you see yourself, Thoresen – as her mentor, her saviour, her lover, her Svengali? Were you her creator, and in the end her destroyer?'

I was getting to him. He was still frozen-faced, but a small bead of perspiration ran from his right temple, and he blinked several times as I threw the words at him. No one else in the bar could have heard them against the low hum of conversation and the chink of glasses. But he heard them: every syllable, every inflection; and he felt the knife as I carved them into him, just as I had intended.

His lips parted in two straight lines, and he pushed his head forward.

'The Gestapo destroyed her. She took the risks knowingly. I was merely the vehicle. Get out there, down to Cannes. I can give you the names of people who knew how she died. The Germans killed her – not I.'

'You put her in front of the execution squad,' I said, and I no longer had to pretend my hatred for him. 'You knew the risks far better than she did. You saved her in 1940 – yes, I know about that, too, because once upon a time she told me herself – but that was not enough. For the greater glorification of your secret soul, she had to do still more. Or was it still revenge, because her mother had rejected you and her father had humiliated you? I know so much, Thoresen, and unless you tell me everything else I want to know, I shall use my knowledge to destroy you publicly, professionally, socially. She cannot suffer now, but unless you help me to understand the rest of her story, I'll guarantee that you will suffer for the rest of your life.'

The bead of perspiration was joined by another; but he was coming to terms with the shock. He straightened in his chair, found his glass and drained it.

'And just supposing I were to go along with you, what guarantee would I have that you would still not vilify me with distortions and exaggerations in your manuscript?' The voice was smooth and confident again, even accusing.

I said: 'None. You have only the certainty of my intent if you do not.'

He looked at his empty glass, turned, and raised a hand to a waiter. Then he looked at me and said: 'You consider yourself thorough, Mr Cameron. I have no such confidence. Penetrating you may be; but I doubt your ability to understand. It may be in my interests to talk to you, not least to demonstrate the extent of your misjudgements up to this time.' To the waiter who appeared beside our table he said: 'Campari and the best malt in your stock, both on the rocks, both large, if you please.' Then to me: 'You understand that I cannot speak to you officially. The war may be over, but there are still restrictions. But on personal matters I am prepared to speak to you confidentially, and on a non-attributable basis. And whatever appears ultimately in your book will, I assure you, be inspected minutely by the appropriate Intelligence department and by my lawyers. So it will pay you well to listen carefully to what I have to say.'

He was mine. He needed to know what I knew, so that he could present his own interpretation of it. He was prepared to trade information for access to my research. It would be coloured by his incredible egoism and his conceit; but I could strip that away and see for myself the final months and weeks of Mitch's life as they really were, and perhaps achieve an understanding of her, and of myself.

MICHELE

---•◆•---

1943–44

1

●—●—●

The Squadron Commander was the one to tell her, in the living room of the little cottage she had rented three miles from the airfield.

Alan had gone out the night before to his Lysander, standing black-painted in the dark, big radial engine raised against the subdued hangar lights behind, wide narrowed wings shadowed overhead. He had volunteered for special duties and now, attached to 138 Squadron at Tangmere in Sussex, was already an acknowledged expert at putting the manoeuvrable Lysander down into small fields in the moonlight. Five times he had done that in France, ferrying agents for the Special Operations Executive. Tonight he would fly to a field near Caen in Normandy where a man and a woman would be waiting. They were French and after a year's dangerous service with the Resistance had been betrayed to the Gestapo. Now SOE wanted them brought back so that they could tell their stories first-hand to Intelligence officers.

A hundred miles away the reception committee were waiting with their signal lights and their primitive flare path. He had flown as low across the water as the moonlight allowed, had lifted up over the coast without a shot being fired against him and had followed poplar-lined roads south, his aircraft's wheels with their big streamlined spats clearing by only twenty feet the power lines which straddled his flight path and were marked in red across the map on his knee.

The landing field was west of Caen, well away from the satellite airfield used by the Luftwaffe south of the town. He flew very slowly, consulting his watch, ensuring that he arrived precisely on time, approaching the field from the planned direction. He could see the ground clearly in the bright moonlight which was essential for operations of this kind and, on schedule, winked his identification light twice. Immediately he received an answer from the ground; a single wink, a three-second pause, then three long ones. He turned in low, banking steeply, flaps extended, and saw the flares flickering into a line of yellow pinpricks. The site had already been checked by RAF photographic reconnaissance aircraft. He had seen the pictures and knew that the approach was down a short avenue between trees. As he dropped he saw the trees dark on either side and the flare path ahead. The moonlight was bright enough for him to see the ground features now, and he knew as he touched down that it was going to be a good landing. He also knew that as he rolled across the field the reception committee would extinguish the flares behind him as quickly as they could.

He did not know, and neither did they, that a patrolling Messerschmitt 110 fighter had picked him up on radar as he had turned in on his final approach.

The reception committee heard the howl of the fighter's twin engines above the lazy growl of the Lysander's single radial as Alan came in, throttle almost closed, but he probably did not see the warning flash of red which was the signal that the Luftwaffe was around. The German came over the trees while Alan was still taxiing and before the flares had been extinguished, and opened fire with cannons and machine guns. The Lysander was raked as it swung into a turn at the end of its landing run, and then exploded in flames. Several of the reception committee and the two fugitives were killed; those who escaped could only run, and later in the night send their news of disaster.

The Squadron Leader went to tell Michele at nine o'clock the next morning. His name was Lloyd Williams, and he was a gentle-voiced Welshman from the Brecon hills whose wife and young daughter lived a few miles away on the outskirts of

Winchester. He stayed with her for an hour, and was astonished that she did not cry. She sat in an armchair, wide-eyed, staring at him, listening to him, and saying: 'We often talked about it. We both knew. It was one of the great things we had, that we could talk about things other people were afraid to mention. He taught me never to be afraid.'

Late in the afternoon she went to Tangmere, to the room he had shared with another pilot, and collected his belongings which had been carefully packed by his batman. Williams was waiting for her when she came out and offered to carry the hold-all, but she shook her head. 'It was Alan's,' she said. 'I must carry it.'

They walked together towards the little car she and Alan had owned and for which they had hoarded their petrol coupons; until they came to the mess, and she saw familiar faces at the windows. Perhaps she knew there were men there who wanted to speak to her but who did not know what to say; so she said: 'Take me to see his friends. Some of them are mine, too.'

Williams did so, and watched wonderingly as she walked in, head high, and talked to the men she had come to know since Alan had arrived at Tangmere. Sad and awkward, they gathered slowly around her, finding that they could converse with her because that was what she wanted; hearing her talk about Alan, not in grief but in pride, realizing that this was her tribute and wanting to share in it. Now and then she even smiled at something recalled, and none of them could believe that he had been dead for eighteen hours for he was still with them in her eyes and her voice and her courage.

Then she said: 'Lloyd is waiting for me. Thank you for being kind to me. I shall always remember you.'

She went to the door. She was very pale now, and her mouth was tight-closed. Then she turned. They were all standing, looking at her, and one put on his uniform cap and saluted, and others did the same, in silence. Beside her, Williams returned their salutes for her, and led her away.

She walked to the car, carrying Alan's hold-all, with tears running down her cheeks and dropping on to the collar of her jacket, but still with her head up and her spirit unquenched.

For the next three weeks she lived with Williams' family, then announced that she would return to London. No, she told them, she had no relatives and there were no friends who would remember her; but somewhere there had to be a new life for her and she would not find it unless she looked for it. Through the Station Commander she was given a name at the Air Ministry and she went there, looking for a job. She was passed on to a French section at the War Office and within another week had started there as an administrative assistant, sharing a flat with an acquaintance from her days with the ambulance service.

Two months later the head of her section sent for her and said: 'There is someone here who would like to see you.' He was an English-born academic who had spent much time before the war at the Sorbonne in Paris, who believed passionately in the rebirth of the French nation and who clearly regarded interest in his staff by outsiders as a personal affront.

She went to a room which had neither number nor departmental identity on the door, and found a man waiting for her. He introduced himself as Graham Granby 'from another department' and after a prolonged casual conversation began to talk about her family life before the war, asking detailed questions yet somehow managing to imply that he already knew a great deal about her. He was well-groomed with, she guessed, a public school background, about forty years old, and although in civilian clothes had the bearing of a soldier. She talked with him patiently, even when he asked for details of her mother's death and led her to tell him how she had taken a rifle and fired on the German aircraft. After that he asked her how she had reached England, and she told the story in a few sentences, omitting any mention of Hugo Thoresen or the identity of the ship in which she had crossed the Channel.

Granby said: 'You got away by yourself? Surely you must have had some help. Do you remember who helped you?'

'I don't know who you are,' she told him calmly. 'I don't know which department you work for, or what you do. In those circumstances, even though you must have the blessing of the War Office to be here at all, I can't tell you any more. Except that I arrived in this country on the 8th of June. That was recorded by the immigration authorities who interviewed me and who were also aware of certain other details.'

He regarded her thoughtfully, critically; then said: 'We'll come back to that, perhaps. But let's talk about what happened next.'

So she told him of her ambulance work and he questioned her about dates and which units she had worked for, noting down some of her answers. Then they moved on to her marriage and her movements afterwards, until he said: 'I'm sorry you lost your husband. The war has treated you badly. Your home, the whole of your life in France, your mother, and now the man you married. You must hate the Germans.'

'I don't try to measure my feelings,' she said. 'When I married Alan I knew the score. We both knew it. I am thankful for what I've had. I try not to grieve for something unknown which has been lost. We all live day by day and minute by minute. Life is a matter of chance, and so is the ending of it. All I know is that the man I loved better than my own life has gone, just as have so many others.'

'Do you know what he was doing when he died?'

'Yes.'

'Will you tell me, please?'

'No.'

'Why not?'

'It is not a matter I can discuss with anyone.'

Granby said: 'Very commendable. So I'll tell you. He was flying into Northern France to pick up two members of the French Resistance who were being hunted by the Gestapo and whom we badly wanted to interview. His mission failed through no fault of his. He had already made a number of similar flights and was earmarked for other, more exacting work, such were his high qualities. You are half French, Mrs Tamworth. You must have a great love of France and the French people, and a high regard for those who are working covertly to help the nation.'

'Of course,' she said. 'Particularly in view of what Alan was doing.'

'Would you like to further his work – and go some way towards avenging his death, and that of your mother?' Granby's voice was quiet and without drama.

Now she was still, watching him, letting his words sink in; until she said: 'Since you are unlikely to be inviting me to fly aeroplanes, would you care to be more specific?'

'I'm sorry.' He shook his head. 'We have not yet reached that stage. The question is one of principle. I think you have the ability to serve this country, and France, much more effectively, much more valuably, than sitting here in this building translating documents for the benefit of Free French units and General de Gaulle. Oh yes,' – he held up a silencing hand – 'I know there's more to it than that. But in comparison with other work, not much more. The most important period of the war since 1940 is coming towards us and we need people of special qualities to ensure that we are successful and that Germany is defeated as quickly as possible. You have special qualities, Mrs Tamworth. Are you willing to discuss further, with one or two of my colleagues, how those qualities might be developed?'

*

For a week she heard nothing; then Granby telephoned, inviting her to meet him at an address in St James's Street. He opened the door himself and led her upstairs to a small, well-furnished flat, and a man whom he introduced as Major Rushworth, a tall well-built soldier of Granby's age whose questioning covered much of the ground already crossed by her earlier conversation.

Again she answered patiently and allowed Rushworth to lead the conversation until, like Granby earlier, he referred to Alan's last flight. Then she asserted herself.

'I think it's time I asked some questions,' she said. 'I don't know who you are or whom you work for, although I can guess. I've told you a great deal about myself, even though some of our talk has been painful to me. So far you have told me absolutely nothing. I don't think I want to go further with this unless you tell me what you have in mind. You obviously want me to work for you. What would that work involve?'

Rushworth nodded, as if satisfied with something.

'Preparation for the Allied invasion of Europe,' he said crisply. 'It is popularly expected that that invasion will take place in 1944. I'm sure even the Supreme Command hasn't yet decided on a date, but we have to assume it will be next year. And since it is now mid-December, we have to make our preparations speedily. Those preparations include the organization of Continental resistance movements into effective guerilla groups which may be mobilized and controlled with precision. In France there are many such groups. We are already in close touch with some of them. But we need greater control and they are looking to us for liaison and leadership. You are effectively native French, and you are an intelligent woman of unusual courage. We believe you could perform a valuable liaison function.'

'By going to France?' No excitement. No sign of tension. But alert and cool.

'Yes. There have been British agents in France since 1940. Most operate in conjunction with the Resistance and, latterly, the Maquis. There is an enormous under-cover army there, waiting for the word. But the organization is not yet good enough. We have found that women can move about more freely than men, with less risk of detection.'

'And what do they do as they move about, Major?'

Rushworth exchanged a glance with Granby who said: 'The details would emerge during your training, if you want to go ahead with this. But, for example, there are arms being dropped by parachute which have to be collected, distributed, stored in safe places, and earmarked for subsequent use. And communications between the groups have to be co-ordinated. There is much more than we can discuss at this stage. But a great deal of organization is involved, and liaison between ourselves and the groups which will eventually operate in the field must be improved.'

Rushworth said: 'I should emphasize that we are not asking you to become a soldier. We shall have military men over there when the times comes, but the fighting will be done by the French, in groups which will hit the Germans where they least expect it, with British leadership and help where appropriate.'

She stared back at him and said quietly: 'I am French. If I am there I shall fight. For my mother and my husband.'

Rushworth's stiff face cracked into the ghost of a smile.

'We are told you were the right person,' he said. 'I'm sure you are.'

'Who told you?'

'Your name emerged,' Granby said vaguely, 'from your husband's files. You'll appreciate that they had to be detailed, in view of the work he was doing latterly. Someone noted that you were born in France of a French mother.'

'That did not tell you I am what you describe as the right person.'

'Of course not. But it led to further inquiries.'

'So who told you I was the right person?'

Granby stood up. He walked to a window sill, moved the drawn curtains aside a little, and picked up a cigarette box. She shook her head when he held it out, so he passed a cigarette to Rushworth and took one for himself. All the time she watched him.

He flicked a lighter and said through a smoke cloud: 'It was deduction.'

She eyed him, then watched Rushworth lighting his own cigarette. She brushed away a wisp of fair hair which had waved across her forehead and said: 'Deduction, Mr Granby? Or the result of an opinion expressed by Hugo Thoresen?'

Rushworth was still. Granby sauntered back to his chair and settled.

'Who is Hugo Thoresen, Mrs Tamworth?' Curiosity; nothing more.

'If you don't know, and I am mistaken, there is no harm done,' she said. 'But I think you do know. Don't lie to me, please. If I found later that you had lied about this, I would suspect that other things might be lies. I need to trust you, just as you need to trust me.'

The two men exchanged glances. Something seemed to pass between them; a flicker of agreement.

'It is not our habit to discuss others,' Granby said easily. 'But we know you are a past acquaintance of Hugo Thoresen's. We know he assisted you in your escape from France, and we know of his friendship with your family before the war. It shouldn't surprise you, therefore, to know that we have consulted him, just as we consulted other people before deciding to put our proposition to you.'

She said: 'I want to know precisely his part in this. Before it goes any further.'

'I'm sorry.' Granby shook his head. 'We can't talk about others in that way, or about how we do things. If you agree to go on with this, I'm sure you will learn a lot more about us. But at present –'

She stood up, the sudden movement interrupting him. They both watched her, expressionless.

'Then I'm sorry, too – that I can't go on. You're not being honest with me. You're asking me to volunteer for very dangerous work, yet you won't tell me the background. So I can't feel confident that in the future you will tell me everything else I want to know.' She picked up her handbag. 'I'm flattered that you should have thought I could do – whatever it is you want doing. Thank you for your courtesy. Will you show me out, please?'

She went, the two men stiff and polite, Rushworth showing her to the door. When he came back Granby had turned out the light in the room and had drawn back the curtains. As Rushworth joined him at the window he nodded down to the street.

'Definitely a girl of unusual calibre.' He held his cigarette behind his back so that the red tip of light should not show at the window. Granby was always careful about details.

They watched her shadow disappear in the blacked-out street. A passing car's masked headlights illuminated her figure for a moment. Then she was gone.

Rushworth said: 'Thoresen was right. She would be a great asset. He won't be pleased.'

Granby shook his head, and drew the curtains.

'He said there might be a problem,' he said in the darkness. His cigarette glowed as he raised it to his mouth. 'She feels we weren't honest with her; I feel he hasn't been entirely honest with us. I'd better have another talk with him. Then he'll have to decide what to do next. Or maybe he'll leave it to the chief.'

*

It was the day before Christmas Eve. Michele walked quickly towards Parliament Square among the five o'clock crowds, her coat collar turned up against a cold wind, a scarf around her hair. Several people kept pace with her and she did not glance at the man beside her until he spoke.

'Mrs Tamworth, I'm a colleague of Major Rushworth. He would like to have another talk with you.'

She kept walking, glancing quickly sideways at the man. He was short, casually dressed, insignificant; perhaps fifty years old, with a drooping moustache.

'I don't think there is anything I want to talk about with Major Rushworth,' she said.

'He asked me to say he had some new information for you.'

'Than why doesn't he come himself to give it to me?' A bus rumbled past, and she raised her voice above its noise.

'I have a car here,' the man said. 'I'm sure you would find it worth just a little of your time to hear what he has to say. Afterwards we'll take you to wherever you want to go.'

She walked on, staring straight ahead, the man beside her. In the darkened street, lit only by the masked lights of passing vehicles and a pale half moon over the river, they bumped shoulder-to-shoulder with others on the pavement. Once the man was obstructed and dropped two or three paces behind her, but he caught up again. Then she nodded.

'All right. Half an hour only.'

The man said: 'Good. I'm sure you won't regret it.' He took her elbow and steered her towards the pavement edge, raising his other hand. A car which had been crawling against the curb just behind them came alongside. The man opened the rear door, followed her into the back, and the driver turned out into the traffic.

'Where are we going?' she asked.

'Not very far. Only ten minutes or so.'

She was silent then, realizing she would get no more information, and watched; expecting the car to turn towards St James's. But it went on across Trafalgar Square, heading north, then turning off Tottenham Court Road; until she recognized Baker Street tube station. There it stopped and the man got out, holding the door open for her. She followed him into the station entrance, watched him buy an evening newspaper, then allowed herself to be led out of the other side of the station into Baker Street itself. A little way along he steered her through the entrance doors of a big building that might have been flats, up a flight of stairs and along a dimly-lit corridor, and used a key to open a door.

The room was a sparsely-furnished office: just two large

filing cabinets, a cupboard, and a wide desk on which there were three telephones. A dark-haired girl looked up from the desk, then came to her feet. She glanced quickly at the man who nodded, and came forward, smiling.

'Hullo. I'm Anne Henshaw-Reid. You're Michele Tamworth.'

Michele nodded. They shook hands formally. When she looked round her escort had gone.

The dark-haired girl said: 'Major Rushworth hoped you would come. Do take off your coat. It's quite warm in these offices.'

Michele slipped out of her coat, shook her hair free from the scarf, and watched as the girl took them to an old-fashioned coat-hanger beside a second door before going back to the desk, picking up a telephone and saying: 'Your visitor is here.' Then she nodded to the second door and said in her pleasant, friendly voice: 'He's waiting. Will you go in?'

She went into an office bigger than the first but similarly furnished, and saw Hugo Thoresen slide the drawer of a filing cabinet closed and turn to face her.

She stood still, staring, silent. He inspected her openly: her hair, her face and her clothes. Then his mouth widened slightly and he inclined his head in casual greeting.

'In the circumstances you look remarkably well. I am pleased to see you again. It's just three and a half years, do you realize?'

He came away from the cabinet, around the desk, and held out a hand. She took it briefly.

'I knew you had something to do with this, Hugo.' She looked around, selected a chair and perched on the edge of it without waiting for his invitation. 'Why did you have to use Major Rushworth as bait?'

He raised his eyebrows, feigning surprise.

'As bait? My dear girl, I assure you he would not appreciate that description. He's here, and he wants to see you. But I wanted to see you first. He told me you had asked about me. I was flattered.'

'You were foolish to think I would not have detected your influence,' she said. She sat erect, pale as she had been ever since Alan's death, her head up and her eyes challenging him. 'But it must have been difficult for you. I'm sure you knew I would not even have discussed the proposition if I had known at the beginning that it came from you.'

Again the raised eyebrows.

'You over-estimate my authority.' His voice was smooth and confident. 'The proposition came from someone much more important than I. There – you have an admission – an acknowledgement that there are a few more important than I.' His bearded face was devoid of humour, although his deep-set eyes shone. 'I am merely an adviser, an intermediary, a talent-spotter. And you have much talent for our peculiar work, Michele. You can render distinguished service to the countries to which you owe allegiance. And you can avenge your husband's tragic death. I have not expressed my regrets over that. I am truly sorry. You and I have had our misunderstandings, but I wished you nothing but happiness. One day I'm sure you'll find it again, even if that seems unlikely to you at the moment.'

She said stiffly: 'The future holds little attraction for me. I don't want to talk about it. But thank you. He and I were very happy, for the short time we had.'

He leaned back in his chair. He had put on weight since she had last seen him in 1940, and it showed.

'Then carry on the fight for him.' He said it softly, and his eyes seemed to recede into their deep sockets, yet still reflected bright lights. 'When Europe is liberated, the battles will be won by men who face the enemy from the front and by others who rise up at their backs. Our business is to ensure that that secondary force is efficient. Your husband knew that and did not hesitate to work towards it. You, his wife, can make an even greater contribution – and know that you are avenging him.' He leaned forward. 'And don't forget your mother, Michele. Germans killed her, too. Right beside you. You fought back then – you told Granby about picking up a rifle and fighting back. We can give you the chance to fight back for both of them, far more devastatingly.'

She retorted: 'You're contemptible, Hugo. You're trying to recruit me by playing on my emotions. I shall need far greater motivation than revenge, much as I loved Alan –'

'Playing on your emotions?' He interrupted her, sharp-voiced now. 'You rebuke me for that, when you are allowing your emotions to dictate your rejection of us? Ask yourself why you said "no" to Granby and Rushworth. Because you were afraid? Because you didn't want to avenge Alan? No – because you thought I was the prime mover and emotion prejudiced your mind. Because you still suspect me of un-worthy motives which were themselves ascribed to me un-worthily. Because you still resent having had to accept my assistance when you left France. Pride and prejudice, my dear Michele. We are all subject to it. Currently it dominates your reasoning. If you are not careful it may cost you the chance to render the most distinguished service to Britain and to France.'

'You're wrong, Hugo.' She shook her head angrily. 'If I refuse it will be because I don't trust you. You are evasive, subversive, ulterior; a plotter and a manipulator. You once called yourself a fixer. It suits you. But you're not going to fix me, or manipulate me.'

'I am simply a cog in a marvellous machine,' he snapped back. 'Whatever you do will be for the service, not for me. Whatever influence I may have is subject totally to the judge-ments and decisions of others. Whether you trust me or not is immaterial. You must decide if the whole is trustworthy, and sufficiently distinguished.'

She was quiet then, studying him and the way he crouched forward over the desk, his eyes sharp and penetrating; then how he leaned back so that his increasing girth showed and the old egoism smoothed his face and the old mockery sparked deep in his half-hidden gaze. And he watched the strange proud courage in every line and every curve of her face, and the slender neck and the hair shining around it, and felt her presence as a charisma which was almost touchable.

Quietly she told him: 'Once you said to me "Let me get you out of hell before the gates close". Do you remember? Why do you want to send me back again?'

'Because now you can carry the weapons to break down the gates from the inside.' His voice was little more than a whisper; but passionate, dedicated, obsessive. 'You would not be going back to hell. You would be going back to havens we have built in hell, from which you could work to destroy it. Once, when the gates closed behind us in 1940, they were impenetrable. But not any more. They are rotting below ground. You can help to tear them down.'

'And what are my chances of survival?' Her whisper matched his in its intensity.

The question jolted him, as if he had not expected to hear it so directly. Then, as quickly, he relaxed, confidence restoring him.

'It's dangerous,' he said. 'We could not pretend otherwise. If you are caught you will be shot, or worse. You will learn all about that in your training. Nothing will be hidden from you. And you can back out at any time. No one will be told if you do. You will simply go back to your desk at the War Office after having been detached for special duties which will remain unspecified and secret. Now –' he put his hands on his desk and pushed himself away from it and upright '– David Rushworth is in Anne's office waiting to talk with you. You will find them both friendly and helpful. But first I want to introduce you to the chief. Colonel Buckman is the man we work for, and the man we love to work for. He is not only a leader but an inspiration. If you decide to stay with us, it is he who will make the final decisions about you, and put the final propositions to you.'

She stood up, her face tight-muscled, her eyes intent upon him. She said quietly: 'And if I accept those final propositions, and am successful, who will take the credit, Hugo? You, because I am your protégé?'

He was genuinely shocked by it. For seconds he stood still; angry, then injured, then, rarest of all for Thoresen, confused; until it all died away and he was controlled again and said: 'Protégé? I may have taught you something, but you flatter me. Once I may have moulded you a little, when you were still young enough to be pliable. But now – now you are mistress of yourself. I am, let us say – your servant.'

2

In the first week of the New Year they sent her to Wanborough Manor in Surrey to learn, in beautiful surroundings, the art of handling explosives, pistols and sub-machine guns. For a time she was unhappy with the modern, compact, plastic explosives, but handled the Thompson sub-machine gun well, and was among the best of the twelve agents under training there when it came to pistol practice in the cellar ranges and the darkened corridors in which target models jumped from hidden recesses and had to be shot down.

They sat in small groups in the lofty rooms of the great house, listening to instructors who included agents who had already spent time in German-occupied territory, watching films shot secretly in France and Holland, learning the tricks of successful operators and the fatal mistakes of others, and the security methods adopted by the police and Gestapo. All the time they were watched and questioned by psychologists; and frequently Major David Rushworth was with her and with two other trainees, for he was the Conducting Officer responsible for their control and welfare throughout their training and assessment.

Michele grew to like him. He was humourless at first, but gradually he relaxed with her and she found herself talking freely with him. She did not know that each week he reported back to Baker Street on her progress and her state of mind, and that his summaries were studied beside reports from the instructors and psychologists. But she did know that he had spent two months in France on special missions, being landed each time by submarine on the west coast, returning once the same way and once by Lysander, and she respected him the more because of it.

From Surrey she went to Scotland for toughening-up on the hills in forced marches and on an assault course – 'just in case you find you have to take to the country for a time,' Rushworth said, with his cautious smile. And then it was south to Ringway, near Manchester, for parachute training; dropping from scaffolding in one of the hangers to find out what it felt like to hit the ground hard, sliding down chutes and learning to roll on impact, then using a parachute for the first time from a captive barrage balloon. She confessed to Rushworth that the night before her first jump she was afraid. But it was the only time he heard her use the word.

The final training stage was at Beaulieu in Hampshire, the SOE's finishing school. And that was where she saw Thoresen for the first time since their meeting at Baker Street.

She was walking down a corridor in the great old house, talking to Rushworth, when he stopped suddenly at a closed door and said: 'There's someone to see you. In here.'

She knew before she entered the room that it would be Thoresen, and said so. 'Hullo, Hugo. I had a feeling about you.'

He lay back in a leather armchair, smoothing his moustache, studying her. Rushworth flushed, embarrassed because he had not stood up to greet her.

'Close the door, David,' he said. 'And pour us something to drink.' He pointed to a small cocktail cabinet. His gaze switched back to Michele. 'I'm told you're doing very well. But I expected that.'

'I'm sure you would have been personally affronted if I had not,' she said. She walked to a chair and sat down, regarding him coolly. He thought the training had given her added confidence, as if she had found an extra barb for her personal armoury.

'Unquestionably. But I came to talk about the future. This

274

is really your last opportunity to change your mind about the whole thing.'

She was watching Rushworth pour a gin and tonic for her. When she took it she said, 'Thank you,' and studied it critically. Thoresen thought she was deliberately keeping him waiting for her response.

Then she looked at him and said: 'I have changed my mind, Hugo.'

He was still, the fingers which had been smoothing his beard arrested. Across the room Rushworth paused, holding a glass he had been about to pass to Thoresen.

'Indeed? I had not expected that.' Smooth and quiet. He held out a hand for his drink, but his eyes did not leave her. 'I thought your nerve would hold. How disappointing.'

She tasted her drink. Her face was a study in control; aloof, almost contemptuous.

'I'm sorry about it,' she said. 'But I've decided I don't want to be a courier. Communications between the resistance groups are vital. But their function is sabotage. Communications are merely a means to an efficient end. There are plenty of people in France who can look after that.'

Rushworth came to life again, pouring his own drink, sampling it. A hint of a smile curved his hard mouth, as if he knew what she was about to say.

'They haven't had the advantage of training,' Thoresen said curtly. 'We need your special skills.'

'No, Hugo.' She shook her head. 'The people you need most out there are trained saboteurs. There may be many enthusiastic operators in France, causing a lot of trouble already to the Germans. But none of them, except your own agents, have had my training with explosives and in field operations. I've been told again and again that a woman has one advantage – somehow the Germans are less inclined to suspect her than they would a man, even now. I can use that advantage much more effectively if I'm handling explosives than if I'm just running messages. If I go, that's what I do.'

He raised his eyebrows, suddenly angry.

'This is a military operation. You cannot decide what you will do. If you go at all, you'll follow instructions to the letter, whatever they may be –'

'I'll follow them as long as they tell me that I join an operational sabotage group,' she snapped back. 'If they don't, I don't go.'

He looked across at Rushworth; then back again, his eyes hooded. Then, visibly, he relaxed further into his chair, and nodded as if pleased with a private thought.

'Your reaction is exactly what I had expected,' he said. He waved a hand imperiously. 'It is worthy of you. You take advantage of your position. But it pleases me. You see, my dear, I came here today to discuss just that change of plan with you. This is an unusual course for us. We have previously sent women saboteurs over there, but very few, very few indeed. We do not like to put women so far into the front line. We still have some sense of gallantry and courtesy. But all the reports which have reached us about you point one way – that you are best suited, tempermentally and physically, to the role you seek. Your own reaction merely demonstrates that we were right.'

She stared at him, not troubling to disguise her astonishment.

'Hugo, you are incorrigible.' She sounded too surprised even to be angry. 'And impertinent. You translate everything into evidence of support for your own contentions. No one is to be allowed initiative, unless you have previously fashioned it. Please don't insult me so.'

He sat up then, pushing himself forward in his chair, clutching his glass, his eyes wide and bright.

'Magnificent,' he breathed. 'Beautiful. You are everything we could have hoped for, and more. You will provide leadership which no group has ever contemplated. They will resent you because you are British, they will resent you because you

276

are a woman; and you will sweep it all aside and they will follow you to the ends of the earth.'

She said: 'Stop it. You are offensive.' She turned to Rushworth. 'David, take me away before I change my mind about everything.' She finished her drink quickly and stood up.

But later, when Thoresen had gone, she sat quietly with Rushworth and said: 'I hate him, for long-gone private reasons. And I hate myself for letting him make me angry. It's as if I feel he's trying to stop me, as if I want to go because I feel he doesn't really expect me to. And that's the worst reason.'

'Why do you want to go?' Rushworth was always looking for motivation. It was part of his job.

'There's nothing left here.' Very quietly; and sadly, as if it were a confession she did not want to make. 'I came with nothing, and I'm left with nothing. I came because I wanted to get away from the Germans. I was afraid of them. When I got here I thought I could make a new life. I did. But it ended. And I'm not afraid any more. Alan taught me that. Maybe I was never really afraid – I just thought I was, because everyone else was. Now I'm going back. And I'm going to prove that I'm as good as Alan.'

Rushworth nodded as if he understood. Again, it was his job to be understanding. 'You don't have to prove that. There's no one to judge you.'

'I'm the judge.' Softly: but with steel at the edges. 'I want to finish it for him. I was happy, and they took it away. My father fought the Germans, too. I didn't know him very well. I think he was a brave man. But he didn't fight an evil as great as this. And they killed Alan.'

'So it's revenge. I thought it was. And there's nothing wrong with that.'

Her eyes narrowed at the corners, as if she was considering it. Then she shrugged; a tiny shoulder movement.

'I don't care what you call it. I've decided. It's for Alan.

And my father. And I meant what I told Hugo, I'm not going to spend my time sitting on trains and waiting in hotels for contacts, just to pass on messages and bits of paper. I saw my mother killed, and I wanted to hit back then. I hauled bodies, and bits of bodies, out of ruins in the Blitz. Once my ambulance was blown across a road and overturned. I got out, but two injured children in it didn't. Alan was hitting back for that, but I wasn't. Now he's dead, and it's my turn. That's all.'

Two days later they sent her on an intensive course in self-defence and silent killing. She was given clothes, some of which contained duplicates of French laundry marks, all of which carried labels from French manufacturers. Everything she was to take with her was checked and checked again to ensure that it could not be traced to British sources. And she was taught the structure of operators' cells which minimized the consequences if someone broke under torture – the triangle, under which each person knew the identities of only two others; the rest were numbers or code names. Like the other trainees she was herself already only a code name; she chose Marie-Claire, after her mother; and she met the radio operator who was to go with her, called Leo. She never knew his real name; only that he was French and was born in Nice and had escaped from Marseille to North Africa in 1941, and thence to Britain. In case their initial reception in a plateau area near Draguignan, west of Cannes, went wrong, they were each told the name of a contact in Grasse and another in Fréjus – but different contacts, so that they had four between them but could betray only two if either was caught. And they were given new identities, with all the necessary documentation, right down to birth certificates.

Michele was Mirielle Roux, born in Calais, and a travelling saleswoman for a clothing manufacturer in Lyon who had quietly added her name to his books. A number of shop and warehouse managers in south-east France had already been told to insert details of purchases from her into their records.

At the same time the leaders of Resistance groups in the area had been warned that she would shortly be with them, that she came with special training, and if they gave her full co-operation they would be provided with fresh supplies of arms and explosives.

Rushworth warned: 'The French are tearing themselves apart in the area. Communists – and there are a lot – won't work with non-Communists; they're already disputing with each other over who will lead local government after the liberation; and they're still settling old political scores which should have been forgotten years ago. We badly need a new face and a new authority to bring some of the splinter groups into line if they're to form an effective guerilla force when the real fighting starts. There are several French leaders you can rely on, of which the man known as André is probably the best; but they're still too few. And there's not much time.'

She asked: 'Is the invasion going to be from the south? Is my area so important?'

'I don't know.' He laughed. 'Churchill hasn't told me. You just have to make your own guesses. I wouldn't be surprised if there are several invasions before it's finished. Our instructions are to improve organisation all the way from Nice to Marseille.'

Then on the 25th May he told her: 'You're ready. And it could be in a couple of days, if the weather's right. The messages have been sent and acknowledged.'

*

The four-engined Halifax stood at dispersals on the RAF airfield near Abingdon, engines idling: a black shadow rising twenty feet and more against the last light of the day, a hundred feet of wing spreading against subdued hangar lighting behind.

She had been there for more than an hour, with Rushworth and the man called Leo, talking French exclusively now. They had had a meal of bacon and eggs, and Rushworth had forced along a little casual chatter: enough to avoid awkward silences. Leo was subdued and thoughtful, and Michele offered little to the conversation even if she gave no other sign of tension. Leo's compact radio set was in the aircraft, and they had already been given their automatic pistols.

When they went into the locker room which had been set aside for them, an RAF corporal handed them parachutes and lifejackets, and when he had gone Rushworth said: 'Just one more thing. The pills.' He held out two small packs: one looked like a lipstick tube and, indeed, at one end was just that, the other was a cigarette lighter with a slightly extended base.

They had both seen such containers before, and knew that they concealed cyanide pills. They accepted them in a moment's awkward silence, staring at them.

Rushworth said: 'We've had people who've thrown those things away when they've got to the other side. I had one agent who refused to accept his. I think that attitude's silly. You don't have to use them. But if you have them, at least the choice is yours.'

Leo nodded curtly and slid the lighter into his pocket. Michele looked at her lipstick tube, turning it over between her fingers, then pressed the catch which released the end cap. For a moment she looked down at the pills inside, then nodded.

'I won't throw them away, David. I'll give them back to you one day.'

'I'll look forward to that,' he said. 'Come on. Time to go.'

He led them out to the crew bus, helping them both inside, carrying Michele's parachute pack for her. She did not know how wretched he felt. It was the first time he had sent a woman agent off, and in the preceding months he had become more fond of Michele than he was prepared to admit even to himself. Now he felt depressed and almost humiliated, as if by sending her away on her mission and staying behind himself, he was somehow guilty of cowardice.

When they reached the aircraft the idling engines had stopped and the airfield was quiet. Rushworth introduced them to the pilot, the rest of the crew, and the despatching officer – a Parachute Regiment sergeant who would supervise their exit from the aircraft. Like the rest, he shook hands with them solemnly; then said: 'We've a lot of admiration for people like you. It's a privilege to fly with you.' He looked at Michele, her hair blowing in the night wind, her face pale against the gathering dark, and added: 'Especially with you, ma'am. It's an honour to have a lady on board.'

She said, 'Thank you, sergeant, you're very kind,' and scooped her hair back so that she could slide her helmet on to her head.

Rushworth shook hands with Leo who turned quickly and climbed the steps leading up into the aircraft. When he turned he saw Michele smoothing her hair around the edges of her helmet, and staring back towards the distant black outlines of the airfield's buildings.

He took a step towards her and she said: 'I was just wondering, David – if he's there, somewhere. Watching.'

'Hugo?' He said it very quietly.

'Yes. It would be like him, to be there but not to show himself. Demonstrating that he doesn't care. Pulling the puppet's strings, but out of sight of the audience.'

Rushworth said: 'He's a strange man. I know there's something bitter between you. It's none of my business. But he cares. I promise you that.'

'I'm glad.' She looked round, seeing the ground crew standing at a respectful distance, watching. 'No one likes to feel that there's someone who – doesn't care. Especially –' she glanced quickly at him and let the word die. He was standing hatless, tall against the black shadow of the Halifax's fuselage, subdued lighting on his face. For a moment they were silent, staring at each other.

281

Then she said quietly: 'Don't look like that, David. I'm – going home.'

He nodded, wordless. Then, awkwardly, he shook hands with her; but he used both hands to enclose hers. He said: 'Good luck. And God bless you.' Then he stepped back, settled his uniform cap on his head, and saluted.

She went up the aircraft steps without looking back.

He watched the door closed and the steps taken away. Then, from high in the nose, he heard the pilot's voice call through the open window of the cockpit and one of the port engines turned, coughed, and fired. He moved away, back to the crew bus, said to the WAAF driver, 'Watch-tower, please,' and twisted in his seat so that he could see the outline of the Halifax receding against the night sky as the bus jolted forward.

When he reached the watch-tower he stood for a moment outside, listening to the distant roar of the aircraft's engines as the pilot taxied slowly along the perimeter track. Then he pushed open the door and ran up the stone stairs.

In the control room shielded lights shone yellow pools from above, and cathode ray tubes glowed in response to the rotating aerials which scanned the sky outside. The duty officer, flanked by a sergeant and two WAAF operators, talked briskly to the pilot.

'Cleared for take off, Able George. Cleared for take off.'

Beyond the windows the last glimpse of the day was a deep red shade coming up from the north-west horizon and fading into the sky's blackness and the silver pinheads of the stars. The Halifax's lights were stationary against the red glow, the aircraft's outline just visible at the end of the runway lights.

Against a window at the back of the control room a figure stirred, the low light catching his face and revealing his civilian clothes.

'Good evening, David. How was she?'

Rushworth glanced back, then went on watching the airfield. 'Excellent. Totally in control.'

'Of course. I expected nothing less.' Almost dismissive.

The Halifax was rolling now, accelerating down the runway's line of lights. In the watch-tower the engines snarled, distant but clear, and louder.

'She said she wondered if you were here.' Rushworth raised his voice slightly above the background noise.

'Did you tell her?' They were side by side now, watching the black aircraft.

'No. She didn't actually ask the question. So I didn't have to.'

The Halifax was airborne; and suddenly the runway lights were extinguished. The airfield was dark again, darker than the sky; and the aircraft was gone, with only the receding thunder of its engines to mark its passing.

'Good. It's better that way.' He leaned forward, staring into the night, as if hoping he still might be able to see the aircraft. The engine noise was dying now. Then he turned away and, almost as if to himself, added: 'But it's pleasing that she remembered.'

3

On the edge of the Plain de St Cassien, above Cannes, the farmhouse and its adjoining buildings were black shadows against the gathering night. Toni Aumont pedalled his bicycle along the road from La Bocca between the scattered parasol pines, glad of the cool breeze after the heat of the day; glad, too, of the silence in the rugged country above the town, because it was easier to pick up the sound of any approaching vehicle. He listened all the time, and his eyes watched the road verges, noting the white mist floating out from the shallow valley he had just left, and the silhouettes of trees and rock outcrop against the bronze and deepening purple of the sky.

He could see the farmhouse clearly now. He knew it well. This was the place where meetings were often held when things became too dangerous in the town. And now, at the beginning of June 1944, things were very dangerous. The Germans were jumpy, and the brutalities of the Gestapo and the Milice – the French secret police who co-operated with the enemy – were becoming even more excessive. The Sicherheitsdiest, or SD – the élite group responsible for Nazi intelligence and security, including the Gestapo – had a new senior officer who, with henchmen he had brought with him, virtually held all the towns along the coast hostage against Resistance activities; yet the word had gone out that the Allied invasion of France was not far away, and the secret armies should be ready, wherever they were, north or south.

Tonight's meeting would draw the heads of three Resistance groups together for news of the next arms drop from the RAF. André and the others would be listening to the radio now, ready for the coded sentence in the BBC broadcast from London.

And the girl would be there.

Toni was not happy about that. Women in the Resistance were bad news. Even if they and the men were sensible enough to avoid the risk of sexual entanglements, there were few who could face the torturers if they were caught. The Gestapo could nearly always find a way to make a woman talk. And that increased the risks for everyone else.

But André had said the London message was that she was a trained saboteur and would teach them to use the new explosives currently being dropped by the RAF. She would also draw several of the groups under one leadership – André's. She would be his liaison officer and aide. Toni did not like that. It made her second-in-command. She might be French, but she was still a woman.

He pedalled up the farm track, still listening and watching; but remembering the night she had landed. He had been one of the reception committee. The drop had been perfect; she and her pianist – Resistance jargon for a radio operator – had landed on the rough heath two miles from Draguignan just a hundred yards apart. Marie-Claire and Leo. God only knew what their real names were – or how many other names they had. But it was better that way. André would know the names on their identity papers; but they would be the invention of someone in London. To everyone else they were Marie-Claire and Leo.

Leo had gone to Nice. But the girl had been taken to a shop in one of the narrow, sloping cobbled streets in the old town of Grasse, and that was where she had held her first meeting.

There had been seven men there, under André's direction, with Toni as his senior section leader in the increasingly formal hierarchy of the Resistance groupings. He had sat cross-legged in one corner, gaunt and thin-faced like the rest after months of cruelly-meagre rations as the Germans had cut back food supplies; watching this crisp-voiced French girl who had been sent by the British Intelligence Service. The invasion is coming, she had said – somewhere. London needs everyone to be ready for a cohesive attack on German communications and services when the word comes; and wants more information sent back by people like Leo on new fortifications along the coasts as the Germans get ready for the attack.

There was plenty to tell about that. Germany's slave labour force, the so-called Todt Organization, had several hundred men working between Nice and Fréjus, and another lot further along the coast beyond St Tropez. Many of them were desperate, pitiful objects, a half-starved conglomerate of nationalities mostly from Eastern Europe. There was one camp he knew about particularly: most of the men were Russians – Mongols and Europeans; plus Poles and Hungarians. And all were the sad dregs of humanity. It was some sort of punishment camp, Toni thought; a sort of mobile concentration camp. Typical of the bastard Germans.

He leaned his bicycle against the wall of a barn and whistled softly, two notes; a pause, then the same notes in reverse. They came back to him, as a faint echo. Then a man materialized from the shadows, a Mauser machine pistol in his hand.

'Toni. You're the last. And you're late, as usual.'

'You've walked fifty yards from the house. I've cycled three miles up hill,' Toni muttered, without acrimony.

The man slapped him on the shoulders as he walked past, along the barn wall, and through a small door. Beyond was a sacking curtain, and beyond that five men sat on the straw-strewn floor. The girl leaned against the frame of a plough. Two oil lamps flickered and spiralled acrid smoke. In the corner a radio played quiet music.

The men murmured greetings and one said: 'Coming up to news time, Toni. No message after the last news, that we heard. But the jamming is heavy.'

The girl, obviously interrupted by his entrance, said: 'If they've done a lot more in the way of under-water booby traps east of Antibes, we need to know something about it: what

286

sort of explosives, whether they're contact-fired or controlled electrically from elsewhere.'

'I've two men working on it,' André growled. He was big, powerful, black-haired, with a dark fuzz growing along his arms and up from the open neck of his shirt. He had been a Resistance leader since the Italians had been replaced by the Germans in the area more than a year ago and his wife had been one of the victims of the first SS purge. He had escaped because he had been down in Marseille at the time, and for some strange reason he had not been molested when he had returned.

'Let's see how fast they can get us something to pass on to London,' she said. 'Now let's have a look at the drawing of the railway cutting. If we can cut the line there and near the bridge outside Golfe Juan, both at the same time, we can delay reinforcements moving either way for days.'

Toni's eyes brightened in the yellow lights.

'When, Marie-Claire? When do we do that?'

'When we're told to,' she said. 'It's risky and it could produce reprisals, so we don't do it until other people ask for it. Then we do it very thoroughly. Right, André?'

The big man grinned and nodded.

'We'll do it thoroughly,' he said. Toni could tell by the way he looked at her that there was already an understanding between them; and that was a tribute to the girl, for André did not take easily to strangers, and particularly female strangers. 'I've had a look at the cutting myself. If we set the charges right we can produce a rock fall.'

He pulled a sheet of brown paper from his pocket, unfolded it and smoothed it out on the floor, and began to point out salient features of the drawing on it. They talked for several minutes about German patrols and the times of trains, especially the armoured train with an 88mm gun on a flat car in the middle, which came up from Italy every night. That was the one they wanted, deep in the cutting so that the gun could not be used.

Toni watched the girl. She wore a cotton skirt and blouse and a rough woollen jacket over her shoulders. She looked like any poor woman out of the town – except that her face showed no sign of the privations which had marked everyone since the turn of the year. He thought that might be a give-away if a sharp-eyed Gestapo agent caught sight of her. He wished London had not sent a woman. If the Gestapo got this one, they'd make her talk. He had to admit to himself that there was something about her eyes and her manner which said she was tough and capable, even though her figure and her face were enough to make any man look at her twice. But being tough and capable were not enough, if you were a woman; not if those bastards got her. London must be ruthless, he thought, to send a woman like this one. He wondered what her background was; then, with the rest, turned to look at the radio as an announcer's voice declared: 'Ici Londres. Ici Londres.' And the morse-coded V was tapped out.

They sat in silence, listening to the news, RAF and American Air Force raids, the battles in Italy, the Russians advancing, the bitter Japanese war. But no hints of invasion moves. Then came the messages, meaningless to anyone who did not know the codes. As soon as they started the jamming increased, distorting the voice. But the radio was powerful and the aerial in the roof of the barn had been expertly erected, and they could still hear the sentences they waited for: 'Marie has a heavy load. It weighs twelve kilos.'

André grinned at them all, his big shoulders hunching.

'That's it. A heavy load for Marie.' He winked at the girl. 'And twelve is the Valbonne dropping zone. No other figure means one o'clock.' He looked at the pocket watch he dragged from his trousers. 'We'll just make it in good time. Toni, Albert – pick up Louis and his team. Let's start.'

Toni looked at the girl and said: 'Are you coming, Marie-Claire?'

'No.' Her eyes met his confidently. No hint of apology. 'It's not my job. You've done this before. I'd be a passenger.'

'And you'd be taking a stupid risk,' André snapped. His black eyes were hard on Toni. 'London didn't send her here to take her chance with a reception committee. She'll take enough risks before we're all much older.'

Toni shrugged. 'I just wondered.' He went out through the sacking curtain and the small door. The guard with the Mauser was still outside.

*

Three days later the massive Allied invasion of Normandy was the trigger for sabotage all over France. In the North it was organised; carefully planned to back up the invading armies. But in the south it was an instinctive, undisciplined reaction to the news that British and American troops were back in France. There were no instructions from London or North Africa, so local groups surged out into the night with long-hidden guns and explosives; and paid dearly for their intemperance as the German army took merciless reprisals.

The group led by André Matthieu known in the London codes as the Seaside group, had the advantage of a strong leader who forbade any activity he had not sanctioned; and for the time being he would agree to nothing unless it was part of a widely co-ordinated plan. Michele had no difficulty in persuading him that it was better to wait until the word came from London or the gathering Free French forces under General Giraud in North Africa.

Then Leo, still operating north of Nice, sent a courier to her with the news that the cue for maximum activity to disrupt the transport of German reinforcements from the south to the north would be the code sentence: 'Put the cork back in the bottle'.

It came a week after the Normandy landings had begun.

*

André said: 'There'll be pitched battles if we go for the bridge at Golfe Juan, because the guards have been doubled and trebled. But there are two stretches of railway line where there's tree cover all around, and one is through that cutting where there could be a rock fall. Here.' He pointed to his map. 'And here. There'll be patrols out all along the coastal line, but they haven't concentrated at those two places. There'll be shooting, but so far they haven't had anything there except small arms.'

'You've twenty-one men,' Michele said. 'Split them in two groups. You take one, I'll take the other.'

He stared down at her, scowling. He was not used to women making decisions like that; or considering themselves his equal. But he had already learned to expect nothing less from her.

'If that's what you want. Toni, you go with her. You know the cutting well. That's yours.' He looked at Michele again. 'And don't take risks you don't have to take. You don't need to prove anything to me.'

She said quietly: 'I won't take risks others haven't taken before me.' But when he raised his eyebrows, not understanding her, she shook her head and concentrated on the map.

*

The Mistral had blown up heavy clouds and the night was densely dark beneath the pines. They could not have wished for anything better as they filtered silently through the trees towards the cutting: Toni on one side of the line with four men, Michele on the other side with five. The patrols had been watched and timed for three nights, and unless they changed their pattern there was a gap of exactly eight minutes when a two hundred metre stretch of line would be unobserved by the guards. That would be enough for Michele and two men to scramble down the rocks on one side and place charges against the rails while two men on the opposite side wedged explosives beneath an overhanging rock which they hoped would split away from the cutting face and add to the damage below. Toni, at the top of the cutting wall, would signal alarms and control the withdrawal.

They lay in the woods, watching the patrols pass on foot along the cutting below; dark shadows, two groups of three men each, with high-powered portable lights which they used intermittently to sweep the cutting and the rock walls overhead. They were vulnerable, and must have known it; but the woods were too dense for regular patrols to be mounted up above, where Michele and Toni crouched with Thompson sub-machine guns slung from their shoulders.

The guards had gone now, the chink and rattle of their boots on the rail bed fading against the sighing wind and rustling, creaking trees. Michele saw a single flash from Toni's hooded torch, responded with her own, then went over the edge on a rope. In daytime the cutting could be climbed easily, but at night and without lights a free descent was dangerous.

She went down, feeling her way, hearing Henri descending close beside her, able to see his outline in spite of the darkness. They reached the bottom almost together, and both unslung bundles of explosives which had been roped to their backs. Above they heard the grunting and scraping of the third member of their party as he scrambled down; then together they moved quickly and fairly quietly to the edge of the track, digging out gaps beneath the rails with the sharp spikes they had brought, placing explosives and detonators, listening to the clinking and scratching of the men operating from Toni's side of the cutting and the sound of the dark trees bending before the restless wind overhead.

Then they had finished, and led wire back to the track side, laying it carefully in the darkness, checking by feel that it was not fouled as Henri unrolled it. He clipped a rope end to his belt, tugged, and began to scramble back up the cutting face, still paying out the wire. Looking up, those below could not see him because the blackness of the overhanging trees was too dense against the night clouds. Nor could they see what was happening on the opposite cutting wall. But there were two ropes, and Michele grabbed the remaining end, pushed it into the hands of the man beside her, and hissed: 'You're next. Go on – now.' When he hesitated she groped for his belt, finding the hook, pulling the rope towards it. So he went, scrabbling and swinging upwards, while she waited for Henri's rope to come snaking back down the rock and held on to the wire to make sure it was not jerked away from the track and the explosives.

She was still waiting when one of the patrols came round the distant bend in the track, two minutes early, a beam of light searching along the rails and the rock walls. Above, Toni saw it too, and flashed his warning – a pointless gesture in the circumstances.

She twisted the Thompson round so that it hung across her waist and began to climb. The patrol, a hundred metres away, came on steadily. Its light was out now, and for seconds she felt her way upwards in the blackness. Then she dislodged a stone and it rolled away down the 60-degree jagged slope, bouncing and rattling, and the light slashed through the night. One of the guards fired indiscriminately and bullets from a machine pistol whined and ricocheted away up the cutting.

Immediately Toni opened fire from his vantage point and the light beam swung along the cutting wall, upwards, as Michele braced herself against the steep slope, wedging her feet between rocks, steadied her own gun, and sent a long burst towards the light and the black area just behind it. The gunfire echoed against the rocks and bullets screeched and bounced. The guards were shouting to each other, and the light was still swinging, then went out and the darkness was even blacker than before. Above, Henri was shouting, 'Marie-Claire – Marie-Claire –' and she scrambled upwards, the clatter of her gun and the scrape of her shoes on the rocks unheard against the numbing gunfire and the whine of the bullets, until she reached the top and suddenly there was silence because the attackers realized there was no longer a response from the track below.

Hands reached for her and steadied her and she panted: 'Flash the signal to Toni. We'll blow the charges. The other patrol will be on its way and radioing for help. We can't wait for the train.'

One of the men found the torch and sent the pre-arranged series of flashes. Immediately there was a response and Michele crouched beside the crude battery box, shouted, 'Now – lie down!' and three seconds later connected the terminals.

*

Toni said: 'You were right. She's good enough.'

André grinned and nodded. He levelled a thick forefinger.

'I told you. I knew as soon as I saw her.'

'She was great that first time, the night we did the cutting. Cool as anyone I've seen. I didn't want her. This job is no work for a woman. But she's different. And since then. That bridge. We just stood by to give covering fire if the guards spotted her. But they didn't hear a thing – until the big bang.' He grinned.

'It's not just the action,' André growled. 'It's organization. We've a proper link now with the Ronde group down at La Lavandou. And she's trying to fix a meeting with that big Maquis gang in the Esterel and beyond, so that we can all operate to a plan.'

'Paul Cardin's maquisards?'* Toni asked. 'They're a dangerous bunch. When the invasion comes we'll be glad of them down here.' His black eyes glittered. 'What's the betting, André? Will the landings be along this coast?'

The big man shrugged his heavy shoulders.

'I don't know. If we're lucky, maybe. It would be great to

* See THE SUCCESSORS

see the bastards on the run, and get out into the open and fight them.' He threw a cigarette to his lieutenant: a German cigarette, taken from a truck hijacked on the Aix road two months before. 'But if we're going to live that long we've got to be very careful. That SD swine Altmann is virtually supreme now, all the way from Menton to the Maures. He's had the Wehrmacht's head of security shot at St Raphael. He can do what he likes. And he's in our area regularly. That's why the Gestapo is getting rougher.'

BRAUNE

—◆◆◆—

1944

1

It started to go wrong when the Gestapo picked up Alain Albert, who lived in Grasse with his wife and three-year-old daughter. His shop, close to the town hall and the former Notre Dame Cathedral, had been used for several meetings, and someone must have talked. By unhappy coincidence SD Major Ernst Altmann was in the town on his way to Cannes. Within two hours Albert's wife and child were found and brought to the room where he stood handcuffed. Altmann, a dapper, fair-haired forty-year-old with light blue eyes and fine features, said to the escorting soldiers: 'Take off their clothes.' He knew the impact upon a man's resolution of seeing his wife and daughter stripped naked by hostile hands. Then he turned to Albert and said in his excellent French: 'Strangers have been seen visiting your shop and staying for long periods. Sometimes at night. I want to know their names, where they come from, why they were there. And I have no time to waste.'

He turned and nodded to a burly sergeant who stood by the door. The sergeant was Karl Braune, Altmann's chauffeur and constant shadow. He turned, opened the door, and barked orders. In came two soldiers, each carrying a long pair of steps. They put them against one wall, ten feet apart, and secured a thick wooden pole between them, almost at ceiling height. By this time the clothes had been torn away from the woman and the child who stood facing Altmann, wide-eyed and terrified, soldiers grasping their wrists.

Altmann's cold eyes stared at the grey-faced Albert. Then he picked up two meat hooks from the desk at which he sat and held them between his hands, their points towards the prisoner.

'Tell me what I want to know, and tell me now, or I'll have one of these driven up under your wife's jaw and into her mouth, and I'll hang her by it from that pole. If you don't talk then, I'll do the same thing to the child. And then you'll stand here and watch them, and listen to them, for as long as it takes them to die. Then if you still haven't talked I'll do the same thing to you and hang you out of the window over the street.' He swung in his chair and a granite-faced junior officer took one of the hooks from him. Two soldiers dragged the twisting, struggling woman to the desk, turned her, and pushed her backwards across it, and Altmann grabbed her hair in both hands and wrenched her head down over the edge of the desk so that her throat was stretched and her jaw jutted upwards. The officer lifted the meat hook with both hands, and the woman began to scream, and then the child's whimpers turned to shrill, piercing screeches.

And Alain Albert, his eyes bulging and sweat streaming down his face, babbled names and places.

Most of the names he knew were code names only and did not help Altmann. But there were two addresses in his hysterical confession, one in Juan Les Pins and the other in Cannes; and at five o'clock in the morning soldiers and police converged on them and took André Matthieu from the one in Juan Les Pins, and two of his Resistance Group from the other. Then one of the security police remembered seeing the big André coming out of a house in Antibes. At seven o'clock they went there and, in a small back room, found a woman whose papers said she was Mirielle Roux.

2

Ernst Altman adjusted the photograph of his wife and two young sons so that the light from the window illuminated it. The photograph was always on his desk, wherever he was; a constant reminder to him of the family who had died in an air raid on Hamburg a year before. Now, on the first floor of the Hotel Montfleury, in the office which was always kept ready for his frequent visits, he pulled a folder towards him and opened it. Without taking his eyes from it he said: 'Cigar, Braune.'

The sergeant who sat on a hard chair beside the door, as he nearly always did wherever Altmann was, rose quickly, produced a cigar case and offered it to his chief. Altmann, still looking at the contents of the folder, took one of the long, thin cigars; then accepted the lighted match which Braune held out.

'Thank you,' he said courteously. He waved a dismissive hand. Braune returned to his chair. He knew his function. Apart from driving the Major's car and carrying his bags, he was a personal attendant and a confidant. He had to sit through hours of Altmann's silences or listen patiently while he debated aloud his latest security problem. Braune had been doing that for eighteen months, ever since he had come back, wounded, from the Russian front. He was frequently sickened by his chief's work and his conduct, but knew that if he asked for a new posting he would be sent back to the east, and he was terrified of that. To a degree he was flattered that such a high-ranking and powerful officer should talk freely to him; although he was intelligent enough to know that, for Altmann, he was often little more than a human mirror before which the SD chief could strut and speak. As long as he remained obedient, impassive in the face of torture and death, and respectfully admiring when Altmann required it, Braune knew his future was reasonably protected; at least until Germany's ultimate defeat.

But in July 1944 Braune was certain that Germany would lose the war. And then he knew there would be ghastly reprisals.

His own hands were clean. He had never been asked to torture or shoot Altmann's captives. It was as if the Major regarded him as inadequate for such duties. But he was Altmann's attendant, and he could not believe he would be excused some responsibility for his ruthless chief's excesses.

Now the British and Americans were established in Northern France; and with the Russians advancing from the east, the Anglo-American armies fighting their way up into Northern Italy, with Corsica and Sardinia in enemy hands and with constant threat of a new invasion somewhere along the Mediterranean coast of France, Karl Braune had no doubt that the days of Hitler, the Nazis and the Third Reich were numbered. This time next year, perhaps, it would all be over. If Altmann and his kind were still alive, they would be facing death in front of firing squads or at the end of the hangman's rope. And with them would go hapless hangers-on like Braune.

He would have to look after himself. Sooner or later he would have to desert, and do it in a way which would prove to the French Underground that he was really on their side. That would be his only hope.

In the meantime he would continue to be Altmann's servant and uncritical confidant.

'Have you seen this, Braune?' Altmann took a photograph from the folder and held it up.

The picture was of a young woman, fair hair waving across her forehead, wide-set eyes, a firm and confident mouth, good features. Very attractive, Braune thought. But he knew who she was, so he said nothing, awaiting his cue.

Altmann said: 'Does she look like a criminal, Braune? Does she look like a terrorist?'

'It's very difficult to tell what people are by the way they look, sir.' Braune, as usual, was cautious.

Altmann nodded. He stuck the cigar into the side of his mouth, wedging it along his teeth so that it slanted upwards. He often smoked like that, especially when he had an audience.

'Of course. But there is frequently something in the eyes, or the set of the lips, which gives away the hardened criminal. This girl betrays no such details. Yet we know she is a criminal, Braune. She has associated with a vicious gang of terrorists. She is linked with the man Matthieu.' He reached for another file and extracted a second photograph. 'Look at that, my friend. Did you ever see a more typical criminal? The vicious eyes, the ruthless mouth, the coarse features. The records show that his wife was executed for terrorism more than a year ago. How he came to be left at large I don't know. Someone will have to account for that.'

'He's obviously a desperate character,' Braune said obediently. 'Has he confessed yet?'

Altmann twisted in his chair to look up at the sergeant.

'Confessed, Braune? Even though you have been with me for so long, you still know very little. But then you have not had the training. No. He has not confessed. And it will be difficult to persuade such a man to confess. He has no relatives we can use as part of the persuasion. And he is the sort of man who regards pain as an honour for his cause.' He took his cigar from his mouth and waved it at the sergeant. 'You were not with me this morning. You would have seen a strong, stubborn, stupid man. He was in great agony, Braune. But he continued to protest his ignorance – in spite of the evidence we already have about him. I fear he will die before he tells us much of value.'

'But it's important that we know more about him, sir,'

Braune said, chanting well-practised phrases. 'The terrorists have to be found, and this man may be an important link.'

Altmann leaned back in his chair. He regarded his sergeant disdainfully.

'There may be better ways, Braune. When one is up against a character like this Matthieu, one has to be far-sighted. I may have made an initial mistake.' He said it as if he did not really think so. 'I started work on the man, knowing that he has been one of the leaders of the terrorists. The other two we picked up in Cannes at the same time were less important – that was obvious after the first interrogation. We shall keep working on them, of course. But I can leave that to subordinates. I decided to concentrate upon Matthieu, assuming that the woman was, like the other two men, of lesser significance. But now I wonder. Do you know one reason why I wonder, Braune?'

'No sir.' The sergeant stood, expectantly, admiringly, beside the desk.

'Because she is intelligent, well educated, and well bred. There is a quality about her which is unusual. And she shows no sign of malnutrition. Isn't that strange these days, Braune?' The cigar came out of the mouth again, and was regarded critically. 'I think it is so strange that, taken in conjunction with her personal qualities which were observed at the first routine interrogation, I wonder if her name is indeed Mirielle Roux.' He swung in the chair suddenly, staring up at the attentive sergeant, his pale eyes bright and piercing. 'I wonder, indeed, if we may have in our hands a full-blown British spy; or at the very least a Frenchwoman who is in close contact with British spies. Now, if that were so, wouldn't it be a valuable prize, Braune?'

The sergeant looked away. The pale eyes always scared him. He concentrated on the photograph on the desk.

'A great prize, sir. And perhaps she would talk more easily than Matthieu.'

Altmann turned. He picked up the photograph and studied it.

'Perhaps. Some women can be very stubborn. But most are a little easier to persuade than men; not least because physiologically they have certain disadvantages, and they know it, and that is a valuable psychological weapon in our hands. I'm sure you understand what these long words mean, Braune.'

He was silent then, staring moodily at the photograph, smoking his cigar rapidly in short, sharp puffs. Braune stared at the back of the rounded head beneath the smooth, fair hair, and wondered what sort of bloody debate was being conducted inside it. He looked back at the photograph and suddenly was desperately, fearfully sorry for the girl.

'Braune.' Altmann was leaning back again, eyes half closed. 'I have a theory about this girl. Female or not, I think she has enough courage to withstand nearly as much pain as the man Matthieu. There is motivation in her face; a secret which I do not understand. I observed it yesterday, when I watched the routine questioning. She acted the innocent; but with pride, Braune. She could be difficult.' He opened his eyes quickly and looked at the sergeant. 'So we must be subtle. Crudities will not suffice in this case. Yet time is pressing. There is evidence that American and British forces are building up in the Mediterranean, which means we could soon be fighting here. Before that happens we must stamp out the terrorists. Otherwise some of us may be shot in the back. Right, Braune?'

'Yes, sir. What sort of subtleties have you in mind, sir?'

'I am not sure. What I do know is that no matter how basically courageous people may be, most have a weak point. If it can be found, they will sometimes submit quite easily. It is a matter of studying character and temperament, Braune. We must study this young woman's character and temperament. And first I must know if she is really French, or if she is British with an excellent command of the French language. The British and the French are different animals, each requiring a different whip. Lieutenant Legrange of the Milice will tell us if she is genuinely French. He is an exceptionally well-educated Frenchman. He also speaks English tolerably well. At Mademoiselle Roux's initial interrogation – when, you will recall, upon my instructions she was not harmed – I remained a spectator. She does not know who I am, or that I speak French quite reasonably. Initially she will remain in ignorance, and we shall see how we progress. How is your French these days, Braune?'

'Much improved, sir. I have been studying hard. So that I may be more useful as your aide, sir.'

The pale eyes surveyed him.

'Very wise. And it will enable you to reach your own conclusions as you watch what is about to take place. You will find it interesting.'

An hour later he was still behind his desk. But now he had been joined by the Milice lieutenant, a tall, sallow-skinned young man in the black uniform of his force; and by two guards, one weighing around 250 pounds and standing well over six feet in height, with heavy jowls and a permanent scowl, the other much smaller with a narrow, expressionless face. The big man had a black rubber cosh hanging from his wrist, the smaller carried a black leather whip coiled in one hand.

Sergeant Braune opened the door in response to a knock, and Michele was pushed into the room by a soldier. She wore a grey cotton skirt and a blue jacket over a crumpled yellow blouse, and her hair was untidy; but her pale face was unmarked.

When she hesitated, looking around the room, the soldier pushed her again and she almost lost her balance. Behind the desk the blue eyes glittered and Altmann barked in German: 'When I want you to treat the prisoner roughly, I'll tell you, soldier.'

The man flushed, drew himself up stiffly, and clicked his heels. Michele walked slowly towards the desk and the empty chair in front of it. She looked at the two guards and their weapons, but her face betrayed nothing. She stood facing Altmann and Legrange, and the Frenchman said in his own language: 'Sit down, Mademoiselle. You must answer questions. The German commandant does not speak French, so I shall act as interpreter.'

Michele sat on the edge of the chair. She stared angrily at Legrange.

'Then start by asking him why I have been arrested. I have not been charged with any offence. I have been told nothing. I have not been given a chance to show that I have nothing to hide.'

Legrange translated; Altmann spoke quietly, almost casually; Legrange said in French: 'The Commandant says that you are not here to ask questions. You are here to answer our questions. That is the best way for you to establish your innocence.'

At the back of the room Braune listened and watched. Legrange started the interrogation with questions about the prisoner's birthplace, her upbringing, her parents, her schooling; went on to talk about her work, her friends, the time she had spent in the Département and at the address where she had been found. The answers came quickly, quietly, firmly; and Altmann listened carefully to the Milice Lieutenant's translations as if he had not understood a word of the French conversation, and responded briskly but never threateningly. Whether or not the girl spoke German, Braune thought, she must get the impression that the Commandant was a reasonable man. But then he knew that Altmann was an accomplished actor; to the extent that even he, his servant and companion, was often unable to decide if he really knew the genuine Ernst Altmann, the inner man behind the pale-eyed facade.

It went on for half-an-hour, until without warning, the Lieutenant said: 'Your answers are most convincing, Mademoiselle. But I know you are a liar.'

The first sentence was in French. The second was in English.

The girl was still, staring at him. Her hands were clasped

in her lap; Braune could see that her knuckles were white.

'I recognise the English language when I hear it,' she said, 'even though I do not understand it. Why did you speak to me like that? What did you say?'

If she's acting, I'll eat my boots, Braune thought. That was as good a trick as I've heard. And it was a waste of time. She just didn't understand.

Legrange looked at Altmann.

'May I speak with you privately, Herr Major?'

Altmann nodded, stood up, and Braune leapt to his feet and opened the door. The two men went out, Braune closed the door quietly, and sat down again. No one else moved.

For ten minutes there was silence in the room. All the time the girl sat quietly in front of the desk, eyes down, fingers locked. Braune noticed that her knuckles were no longer white. She seemed to be relaxed; as if she had not grasped the danger she was in.

Then Altmann came back, alone. He moved briskly across the room to Michele's side, paused, and extended one hand. His forefinger and thumb took her chin and turned her head so that she looked up at him. For seconds he held her like that, staring at her with his pale blue eyes; then abruptly he released her and walked to his chair.

'Do you speak any German, Mademoiselle?' he asked in his own language.

She blinked at him, as if struggling with the memory of words. Then, haltingly, she replied: 'A little, Major. But badly. I understand more than I speak.'

He nodded, and said in fluent French: 'That is not unusual. So it is as well that I speak your language. From now on we shall use it.'

Her eyes opened wide, and anger tightened her face.

'Then why have we just had that charade with the Milice Lieutenant? Why did you have everything translated –'

He held up a hand to silence her.

'Mademoiselle, you must stop asking questions. Only I have

that privilege. My questions – your answers. And I have the means to encourage your co-operation. Some are elsewhere. But you must realise how effective the most basic could be.' He nodded curtly to the fat man. 'Show her.'

The fat man left his place against the wall. He was quick and quiet on his feet. When he reached Michele he held the black cosh in front of her face. She stared at it, then looked up at him. His thick lips parted in an obscene grin and the heavy flesh creased beneath his eyes and around his jaw. Then he jerked the cosh as if to strike her. She flinched, closing her eyes. He waited until she opened them; then whirled and hammered the cosh down on the edge of the desk. Michele's nerves jolted her body.

'Imagine what that would do to your pretty face, Mademoiselle.' Altmann's voice was gentle in the stillness. 'Or to the bones in your legs and arms and hands.'

He nodded again, and the fat man's place was taken by the thin man. He stood in front of Michele, caressing the thong of the whip. It was four feet long, thin plaited leather tapering to a single strand. He let it dangle, drawing it slowly across her thighs. His face was wax-like, expressionless. But his eyes stared into hers; until his stare shifted, down to her shoulders, her breasts, her stomach and her legs. Then he stepped back and raised the whip as if to lash her, and cracked it at his side. The sound was like a thin pistol shot. Michele blinked, once.

Altmann's voice said: 'If I allowed him to do so, he would strip you and suspend you by a rope around your wrists, with your feet off the ground, before he started to work.' He sounded indifferent; an academic explanation.

The thin man went back to his place, coiling the whip. Michele said: 'Why are you threatening me? You tell me not to ask questions, but you don't tell me what you want. I've nothing to hide, but you don't give me a chance to show you that.' Her head was up, and from his place by the door Braune recalled Altmann's reference to her pride.

Altmann said: 'I want you to see your position realistically.

I am going to ask you many questions. It is essential that you answer quickly and truthfully, otherwise we shall force the answers from you. The cosh and the whip are only the start of the process. Come with me.'

He nodded dismissal to the two threatening figures against the wall, snapped, 'Braune – guards – escort her,' and marched from the room.

They went along the corridor in a line: Altmann followed by Braune alongside Michele, the two guards behind. As they went Braune contrived to glance at her without making it obvious to the guards, but she looked straight ahead. He thought she was unnaturally pale, but otherwise showed no apprehension.

They climbed two flights of stairs and Altmann opened a door. Beyond was a small vestibule and another door: before the war probably the entrance to a high-priced suite. He opened the second door and Michele moved to follow him. Then she stopped, but the two guards closed on her, hustling her forward. Braune heard her breath hiss between her teeth.

The room was twenty feet square. It contained an electric oven with rings on top, a large bath with poles above it and straps hanging from them, a square metal frame the height of a man with ropes looped at the four corners, a small table carrying surgical instruments and several bottles, a hook in the ceiling from which a rope dangled; and a large metal table in the centre.

On the table, wrists and ankles strapped down, was André Matthieu.

He was naked, there were streaks of blood across his body and a pool of blood on the floor, and his face was distorted by bruisings and swellings. His mouth, rimmed with blood, was open and his breathing was shallow and rapid. He seemed to be unconscious. Two pale-faced men in civilian clothes, jacketless, stood beside the table.

Altmann said coldly: 'If common sense does not produce the answers we need, and the whip and cosh are insufficient, this room is the next stage in the unhappy process. Few come out of here without telling us the truth, quickly. This man is stubborn. But you know him, so I'm sure you would expect that.'

Michele was still and straight between the guards. Her pale face seemed to shrink, and became grey. It took her several seconds to reply. Then she whispered: 'I don't know him. But – what have you done to him?'

Altmann's mouth widened into what might have been the hint of a smile, as if the gesture would somehow reduce the horror.

'I won't distress you with the details, Mademoiselle. We have persuaded him to tell us things. But he knows more. After I have spoken with you I shall supervise the next stage of his interrogation. If he does not answer my further questions, we shall inject acid into his urethra and bladder.' He looked at her and his smile faded. 'Unless you tell us what we want to know. That would save both of you a great deal of suffering.'

He turned abruptly and walked out of the room. The guards moved up on either side of her, but she was rigid, staring at the big man on the table. And as she did so his eyes opened. His head was on one side so that he looked straight at her. And the black eyes glittered with a ferocity and courage which was unmistakable. She, and the watchful Braune, were the only ones to see it.

Then the guards took her out, and Braune closed both doors and followed the others down to the lower floor.

Back in his own room Altmann dismissed the guards and settled behind his desk. Michele took the chair in front of it.

'I'm sorry you lied to me,' Altmann said. 'That was not a good start. The man upstairs is well known to you. He has told me so. And also he was seen by the security police visiting the house in which you were found. Indeed, that was how we found you.'

She stared at him. Her face was still ashen, and her fingers, locked together on her knee, were strained.

'It doesn't matter who he is. It's – dreadful. To see a man like that.' Her voice was husky. 'Please – may I have a drink of water?'

'Of course. There is no hurry, Mademoiselle.' He waved a hand to Braune. 'We have much to talk about, and plenty of time. I'm sorry it was necessary to demonstrate to you so graphically just how serious your situation is.'

When Braune came back with a glass of water she took it in both hands. For an instant her eyes met his, and he saw shock still lurking in them. Again he felt sorry for her. Braune was old-fashioned about these things. He thought war was for men, and that somehow women should be protected from it.

She sipped the water; then straightened in the chair as if disciplining herself.

'I am sorry, Major. I am not used to seeing men who have been tortured. I am surprised that the proud German army should descend to such bestialities.'

'Armies, by their nature, are violent,' Altmann said. 'They become more violent when they are threatened not only by the enemy they can see but by secret and subversive enemies – terrorists who kill in the night and who plot with the enemy to destroy the new world which Germany is seeking to establish. Most French people welcome that new world. We are dealing with only a handful of extremists who still resist. Why are you associating with such people, Mademoiselle?'

She shook her head quickly.

'I don't know what you mean.'

'The man upstairs was seen visiting your house – and he is a well-known terrorist. Why do you deny knowing him?'

'There are many houses where I live, close together and confusing. Your police have been mistaken. He must have been visiting another house.'

'Then why does he say he knows you?'

'He cannot have said that.' Abruptly she was angry, the

colour coming back to her face. 'Unless your tortures have made him agree to anything, just to save himself from further pain.'

Altmann raised a hand; said sharply: 'Cigar, Braune.' Then his voice softened. 'You are foolish. We know much more than you think. For example, I know you are not French. What is your real name?'

Braune appeared at his side, and Altmann selected a cigar from the case offered by the sergeant. He accepted a light, too; but not for an instant did his pale eyes leave the face of the girl beyond the desk.

She said steadily: 'My name is Mirielle Roux, and I am French.'

He inhaled smoke; then blew it out in a thin stream.

'Lieutenant Legrange does not think so. He tells me there is a subtlety in your accent which only a well educated and extremely sensitive French ear might detect but which betrays some foreign influence. And he believes that influence might be English.'

'I am not English.' She snapped the words at him. 'I was born in France and I am as French as anyone in this town.'

He wedged his cigar in the side of his mouth.

'We shall see. I have sent for someone who knows Calais. And someone else who knows Lyon. They will question you about both, since you say you were born in one and know the other well.'

'I do not say I know either well,' she retorted. 'I was born in Calais but only have childhood memories of it. I visited Lyon to get a job. Send for someone who knows Cambrai and Arras.'

'You argue confidently. That means you know those towns. Why did you not mention them in your initial interrogation?'

'Because I was not asked.' She leaned forward. Braune thought she was showing remarkable spirit. He would not have been able to face Altmann's pale blue eyes so aggressively. But then he knew Altmann very well. 'I know you are trying to frighten me. Well, I am not frightened. But I am confused – too confused to be able to anticipate the things which interest you.'

Altmann took his cigar from his mouth, put his elbows on the desk, and rested his chin on his clasped hands. Except for his eyes, he looked friendly and relaxed.

'You are not afraid? I believe you. You are an unusually brave woman. And you will have no need to be afraid if you talk to me as honestly as I talk to you. Let's see if we can remove some of this confusion which troubles you. When did you first meet André Matthieu?'

She said: 'I don't know him. Who is he?'

Altmann raised his eyebrows, as if in good-humoured surprise.

'You don't know him? The man who is your principal link with what the British and French are pleased to call the Resistance movement? The man who perhaps met you when you parachuted into France? Or did you come by submarine into one of the beautiful little bays along the coast?'

'I did not come by submarine.' Now she was being as artificially patient as he. 'Nor by parachute. I am French-born and have lived in France all my life. And I have always been careful to keep away from the Resistance movement because it has brought nothing but trouble to France.'

He nodded approvingly.

'Very sensible. But hardly what Major Rushworth had in mind when he sent you. How is Major Rushworth these days, Mademoiselle? Still the same gambler with other people's lives? The man who stays safely at home while he sends others into highly dangerous situations? I'm sure he hasn't changed.'

She studied him, eyes narrowed in concentration.

'You said you were going to remove my confusion.' Her voice was tipped with anger again. 'You are making it worse. Who is Major Rushworth? I'm sorry – I just don't understand you.'

'Don't you know Major Rushworth?' He was still being

reasonable; a man dealing with a tiresome situation which duty demanded he should pursue. 'Perhaps now he has found some other way to sit out the war in safety. It must have been one of the others who sent you, then. We know a lot about them, of course. The Abwehr is very efficient. You know what that is. The German espionage service. They have many agents in Britain, some in high places. And of course we have captured British agents here in France, and they have told us many things. You are not in an unusual situation, Mademoiselle. So don't try to be a heroine.'

'I don't want to be a heroine,' she retorted. 'I just want to make sense of the things you are saying. And I can't. The only thing which is obvious to me is that you think I am not French but am a British spy. But whether you really think that or are playing some other game with me I don't know.' Suddenly tension seemed to get the better of her and tears brimmed in her eyes. 'You can't prove any of the things you're saying and you know you can't, because they're not true.'

'Lieutenant Legrange says you are not French,' Altmann said smoothly. 'I believe him. He has advised us on other occasions, and has never been wrong. He says you must have lived in France for many years; but you have lived in another country for a long time, too. What other country was that?'

'I haven't lived in another country.' The tears got the better of her and she covered her face with her hands. He watched her, as if tolerant of an inadequate child. She stayed like that, behind her hands; until she pushed her fingers up into her untidy hair and stared at him in despair and whispered: 'I can't tell you about another country, or about the people you talk about, about this Major or André whoever-it-was. And I've never been in a submarine or an aeroplane in my life.' Her fingers combed through her hair again and she tried vainly to smoothe it and disentangle it, then wiped her fingers across her cheeks. 'Please let me have my handbag. It was taken from me. I have no handkerchief, no comb. Please let me have my bag.'

He nodded. Without turning, he waved a hand at Braune who got up and went out, closing the door quietly. Then he picked up his cigar, frowned when he found that it was no longer alight, and took matches from a drawer. He concentrated upon relighting the cigar; then rose, went round the desk, and stood beside her. She did not look up at him, so he reached out, took a handful of her hair, and tilted her head back. He held her like that for seconds, staring down at her tear-rimmed eyes, the cigar jutting from one corner of his mouth. Then his other hand lashed across her face, and back again, and Braune heard the sharp, sickening sound as he came back through the door, and saw the red lines of Altmann's fingers streak red across her cheeks and jaw and heard her gasp, a small sound quickly strangled.

Cigar still between his teeth, Altmann returned to his chair. He looked contemptuously at Michele's marked face and the hair which had now fallen across her forehead and the eyes which stared back at him in bruised defiance, and said: 'You're a stupid woman. Here – straighten yourself up.' He took the handbag held out by Braune and slid it across the desk so that it fell from the other side at Michele's feet.

For a moment she looked down at it, then slowly bent forward and picked it up. It was grey, smooth leather with a large handstrap. She opened a flap and took out a comb, dragging it through her hair, across the top, then the sides, then the back; found a mirror and a small handkerchief and dabbed her eyes. She studied the reflection and the marks of Altmann's fingers, drawing her own finger ends down her cheeks. Then she searched the handbag again and found a lipstick, taking off the cap and applying the end sparingly to her lips. She put it back into the bag, fiddling with it, unable to get the cap into place. Altmann leaned back in his chair, blue smoke curling around his head, his pale eyes watching her hands as they came out of the handbag. She coughed and put one hand up to cover her mouth; and Braune shouted involuntarily as he saw something between her fingers and her lips parting and her eyes closed as she swallowed. He darted from his chair by the door, then checked as Altmann held up an arresting hand. It was the SD major's only movement; otherwise he only watched, waiting for the girl to open her eyes so that she could see the way his mouth widened in a tight, humourless smile.

'Cyanide pills,' he said softly. 'In ten seconds you should be on the floor, clutching your body in appalling agony. But it will pass quickly, they tell you, and you will die and be beyond my reach. But not this time, Mademoiselle.' He extended a closed hand towards her. 'Because they were discovered in your handbag yesterday.' His fingers uncurled. Two small white pills lay on his palm. 'Here they are. The pills you have taken were harmless. You will not die; not today, at least. And certainly not quickly, or until I have finished with you.'

She seemed to have stopped breathing. She stared at him, unblinking, her marked face frozen. Braune, poised beside the desk, was fascinated and fearful.

'So I knew all the time, you see,' Altmann said. He tapped his cigar carefully into an ashtray. 'You are a spy. We have seen these things before. They come from Britain.' He looked at the startled Sergeant. 'And what did you think of all that, Braune? I kept that titbit from you. Now we have had the ultimate evidence.' He levelled his cigar at Michele. 'You will either tell me immediately who sent you, and why, and the names of the stupid people who have helped you here, or I shall personally take you to the room above and strip the clothes from your body and start work on you. If you do not talk, in thirty minutes you will be in that room.' He stood up, leaning forward with his hands on the desk, his pale eyes wide and unblinking. 'As soon as you get to that room, I shall give you to Krupp. You have met him already. He is the fat man with the cosh. Remember? A coarse and disgusting man. We shall take his cosh away from him, then we shall give him permission to vent his sexual frustrations upon you. Krupp has unlimited vigour. Because he is so revolting no woman

315

will tolerate him voluntarily. So when a woman is given to him, he is anxious to show everyone what he can do to her. We shall all find it an interesting spectacle. And after he has paused for breath and we have dragged him away from you, I shall begin the serious business, with the instruments and the other aids we have there. Or you can talk to me now.'

She did not flinch. But her face seemed to be smaller, as if the skin was shrinking beneath her eyes, down her nose and around her mouth; smaller, thinner, tighter. And the marks of Altmann's violence were brighter spots of colour as if she had paled further. They were waxen images facing each other. Braune stared at them, horrified by the picture painted by Altmann's words, horrified by its inevitability, and horrified by the girl's unyielding silence.

Then she shook her head.

'I don't know anybody. There's nothing to tell.' Quiet; tense but disciplined.

Altmann stubbed out his cigar. He said to Braune 'Have the guards take her to her cell. In thirty minutes tell them to take her upstairs. And tell Krupp to be there.'

He settled back in his chair; and watched Michele with his strange eyes all the way to the door, until she had gone.

When Braune returned he was still there, staring at the door. For several minutes he remained motionless, ignoring the Sergeant's presence; eyes half closed and unwavering as if he could still see the girl in the doorway.

Then he said distantly: 'What is your opinion, Braune?'

'You were brilliant, sir,' the Sergeant said stiffly. 'You tricked her into protesting her innocence when all the time you had proof of her guilt. And then you tricked her into attempting suicide, so making her situation worse. She must now be totally demoralised.'

'Demoralised – and frightened, Braune. But do you think she is frightened enough? And what is she frightened of?'

'She is difficult to interpret,' Braune said, taking his cue. 'She is a brave and intelligent woman.'

316

Altmann was nodding; small, repeated movements of his head.

'I agree. She is also an excellent actress. Remember how she simulated anger, then calmness, then tears and frustration. All artificial. But she fooled you, didn't she, Braune? Don't be ashamed to admit it. She might even have fooled me for a time, had I not known already that she was a spy. And recall the manner with which she faced the final revelation. Impassive. No sign of fear. How will such a woman stand up to our persuasion in the room above?'

'She may be difficult to break, sir,' Braune said cautiously, and was pleased when the Major nodded again.

'So we must be cunning. And I have seen something deep in her eyes which gives me an idea. Wait here for me.'

Braune clicked his heels, opening and closing the door for his superior. Then he sat down on his hard chair. Well as he knew Altmann, the man's dispassionate, academic attitude made him feel physically sick. He discussed the psychological approach to questioning a prisoner with total disregard for the torture and mutilation which was an integral part of it. He might have been a detective contemplating the breaking of a petty criminal's alibi, with a court appearance and a short jail sentence as the end result. It was no novelty to Braune; but he could never accustom himself to it. He had seen Altmann inflict the most monstrous agony, or watch others do it for him, with total indifference to the victim's screams. Death on the torture table was annoying if it occurred before he had learned everything he believed was to be learned; otherwise, while a spark of shattered life remained, he would continue to debate, study, contemplate and experiment with the concern which others might give to a difficult game of chess. Mirielle Roux represented to him as much a personal challenge as a security threat. He wanted to break her will and her spirit to demonstrate as much as anything that he, Ernst Altmann, was the master, the irresistible interrogator, the supreme authority upon the human mind and its disciplines. That was a driving force even more powerful than his devotion to the Nazi Party and the Third Reich.

Braune stood up and walked to the window. It looked out over a busy street. He stared down at men and women hurrying past. They knew what went on in this building. They also knew who worked here. They would certainly know about Altmann, just as the people of Nice and Grasse and St Raphael and all the other towns knew about him. And they would know about his sergeant, too: the man who drove his car and walked a step behind him and was present through some of his interrogations, stiff faced and apparently indifferent. And when the end came and the enemy destroyed the Third Reich, if the people of these towns could catch Altmann and his sergeant they would tear off their limbs and put out their eyes and hang them from street lamps; or if the enemy armies caught them first, they would be paraded before military courts and tied to posts and shot. No one would listen when the sergeant protested that he had never harmed anyone, that he was only Altmann's servant, that he was a soldier who had been given this job after being wounded in action and that if he had refused to do it he would have been sent back to face the murderous Russians who took no prisoners.

He would have to desert. He would have to do something to convince the Resistance that he was not a brute and a sadist; that he was tired of war and that he hated Hitler and the Nazis who had taken him from his comfortable job as a clerk in a Leipzig factory and turned him into fodder for the enemy's guns. He did not care what happened, as long as he stayed alive. He was unmarried, with no close family. It would not matter if he could not go back to Germany. When this war ended Germany would be one vast ruin. He could live here, in France, if he could show the French that he was really on their side.

But he would have to be quick about it. The enemy was at the gates.

Perhaps he could help the girl to escape. Altmann was right

318

– if she carried cyanide pills, she must be a spy. So she would be important to the Resistance. If he could get her out, or tell the Resistance how to do it, they might shelter him until the war was over. But he would have to do more than that. He would have to take papers giving details of German security – something to help the French when the war came to this part of France; papers about the German plans to blow up bridges and buildings if they had to withdraw. They would destroy half of Cannes and Nice unless someone stopped them. The French Resistance could stop them – with his help. And he knew where the plans were.

But he would have to be quick. Tonight would not be too soon. If he could find a way to help the girl as well.

Then he felt sick again. Half an hour. Altmann had said. Then she would be in the room above.

He wanted to run away, so that he would not have to watch it.

But he dared not do that. Not yet.

In half an hour they brought her, between two guards. She came in pale and proud and tight-faced, and looked at the table as if she half expected to see André Matthieu still strapped to it. But Braune knew that Matthieu was back in his cell. He was incredibly strong. In spite of his agony and the way they had mutilated him, he had been seen by the guards to be on his feet, trying to walk, an hour after they had taken him there.

By tomorrow he would be fit enough for more torture, Braune thought.

She faced Altmann, and the two men in shirt sleeves who were Altmann's sadistic instruments of horror: they were low-grade Gestapo, capable of whatever inhumanity the Major demanded, professional torturers. Then she looked at Braune, and he turned away and concentrated on Altmann so that he would not have to see the way she stared at him.

Last of all, she looked at Krupp.

He was gross. Untidy, with a bulging belly and fat hips and wide thighs. Flesh hung from his jaw and puffed beneath his eyes. He licked his thick lips as he stared at her, and the blood rose and flushed his coarse face.

They took her to the centre of the room, close to the table. He towered over her as he shuffled forward. The guards stood on either side of her, holding her wrists and upper arms.

He said hoarsely: 'Let her go.'

The guards released her and stepped back. She stood still, and closed her eyes. One of the Gestapo torturers muttered: 'Go on, Krupp. Let's see how long it takes you.' Krupp grinned and grated: 'I'm going to make this one last.'

They were motionless, staring; their excitement charging the air, their breathing loud. And they heard her small despairing whisper: 'Why can't you all go away – why do you have to watch?' Even before Krupp touched her she shuddered violently, and her eyes opened and she looked not at the huge man in front of her with his red face and thick grinning lips but at the spectators with their open mouths and lusting eyes.

Then Krupp reached out and took her by the hair, and the thick fingers of his other hand dragged down the front of her body, hooked into the waistband of her skirt and jerked it violently. The hooks gave way and he forced his hand down behind it, pulling her head back by her hair, his breath rasping. Stitching and cloth tore and a spasm shook her and a little strangled cry wrenched from her.

And then she hit him.

Without warning, straight knuckles into the windpipe, straight fingers into the right eye. Two fast jabbing movements, so fast they were hardly recognized by the spectators.

Krupp bellowed, one hand to his eye, clutching at his throat, staggering back, retching. The guards snatched for their pistols, the Gestapo torturers pounced, and one slammed his clenched fist into her stomach. She catapulted backwards, the Gestapo men following her, grabbing her arms, twisting them back and up, and she screamed and Altmann's voice cracked through the room: 'Stand still. Every one of you. Stand still.'

Only Krupp moved then. He was moaning, his mouth open

and saliva dribbling down his chin. He seemed to be trying to vomit. His hands covered both his eyes and he leaned against the table, swayed, then fell to his knees, choking.

Altmann barked: 'Kiechle – take him out. Take him to the Medical Room.' One of the guards holstered his pistol, grabbed Krupp under the arms and heaved him to his feet. Krupp swung away, words bubbling up through his injured throat – 'Want her – kill – kill her –' But the guard was strong and dragged him away to the door, and he went out, staggering and retching, still covering his eyes.

'You're a dangerous lady.' Altmann's voice was razor-edged. He went across to her, flanked by the second guard and by Braune, both with their pistols drawn. He gestured, and the Gestapo torturers released her. She clasped both hands to her stomach and stood for seconds, head down, shoulders hunched, breathing hard.

Then she looked up into his pale eyes and slowly straightened. One hand came up and pushed hair away from her face.

'You must have done well on your combat course,' he said. 'That's just the sort of thing the military schools teach. Your instructor would have been proud of you.' He was staring at her intently, and made no move to stop her as she dragged her torn skirt up around her hips. She held it there, the fingers of her other hand covering her stomach where she had been hit. Her grey-pale face was old and hurt; yet her eyes were not afraid.

Then, abruptly, Altmann turned. He snapped: 'Keep her here. Guard her well. But unless she becomes violent, do not harm her. Hear me? I want her unhurt. I'll send for her in a few minutes. Give her pins or something to repair her clothes.' He marched out, jerking his head for Braune to follow.

In his office on the floor below he snapped: 'Get on the telephone. Ring Coastal Defence Work Camp Three and tell the Commandant I want as many men as possible in the compound in one hour. Understand? Work Camp Three.

I don't care what state the men are in. I want them waiting there when I arrive.'

Braune jumped for the telephone, and Altmann slumped into his chair, staring at the window, thinking. He remained like that for ten minutes; then said to the silent, attentive Sergeant: 'Do you know what we're going to do, Braune?'

'No, sir.'

'I'll tell you.' Distant voice; still thinking; pale eyes half closed. 'We're going to search for the most secret place in her mind. Consider what we have just seen. I'm sure she had conditioned herself to accept whatever Krupp was going to do. But then her plea, Braune. Remember? Why do you have to watch? She was revolted by Krupp. But she did not resist. Then something happened to her. In the instant before she attacked him I saw her eyes open. But she didn't look at Krupp. She looked to me, and at you. Then it was too much and she lashed out. Very skilfully, but in panic. She was making things infinitely worse for herself, she was inviting retribution, she had no hope of escape. Yet she did it.' He reached for a cold, half-smoked cigar in an ashtray, inspected it, then struck a match. 'No hell is more vile that the dread we hide from ourselves, Braune,' he said through a cloud of smoke. 'The unthinkable, the unspeakable, the unimaginable lurks in all of us. All women are afraid of rape. That girl is afraid of it, but if we had left her in the room alone with Krupp she would not have pleaded for mercy, or confessed the things I want to hear. Her spirit is too strong. It may be still too strong if we perform crude surgery upon her without anaesthetic, or flog her or burn her or inject acid into her. And if we do those things she may die before she has talked. So we shall be more subtle. And we have seen something today which shows us the way. Have a closed van waiting, and six guards to follow in another vehicle, all armed with sub-machine guns.'

*

The sun was low beyond the Esterel, the heat of the day tempered by an evening breeze stirring the dust. The long, grey Mercedes van left the Hotel Montfleury and headed west along the coast road; then at La Napoule turned inland under the railway track, crossed the River Siagne, and headed for Fréjus. Behind, in an open truck, rode six soldiers.

Braune drove the first vehicle with Altmann beside him, and Michele in the dark enclosure between two guards.

After four or five miles, climbing into the beginning of the Esterel range between stunted trees and rock outcrop, they turned into a narrower road between two large signs declaring *Eintrit Verboten*; and, beneath, the French translation, *Entrée Interdite*. Within two hundred metres they reached the gates of the camp, set in an eight-foot high wire fence stretching around a dirt compound in the centre of which were a cluster of long wooden huts. At the corners were watch-towers, twelve feet high, carrying searchlights.

Guards checked Altmann's identity and admitted the two vehicles. Braune looked critically at the wire and the gates, and concluded that they would not contain a really determined group of escapers. But he also knew that the men who lived in this camp were beyond thoughts of escape.

They were gathered now, outside the huts. Fifty, seventy, maybe more men in ragged clothes, mostly bearded; gaunt, with thin limbs and sullen eyes. At sixty metres they were repulsive, and there was a faint sickly smell hanging in the hot air. Death and disinfectant, Braune thought.

'Turn the van round so that the back doors open into the compound,' Altmann ordered, and the Sergeant swung the wheel. The armed escort did the same and the soldiers climbed down and spread out in pairs, guns levelled. The gate guard stayed at their posts, watching, while a handful of others walked slowly towards the vehicles then stopped at a distance, staring curiously, rifles slung.

Altmann climbed out and went to the back of the van, Braune following. He used a key to open the doors and swung them wide. The two guards clambered out, leaving Michele in the interior. Altmann stepped inside and sat down opposite to her.

He pointed across the dusty compound to the huts and the groups of men who shuffled slowly nearer, and said: 'This is one of the camps where foreign labourers live. They were brought here to build defences along the coast. I'm sure you were told in London about that.'

'Everyone knows the Germans use slave labour,' she said quietly; and Braune marvelled that she sounded so controlled. She had repaired her torn skirt and had even combed her hair. She sat now, looking smaller than she really was, her face pale and tense; yet still proud and disciplined. Braune thought she must be terrified; yet she did not show it.

'These men are prisoners of war,' Altmann said crisply. 'But they are special prisoners. There are other work camps along this coast; but the men here have been separated from the rest.' He waved a hand towards the compound and the men standing, staring, in the late sun, their long shadows across the dust. 'They are criminals, Mademoiselle. Violent men beyond discipline. Half-wits, too. See their faces. Out of Mongolian Russia and the fringes of Afghanistan, out of Poland and Bulgaria and other eastern states. But more then that, they are diseased. In the mind and in the body. Respiratory diseases, dreadful skin diseases, every venereal disease in the book and some we've never seen before. They rot as they stand there. They are isolated in order to preserve the rest of the workforce. They work until they die.' He leaned forward, his pale eyes bright in the dim interior of the van, staring intently at her. 'Imagine what they would do to a woman, if they had the chance. None of them has had a woman for a year, two years, longer. Homosexuality is rife. When they have the strength they masturbate, watching each other. There hasn't been a woman inside this camp since it was built last autumn. They don't know there's a woman here now. But they will soon see you, Mademoiselle.'

In spite of the almost hypnotic intensity of his stare, she turned her head slowly away from him, and looked outside. The men were thirty metres away in a half-circle, silent. Then she saw there were guards behind them, guards who had been edging them forward. Some of the men looked back, as if they wanted to return to their huts, but dared not move. Thin, fleshless faces, scrawny necks, dangling limbs. Skin, patchy red and grey and dirty parchment. Torn, filthy clothes.

And she could smell them. At thirty metres and in spite of the stirring evening breeze, the odour drifted in an unseen cloud across the vehicles and the soldiers and the still, wide-eyed ashen girl in the dark van; sickening, contaminating clothing, hair and lungs. Outside, Braune wanted to put a handkerchief across his nose. But he was a soldier and he dared not.

Then Altmann said: 'Get out, Mademoiselle.' He swivelled on his seat, crouched, and jumped to the ground. When he looked back she had not moved. 'If you don't get out of your own accord, I'll have the guards throw you out,' he said conversationally. That was Altmann's style. He rarely showed anger.

He stood there then, looking at her. Braune looked at her too, and the two guards who had ridden with her. Slowly, she moved, sliding along the bench seat; then, abruptly, as if she had found new courage and resolve, ducking out into the sunlight and dropping to the ground.

And the crowd rumbled. A low muttering, not of words but of harsh breath across broken vocal chords, senseless syllables merging; feet shuffling and dust stirring, a swaying as if an unseen sea shifted bodies back and forth against each other.

On each side, the soldiers levelled their rapid-fire automatic weapons, and the movement died.

Altmann took her by the wrist and stepped out away from the van. The sun threw their shadows across the brown earth and lit up her hair. She looked straight ahead, her eyes fixed on some point low in the sky, above and beyond the human nightmare facing her. Altmann walked forward until the nearest men were only four or five strides away. Then he stopped, his fingers iron bands around her wrist. The foulness of their breath and their bodies swept across her, and she swayed.

Altmann's soft voice said: 'See them, Mademoiselle. See the running sores around their mouths, and their diseased eyes and hands. Imagine what exists beneath those filthy rags. I'm going to give you to them. I'm going to let them fight over you, tear your clothes from you, cover you with their spittal and their urine and their sperm. But I won't let them kill you. We shall all be watching what happens to you, and listening to the indescribable sounds you will make. And then we shall drag you out and take you back to Cannes and throw you into a disinfectant bath. And tomorrow I will bring you back, for the same thing all over again. And it will go on, until you die from their diseases and their foulness inside your body and the injuries they will inflict on you – or talk. That's all I want, Mademoiselle. Talk. So easy. So much better than lying here struggling in the dust, in public degredation and agony, in a never-ending living hell.'

She was quivering. A vibration, starting in her head and running down her body to her arms and hands and thighs. Braune could see it from where he stood behind them in fascinated, sweating horror. Fear, revulsion, the unimaginable, the unbelievable, facing her; hot stinking breath in the sun, hungry desperate eyes, hands reaching.

Altmann snapped: 'You. Come here.' The smooth, persuasive eloquence gone: a hard crack of sound. He pointed.

A man blinked at him. The low sun lit his face yellow. He might have been thirty, or sixty years old. Lined face with dirt ingrained; eyes and lips out of the Asiatic plain; high bony forehead and thin straggling hair, veins blue knotted above emaciated cheeks. An ulcer oozed below one ear and saliva trickled from the corner of his mouth. When he moved from the front rank of gaping, shifting men in answer to Altmann's summons, he dragged one leg. But he was big and still strong, and his lusting stare stripped her and stroked her body like hands. He leered at Altmann.

'You want her?' Altmann asked curtly. 'You want this woman?'

Whatever his nationality, the man knew what was meant, and he grinned, showing toothless gums except for two fangs on one side. He stretched out hands, clawing for her, and the crowd behind him shifted as heads moved and necks strained, and the low ugly rumble surged across the compound again.

But before he could touch her Altmann stepped across and with one savage hand tore the clothing away from the upper half of her body, dragging it down from her shoulders. He still held her wrist, and just once she jerked, twisting; then put her head back and stared up at the fading sky and whimpered as the reaching hands clawed again and touched her breasts and two men close by began to wrench at the front of their baggy trousers and there was a surge of movement at the back, pushing the circle of panting foul-smelling men closer and the man with the bony forehead tried to get his wet mouth to one of her breasts and his fingers searched down her body and she began to shake her head, moaning.

And Altmann shot him at close range through the chest.

He slammed backwards against the men behind, and some-one screamed as the sound of the shot echoed across the compound. The crush of men swayed and the animal rumble was anger and fear, and the dead man with the bony forehead vomited blood as he fell across the legs of one of the men who had been tearing at the crotch of his trousers. Then a soldier fired a burst from his submachine gun into the air, and the crowd stumbled backwards, men falling and scrambling and shouting, dragging themselves desperately away towards the huts, frantic eyes looking back.

Altmann stood still, Luger in one hand, Michele's wrist still clamped in the other. She was staring at him, breath gasping, breasts white in the yellow sun, reprieved yet seeing only worse horror in his cold eyes. Then he released her hand and snapped: 'You can go back to the van if you like.'

She went, trying to drag the remains of her blouse across her shoulders, grinning soldiers staring. She did not run; just came on steadily, like a blind woman who saw nothing but was guided by memory pictures. She reached the van, and Braune was there and he wanted to help her into it but did not dare. She scrambled up, dragging herself on to a seat; and then Altmann was there too. She clutched her blouse and it tore further, and then she stopped trying to hide herself and let the tears come, shuddering violently again and again but making no sound.

Altmann's voice, soft now, said: 'That was a glimpse, Mademoiselle. Hell, so close. Next time I shall not be with you. I shall send you through the gates alone. Tomorrow. Unless you talk to me tonight. Tell me your real name. That can't harm anyone. Tell me that now. What is your name?'

A tiny quiver of sound came from her. She covered her face, fingers into her hair. Twice more the sound came. Then she took a deep breath, and the shaking grew less, and she whispered, 'Michele – Tamworth.'

*

Altmann rode back to Cannes with her. Talking quietly, promising her protection as long as she talked to him that night. He called her by her name and he was persuasive, reasonable, comforting; regretting that he had caused her so much distress, wanting now to take it all away. She sat through it in silence, eyes closed, swaying with the jolting of the van, a pale shadow in the dim interior. When they reached the Montfluery he took a jacket from a guard so that she could cover herself, and said: 'You may have a bath if you like. Then, in two or three hours, when you've had time to think, I'll send for you.'

He went back to his office and said to Braune: 'It wasn't the thought of mass rape that broke her. I think she would have been strong enough to take that. It was the filth that went with it, and above all the spectators. She's now deeply shocked. And while she's shocked she'll see me as her protector. I think we shall learn a lot from her.'

He was still in his office an hour later when the telephone rang. He sent Braune outside, and the Sergeant stood in the corridor for a long time, wondering; until Altmann called him.

'A change of plan. For all of us.' Brisk words, but the voice was strained. Some of the confidence was gone. Braune had never seen him like that. 'Orders from Berlin. Have Weise and Schumann here immediately, with their aides.'

Within five minutes he was telling his senior officers: 'This is confidential information which must not be communicated to the Wehrmacht. The enemy has broken out of the invasion area. Our armies are retreating. I am informed that although the enemy doesn't yet know it, this is a serious defeat which could lead to the whole of North-West France being evacuated. It is also likely to hasten the expected invasion of the South of France which is now regarded as imminent and which we are inadequately equipped to resist. Further, our heroic resistance in Northern Italy is crumbling, and the Russian advance is gaining momentum. I have been given authority to destroy certain records. Go back to your offices and decide what you must take with you if the army has to withdraw from this region, and what would be better destroyed here. I have also been instructed that prisoners who have survived intensive interrogation must be executed. Weise, make the arrangements for six in the morning, and have it done somewhere outside the town. We shall then have less to think about in the coming days, when security in this area may become increasingly difficult to maintain.'

When the others had gone he turned to Braune.

'The war is going against us. The news is as bad as it could be. I don't know what will happen. Every man may ultimately have to care for himself. But I shall expect you to fight with the rest, Braune. You are an experienced infantryman. I shall have you transferred back to normal duties. Now bring me a list of the prisoners. There won't be time to talk to the girl. A pity, after all that work.'

Braune did not go to bed that night. He spent most of the time between Altmann's office and the rooms occupied by Weise and Schumann. And as he worked he knew the time had come for his own private decision. Every man may have to care for himself, Altmann had said. Karl Braune would do just that. So as he worked, with access to papers he had never seen before, he secreted some of them, stuffing them behind a water tank in one of the lavatories. They would be his passport.

At 5.15 in the morning Weise rang. 'Wake the Major,' he said. 'Tell him that everything is arranged. The convoy will leave at six o'clock.'

At 5.45 Braune stood behind Altmann and Weise in the hotel yard. The prisoners were brought out, looking around in the chill morning air, apprehensive and wondering. Braune saw her among them, walking with her eyes down. There were three lorries, one laden with prisoners from the hospital in the Grande-Bretagne nearby. André Matthieu was one of those, Braune knew. He had been taken to the hospital the previous afternoon, and if Altmann had not had that telephone call last night would have been taken back to the third floor room at the Montfleury that morning. At least he had been saved that, thought Braune. He, and some of the others.

Braune knew what this was all about. Not only were records to be destroyed. Evidence, to: evidence of Gestapo atrocities. The victims of the torturers were to die, so that they could not talk. It was futile, the Sergeant thought gloomily. So many people knew. Even if none of the victims survived, there would still be enough evidence to send everyone here to the firing squad when the British and Americans came; when the French took control again.

Panic gripped him then. Time was running out fast. He snapped to attention, asked Altmann's permission to return to the office to ensure that doors were locked, and ran back into the building. He went to the office, picked up an envelope, ran down to the lavatories, scrambled up to the water tank, and stuffed the hidden papers into the envelope. He was taking an enormous, terrifying chance. If he was caught with the papers he would be shot immediately. But something drove him and he did not try to understand it. He only knew that his whole life seemed to have reached a crisis point on that dreadful morning with the prisoners outside waiting for execution and the firing squad already on its way to the chosen place. When he ran out of the building again, with the envelope inside his uniform jacket, he knew he was leaving it for ever.

The prisoners were in the lorries and the canvas flaps secured. Altmann and SS Hauptmann Weise were seated in Altmann's Mercedes staff car. Braune climbed in, started the engine, and Altmann raised an arm. The convoy moved.

They went east, towards the observatory on the great hill behind the old port, climbing up the winding roads past the blockhouse at the Col St Antoine where the Wehrmacht had a battery of big guns. Down below in La Californie several thousand soldiers were quartered; but up here among the pines and the small houses only the blockhouse was a reminder of the war and the German presence – the blockhouse and the ruined buildings around it where many civilians had died in American and British air attacks on the gun emplacement.

Higher up, beyond Vallauris, the houses were scattered and soon the road wound through pines and outcrop rock, still and deserted in the cool of the early daylight.

Then they came to the clearing; sun-scorched grasses across a flat earth plateau with the pines clustered close and scrub undergrowth filling in below. As Weise told him to turn, Braune saw a scout car and a tractor-mounted earth shovel in the trees, and felt a spasm of sick fear. He knew why they were there: the scout car carried the machine gun, the earth shovel would bury the bodies afterwards.

He swung the car round and the lorries followed, lining up close together. Soldiers dismounted, and four climbed out of the scout car carrying a machine gun. Weise marched over to them and gave directions. They mounted the gun on a tripod and fixed the ammunition trays. Then they stood in a line in front of the gun, close together, partly concealing it from the three lorries.

Altmann leaned on the door of his car, watching; his face expressionless. When Weise marched across to him, clicked his heels and snapped, 'Everything is ready, sir,' he just said quietly: 'Carry on, please.'

The Hauptmann, a tall thin man with a narrow face and a broken nose, swung on his heel and bellowed: 'Bring out the prisoners.' Soldiers stood in a half circle on either side of the machine gun, rifles levelled; others released the canvas sheets at the rear of the lorries and ordered the prisoners out.

They climbed down slowly, looking round. Some had to be helped; there were broken limbs and battered faces. Others were upright, apparently strong, with quick, wary eyes. The big figure of André Matthieu was one of the last to appear from the Grande-Bretagne lorry. Black hair fell across his forehead as he slid to the ground, dropped to his knees, then dragged himself upright. His nose was broken and one eye was swollen and closed with a great purple bruise covering half his face. He stood with both hands clutching his abdomen; then, slowly, straightened his back, lifted his battered head, and looked around with his one good eye, searching faces.

There were only two women. One was small, dark, middle-aged, apparently blind. The other was Michele.

She stood, blinking in the bright rose light of the dawn, staring at the soldiers and the prisoners. Then she saw André and tried to edge towards him as the guards shouted orders and the prisoners shuffled towards the centre of the clearing.

They gave no sign of knowing each other, but Braune saw the way they came together. Altmann saw it too and said to his Sergeant: 'Look – the girl and Matthieu. He was looking for her. Watch them.'

Then the soldiers stepped away from the machine gun, and the prisoners saw it, and their shuffling stopped and their muttered questioning died and there was only the call of seagulls and the cicadas wakening; until someone began to weep quietly and André's thick shoulders pushed between the others and he reached Michele.

She turned her head away from the gun and looked up at him. Braune saw him speak, and the girl replied, and put up a hand to touch his injured face, and he reached for her and circled her shoulders with his great arm. The sun tipped the pines and slanted through the leaves, and in all that doomed crowd Braune thought there were only two people, holding each other, eyes on each other, the man a head taller than all the rest, the girl's hair shining in a shaft of sunlight, giving each other courage as the machine gun shattered the dawn.

Braune closed his eyes, but he could not close his ears to the horror. When he looked again most of the prisoners had fallen, some still, some writhing, a few on their knees. Several were screaming through the noise of the gun and bodies tossed and jerked like rag dolls. He could not see the man and the girl and thought they must have been among the first to go down.

Then it was still. No gun, no screams, no birds or insects. Still until Weise drew his pistol. The *coup de grâce*. If anyone should need it. Distant thunder. It happened sometimes, out of the heat. The sun was on the pistol in the Hauptmann's hand. Thunder? Braune's head snapped round. Aircraft fast and low. They came up the face of the hill from the sea, over the trees, gull wings, great radial engines. Corsairs. Oh Christ. Under the howling engines soldiers were shouting. The Corsairs came round in tight turns, seeming to clip the tops of the pines, and their guns hammered through the deafening engines. Braune began to run, fell down, saw Altmann's body shatter and explode in gouts of blood and flesh. A lorry burst into flames with a great rushing sound, then another. Soldiers reared and cartwheeled. The scout car blew up, roaring into the air and falling back in sheets of fire and spinning metal onto the remains of the machine gun crew. And still the Corsairs' engines and guns split the morning and Braune ran through the trees as he had never run in his life. He could hear his voice swearing and calling on God for help. He collided with bushes and a branch swept his cap from his head and gashed his eyebrows. But he went on, leaping, scrambling, chest heaving, blood pounding through him.

Until it was far away.

The engines were distant, snarling across the slopes, down towards the Esterel. And the guns had stopped.

He leaned against a tree, fighting for breath; then slid to the ground, on his hands and knees. Blood dripped from his forehead, and he wiped the back of his hand across it. He stayed like that for minutes, until he began to recover. Then he stood up, looking around, listening.

No one was there. Just the trees, and the cicadas calling, and the sun rising. And Sergeant Karl Braune.

Very slowly, he took out his pistol and stuffed it into his trouser pocket, discarded the belt and holster, then took off his uniform jacket. He slid the thick envelope from the inside pocket of the jacket and stood, looking at it, for several seconds. Then holding the envelope tightly in one hand, he began to walk away through the trees, leaving the jacket with its badges and stripes on the ground.

Not once did he look back.

PART THREE

◆━●━◆

NEIL

———•◆•———

1947

1

Red tiled roofs and grey walls hemming in narrow winding streets: old Cannes, climbing up towards the observatory hill, a world away from the great hotels and the tree-lined promenade along the Croisette.

This was where she had been, here and along the coast to Antibes and St Laurent; and where I had met Toni, who still lived in a narrow house with plaster chipped from the walls and small windows which kept it dark and cool inside. He had a suspicious wife and noisy children, so when I had overcome his initial reluctance we went out to a small restaurant and spent three hours over lunch while he remembered 1944 and the days when he had been important. Now the sickening danger was forgotten; only the excitement and the secret glories and the ultimate triumph survived as he talked.

Peter was there because I had promised to take him. When the time had come I had been reluctant; it would have been far easier to move around and to talk if I had been by myself. I might have got more out of Toni, too. But Peter was so anxious to come, so eager to make this final pilgrimage, and so much in need of a companion and a guide, that I could not bring myself to refuse him.

I had not told him that I had found Thoresen, and that he had told me where to look for the people who had been part of Michele's final days. There would be time enough for that when he had absorbed the shock of learning how she had died, and finding her grave.

He sat quietly through that first long lunch; and then through an evening meeting at a pavement table when I plied

Toni with as much wine as he would take in a bid to overcome his reserve. He talked freely enough; yet I sensed a subtle withdrawal as we came to the end of his story. Perhaps it was Peter's presence; the knowledge that his recollections were not only being recorded by a professional writer but heard by the father of the girl who had become a victim of the dreadful Gestapo machine.

Perhaps he felt guilty, too: as if the Resistance movement itself had been responsible for her ultimate sacrifice because one of its minor members had confessed in the face of an alternative too ghastly to contemplate. He implied no criticism of Alain Albert; yet tried to push the conversation on as quickly as he could as if afraid I would ask his opinion of the incident.

It was only at the end of our second meeting that Peter asked a question of his own: the question he had travelled more than eight hundred miles to ask: 'Where is she buried?' I translated. But Toni, with more than a bottle of wine inside him, shook his head as if he did not want to talk about that.

'It's a mass grave. The bastards shot a lot of them. Then buried them all together. There are a lot of graves like that. I don't know which is hers. I'll ask – see if anyone remembers.'

I didn't believe he would. Again, it was as if he felt some element of responsibility for what had happened. Perhaps he, and others, had deliberately turned their backs on it for three years and did not welcome the appearance of probing strangers.

But at that stage there was an alternative which I was sure would yield the rest of the story: Karl Braune.

Thoresen had given me his name and his last-known address in one of the mountain villages above Antibes. He had deserted on the day of the shooting and had found his way to a house on the edge of Le Cannet where he had asked to see a Resistance leader. He had handed over his papers, which included German plans to destroy Riviera towns and bridges, and these were passed on to Toni and others who had succeeded André Matthieu. Then he had been sent up into the mountains where a Maquis unit had kept him in a cave until the Allied armies had liberated the area at the end of August when they gave him to the Americans; and after three months in custody and a lot of questioning he was released. One of Thoresen's men talked to him, after which the SIS discarded him as of no further use.

When I went to find him I did not take Peter. If Braune knew anything about Michele's torture it would be better if her father did not hear his story. And when I met him I knew I had been right for another reason: Braune was an outcast, allowed to live there but shunned by his neighbours, and deeply troubled by his past. He was nervous, he pleaded with me to understand his predicament and to accept that he had not harmed Michele or anyone else, and twice he broke down and wept when I pressed my questions. The presence of someone else would have made the interview even more painful and probably less informative.

At the end I said: 'I want to know where it happened, and where she's buried.'

He looked at me apprehensively.

'Do you know that it's nearly the anniversary? That it was on the 19th of July in 1944, and today is the 18th? It was three years ago tomorrow. Did you plan it like that?'

'No. I didn't know the exact date.' For some reason the information disturbed me; as if I was suddenly closer to her than I had expected. 'No one had told me. I just knew it was in July. Perhaps no one else knew.'

'Others knew,' he said. 'Others must have known. These things were always known. And yet perhaps not. They might have known there was an execution without being certain who was there.'

'But you were there,' I said. 'Where did it happen? And where did they bury her?'

We were sat at the window of his little apartment at the top of a crumbling building overlooking meadows which ran up towards the backdrop of rock outcrop and trees and distant mountains. He looked out, biting his lower lip, as if forcing himself to remember something he had tried to forget.

'It was on the slopes above Cannes. High up there, in a clearing amongst the trees. It was a beautiful place. But no one goes there now. People say the grass is still bloodstained. But that's not true. They're all buried there. The army dug out a mass grave. I can show you on a map. The exact place. And you'll know it when you get there. The Resistance put a stone in the clearing and carved something on it.'

'The Resistance did that?' I stared at him. 'Then why did Toni tell me he didn't know? He must know.'

Braune shrugged. He moved his shoulders as the French do, exaggerating.

'Some of these people resent foreigners. Even the British. Maybe he was too drunk after all the wine you said you gave him, or maybe he was afraid you would ask him to go there with you. I've been back. And I was sorry I went. It's lonely. And when you know what happened there it's – a bit frightening. Or perhaps that was just my conscience.' He looked down, and a shiver ran through him. I wondered if it was an act for my benefit, if he was just sorry for himself, or if he really cared about Michele and André and the others.

'Let's find a map,' I said. 'I want to go.'

He looked tired; and afraid.

'You won't like it. No one goes there. Not even the birds. People say it's – an evil place.'

'You mean they say it's haunted?'

'Yes. I don't believe it. But I don't want to go again.'

'I don't believe it either,' I said.

*

I dressed quietly, went down to the hotel foyer and asked the night porter for a cup of coffee, then went out to my car. It was half past five and the morning light was clear in the town's fresh streets. I was the only person moving.

Maybe it had been like this three years ago, on this same

day. Pale blue sky and high wispy cloud picking up the golden light of the new sun: still air heralding the heat to come: smooth sea stretching away to the hazy horizon.

Her last day. Her salvation day, when death had rescued her.

I drove out into the streets and along the promenade. I could see the sea and the sky, and the hills rising to the distant mountains. There was a mist on the hills; thin white clouds drifting through the valleys. I didn't want to go. I was getting too close. I was reaching out, trying to touch her, and when I failed I would be desperately sad.

But I had to see the place. It was there, and I had to go.

Not with Peter, though. Not this first time. I hadn't told him that I knew where it was. Later, maybe. But this was the anniversary, and the hour. I had to be by myself.

I drove past the railway station and up into the jagged streets between the tiered houses climbing the pale sky; quickly, tyres singing on the tight corners.

Above the observatory the mist hung. I felt the chill in the car. White and drifting, with the bright sky lighting it from above. Then it cleared, but there was another white sheet ahead, hovering above the road, clinging to the red roofs and the scattered pines.

When the houses were gone and there were only the pines and the outcrop I knew I was almost there. The mist still hung in silent ribbons, parting to admit a shaft of pale sun, then closing. Perhaps it was because of the mist that I stopped at the wrong clearing. I drove the car off the road and got out, but somehow knew straight away that this was not the place. And there was no stone. So I went back to the car; then changed my mind and walked on.

Until I found it.

The pines were close to the road, and because of the mist I didn't see it until I was there: a narrow entrance, maybe thirty metres, with outcrop on either side, then widening away from the road to seventy or eighty metres and more than that in depth. The mist shifted, wraith-like, between the tall tree sentinels surrounding, and then there was blue sky overhead and the new sun slanted across the trees and down to the scorched grasses.

The stone was in the centre. A block of limestone cut and smoothed by nature, with one flat surface. It had been placed carefully so that the flat face could be seen from the road. I stood for a long time looking at it, and at the low mound behind it.

This was what I had come to see. Because she was here.

And it was still. Silent. Isolated from the world. No birds, Braune had said. Neither birds nor insects. Just trees and the sun through mist.

I pushed my hands deep into the pockets of my coat and walked across to the stone. It was more than two feet high and I could read the inscription without stooping.

Here lie heroes.
Remember them even if you did not know them.
For if you love liberty
Their pain and their sacrifice was for you.
Even you.
Weep in shame for man's inhumanity.

July 1944

I stood there for a long time. And had no shame for my own tears.

She was with me. In that far-off room where she had lived close to the airfield so that she could hear her husband go out each night to meet the guns. In a hotel restaurant with laughter in her eyes. In a nightmare beneath broken stones, warm and clinging in the startling dawn of an unwanted, undeniable understanding. Don't let it show again. It never did. But the dawn mist in my nostrils was gone and her perfume was there and the eerie silence was broken by her voice, and I could feel her hair against my face. Innocence and sin. Neither, for we were not innocent and we did not sin. I had turned away and so had she; until now, when I had gone back to find her and

344

she was here beneath my feet, rotting in this cold dawn with no voice and no laughter and no understanding.

When I could see again the mist had drifted cold through the trees, hiding her last day.

I forced myself away from the stone and wandered to the edge of the clearing. My watch said six o'clock. But there was no thunder of great engines coming up from the sea. Only the sound of my own footsteps, muffled on the damp earth. This was where the lorries had stood, and the machine gun. I poked with the toe of my shoe and found a piece of metal. Twisted, rusty, six inches long and jagged. I picked it up, shaking away the earth which clung to it. Then I looked up, seeing Corsairs howling in over the dark trees.

Karl Braune had been here. Then he had run away through the pines on my left. I dropped the piece of metal and walked away from the clearing. He had gone downhill, he had said; the way I was going. A gentle slope. The mist chilled me. I walked carefully through the trees. The silence chilled me, too. After a minute or two I stopped. This must have been where he had left his uniform jacket. I looked around, half expecting to see it. Then, slowly, I turned back.

When I reached the clearing again the mist was dense; a slow moving, ethereal sea. Silent, lying like a shroud across this awful place. The stone was dark, blurred at the edges; the trunks of the trees beyond almost concealed, shadowy lines, advancing and receding.

I was afraid.

The silence lay over me, suffocating. But the stillness was disturbed. The mist curling. No. More than that. Something drifting. Out there, across the clearing, grey-white, part of it yet not part of it. The mist thickened and the stone was almost gone; and the silence too, wiped away by a whispering, shivering breath of sound filling this hidden sanctuary, cold on my face, cold in my soul.

A breeze up from the sea rustling a million damp leaves, thinning the mist.

And something was close to the stone.

A white shape, gliding. White from head to foot. But there was no head and no feet, and the mist drifted across again, and I came away from the shelter of the trees, softly, not breathing, horrified, closer as the breeze stirred through the mist and the figure materialised and was bending, kneeling, reaching.

Flowers against the stone. Red and white flowers.

And the breeze was a wind, and the orchestra of the leaves and the grasses greeted it, and the mist swirled and yielded before the sun and the new day came in a crescendo of light and movement. The figure rose, leaving the flowers, and turned quickly as a twig crackled beneath my feet and the white hood fell back.

And I saw her.

There.

Against the stone and the mound where she lay rotting. There, with clear eyes startled, there with fair hair shining in the new sun, there with colour and form and life. And life. And life.

She turned slowly to face me, and the white cloak was parted by the stirring wind, and she wore a simple black dress because this was her day of mourning beside the stone and the red and white flowers and the dreadful mound where she lay rotting.

I moved. Hands against cloth. Fingers holding. I had to move, to know that I was real and could feel and my hand hurt when I dug my nails into my palm. I waited, but she was still, as still as the stone; yet I saw her eyes searching my face, wide and fearful.

Then I heard my voice. A distant echo, lost inside my head; not loud enough for her to hear. Yet I heard.

'I don't understand. But if you are alive, please speak to me.'

The breeze died and the first warmth of the sun flooded across the clearing, and she swayed, a tiny movement from side to side, an uncertain movement quickly gone.

She said: 'Neil.'

2

There are rare moments in every life for which there are no words: moments too tragic, too exciting, too fearful or ecstatic; or moments so far beyond understanding that men have never invented words to describe them.

Afterwards those who have known such moments can rarely remember how the spell was broken, how communication returned, how life was resumed after being suspended in disbelief.

I know it was a long time before we touched. I was afraid to touch her in case I destroyed the dream. The words are lost; but the moment is carved across my soul: her fingers against mine, a hesitant, almost formal gesture, an experiment quickly ended. She was real.

Talk; scattered words, confused, trying to explain the impossible; questions without answers; answers without questions. How, when, and how again.

But what is rebirth, when the world itself is recreated too?

After some time we came away from that place. Her car was parked off the road nearby, and I ignored mine because I would not allow myself to leave her side. The magic which had conjured her out of the mist could so easily dissolve her into the bright sun if I looked away even for a moment.

Then we were on the beach, because it was wide and deserted and we had to be away from people. The sea edged in across the warm shingle in straight, thin lines pushed gently by an on-shore breeze which plucked at her neat black skirt as we wandered beside the water and sorted the scattered fragments of life and death, hope and despair into recognisable patterns.

How. Have mercy and tell me how, so that I may believe.

Back to Karl Braune's story, and the big, stooping André with his arm about her as if even then he could save her as the machine gun shattered the morning. He had turned her away in a last, forlorn gesture of protection, putting himself between her and the gun. She had felt him jerk against her and pain searing her side, then he had fallen on her, crushing her, smothering her, hiding her from the awful cacophony of death and hell reaching for her. When the gun stopped she wanted to scream but his voice whispered 'Lie still, lie still,' and then the remains of the world were split apart by roaring, shrieking thunder and more guns, different guns, and it went on forever as she lay under him with fire in her side and his blood running down her face.

But she was alive.

For a long time they lay still in the silence. She was breathing, hurting, trying to think. And André was breathing too, in struggling gasps against her hair. When she opened her eyes she saw blood trickling from his twisted mouth. She edged sideways and he slid away from her, grunting, then whispering, 'Don't move.'

But she was moving now, trying to look around, raising her head and seeing the carnage, the bodies tumbled and pressing around her, none stirring; and the flame and smoke belching from vehicles and the German guards dead, killers killed, and the pines climbing against the morning sky.

She was bleeding. From her side, where the agony was; spreading agony. She moved her arms and legs and pain tore at her. For a time she lay still; then heard André coughing and knew that however badly she was hurt, he was worse. So she rolled over and struggled to her knees, crying out but pushing herself towards him, crouching at his side, staring at his twisted bloody face and closed eyes, hearing his breathing struggle and bubble in his mouth. And there was nothing she could do.

She put her head against his chest and wept.

That was how Toni and the others found her. And André was still alive.

They made rough stretchers and carried them into the trees and away to a nearby farmhouse; then found an old van and took them further away to another farm, up beyond Grasse. A doctor came to them secretly, then another, and they took away a bullet which had broken two of her ribs and had lodged below her left lung, miraculously without touching anything vital. They operated on André, too, as best they could; but there were four bullets in him and a fifth had passed through him – probably, they said, the one they found in Michele – a kidney was shattered, a lung torn and worst of all, one had broken his spine. If he survived he would be paralysed from the chest down.

Before the Americans landed along the coast on either side of St Tropez on the 15th August, she was able to spend part of each day sitting at his bedside, holding his hand, talking to him, encouraging him. And when the Germans were driven out of the area less than two weeks later and the Maquis and the Resistance had had their revenge on collaborators and had taken over civil administration she went with him to the Cannes hospital, then to a bigger one in Nice, and they let her sit with him every day.

She said to me: 'He was such a big man. And he had been so big in spirit. But now he was like a child. Weak and ill and unable to move except for his head and his arms. And he was frightened, because he had no one, no relatives, and no hope.'

'Was that why you stayed with him, instead of going to the Americans and telling them who you were?'

'I had to stay,' she said. 'I think he would have died if I had gone. And he was crippled because he had tried to save me. One bullet went right through him and into me. Some of the others would have hit me, and killed me, if he hadn't put himself

349

between me and the gun. Maybe the bullet which hit his spine. He saved me, Neil; and he paid for it dreadfully.'

We were walking along the beach now, with the water lapping close to our shoes. She had left her white cloak in the car and was a small, black-clad figure beside me; paler and thinner than when I had known her in another world; quiet and defensive. The initial shock had left us both and we were talking rationally. Or rather she was talking, because there was so much for her to tell. I just provided the punctuation.

'But you could have let London know you were alive.'

She bent down and picked up a pebble. It was veined with shades of grey and red. She studied it as if she were interested in it.

'Yes. I could have. But I didn't want to.'

'Why?'

She looked up at me, then threw the pebble into the water and watched the splash. We had stopped walking now, and she stood in front of me, defiantly.

'Because they would have sent for me. And when I'd refused to come, they'd have sent somebody here. Maybe Hugo himself. I couldn't stand that. He'd have come here with his platitudes and his sermonising. And he'd have questioned me. Over and over. Debriefing, they called it. Every detail.'

She stopped then, and turned quickly and began to walk. I watched her, and saw her pride in the way she held her shoulders and her head. But I saw fear, too; and knew she was running away. Not from me, but from memory. And at that moment I knew she had been running away for three years. Hiding from the world she had left, which she could no longer face.

When I caught up with her she did not look at me, so I took her hand. She did not try to resist, and I slowed our walk until we were idling again. But she was stiff now, and distant.

As gently as I could, I said: 'I know what happened, Mitch. I know everything. All the details Hugo would have wanted. And more besides. Don't be afraid of it.'

She stared. She did not believe me.

'What do you mean? How could you? You weren't there. I'm the only one. All the others are dead.'

That was the way she wanted it, with all the others dead.

I said: 'I know everything. I'll tell you how – later. I know about Ernst Altmann, and the Milice Lieutenant, and how you tried to kill yourself with the cyanide pills. I know what was said to you and what you said in return. I know about Krupp and what he did in that room, and what you did to him. And I know about the slave labour camp, and the dreadful thing that happened there.' Although I was being as gentle as I could make myself, I saw her shock, then anger suddenly giving way to fear; and shame. I held her hand tightly and said: 'Don't be afraid of it. Only one other person in the world knows, and he will never have any reason to tell.'

'You know.' She whispered it, as if it were a sentence to eternal darkness.

'Yes. And I'm glad. Because suddenly I understand more than you could ever tell me.' I held both her hands now, trying to give her courage.

Her eyes were wide, and the shock was still in them. She shook her head, quick little jerks. For seconds she made no sound. Then when she spoke I heard the depth of her despair.

She said: 'I failed them. If Altmann hadn't taken me out to shoot me, I'd have told him everything, anything to save myself.' And she put her head down and sobbed, her shoulders shaking, and it was as if all the secret tensions of a lifetime were being released. I put an arm about her and pulled her close to me and she clung like a child, hiding her face.

We stood like that on the empty beach, the water rippling around our feet, the morning sun hot on our heads, for a long time; until she quietened and her body was still and I felt her taking comfort from my closeness because she knew I shared her secret and did not despise her for it. She had stayed here because she was among men and women who understood. In their different ways they had been part of it. If she went anywhere else she would have to lie, and live for ever with the fear of detection. She had nothing in Britain, no one except a father whom she had not seen since he had left home, despised, when she had been little more than a child. Here, she was with friends.

And Britain meant Thoresen. He was the ultimate barrier. He more than anyone in her life had come close to her soul; not because she had loved him as she had loved her husband, but because he had been the first to reveal her to herself. Not for Thoresen the conventional lovers' relationship, the experienced and sophisticated man teaching the young and flattered girl the joys of the flesh. He was the analyst, the searcher. He had penetrated her mind as well as her body. Through him she had learned not only passion and ecstacy and deception, but the innermost truths of her own personality. And because he was her teacher he was also her master, and could be so again. If he had questioned her, he would have exposed her failure in the face of horror, would have probed her motives and conflicts and reactions and would have heaped his own interpretations upon them with oppressive authority, stripping away her last secret defences against the torture she had inflicted upon herself.

That, above all, she could not face.

*

She had married André. She told me while we sat at a pavement café, looking out at the flat sea, glad of the shelter of the table umbrella as the sun climbed higher. Other people were around now and we had been watching them idly as we had talked about Toni and the others and how she had made them swear that if anyone came, searching for her, they would never reveal that she had survived the massacre. The French Resistance was used to keeping secrets.

She had wanted to stay with André. She owed her life to

him. She could not have left him to die in despair. And he was her refuge.

He had urged her to go – anywhere, to a new life in France if not in Britain. You need freedom, he said; not to be tied to a helpless cripple you have known for only a few weeks. And what about your decaying chateau at Montargis, and the old man who lives there? But she had said no, she could never go back to him because he belonged to part of her life which was gone and she would be suffocated. It was enough to know that he had been provided with a home; and through a lawyer to check that he was still alive and living there. She had no money, but she could earn enough to keep herself and André, and the others in the old Resistance group promised to help their crippled leader.

But still he would not believe her, and every day he per-suaded himself that she was going to leave; until in pity she brought in the abbé to talk to him, and then the mayor to marry them so that he would know that she would never go away.

I heard it all quietly, as if I had no part in it, like a doctor listening to a patient asking to be understood.

When I asked, 'But what about your pension after Alan's death?' she said: 'We've had enough to live on. Nursing him was what I had to do. I owed him much more than a pension.' No mention of her own crumbled world, as if she had forgotten it.

And it would have gone on, I thought, if I hadn't made my pilgrimage to her grave on the anniversary of the massacre, and if she hadn't made her annual visit to the place in memory of all the others; and if we had not both been so sentimental and dedicated that we had chosen the hour and the minute of the terror as our moment.

But what now? Would I be able to leave her to her anonymity and her selfless labour? Would I be able to take her father to the stone on the hill, and watch his grief, and never tell him that she was alive and I had seen her and held her while she had wept out her confession? Would the helpless man I had never met survive my intrusion? And could I survive her loss after the revelation of this extraordinary day?

I could not find the answers. I said: 'I have something to tell you. I didn't come here by myself. I brought your father. I've come to know him well, and to respect him. He wanted to see your grave. What shall I do?'

For a little while she looked at me in silence, playing with her coffee cup and then drinking a little from it to give herself extra time before she said: 'I hadn't expected that. I haven't seen him since 1932. I haven't thought about him much; not after the first few years. Does he really care so much about me?'

'Fifteen years ago he lost a daughter,' I said. 'It's been the great grief of his life.' I put up a hand when she started to object. 'I don't think you'd recognise him. He's not sorry for himself. He thinks the old Peter Armstrong wasn't much of a feller, and probably got what he deserved. I don't know how much he regrets the way he used to live; but I do know he regrets enormously one consequence of it – his estrangement from you. He met Chuck Feldman once, during the war.' Her eyes opened wide, and I smiled. 'Yes. I know about Chuck, too. And that you met him in the RAF Club in London. Your father ran across him a couple of months later and asked him to find you again if he could. Chuck couldn't. And your father wouldn't try in case you rejected him. He had to have a go-between to protect himself from that because he was terrified of it. Well, I guess I'm the go-between now.'

She held the coffee cup with both hands, as if trying to warm her fingers on this hot day. And she was small and afraid again.

'I don't know what to do.' Her voice was small too. 'Because I don't know what you're going to do. You know so much. I feel kind of – naked. You seem to know more about me than I know myself. Please tell me how you're going to use it all.'

The question shocked me. I had been writing a tribute to

a memory; to courage and vitality lost, and a tablet to my own grief. But now the memory had been thrust miraculously into the present and grief had been wiped away. The strange magic of long ago was wakening while I struggled to accept the impossible. What it might mean to me in the end was beyond my imagination at the moment.

She was watching me; tense and apprehensive.

'I loved you once,' I said. 'No words. But we both knew. And you felt something, too. I promised it would never show to anyone else, and I went away to make sure I could never break that promise. Now I'll promise you something else. I know more about you than any man has ever known of a woman. But I will never tell, unless you want me to.'

For a long time she stared at me with unfathomable eyes. Then she looked out across the promenade and the beach and the sea, and seemed lost to me; until she whispered: 'How strange that it should be you who came to find me; you who have haunted me because I was unfaithful with you. I would never have left Alan for you; but I knew that if you had asked me, secretly I would have been tempted. That was my infidelity.' She looked at me again. 'It turned a knife in me so many times, before Alan died. My consolation was that I knew you would never come back. I trusted you then. I still trust you.'

'I seem to be making a habit of being trusted by other men's wives.' I could not disguise the bitterness. 'The same wife, even if the men are different. I'm sorry. That was cruel. Please forgive me. I had nothing but admiration for Alan. And I know André must be a very special man for you to give your life to him –'

I stopped, because she was shaking her head; and then she put out her hand and her fingers pressed across my mouth for a moment to silence me.

'I'm the one to ask forgiveness,' she said softly. 'It's been so confusing. I didn't realise I had told you only part of it. I'm not another man's wife. André fought so hard. But he couldn't win. He died three months ago. I was married for two years and eight months. I don't regret a day of it. But it's over. I'm sorry I didn't tell you.'

A great stillness settled inside me. 'Thank you for telling me now. I – I'm sorry, of course.' I couldn't think of anything else to say.

'I am,' she said, 'because he deserved so much more from life. And he gave it away for me.'

The stillness eased, and I could move again. I reached out and touched her finger tips on the table.

'We knew each other in another world, Mitch. Now we have to find our way in a new one. It's different. And there'll be some difficult things to do, and difficult decisions to make. Like deciding about your father.'

She searched my face and did not move her fingers away from mine.

'He's a stranger to me, Neil. Tell me what to do.'

'If you're not going to see him, and try to be nice to him, it would be cruel if I told him the truth. It would be better if he went on believing you're dead.'

'I can't do that.' She made up her mind instantly. 'I don't know what's going to happen to us all after today. But I couldn't ask you to keep this from him. Maybe we won't find much together, after all this time. But at least we can try.'

*

I didn't want to let her go. Even now, after the morning, after a quiet lunch at a little bistro with a view over the water and a proprietor who made a great fuss when she said I was one of her most special friends, after so much talk and silences too, after thinking and wondering and marvelling, I had the awful feeling that if she left me it would all turn into a dream and I would never see her again. When she had gone I felt a kind of despair, a desolation and an aching apprehension.

She must have known, because before she got into her little

car she stood very close and said: 'Don't be afraid. I'm coming back.'

When I took a taxi up to the hill so that I could reclaim my abandoned car, I couldn't make myself walk along the road to see the clearing and the stone again because I was still not sure what was truth and what was the product of imagination which had become strangely fevered, and a false step now might destroy it all. So I drove straight back down into the town and to the hotel, and found Peter.

He needed a little time to accept what I had to tell him. He sat in his room, shoulders hunched, staring at me with faraway eyes. For a few minutes he looked older, and held his head between his hands. I told him practically nothing about Karl Braune and what had happened to her; only about the miracle of her survival and why she had chosen to nurse André and turn her back on the rest of the world. Then, suddenly, he was ecstatic, laughing, shaking my hand, saying, 'Where is she – tell me – take me to her,' and I knew he had to react like that if he was to fight away tears.

An hour later, because that was how we had arranged it, I went down to the foyer and found her there. She wore a simple white dress with blue palm tree motifs, and when she saw me her eyes were alive with light and pleasure and she squeezed my hand. I took her up to his room and she stood outside the door, summoning courage; then whispered, 'Wish me luck,' and kissed me quickly on the cheek.

3

⊶⊶⊷

I wanted to see him take the full impact of it. I wanted to see it shock him. I wanted him to suffer.

I didn't know where he lived, and in the circumstances I knew Anne would not tell me. So I rang the Ministry of Defence and asked the operator to convey a message to Hugo Thoresen – probably in MI6, I said – that Neil Cameron had some exceptionally interesting information for him. I gave my telephone number. The operator started to say 'I can't –' but I snapped: 'You'd better, or he'll burn your pension in front of your eyes.'

Sure enough, two days later he rang. I said: 'Come to my flat.' When he objected I said: 'There – or nowhere. But you won't want to miss it.'

At six in the evening he stood on the doorstep, in cold winter rain. I avoided any suggestion of a handshake and led him into the small hallway. He shrugged off his wet coat and I hung it for him.

'I hope this is going to be worth the journey,' he said caustically. 'Our last meeting was hardly memorable for its cordiality – although I confess that after so long I forget the unpleasant detail. It must be five months. Your complexion suggests that you've been out of the country for most of the time.' He regarded me with that characteristic lift of the brows above deep, unreadable eyes. 'So what is this about? What revelation have you in store?'

I said, 'The word is well chosen, Thoresen,' and opened the living room door.

He was still; rock-steady and expressionless. Only his

breathing registered reaction. She had been sitting in a winged chair, her back to the door, and he saw her only when she moved, rising and turning slowly, staring at him. She had wanted to hurt him, and she succeeded.

After a long time he said: 'You were the last person I expected to see.' He pronounced each word carefully, as if unsure of his diction, and I heard his breath shudder in his throat.

'And you were the last person I wanted to see. I had to be persuaded.' Cool and precise, almost indifferent.

I had to admire him. He looked her up and down, giving himself time, controlling that tell-tale breathing. His fingers opened and closed at his sides. Then he nodded, as if confirming a private suspicion.

'Of course. Your friend' – he inclined his head slightly towards me – 'had to make the most of his dramatic moment.' Another pause. He drew himself up slightly, squaring his shoulders, 'But I am sorry you're not more welcoming. This – this is marvellous. Incredible. I long to hear the story.' He held out both his hands, but made no move towards her. The requirement was clear: she had to come to him, to return to the fold and the shepherd.

But she did not. She left him standing there with his hands extended as if frozen in sightless search.

'I doubt if you ever will,' she said. 'I did not come here to tell it to you.'

He lowered his hands and walked into the room, her rejection passed over as the gesture of a petulant child.

'Then your friend' – again the nod towards me – 'must have invited me for some other reason. Perhaps he wanted to present you as a prize, ferreted out by the astute writer-turned-detective. Clever. But unbecoming. And I'm unimpressed by your rabbit-from-the-hat trick. I am only delighted. This is an exquisite moment.' He turned to me, his mouth smiling, his eyes shielded. 'Surely you will extend hospitality to an appropriate drink, Cameron. The moment demands a toast. There can never have been a greater surprise.'

I said: 'Perhaps greater for you than for anyone, since you started it all when you told your cousin about the girl who went to France as a spy, and who died there, and how sure you were that her story deserved a book. What made the story for you, Thoresen? Her heroism and death? Or your own secret memories and desire to see her immortalised in print? I cannot imagine that you would have told Anne about her if you had guessed she might be alive.'

'You're trying to be insulting, and failing miserably,' he retorted. 'You think you know so much and in reality understand little. If you were now considerate you would allow us a few private minutes together.'

'Do you want a few private minutes with him, Mitch?'

She looked at me as if surprised by the question. She was poised, aloof.

'Neither minutes nor seconds. Would you have told your version of my story to a publisher if you had thought I might still be alive, Hugo?'

'There is no sensible answer to that.' He waved a hand deprecatingly. 'Because the question is not sensible. I wanted your story to be told because I believed you were worthy of the highest tribute. Perhaps if I knew how you came to survive, and why you chose to remain hidden away until now, I might still feel the same way, or even more so. The question is not who started it, but how it comes to this conclusion.'

'It's not yet concluded,' I said. 'And it didn't start when you talked to Anne. It started when you began to hate Mitch's parents. And ever since you've been at the heart of it. Even when you thought she was dead you wanted to be centre stage, the man who discovered her, moulded her, chose her for her mission. And pointed her towards horror beyond, I suspect, your imagination. The only surviving witness was a renegade German sergeant named Braune. But he didn't tell you in 1945 what he told me last July. He was too scared then. If you had known what really happened to her, I doubt that even your distorted reasoning would have persuaded you to have her story told.'

That hurt him. He turned quickly, facing me, his eyes no longer hidden, but hating. He jabbed a finger at me.

'You are impertinent. And you live dangerously. I don't know what you are talking about. And I do not have to listen. I would have preferred to have been able to talk to Michele quietly and personally, and to celebrate her return gently. Your coarseness denies that. If I am to keep my hands off you, I have to leave –'

'No, Hugo.' She stopped him. 'Not until I've finished. You wanted to know why you had been invited here. I'll tell you. It was so that I may give you a minute hint of what happened to me after you sent me to France. And what it did to me – and still does when I see you. Because I know I wasn't really a volunteer for that work. I was pre-conditioned, maybe, by Alan's death. But I was also sought out by you and your agents, and persuaded by you. Because you couldn't leave me alone. Now you're going to hear how it ended.'

He didn't know. I was sure of that. But instinct warned him. He looked quickly at me, as if wanting to escape. I stared back.

She said quietly: 'Their torture for me was to give me to the men in a slave labour camp. But not just any labour camp, Hugo. A special one, where they kept the criminals, the insane and the diseased. The ultimate in human degradation, crowded together. Tell us about your French contacts and about the intelligence department which sent you, they said, or we'll let them have you for a plaything. We'll keep dragging you out for questions, then throwing you back into the cage with them while we stand and laugh.'

The horror registered. It showed in the curve of his mouth and in his eyes. He did not try to interrupt: he just stared, a reluctant witness numbed into silence by the dreadful picture before him.

'The Gestapo officer ripped open my clothes so they could see my body.' Her calmness and control made it worse. 'They had running sores on their faces and drooling mouths and wild eyes. They didn't speak or shout. They mumbled unrecognisable words. The smell of them was like vomit. And when they reached for me I saw you, Hugo. You were Ernst Altmann. I saw your face instead of his. Because if you had been German you would have been doing what he did. Watching my terror, calculating it, using it. He manipulated me like a doll – just as you did. You and he were out of the same mould.'

He stirred then, as if breaking away from a clamp, and his voice rumbled: 'That's a lie. Altmann was one of the worst. He was notorious. It's a dreadful insult –'

'No, Hugo. You were different only because the demands of your service were different.' Her voice had sharpened and cut across his. 'But there's more. Because I saw you in that foul crowd, too. Every face was a twisted, corrupted version of yours. You had haunted me all my life, through my parents then through my own foolishness. You may have repaid some of the debt when you helped me to escape from France – but then you sought me out and sent me back, knowing what could be waiting for me. I stood on the very edge of hell, Hugo – and saw you there, pushing me and then waiting for me on the other side. And if I had had the strength to scream it would have been your name they would have heard.'

He crumpled. His breathing was a small gulp of sound and his handsome face shrivelled behind his greying beard. His hands went up and covered his eyes and he whispered: 'No. No. That isn't true. I worshipped you.'

'As a prize for your ego.' She was merciless. She had been afraid of him for so long; even when, once, she had imagined she loved him. Now there was no limit to her retaliation. 'You have only ever worshipped yourself. I was just a sacrifice on your secret altar. A devil's altar. I saw you in hell, Hugo. It was the right place for you. And I'll never think of you in any other way.'

His hands came down from his face. He was fighting to recover. His breath snatched in his throat and he choked: 'Lies. Lies. What did they do to make you lie?' She flashed back: 'What did you do to show me the truth?' And then I moved, because it was enough.

'Time to go, Thoresen. You've seen the miracle. There's nothing else for you.' I opened the door, and to my surprise he backed towards it without argument. But he was still fighting.

'Have you corrupted her, Cameron? To sensationalise your story?' He pointed at her with an unsteady finger. 'Don't trust him. He'll betray you. He's a hack writer, in it for the money.' He swung back to me. 'If you print a word to my detriment, or to her's, I'll take every penny you have.'

She smiled a small, cold, secret smile, and I said: 'Don't concern yourself. There isn't going to be a book.'

'No book?' His confidence was coming back. 'You must have the story of a lifetime. However she escaped, the details must be sensational. A better story than if she had died. I can't believe that you, who grub your living from words, would turn down such an opportunity.'

'I was commissioned to write a story about a girl who died,' I said. 'She didn't. So no story. Charles Le Page and I have settled our differences. And no one else can write it, because now they couldn't get the details. You're the only one who might have been willing to talk to someone else, if you were still looking for your ego trip. But in the circumstances, I don't think you will.'

'Circumstances?' He snapped the word. He knew, as I'd intended he should, that there was something else.

'Peter Armstrong,' I said.

He stood in the little hallway, staring; at Mitch, then at me.

'Armstrong? What are you talking about?'

I said: 'He's looking for you. He knows what you did, in Berne in 1937, in London in 1943 and 44. He knows what happened – because of you. From now on you might meet him on any street corner. He could be waiting for you, anywhere. He wants you, Thoresen. We haven't told him how to find you. But if you ever show up in Michele's life again, no matter in what way – we will.'

I pushed his raincoat into his hand. He took it, hardly aware of it. I heard a movement behind me, and Mitch came into the hall. She stood close to me and I slid an arm around her waist. She was tense, but I could feel her warmth.

He was watching us; eyes darting from my face to hers, and back again.

'What is she to you, Cameron?' Quietly; an acceptance, and a resignation.

'My wife,' I said. And opened the door for him.

He walked backwards, without a word, into the cold night.

Patrick O'Brian

Writing recently in the *London Review of Books*, John Bayley compared Patrick O'Brian's writing with that of his compatriot, J. G. Farrell:

'O'Brian, a similar and at least as great a talent [as Farrell] has to have a ship and the sea for his marvellously delicate and humorous fantasies set in Napoleon's day. They are emphatically not the kind of mechanical marine thrillers which sprang up in the wake of C. S. Forester. Smollett and Marryat are here being rewritten less for the excitement than for the feeling, as Dr Johnson said of Richardson: both O'Brian and Farrell share the wholly civilised, entirely good-humoured champagne Irishness of Laurence Sterne. . . .

'Like Farrell, O'Brian has solved in his own individual way the problem of getting history – in terms of habits, assumptions and ideas – into the texture of the novel . . . [Jack Aubrey] is a Lord Jim without the author's philosophic pretension, and in his context far more convincingly contrived. [In him] O'Brian's combination of sagacity and magic is at its best.'

Master and Commander
Post Captain
HMS *Surprise*
The Mauritius Command
The Fortune of War
The Surgeon's Mate
The Ionian Mission

Treason's Harbour
Desolation Island
The Far Side of the World
The Reverse of the Medal

and in July 1989
The Letter of Marque

FONTANA PAPERBACKS

Kara Kush
Idries Shah

'Unputdownable . . . the best war novel I have read' Doris Lessing, *Sunday Times*

In the depths of an Afghan winter, the Russians descend upon Central Asia, terrorising the patchwork of peoples whose land extends from China to Iran.

Rallied by Adam Durany, the man known as Kara Kush – The Eagle – the ill-equipped patriots fight back and win one battle after another against the slow-moving Russian bear. And they deny the enemy the golden Hoard of Ahmed Shah, the greatest treasure the world has ever seen . . .

'Thrilling fiction with ancient tales and legends interwoven . . . the stuff of epic' Pat Williams, *New Society*

'Impossible to put down' David Wade, *The Times*

FONTANA PAPERBACKS

Herman Wouk

One of the most talented novelists writing in America today. All his novels have been highly praised bestsellers, and *The Caine Mutiny* won the Pulitzer Prize.

His books include

WAR AND REMEMBRANCE
THE WINDS OF WAR
DON'T STOP THE CARNIVAL
THE CAINE MUTINY

FONTANA PAPERBACKS